THE BEST FROM

FANTASY
&
SCIENCE FICTION

THE BEST FROM

FANTASY
&
SCIENCE FICTION

A 45th Anniversary Anthology

◆ ◆ ◆

Edited by
Kristine Kathryn Rusch
and
Edward L. Ferman

St. Martin's Press New York

THE BEST FROM FANTASY & SCIENCE FICTION: A 45TH ANNIVERSARY AN-
THOLOGY. Copyright © 1994 by Mercury Press, Inc. All rights reserved.
Printed in the United States of America. No part of this book may be
used or reproduced in any manner whatsoever without written permission
except in the case of brief quotations embodied in critical articles or
reviews. For information, address St. Martin's Press, 175 Fifth Avenue,
New York, N.Y. 10010.

Design by Basha Zapatka

Library of Congress Cataloging-in-Publication Data

The Best from Fantasy & science fiction : a 45th anniversary anthology
/ Edward L. Ferman and Kristine Kathryn Rusch, editors.
    p. cm.
  ISBN 0-312-11246-7
  1. Fantastic fiction, American. 2. Science fiction, American.
I. Ferman, Edward L. II. Rusch, Kristine Kathryn. III. Magazine
of fantasy and science fiction (Cornwall, Conn.) IV. Title: Best from
Fantasy and science fiction.
PS648.F3B473 1994
813'.087608—dc20   94-20632
                                                      CIP

First Edition: October 1994

10 9 8 7 6 5 4 3 2 1

For Harlan Ellison
and
In memory of Isaac Asimov

Contents

Introduction: Changes

◆　　◆　　◆

The last five years have been a period of change for *F&SF*, and the most significant one began sometime during the summer of 1990, when it dawned on me that it would be a smart idea—for both me and the magazine—to replace myself as editor. I had been at the job for twenty-five years, and while I have yet to consider myself actually *old*, the fires of enthusiasm were beginning to look a bit more like embers, especially when I was faced with a mountain of manuscripts to read.

I think of SF as a young person's literature, and as proof I need only point to the contributors to this book. I'm pretty sure that there are only two besides myself who are older than the magazine itself. So—some new blood seemed in order. I could still be publisher. After all, other magazines had complete departments to deal with things like circulation, advertising, finances; there would be plenty to keep me busy. And even if not, there was always tennis, or long walks in the woods, or longer naps.

That fall I made a few phone calls for advice and suggestions and drew up a short list of candidates. It consisted of a well-known writer from the South, another prominent writer/editor from the Midwest, and two New York editors. All very good people, and all fairly well known by me. It would be a tough choice, but I felt I couldn't go wrong with any of them.

I typed up a long list of topics to discuss and talked to these people at length about the job. Somewhere in the middle of all this, Harlan Ellison (who is not only one of the few older-than-*F&SF* contributors here, but also the magazine's film editor and unofficial watchdog) mentioned another name, a writer/editor in her early thirties named Kristine Kathryn Rusch. I had bought several of her stories and heard good things about her editing at Pulphouse Publishing, but I had never met her.

Kris flew to Hartford from Oregon in early December, and my

first thoughts were: This is not only new blood, this is *young* new blood. (Kris looks about ten years younger than her age.) And SF is a young person's game! We'd make a perfect team, an editor bursting with youth and vitality, along with an older and wiser voice (me), whom would rouse himself from long naps on the rare occasions when it would be necessary to lend a guiding hand.

And that's pretty much the way it turned out. A largely intuitive decision, and a good one. The guiding hand has hardly been necessary, despite the fact that Kris has been faced with some difficult changes and decisions.

If there was one writer who seemed essential to *F&SF*, it was Isaac Asimov, whom we all loved and assumed would go on forever. His first Science essay for *F&SF* appeared in the November 1958 issue, and the series continued without interruption for thirty-four years. Late in 1991 Isaac became seriously ill and had to stop writing the column. He died in the spring of 1992. Even through his illness, Isaac was considerate of his publishers' needs and gave us enough notice to plan for a replacement. Kris's choices were Gregory Benford and Bruce Sterling, and while we still miss Isaac, the new tandem has proved inspired.

Later in 1992, Algis Budrys, *F&SF*'s longtime book reviewer, left to start up a new magazine called *Tomorrow*. Kris coaxed an equally prominent author, John Kessel, into contributing six columns a year, and they have been models of clarity and insight.

The backbone of *F&SF* is its fiction, and here the changes have been both subtle and simple. *F&SF* has been what I would call a writer's magazine rather than an editor's magazine. Its definition of SF is broad and flexible; there is no formula, no agenda; anything of quality goes. I think Kris has always understood this.

Let me contrast another editorial change. Recently, in the fast lane of magazine publishing, a new editor took over the venerable *New Yorker*, presumably to sweep out the cobwebs and attract advertising. She appears to have done that, but she has drastically altered the magazine. Any longtime reader would concede that the old *New Yorker* was eccentric and self-indulgent, but you found stuff in it you would find nowhere else. Long articles on offbeat subjects and people turned out to be compelling, because the pieces were so deeply felt by the writers. The new *New Yorker* runs shorter, trendier, more timely articles. To a certain audience it's more attractive, but it's no longer unique. It has been turned into an editor's magazine, possibly to the benefit of the bottom line, but in the long run I have my doubts about the wisdom of taking something singular, if limited in appeal, and turning it into just another snappy read.

There were no such drastic changes to the fiction in *F&SF*. It remains a writer's magazine. To recognize the changes in the fiction, one need look no further than the names of some of the new, young writers Kris has encouraged and published, writers whose work I was either not seeing or not recognizing, people like Jonathan Lethem, Dale Bailey, Nina Kiriki Hoffman, Marcos Donnelly, Elizabeth Hand. This is not so much a change as a renewal, a breath of fresh air. It's just what I had hoped for in the summer of 1990, and I hope it adds to your enjoyment of this book.

—Edward L. Ferman
West Cornwall, Connecticut

Introduction

◆   ◆   ◆

Faithful readers of the magazine will disagree.

About, of course, these being the best stories printed in the last five years from *The Magazine of Fantasy & Science Fiction*. Some readers will complain that Ed or I will have left out Story X or Novella Y, and other readers would have put together a slightly different volume, with a different slant, and a different focus.

So would I, in a perfect world.

Let me explain. This volume of *The Best from Fantasy & Science Fiction* (the 26th volume for you completists out there) covers a five-year span. Two and a half years were under Ed Ferman's editorship, and two and a half years were under mine. During that time we published hundreds of pieces of fiction, and some rather amazing nonfiction by our regular columnists. I actually thought of compiling a list of the noteworthy fiction and appending it to this volume before I realized that we had—each issue of the magazine provides its own list. Choosing from that list required some arbitrary criteria.

First, we divided the book. Ed chose 60,000* words and I chose 60,000 words. A typical issue of the magazine has 65,000 words—so we each had to narrow our choices (from all this material) to less than the average size of a regular issue of *F&SF* each. When Ed gave me the word count, I teased him: "Well," I said, "I will just choose Algis Budrys's *Hard Landing* and be done with it." (*Hard Landing* is a novel of 60,000 words which we published in its entirety in our October/November 1992 issue.) There was a long pause before Ed began to chuckle.

Only I was half serious. The novel is excellent and received a terrific response from the critics and the readers. I didn't tell Ed about the other options I explored, such as combining Jack Cady's

---

*Actually, I chose 70,000—privilege of seniority.—E.F.

award-winning novella, "The Night We Buried Road Dog" (30,000 words) with Kate Wilhelm's critically acclaimed novella, "Naming the Flowers" (30,000 words). Or perhaps I would pull a set of four novelettes, each at 15,000 words.

The combinations were endless, and unsatisfying. In each case, I left out a dozen marvelous stories. We couldn't even get all of our award-winners and nominees in here. From my tenure, we are missing Ed Gorman's "The Face" (which won a Golden Spur Award from the Western Writers of America), for example, and award nominees from Bradley Denton's "The Territory" (a novella) to Charles de Lint's "PaperJacks" (a novelette). My original can't-do-without list of short stories ran over a page. I finally had to cull that down to ten representative pieces of fiction.

Representative is the key word. We want to give you a short sampling of what the magazine has been about in the last five years. We have some *F&SF* regulars in here, some favorites, and some newcomers. We have a fairly even mix of science fiction, fantasy, and horror. We made sure that this volume also has a touch of humor, because humor in both fiction and cartoon is very important to the magazine.

Unfortunately we weren't able to squeeze in a sample column or two. In recent years, Bruce Sterling wrote an excellent essay on the human brain (which, I had hoped, would be picked up by the Best Essays of the Year). Gregory Benford wrote a column on time travel which I recommend to anyone who has an interest in that subject. The film columns by Harlan Ellison and Kathi Maio have stirred much debate and controversy, and the books columns under Algis Budrys, Orson Scott Card, and John Kessel have explored the changes in SF literature over the past few years. We also lacked space to include the final few columns by Isaac Asimov—whom we all still miss greatly.

Now that I have told you what isn't here, I'll tell you what is. The 130,000 words of fiction that follow are our personal favorites from the shorter lengths. For example:

Madeleine Robins's story "Willie" so tickled me when I first read it that I immediately read it to my assistant, then to my husband, and then to a friend who had happened to drop by. They were as enchanted as I was. The story later became a cover for our December 1992 issue.

I include Marcos Donnelly's story "The Resurrection of Alonso Quijana" as an example of one of the few recent stories that has used the Gulf War as its heart. The story is about more than that, of course—and manages to have some of the funniest footnotes I have ever read.

Harlan Ellison read his story "Susan" aloud to me one afternoon in the presence of his wife, whom the story is about. The story is based on a painting by Jacek Yerka, a Polish artist, and the painting was the cover of our December 1993 issue. One look at that piece of art and the visceral punch-to-the-gut I felt when the story was finished comes back to me in all of a piece.

Each story in this volume has that kind of memory attached to it—the moment that makes editing so special. The joy of an emotional roller-coaster ride, the glimpse of a new world, the look inside a vision so powerful that it takes your breath away. I am especially pleased to include so many newcomers, from Dale Bailey to Ray Vukcevich.

Despite my wish that the book could be 500,000 words long, I am very pleased with this volume. For those of you who are just discovering *F&SF*, you will find the center of the magazine here—the short works we are most proud of. For those of you who read the magazine regularly, you will have a chance to revisit old friends and to figure out what you would have done differently, had you been in our shoes.

Enjoy.

—Kristine Kathryn Rusch
Eugene, Oregon
November 3, 1993

KIRINYAGA

♦   ♦   ♦

Mike Resnick

The prolific Mike Resnick is a novelist and anthologist, but we confess we like him best as a short story writer, and fortunately he still finds time to produce quality short fiction. "Kirinyaga" was the first of several stories with an African background, and it won a Hugo Award in 1989. It's about the power of tradition in the far future; the hero is a witch doctor of sorts, but one who uses a computer.

In the beginning, Ngai lived alone atop the mountain called Kirinyaga. In the fullness of time, he created three sons, who became fathers of the Maasai, the Kamba, and the Kikuyu races; and to each son he offered a spear, a bow, and a digging stick. The Maasai chose the spear, and was told to tend herds on the vast savanna. The Kamba chose the bow, and was sent to the dense forests to hunt for game. But Gikuyu, the first Kikuyu, knew that Ngai loved the earth and the seasons, and chose the digging stick. To reward him for this, Ngai not only taught him the secrets of the seed and the harvest, but gave him Kirinyaga, with its holy fig tree and rich lands.

The sons and daughters of Gikuyu remained on Kirinyaga until the white man came and took their lands away; and even when the white man had been banished, they did not return, but chose to remain in the cities, wearing Western clothes and using Western machines and living Western lives. Even I, who am a *mundu-mugu*—a witch doctor—was born in the city. I have never seen the lion or the elephant or the rhinoceros, for all of them were extinct

1

before my birth; nor have I seen Kirinyaga as Ngai meant it to be seen, for a bustling, overcrowded city of 3 million inhabitants covers its slopes, every year approaching closer and closer to Ngai's throne at the summit. Even the Kikuyu have forgotten its true name, and now know it only as Mount Kenya.

To be thrown out of Paradise, as were the Christian Adam and Eve, is a terrible fate, but to live beside a debased Paradise is infinitely worse. I think about them frequently, the descendants of Gikuyu who have forgotten their origin and their traditions and are now merely Kenyans, and I wonder why more of them did not join with us when we created the Eutopian world of Kirinyaga.

True, it is a harsh life, for Ngai never meant life to be easy; but it is also a satisfying life. We live in harmony with our environment; we offer sacrifices when Ngai's tears of compassion fall upon our fields and give sustenance to our crops; we slaughter a goat to thank him for the harvest.

Our pleasures are simple: a gourd of *pombe* to drink, the warmth of a *boma* when the sun has gone down, the wail of a newborn son or daughter, the foot races and spear throwing and other contests, the nightly singing and dancing.

Maintenance watches Kirinyaga discreetly, making minor orbital adjustments when necessary, assuring that our tropical climate remains constant. From time to time they have subtly suggested that we might wish to draw upon their medical expertise, or perhaps allow our children to make use of their educational facilities, but they have taken our refusal with good grace, and have never shown any desire to interfere in our affairs.

Until I strangled the baby.

It was less than an hour later that Koinnage, our paramount chief, sought me out.

"That was an unwise thing to do, Koriba," he said grimly.

"It was not a matter of choice," I replied. "You know that."

"Of course you had a choice," he responded. "You could have let the infant live." He paused, trying to control his anger and his fear. "Maintenance has never set foot on Kirinyaga before, but now they will come."

"Let them," I said with a shrug. "No law has been broken."

"We have killed a baby," he replied. "They will come, and they will revoke our charter!"

I shook my head. "No one will revoke our charter."

"Do not be too certain of that, Koriba," he warned me. "You can bury a goat alive, and they will monitor us and shake their heads and speak contemptuously among themselves about our religion. You can leave the aged and the infirm out for the hyenas to eat, and they will look upon us with disgust and call us godless heathens. But I tell you that killing a newborn infant is another matter. They will not sit idly by; they will come."

"If they do, I shall explain why I killed it," I replied calmly.

"They will not accept your answers," said Koinnage. "They will not understand."

"They will have no choice but to accept my answers," I said. "This is Kirinyaga, and they are not permitted to interfere."

"They will find a way," he said with an air of certainty. "We must apologize and tell them that it will not happen again."

"We will not apologize," I said sternly. "Nor can we promise that it will not happen again."

"Then, as paramount chief, *I* will apologize."

I stared at him for a long moment, then shrugged. "Do what you must do," I said.

Suddenly I could see the terror in his eyes.

"What will you do to me?" he asked fearfully.

"I? Nothing at all," I said. "Are you not my chief?" As he relaxed, I added: "But if I were you, I would beware of insects."

"Insects?" he repeated. "Why?"

"Because the next insect that bites you, be it spider or mosquito or fly, will surely kill you," I said. "Your blood will boil within your body, and your bones will melt. You will want to scream out your agony, yet you will be unable to utter a sound." I paused. "It is not a death I would wish on a friend," I added seriously.

"Are we not friends, Koriba?" he said, his ebon face turning an ash gray.

"I thought we were," I said. "But my friends honor our traditions. They do not apologize for them to the white man."

"I will not apologize!" he promised fervently. He spat on both his hands as a gesture of his sincerity.

I opened one of the pouches I kept around my waist and withdrew a small polished stone, from the shore of our nearby river. "Wear this around your neck," I said, handing it to him, "and it shall protect you from the bites of insects."

"Thank you, Koriba!" he said with sincere gratitude, and another crisis had been averted.

We spoke about the affairs of the village for a few more minutes, and finally he left me. I sent for Wambu, the infant's mother, and led her through the ritual of purification, so that she might conceive again. I also gave her an ointment to relieve the pain in her breasts, since they were heavy with milk. Then I sat down by the fire before my *boma* and made myself available to my people, settling disputes over the ownership of chickens and goats, and supplying charms against demons, and instructing my people in the ancient ways.

By the time of the evening meal, no one had a thought for the dead baby. I ate alone in my *boma*, as befitted my status, for the *mundumugu* always lives and eats apart from his people. When I had finished, I wrapped a blanket around my body to protect me from the cold and walked down the dirt path to where all the other *bomas* were clustered. The cattle and goats and chickens were penned up for the night, and my people, who had slaughtered and eaten a cow, were now singing and dancing and drinking great quantities of *pombe*. As they made way for me, I walked over to the caldron and took a drink of *pombe*, and then, at Kanjara's request, I slit open a goat and read its entrails and saw that his youngest wife would soon conceive, which was cause for more celebration. Finally the children urged me to tell them a story.

"But not a story of Earth," complained one of the taller boys. "We hear those all the time. This must be a story about Kirinyaga."

"All right," I said. "If you will all gather around, I will tell you a story of Kirinyaga." The youngsters all moved closer. "This," I said, "is the story of the Lion and the Hare." I paused until I was sure that I had everyone's attention, especially that of the adults. "A hare was chosen by his people to be sacrificed to a lion, so that the lion would not bring disaster to their village. The hare might have run away, but he knew that sooner or later the lion would catch him, so instead he sought out the lion and walked right up to him, and as the lion opened his mouth to swallow him, the hare said, 'I apologize, Great Lion.'

" 'For what?' asked the lion curiously.

" 'Because I am such a small meal,' answered the hare. 'For that reason, I brought honey for you as well.'

" 'I see no honey,' said the lion.

" 'That is why I apologized,' answered the hare. 'Another lion stole it from me. He is a ferocious creature, and says that he is not afraid of you.'

"The lion rose to his feet. 'Where is this other lion?' he roared.

"The hare pointed to a hole in the earth. 'Down there,' he said, 'but he will not give you back your honey.'

" 'We shall see about that!' growled the lion.

"He jumped into the hole, roaring furiously, and was never seen again, for the hare had chosen a very deep hole indeed. Then the hare went home to his people and told them that the lion would never bother them again."

Most of the children laughed and clapped their hands in delight, but the same young boy voiced his objection.

"That is not a story of Kirinyaga," he said scornfully. "We have no lions here."

"It *is* a story of Kirinyaga," I replied. "What is important about the story is not that it concerned a lion and a hare, but that it shows that the weaker can defeat the stronger if he uses his intelligence."

"What has that to do with Kirinyaga?" asked the boy.

"What if we pretend that the men of Maintenance, who have ships and weapons, are the lion, and the Kikuyu are the hares?" I suggested. "What shall the hares do if the lion demands a sacrifice?"

The boy suddenly grinned. "Now I understand! We shall throw the lion down a hole!"

"But we have no holes here," I pointed out.

"Then what shall we do?"

"The hare did not know that he would find the lion near a hole," I replied. "Had he found him by a deep lake, he would have said that a large fish took the honey."

"We have no deep lakes."

"But we do have intelligence," I said. "And if Maintenance ever interferes with us, we will use our intelligence to destroy the lion of Maintenance, just as the hare used his intelligence to destroy the lion of the fable."

"Let us think how to destroy Maintenance right now!" cried the boy. He picked up a stick and brandished it at an imaginary lion as if it were a spear and he a great hunter.

I shook my head. "The hare does not hunt the lion, and the Kikuyu do not make war. The hare merely protects himself, and the Kikuyu do the same."

"Why would Maintenance interfere with us?" asked another

boy, pushing his way to the front of the group. "They are our friends."

"Perhaps they will not," I answered reassuringly. "But you must always remember that the Kikuyu have no true friends except themselves."

"Tell us another story, Koriba!" cried a young girl.

"I am an old man," I said. "The night has turned cold, and I must sleep."

"Tomorrow?" she asked. "Will you tell us another tomorrow?"

I smiled. "Ask me tomorrow, after all the fields are planted and the cattle and goats are in their enclosures and the food has been made and the fabrics have been woven."

"But girls do not herd the cattle and goats," she protested. "What if my brothers do not bring all their animals to the enclosure?"

"Then I will tell a story just to the girls," I said.

"It must be a long story," she insisted seriously, "for we work much harder than the boys."

"I will watch you in particular, little one," I replied, "and the story will be as long or as short as your work merits."

The adults all laughed, and suddenly she looked very uncomfortable, but then I chuckled and hugged her and patted her head, for it was necessary that the children learn to love their *mundumugu* as well as hold him in awe, and finally she ran off to play and dance with the other girls, while I retired to my *boma*.

Once inside, I activated my computer and discovered that a message was waiting for me from Maintenance, informing me that one of their number would be visiting me the following morning. I made a very brief reply—"Article II, Paragraph 5," which is the ordinance forbidding intervention—and lay down on my sleeping blanket, letting the rhythmic chanting of the singers carry me off to sleep.

I awoke with the sun the next morning and instructed my computer to let me know when the Maintenance ship had landed. Then I inspected my cattle and my goats—I, alone of my people, planted no crops, for the Kikuyu feed their *mundumugu*, just as they tend his herds and weave his blankets and keep his *boma* clean—and stopped by Simani's *boma* to deliver a balm to fight the disease that was afflicting his joints. Then, as the sun began warming the earth,

I returned to my own *boma*, skirting the pastures where the young men were tending their animals. When I arrived, I knew the ship had landed, for I found the droppings of a hyena on the ground near my hut, and that is the surest sign of a curse.

I learned what I could from the computer, then walked outside and scanned the horizon while two naked children took turns chasing a small dog and running away from it. When they began frightening my chickens, I gently sent them back to their own *boma*, and then seated myself beside my fire. At last I saw my visitor from Maintenance, coming up the path from Haven. She was obviously uncomfortable in the heat, and she slapped futilely at the flies that circled her head. Her blond hair was starting to turn gray, and I could tell by the ungainly way she negotiated the steep, rocky path that she was unused to such terrain. She almost lost her balance a number of times, and it was obvious that her proximity to so many animals frightened her, but she never slowed her pace, and within another ten minutes she stood before me.

"Good morning," she said.

"*Jambo, Memsaab*," I replied.

"You are Koriba, are you not?"

I briefly studied the face of my enemy; middle-aged and weary, it did not appear formidable. "I am Koriba," I replied.

"Good," she said. "My name is—"

"I know who you are," I said, for it is best, if conflict cannot be avoided, to take the offensive.

"You do?"

I pulled the bones out of my pouch and cast them on the dirt. "You are Barbara Eaton, born of Earth," I intoned, studying her reactions as I picked up the bones and cast them again. "You are married to Robert Eaton, and you have worked for Maintenance for nine years." A final cast of the bones. "You are forty-one years old, and you are barren."

"How did you know all that?" she asked with an expression of surprise.

"Am I not the *mundumugu*?"

She stared at me for a long minute. "You read my biography on your computer," she concluded at last.

"As long as the facts are correct, what difference does it make whether I read them from the bones or the computer?" I responded, refusing to confirm her statement. "Please sit down, *Memsaab* Eaton."

She lowered herself awkwardly to the ground, wrinkling her face as she raised a cloud of dust.

"It's very hot," she noted uncomfortably.

"It is very hot in Kenya," I replied.

"You could have created any climate you desired," she pointed out.

"We *did* create the climate we desired," I answered.

"Are there predators out there?" she asked, looking out over the savanna.

"A few," I replied.

"What kind?"

"Hyenas."

"Nothing larger?" she asked.

"There *is* nothing larger anymore," I said.

"I wonder why they didn't attack me?"

"Perhaps because you are an intruder," I suggested.

"Will they leave me alone on my way back to Haven?" she asked nervously, ignoring my comment.

"I will give you a charm to keep them away."

"I'd prefer an escort."

"Very well," I said.

"They're such ugly animals," she said with a shudder. "I saw them once when we were monitoring your world."

"They are very useful animals," I answered, "for they bring many omens, both good and bad."

"Really?"

I nodded. "A hyena left me an evil omen this morning."

"And?" she asked curiously.

"And here you are," I said.

She laughed. "They told me you were a sharp old man."

"They are mistaken," I replied. "I am a feeble old man who sits in front of his *boma* and watches younger men tend his cattle and goats."

"You are a feeble old man who graduated with honors from Cambridge and then acquired two postgraduate degrees from Yale," she replied.

"Who told you that?"

She smiled. "You're not the only one who reads biographies."

I shrugged. "My degrees did not help me become a better *mundumugu*," I said. "The time was wasted."

"You keep using that word. What, exactly, *is* a *mundumugu?*"

"You would call him a witch doctor," I answered. "But in truth the *mundumugu*, while he occasionally casts spells and interprets omens, is more a repository of the collected wisdom and traditions of his race."

"It sounds like an interesting occupation," she said.

"It is not without its compensations."

"And *such* compensations!" she said with false enthusiasm as a goat bleated in the distance and a young man yelled at it in Swahili. "Imagine having the power of life and death over an entire Eutopian world!"

So now it comes, I thought. Aloud I said: "It is not a matter of exercising power, *Memsaab* Eaton, but of maintaining traditions."

"I rather doubt that," she said bluntly.

"Why should you doubt what I say?" I asked.

"Because if it were traditional to kill newborn infants, the Kikuyu would have died out after a single generation."

"If the slaying of the infant arouses your disapproval," I said calmly, "I am surprised Maintenance has not previously asked about our custom of leaving the old and the feeble out for the hyenas."

"We know that the elderly and the infirm have consented to your treatment of them, much as we may disapprove of it," she replied. "We also know that a newborn infant could not possibly consent to its own death." She paused, staring at me. "May I ask why this particular baby was killed?"

"That *is* why you have come here, is it not?"

"I have been sent here to evaluate the situation," she replied, brushing an insect from her cheek and shifting her position on the ground. "A newborn child was killed. We would like to know why."

I shrugged. "It was killed because it was born with a terrible *thahu* upon it."

She frowned. "A *thahu*? What is that?"

"A curse."

"Do you mean that it was deformed?" she asked.

"It was not deformed."

"Then what was this curse that you refer to?"

"It was born feetfirst," I said.

"That's it?" she asked, surprised. "That's the curse?"

"Yes."

"It was murdered simply because it came out feetfirst?"

"It is not murder to put a demon to death," I explained patiently. "Our tradition tells us that a child born in this manner is actually a demon."

"You are an educated man, Koriba," she said. "How can you kill a perfectly healthy infant and blame it on some primitive tradition?"

"You must never underestimate the power of tradition, *Memsaab* Eaton," I said. "The Kikuyu turned their backs on their traditions once; the result is a mechanized, impoverished, overcrowded country that is no longer populated by Kikuyu, or Maasai, or Luo, or Wakamba, but by a new, artificial tribe known only as Kenyans. We here on Kirinyaga are true Kikuyu, and we will not make that mistake again. If the rains are late, a ram must be sacrificed. If a man's veracity if questioned, he must undergo the ordeal of the *githani* trial. If an infant is born with a *thahu* upon it, it must be put to death."

"Then you intend to continue killing any children that are born feetfirst?" she asked.

"That is correct," I responded.

A drop of sweat rolled down her face as she looked directly at me and said. "I don't know what Maintenance's reaction will be."

"According to our charter, Maintenance is not permitted to interfere with us," I reminded her.

"It's not that simple, Koriba," she said. "According to your charter, any member of your community who wishes to leave your world is allowed free passage to Haven, from which he or she can board a ship to Earth." She paused. "Was that baby you killed given such a choice?"

"I did not kill a baby, but a demon," I replied, turning my head slightly as a hot breeze stirred up the dust around us.

She waited until the breeze died down, then coughed before speaking. "You do understand that not everyone in Maintenance may share that opinion?"

"What Maintenance thinks is of no concern to us," I said.

"When innocent children are murdered, what Maintenance thinks is of supreme importance to you," she responded. "I am sure you do not want to defend your practices in the Eutopian Court."

"Are you here to evaluate the situation, as you said, or to threaten us?" I asked calmly.

"To evaluate the situation," she replied. "But there seems to be only one conclusion that I can draw from the facts that you have presented to me."

"Then you have not been listening to me," I said, briefly closing my eyes as another, stronger, breeze swept past us.

"Koriba, I know that Kirinyaga was created so that you could emulate the ways of your forefathers—but surely you must see the difference between the torture of animals as a religious ritual and the murder of a human baby."

I shook my head. "They are one and the same," I replied. "We cannot change our way of life because it makes *you* uncomfortable. We did that once before, and within a mere handful of years, your culture had corrupted our society. With every factory we built, with every job we created, with every bit of Western technology we accepted, with every Kikuyu who converted to Christianity, we became something we were not meant to be." I stared directly into her eyes. "I am the *mundumugu*, entrusted with preserving all that makes us Kikuyu, and I will not allow that to happen again."

"There are alternatives," she said.

"Not for the Kikuyu," I replied adamantly.

"There *are*," she insisted, so intent upon what she had to say that she paid no attention to a black-and-gold centipede that crawled over her boot. "For example, years spent in space can cause certain physiological and hormonal changes in humans. You noted when I arrived that I am forty-one years old and childless. That is true. In fact, many of the women in Maintenance are childless. If you will turn the babies over to us, I am sure we can find families for them. This would effectively remove them from your society without the necessity of killing them. I could speak to my superiors about it; I think that there is an excellent chance that they would approve."

"That is a thoughtful and innovative suggestion, *Memsaab* Eaton," I said truthfully. "I am sorry that I must reject it."

"But why?" she demanded.

"Because the first time we betray our traditions, this world will cease to be Kirinyaga, and will become merely another Kenya, a nation of men awkwardly pretending to be something they are not."

"I could speak to Koinnage and the other chiefs about it," she suggested meaningfully.

"They will not disobey my instructions," I replied confidently.

"You hold that much power?"

"I hold that much respect," I answered. "A chief may enforce the law, but it is the *mundumugu* who interprets it."

"Then let us consider other alternatives."

"No."

"I am trying to avoid a conflict between Maintenance and your people," she said, her voice heavy with frustration. "It seems to me that you could at least make the effort to meet me halfway."

"I do not question your motives, *Memsaab* Eaton," I replied, "but you are an intruder representing an organization that has no legal right to interfere with our culture. We do not impose our religion or our morality upon Maintenance, and Maintenance may not impose its religion or morality upon us."

"It is not that simple."

"It is precisely that simple," I said.

"That is your last word on the subject?" she asked.

"Yes."

She stood up. "Then I think it is time for me to leave and make my report."

I stood up as well, and a shift in the wind brought the odors of the village: the scent of bananas, the smell of a fresh caldron of *pombe*, even the pungent odor of a bull that had been slaughtered that morning.

"As you wish, *Memsaab* Eaton," I said. "I will arrange for your escort." I signaled to a small boy who was tending three goats and instructed him to go to the village and send back two young men.

"Thank you," she said. "I know it's an inconvenience, but I just don't feel safe with hyenas roaming loose out there."

"You are welcome," I said. "Perhaps, while we are waiting for the men who will accompany you, you would like to hear a story about the hyena."

She shuddered involuntarily. "They are such ugly beasts!" she said distastefully. "Their hind legs seem almost deformed." She shook her head. "No, I don't think I'd be interested in hearing a story about a hyena."

"You will be interested in *this* story," I told her.

She stared at me curiously and shrugged. "All right," she said. "Go ahead."

"It is true that hyenas are deformed, ugly animals," I began, "but once, a long time ago, they were as lovely and graceful as the impala. Then one day a Kikuyu chief gave a hyena a young goat to take as a gift to Ngai, who lives atop the holy mountain Kirinyaga. The hyena took the goat between his powerful jaws and headed toward the distant mountain—but on the way he passed a settlement filled with Europeans and Arabs. It abounded in guns and machines and other wonders he had never seen before, and he stopped to look, fascinated. Finally an Arab noticed him staring intently, and asked if he, too, would like to become a civilized man—and as he opened his mouth to say that he would, the goat fell to the ground and ran away. As the goat raced out of sight, the Arab laughed and explained that he was only joking, that of course no hyena could become a man." I paused for a moment, and then continued. "So the hyena proceeded to Kirinyaga, and when he reached the summit, Ngai asked him what had become of the goat. When the hyena told him, Ngai hurled him off the mountaintop for having the audacity to believe he could become a man. He did not die from the fall, but his rear legs were crippled, and Ngai declared that from that day forward, all hyenas would appear thus—and to remind them of the foolishness of trying to become something that they were not, he also gave then a fool's laugh." I paused again, and stared at her. "*Memsaab* Eaton, you do not hear the Kikuyu laugh like fools, and I will not let them become crippled like the hyena. Do you understand what I am saying?"

She considered my statement for a moment, then looked into my eyes. "I think we understand each other perfectly, Koriba," she said.

The two young men I had sent for arrived just then, and I instructed them to accompany her to Haven. A moment later they set off across the dry savanna, and I returned to my duties.

I began by walking through the fields, blessing the scarecrows. Since a number of the smaller children followed me, I rested beneath the trees more often than necessary, and always, whenever we paused, they begged me to tell them more stories. I told them the tale of the Elephant and the Buffalo, and how the Maasai *elmoran* cut the rainbow with his spear so that it never again came to rest upon the earth, and why the nine Kikuyu tribes are named after Gikuyu's nine daughters; and when the sun became too hot, I led them back to the village.

Then, in the afternoon, I gathered the older boys about me and explained once more how they must paint their faces and bodies for their forthcoming circumcision ceremony. Ndemi, the boy who had insisted upon a story about Kirinyaga the night before, sought me out privately to complain that he had been unable to slay a small gazelle with his spear, and asked for a charm to make its flight more accurate. I explained to him that there would come a day when he faced a buffalo or a hyena with no charm, and that he must practice more before he came to me again. He was one to watch, this little Ndemi, for he was impetuous and totally without fear; in the old days, he would have made a great warrior, but on Kirinyaga we had no warriors. If we remained fruitful and fecund, however, we would someday need more chiefs and even another *mundumugu*, and I made up my mind to observe him closely.

In the evening, after I ate my solitary meal, I returned to the village, for Njogu, one of our young men, was to marry Kamiri, a girl from the next village. The bride-price had been decided upon, and the two families were waiting for me to preside at the ceremony.

Njogu, his face streaked with paint, wore an ostrich-feather headdress, and looked very uneasy as he and his betrothed stood before me. I slit the throat of a fat ram that Kamiri's father had brought for the occasion, and then I turned to Njogu.

"What have you to say?" I asked.

He took a step forward. "I want Kamiri to come and till the fields of my *shamba*," he said, his voice cracking with nervousness as he spoke the prescribed words, "for I am a man, and I need a woman to tend to my *shamba* and dig deep around the roots of my plantings, that they may grow well and bring prosperity to my house."

He spit on both his hands to show his sincerity, and then, exhaling deeply with relief, he stepped back.

I turned to Kamiri.

"Do you consent to till the *shamba* of Njogu, son of Muchiri?" I asked her.

"Yes," she said softly, bowing her head. "I consent."

I held out my right hand, and the bride's mother placed a gourd of *pombe* in it.

"If this man does not please you," I said to Kamiri, "I will spill the *pombe* upon the ground."

"Do not spill it," she replied.

"Then drink," I said, handing the gourd to her.

She lifted it to her lips and took a swallow, then handed it to Njogu, who did the same.

When the gourd was empty, the parents of Njogu and Kamiri stuffed it with grass, signifying the friendship between the two clans.

Then a cheer rose from the onlookers, the ram was carried off to be roasted, more *pombe* appeared as if by magic, and while the groom took the bride off to his *boma*, the remainder of the people celebrated far into the night. They stopped only when the bleating of the goats told them that some hyenas were nearby, and then the women and children went off to their *bomas* while the men took their spears and went into the fields to frighten the hyenas away.

Koinnage came up to me as I was about to leave.

"Did you speak to the woman from Maintenance?" he asked.

"I did," I replied.

"What did she say?"

"She said that they do not approve of killing babies who are born feetfirst."

"And what did *you* say?" he asked nervously.

"I told her that we did not need the approval of Maintenance to practice our religion," I replied.

"Will Maintenance listen?"

"They have no choice," I said. "And *we* have no choice, either," I added. "Let them dictate one thing that we must or must not do, and soon they will dictate all things. Give them their way, and Njogu and Kamiri would have recited wedding vows from the Bible or the Koran. It happened to us in Kenya; we cannot permit it to happen on Kirinyaga."

"But they will not punish us?" he persisted.

"They will not punish us," I replied.

Satisfied, he walked off to his *boma* while I took the narrow, winding path to my own. I stopped by the enclosure where my animals were kept and saw that there were two new goats there, gifts from the bride's and groom's families in gratitude for my services. A few minutes later I was asleep within the walls of my own *boma*.

The computer woke me a few minutes before sunrise. I stood up, splashed my face with water from the gourd I keep by my sleeping blanket, and walked over to the terminal.

There was a mesage for me from Barbara Eaton, brief and to the point:

It is the preliminary finding of Maintenance that infanticide, for any reason, is a direct violation of Kirinyaga's charter. No action will be taken for past offenses.

We are also evaluating your practice of euthanasia, and may require further testimony from you at some point in the future.

Barbara Eaton

A runner from Koinnage arrived a moment later, asking me to attend a meeting of the Council of Elders, and I knew that he had received the same message.

I wrapped my blanket around my shoulders and began walking to Koinnage's *shamba*, which consisted of his *boma* as well as those of his three sons and their wives. When I arrived, I found not only the local elders waiting for me, but also two chiefs from neighboring villages.

"Did you receive the message from Maintenance?" demanded Koinnage, as I seated myself opposite him.

"I did."

"I warned you that this would happen!" he said. "What will we do now?"

"We will do what we have always done," I answered calmly.

"We cannot," said one of the neighboring chiefs. "They have forbidden it."

"They have no right to forbid it," I replied.

"There is a woman in my village whose time is near," continued the chief, "and all of the signs and omens point to the birth of twins. We have been taught that the firstborn must be killed, for one mother cannot produce two souls—but now Maintenance has forbidden it. What are we to do?"

"We must kill the firstborn," I said, "for it will be a demon."

"And then Maintenance will make us leave Kirinyaga!" said Koinnage bitterly.

"Perhaps we could let the child live," said the chief. "That might satisfy them, and then they might leave us alone."

I shook my head. "They will not leave you alone. Already they speak about the way we leave the old and feeble out for the hyenas, as if this were some enormous sin against their God. If you give in on the one, the day will come when you must give in on the other."

"Would that be so terrible?" persisted the chief. "They have medicines that we do not possess; perhaps they could make the old young again."

"You do not understand," I said, rising to my feet. "Our society is not a collection of separate people and customs and traditions. No, it is a complex system, with all the pieces as dependent upon each other as the animals and vegetation of the savannah. If you burn the grass, you will not only kill the impala who feeds upon it, but the predator who feeds upon the impala, and the ticks and flies who live upon the predator, and the vultures and maribou storks who feed upon his remains when he dies. You cannot destroy the part without destroying the whole."

I paused to let them consider what I had said, and then continued speaking: "Kirinyaga is like the savannah. If we do not leave the old and feeble out for the hyenas, the hyenas will starve. If the hyenas starve, the grass eaters will become so numerous that there is no land left for our cattle and goats to graze. If the old and feeble do not die when Ngai decrees it, then soon we will not have enough food to go around."

I picked up a stick and balanced it precariously on my forefinger.

"This stick," I said, "is the Kikuyu people, and my finger is Kirinyaga. They are in perfect balance." I stared at the neighboring chief. "But what will happen if I alter the balance and put my finger *here*?" I asked, gesturing to the end of the stick.

"The stick will fall to the ground."

"And here?" I asked, pointing to a stop an inch away from the center.

"It will fall."

"Thus is it with us," I explained. "Whether we yield on one point or all points, the result will be the same: the Kikuyu will fall as surely as the stick will fall. Have we learned nothing from our past? We *must* adhere to our traditions; they are all that we have!"

"But Maintenance will not allow us to do so!" protested Koinnage.

"They are not warriors, but civilized men," I said, allowing a touch of contempt to creep into my voice. "Their chiefs and their *mundumugus* will not send them to Kirinyaga with guns and spears. They will issue warnings and findings and declarations, and finally, when that fails, they will go to the Eutopian Court and plead their case, and the trial will be postponed many times and reheard many more times." I could see them finally relaxing, and I smiled confidently at them. "Each of you will have died from the burden of your years before Maintenance does anything other than talk. I am your *mundumugu*; I have lived among civilized men, and I tell you that this is the truth."

The neighboring chief stood up and faced me. "I will send for you when the twins are born," he pledged.

"I will come," I promised him.

We spoke further, and then the meeting ended and the old men began wandering off to their *bomas*, while I looked to the future, which I could see more clearly than Koinnage or the elders.

I walked through the village until I found the bold young Ndemi, brandishing his spear and hurling it at a buffalo he had constructed out of dried grasses.

"*Jambo*, Koriba!" he greeted me.

"*Jambo*, my brave young warrior," I replied.

"I have been practicing, as you ordered."

"I thought you wanted to hunt the gazelle," I noted.

"Gazelles are for children," he answered. "I will slay *mbogo*, the buffalo."

"*Mbogo* may feel differently about it," I said.

"So much the better," he said confidently. "I have no wish to kill an animal as it runs away from me."

"And when will you go out to slay the fierce *mbogo*?"

He shrugged. "When I am more accurate." He smiled up at me. "Perhaps tomorrow."

I stared at him thoughtfully for a moment, and then spoke: "Tomorrow is a long time away. We have business tonight."

"What business?" he asked.

"You must find ten friends, none of them yet of circumcision age, and tell them to come to the pond within the forest to the south. They must come after the sun has set, and you must tell them that Koriba the *mundumugu* commands that they tell no one, not even their parents, that they are coming." I paused. "Do you understand, Ndemi?"

"I understand."

"Then go," I said. "Take my message to them."

He retrieved his spear from the straw buffalo and set off at a trot, young and tall and strong and fearless.

You are the future, I thought, as I watched him run toward the village. *Not Koinnage, not myself, not even the young bridegroom Njogu, for their time will have come and gone before the battle is joined. It is you, Ndemi, upon whom Kirinyaga must depend if it is to survive.*

Once before, the Kikuyu had to fight for their freedom. Under the leadership of Jomo Kenyatta, whose name has been forgotten by most of your parents, we took the terrible oath of Mau Mau, and we maimed and we killed and we committed such atrocities that finally we achieved Uhuru, for against such butchery civilized men have no defense but to depart.

And tonight, young Ndemi, while your parents are asleep, you and your companions will meet me deep in the woods, and you in your turn and they in theirs will learn one last tradition of the Kikuyu, for I will invoke not only the strength of Ngai but also the indomitable spirit of Jomo Kenyatta. I will administer a hideous oath and force you to do unspeakable things to prove your fealty, and I will teach each of you, in turn, how to administer the oath to those who come after you.

There is a season for all things: for birth, for growth, for death. There is unquestionably a season for Utopia, but it will have to wait.

For the season of Uhuru is upon us.

TOUCHED

✦ ✦ ✦

Dale Bailey

*Dale Bailey went to the Clarion Writers Workshop in 1992 and
has since sold a number of stories to F&SF. He is hard at work on
a novel.*

*About "Touched" he writes, "I was born in southern West Virginia and spent most of my life there. Since I was a teenager I'd
been fascinated by the coal-field wars that consumed the state in
the 1920s, when it was organized by the United Mine Workers of
America. . . . I'd long wished to set a story in this milieu, but I
couldn't figure out how to do it until I one day happened to recall
an old Appalachian superstition—the idea that the mentally handicapped child is in some way compensated for his disability. This
single notion opened up the whole story for me."*

Oh, Mama, you say. And again: Oh, Mama.
Your chest hurts with a dull unceasing ache, but you
say it quietlike, half afraid she'll hear you.

Mama wishes you would die.

And anyway, she mostly listens to Cade, when Cade is here. Pap,
too, and Gramma sometimes.

Gramma now, rocking here in her place by the stove, saying:
That one's a half-wit. That one's touched. The old woman lowers
a trembling finger at you, huddled beside her, here by the stove.

Coughing the steady, hacking cough that has been with you for
days, you move closer to the firebox, but even here you feel the
draft from the broken windowpane, like icy fingers beneath your
clothes. Mama's asked the company to patch up that hole, maybe
a thousand times, but the company takes its time about things. And

the cardboard—well, it doesn't do much good. So you huddle closer to the firebox and watch Mama like you do sometimes when she doesn't think you're looking. Mama is churning butter. And every once in a while, if she thinks you're not watching, she steals a glance at you.

The coughing's got her hopeful.

Touched, Gramma says again, and Mama's pretty face twists up like she just bit into a green apple. She stops churning and wipes at her forehead with her hand. What do you mean, old woman? she says. Touched?

But Gramma just rocks, back and forth, back and forth. Her rocker squeaks against the floor, squeak, squeak, a noise like a mouse might make. This sound, the cold draft, the heavy scent of beans simmering atop the stove, and Gramma looming over you. Her mouth caves in, wrinkled as a prune. White hairs poke out of her chin.

Mama starts to churn again. The dasher thumps against the wooden crock.

Out the window, pallid winter light climbs the high ridges. Evening coming on. Cade will be home from school soon. And in a little while Pap will be back too, carrying his tool poke across his shoulder, his face black with coal dust.

Gramma says, Touched. Touched by the hand of God. Idiot child'll have a talent.

Mama snorts, and crosses the room to stir the beans. Then she hunkers down beside you and her rough fingers touch your face. Jorey, Mama says. Her voice is cold and hollow-sounding. Jorey doesn't have a talent, old woman. Jorey doesn't have anything at all.

Your coughing starts again, but just then the plank door swings open. Cade sweeps into the room, sweeping in the cold.

Cade, Mama says, her voice filling up. You're home.

Mama stands and you cough hard, jarring congestion loose in your chest. You inch closer to the firebox, almost against the cast iron stove.

Oh, Mama, you say.

But Mama, she doesn't even look around.

High above the number five hole, the chill silence folds around you like a blanket. No shrill voices jeer you; no fingers point. Up here, no one sneaks along behind you to throw you to the frozen ground.

Just the cold, your breath smoky in the still air, and the gaunt trees, dark against the ridges as far as you can see. In the stillness, electric cars clank out of the shaft beneath you, bearing load after rattling load of coal. Far below, railroad tracks veer away from the coal tipple into the steep-walled valley. And if you squint your eyes you can just see the tar-paper roofs of the Copperhead coal camp, black squares against the barren earth.

Home. Mama's waiting.

You jingle the scrip in your pocket, rocking a little in your flannel coat to keep warm. Somehow you can't quite bring yourself to go. It's not the other kids so much as it is your pap, down there somewhere, deep under the mountain. That and the sun, falling against your face as it sets toward the rim of the valley, and a squirrel, perched at the edge of the precipice, gnawing at a frozen nut. You used to bring chunks of bread to feed that squirrel, but you haven't done that since Mama whipped you for stealing bread.

With a rustle of dry leaves, Cade appears at the edge of the woods. He hunkers down beside you, resting his elbows on his thighs. The squirrel hurries into the safety of a looming hickory to scold him, but you just laugh.

Pretty funny, huh, Jorey, Cade says.

But the laughter turns to coughing, the coughing into the hot shameful sting of tears.

Them kids been giving you a hard time again? Cade asks.

You nod, ashamed for Cade to see you cry. Boys aren't supposed to cry.

But Cade just squats there, peers out into the sky, and lets you have your cry. After a while you stop crying and look up at his slim brown face, his blue eyes narrowed against the sun. Nobody's got blue eyes like my Cade, Mama says. And it's true. Cade's face is so handsome and regular that you almost want to reach out and touch it. Perhaps that is what you are extending your short fingers to do when he turns abruptly to look at you.

Feel better? Cade asks. He breaks into a wide smile and reaches out to ruffle your hair.

Okay, you say. What Mama says don't work.

What's Mama say? Cade asks.

Tell them to go jump in a lake.

Cade laughs and sits down. His breath hangs in the cold air. You laugh, too. Everybody laughs when Cade laughs, except Pap. Maybe because Mama specially likes Cade, but you're not sure. You wish Mama talked to you the way she talks to Cade, her voice all full up instead of thin and sorry-sounding.

Nah, Cade says, pulling his legs up against his chest and resting his chin on his knees. I reckon telling them to go jump in a lake wouldn't do much good.

You say nothing, like you always do, mostly because you don't know what to say. It's okay to be quiet though, especially with Cade. He showed you this place, Cade did. Said it was his special place for thinking, and now it's your special place, too, though you don't think much.

Cade is humming a snatch of something under his breath when you speak again. Mama send you to find me? you ask.

Mama said you done run off with the lamp oil money, that's all, Cade says. I reckoned you were up here.

Mama's going to be mad, you say. You jingle the scrip in your pocket.

Mama ain't going to be mad, Cade says. I'll take care of Mama. She don't understand you, that's all.

Understand me how? you ask.

Cade turns to study you with his clear blue eyes. Mama's funny that way, Jorey. Sometimes, she forgets how special you are.

I ain't special, you say. Stupid, maybe.

Cade chuckles. Well, you ain't no professor, Jorey, that's for sure. But you're special all right.

Cade tousles your hair and laughs again and stands. But you don't move, not for a long moment. Cade's words jolt some memory: Gramma saying, That one's touched. Those words rattling around in your head.

C'mon, lazy, Cade says, prodding at you with his boot. C'mon, we gotta get back.

You stand and the scrip jingles in your pocket again. You think of the lamp oil, and the commissary, closed till morning, and you say, Mama's going to be mad.

But Cade says, Don't you worry. Company's sending in some Baldwin-Felts men on the afternoon train. Mama's got plenty to worry her tonight without bothering about you.

He laughs again, but this time there's something underneath the laugh, something shrill and excited and maybe a little scared—something you can't quite put a name to. An uneasy feeling swirls through your belly.

Then Cade says, shivering, Let's go. It's cold out here.

He throws his arm around your shoulders and together you strike off into the woods, angling away from the mine, down toward the tracks and home. Looking back, you see the squirrel come down out of the hickory to sniff around on the rock. Something warm and pleasant opens up inside you, and that uneasy feeling is gone, for a little while anyway.

It's worse at night, the coughing is, and with it a kind of tightness that closes in around your lungs. But no one really notices, not tonight.

Pap, Mama, and Cade are deep in talk, hunched around the table, the kerosene lamp between them. Their long twisting shadows skulk away behind them. The shack is a fitful menagerie of shadows. Gramma's snakes along the floor here by the stove, and yours rocks close beside it: a small boy's shadow, just like any other.

Mama's face is pale in the red gleam, saying, with a tremble in her voice you've never heard there, The boy's too young, Jack.

Pap, his gray hair thin, dark lines of coal dust beneath his eyes, Pap says, We ain't got any choice. Copperhead won't stop at nothing to keep the union out of West Virginia. We got to make a show of force.

Cade leans forward and places his big hands, knotting and unknotting, against the table. His shadow seems to follow him, up along the rough wall and ceiling, looming over him. Cade says, He's right, Mama.

What do you mean, he's right? What about school?

It's only one day, Pap says.

Cade isn't a miner, says Mama.

Ain't nothing else you can be in these parts, Gramma says from her rocker. You ought to know that, Lilla.

Them Baldwin-Felts men coming up from Bluefield tomorrow, Pap says. They're bringing scabs with them.

Let them come, Mama says, but my boy is going to school.

Goddammit, Pap says, he ain't no boy anymore. He's near six-teen years old.

He's fifteen, Mama says. Just a boy. I won't let you use him. People might die there tomorrow. Cade might die.

Pap curses and stands, his chair clattering to the floor behind him. He strides to the window with long angry steps. In the silence, Cade looks into Mama's eyes with that way he has. Cade could charm a snake, Mama says sometimes, and she looks back at him now with shiny, fearful eyes.

Mama, you want to live in them tents again? Cade asks with a voice smooth like syrup.

Mama sniffles and shakes her head. Pap turns from the window to watch, and in the flickering light you can see his eyes are wet, too. Suddenly, without knowing why, you want to go to him, to press your face against his rough shirt, but you hold your peace here by the stove, watching.

Cade says, The strike's going to happen, Mama. There ain't nothing we can do about it. Tomorrow them Baldwin-Felts men are going to throw us out of here and we'll be in those tents again.

You want to live in them goddamned tents all winter? Pap says from across the room. Half-starved and freezing, with Jorey coughing like he is?

Mama doesn't even look at you.

What about Ma, Pap says, jabbing his finger at the old woman.

Cade silences him with a look. For a moment, the only sounds are Gramma's rocker, squeaking, and the lamp, sputtering, nearly dry. Cade says, They'll throw us out, Mama. Put niggers to work in the mines, let niggers live in our houses.

Pap says, Anybody going to take that coal out of the mountain, it's going to be us. It's only right.

But why Cade? Take Jorey if you have to, but not Cade, Mama says. She starts to cry.

Pap laughs. Jorey, he says. You know better, Lilla.

And Cade says, Mama, we got to stand up to them tomorrow. And every man as can help ought to help.

Just then, the kerosene is gone. The lamp flickers and dies. In the half-darkness, the room red with the gleam of the stove, Mama says, Stupid child. That's all the lamp oil.

Pap curses and moves to the door. You follow, the room suddenly too close with the smell of kerosene and burning coal, with Mama crying in the gloom. You slip out behind Pap, out into a cutting wind, somehow pure in its iciness. The door slams behind you.

Dark mountains loom against the sky. It has begun to snow, tiny wind-driven flakes, like grains of sand flung against your face. You shiver.

Pap, standing out on the other side of the road, at the edge of an icy creek, turns to face you. Jorey, he says.

Yes sir, Pap, you say.

What are you doing out here, boy? Too cold for you, with that cough.

You cross the road, scuffing your feet against the dirt. Too hot inside, you say. I want to be with you.

Pap shrugs out of his flannel coat and drapes it around your shoulders. He stands there for a minute, then says, Let's walk.

Together, Pap's arm heavy across your shoulders, you head down into the coal camp. Beyond the stream, dark woods press close. The other side of the road is lined with shacks, shuttered against the cold, trailing wind-blown streams of smoke. The stench of burning coal hangs like a pall over the valley.

Wish I could help tomorrow, you say.

I know, Pap says.

You walk in silence for a while. The stream chatters along beside you. In daylight, it runs black with coal dust, that stream, but now it shines silvery in the falling snow, clean-looking. The blackness is still there. You just can't see it.

Mama wants me to help, you say.

Pap sighs, his breath gray and cloudy in the darkness. Your mama don't know what she wants, most of the time, he says. You ain't to judge her, Jorey.

At last, the stream turns away into the woods. You emerge into a rutted street, bordered on this side by a network of railroad tracks that runs the length of the camp. Beyond them, a weather-beaten line of buildings, black behind the shifting curtain of snow, straggles along the dirt lane.

Together, you and Pap cross the tracks and mount the steps to the commissary porch. A single electric lamp glows within the store, casting a narrow rectangle of light across the porch and the wooden walkway that fronts the street. Pap lowers himself to the oaken bench in one shadowy corner, and cradles his face in cupped palms. You move close against him, against his heat.

Shouts and piano music drift up the street from Janey's Saloon, two blocks away. After a while, Pap raises his head and says, You hear me, Jorey? You ain't to judge your Mama.

Okay, you say.

She ain't from these parts, Pap says. She's from down Bluefield, and that ain't mining country. You remember Bluefield.

And you do. A long time ago, three, four years maybe, that was. Pap said you needed a real doctor, not a coal field quack, so he and Mama saved up for a while, and then one spring morning you and Mama took the morning train to Bluefield, nearly an hour away. But the doctor, he just shook his head. Nothing I can do, the doctor said. Boy's a mongoloid. Nothing anybody can do.

Afterward, Mama showed you the house where your grandpa lived. It was a big house with columns, all shining white, and you wanted to go in and see Grandpa. You hadn't ever seen him. But Mama tightened her lips till they turned white and led you away. On the train back to Copperhead, Mama wept. You just sat there, watching the mountains roll by.

No one has ever said a word about that trip, not ever. But Mama hasn't been the same.

Ahh, Jorey, Pap says now. These mountains call you back. You can't never get away.

You don't know what Pap means by this, so you don't say a word. Just shiver, listen to the music from Janey's, and watch the snow spit heavier out of the night sky. It's beginning to stick, the snow is, a gray shroud across all of Copperhead. After a while, you hear the muffled beat of footsteps against the wooden sidewalk. A long figure ambles in front of the commissary, but you and Pap, submerged in shadow, don't say a word until the cough betrays you.

Then Pap stands, pulling you up with him, pulling you into the light. Evening, Granville, Pap says.

Granville Snidow tips a finger to his black hat and crosses his arms against the porch railing. He wears pearl-handled revolvers strapped low to either hip. At home, Pap calls Snidow a Baldwin-Felts s.o.b., but up here on the porch of the commissary, he just smiles in a private kind of way.

Snidow laughs, a harsh sound. The star pinned to his overcoat glints in the light from the electric lamp. His lips widen beneath his mustache—a handsome affair, your mama calls it—thick and bristling, with ends coiled into tight circles. Well, Jack, Snidow says, how come you ain't down at Janey's drinking up some courage?

I don't need to drink my courage, Granville, Pap says. I ain't a drinking man.

Kind of cold for you all to be out tonight, ain't it?

We was just leaving, Pap says. He grips your shoulder tightly and steers you down to the sidewalk. Together, you cross the tracks and start up the dirt road toward home.

Hey, Jack! Snidow shouts a minute later.

You feel Pap tense as he turns. Granville Snidow is almost lost in the snow that pelts down now out of the sky.

Hey, Jack! Snidow calls. It's a good thing you're heading in! I wouldn't want your half-wit to catch cold!

But Pap doesn't say a word. He just turns away and leads you home. Inside, the tiny shack seems warm after the cold night. In the red glow of the firebox, it is a relief to climb into the warm bed with Cade, stealing his heat. Gramma snores in the dark and you hear Pap shuck his clothes before he crawls in bed with Mama. Then the room falls quiet and you sleep.

Sometime in the night, the coughing wakes you. The whole room is bright with moonlight. Outside, the snow has stopped, but you don't pay it much mind. You just lie there, watching Pap. He sits by the window in a cane-backed chair and his long johns seem to shine in the moonlight. He's humming quietly to himself, Pap is, humming as he cleans his rifle.

You wake again to the chill glow that precedes dawn, your nerves tingling with the awareness of someone watching you: Gramma, awake, though the others still sleep. The old woman eyes you wordlessly from her place by the stove as you clamber away from Cade's heat, out into the cold air. She doesn't speak as you dress. And when you offer her a hunk of bread to breakfast on, she merely shakes her head and sucks at her toothless gums.

She just watches you with her pale eyes, and never says a word. Perhaps it's because you're touched.

Touched.

That word, and all its vast mystery, rattles around in your head like a seed in a dry gourd. And together with Gramma's unflinching gaze, somehow awful in the sleeping cabin, it is at last enough to chase you out into the frigid dawn, still holding a half-eaten chunk of bread.

Silent as a wraith, you flee through row after row of squalid shacks. With every step your feet punch through frozen drifts and gray snow clutches at your ankles. Gramma's stare seems to follow you, that word—

—*touched*—

—to linger in your mind.

Only when you reach the edge of the coal camp and turn up the tracks toward the mines, does Gramma's persistent stare seem to fall away behind you, your hunger to return. You start to gnaw at the bread, but the memory of the squirrel probing hungrily about the edge of the precipice returns. A kind of warm feeling opens up in your belly, and you tuck the dry crust into a pocket.

But when at last you reach the special place, up above the number five shaft, the squirrel is dead, curled into a frozen knot at the edge of the cliff.

For a moment, standing there, a terrible sense of vertigo sweeps through you—as if you are falling, falling back into a well of memory. Last winter. An explosion in the number three shaft. Fifteen miners dead.

You won't ever forget those bodies, stiff and bloody, beginning to stink when they were finally dragged from the rubble. You won't ever forget the funeral: the sound of shovels scraping at mounds of frozen earth; the voices of the miners and their families rising in song together, dry and lonely sounding as night wind in the hollers. Death is real to you, palpable, though you can never understand it.

Now, remembering, Mama's words return to you: *People might die there. Cade might die.*

Today.

And then that endless moment snaps; the world settles into place around you. A sob escapes you, and you step forward, falling to your knees, the crust of bread dropped on the ground behind you, forgotten.

The squirrel is rigid and cold to the touch. Frost rimes its whiskers. Its small skull is cracked as neatly as you have seen Pap crack an acorn beneath his heel, and a single dark streak of blood mats the stiff fur above one eye. Perhaps it has fallen from the icy branches of the overhanging hickory. You don't know.

Somehow, though, in the midst of large griefs which surpass your understanding, this small grief touches you. Loss suffuses you, and for a time you clasp the tiny corpse to your chest, unawares.

When you finally look up again, the pale glow of dawn has given way to the broad luster of midmorning. The chill has crept beneath your flannel coat. It clings close about your feet, wet from the long hike up the mountain. You feel as stiff and cold as the corpse you cradle in your hands.

As the squirrel. Dead.

You cannot help but recall how the squirrel would nuzzle your empty fingers when the bread was gone, and with that memory a dry emptiness yawns within you. Almost without realizing it, you speak, a single word, whispered in the stillness of morning: No. Something surges within you, a power almost electric. That one word seems to blow away the fog of confusion that clouds your mind. That one word seems to fill you up.

Your fingers, numb with cold mere moments before, grow suddenly warm and flex of their own accord. Your hands flare with sharp sudden pain. The squirrel twists in your grasp, twists again, and tiny jaws clamp around your finger. Sharp teeth grind your flesh, drawing a sudden welter of blood, dark against your pale flesh.

With a cry of fear and astonishment, you release the squirrel's writhing body. It springs away, turns to scold you briefly, and then escapes into the overhanging hickory. You do not move, not even to lift the bleeding finger to your lips.

A sense of mystery and awe you can never articulate rushes through you. That power, that moment of stunning clarity is again eclipsed by fog and confusion. For long hours you turn all your will to dispel that fog, to try to understand. But it is no use. You can never understand anything.

Through all the fog that fills your mind, there is only this mystery: Gramma's voice, saying, *Touched. Touched by the hand of God. Idiot child'll have a talent.*

Though you cannot understand those words, you think of them over and over through the morning. And despite the cold, you do not move again, not till the long rising whine of the afternoon train calls you out of your torpor.

Cade, you think.

And then you are running down the mountain toward the railroad tracks and home.

By the time you reach Copperhead, clouds have settled in and gray snow spits from the lowering sky.

Standing breathlessly in the street across from the commissary, you watch Pap and three other men stride down the tracks toward the railway station by Janey's Saloon. They carry long rifles cradled in their arms. Twenty yards behind them follows a ragged crescent of ten or eleven armed men. Cade is among them, his face pale and thin, so young-looking. From the other direction, a loose band of men led by Granville Snidow walks up the tracks. Snidow's palms rest easily on the pearl-handled revolvers that ride low on his hips. His hatchet face is still and expressionless.

When they are ten or fifteen yards apart, the two camps stop to study one another. Both groups of men shift restlessly about. Fingers curl white around the stocks of shotguns and rifles. Pap and Snidow alone stand motionless, facing one another.

In the stillness, you can hear the wind sough among the trees in the hollers. Across the street, a curtain twitches in the commissary window and your eyes are drawn to your mama's face, peering through the glass at the gloomy afternoon.

And then Pap's voice, loud in the silence, draws your attention back to the cluster of men in the street.

Granville, Pap says. He inclines his head, the barest nod.

Well, Granville says. To listen to the talk at Janey's last night, I'd have thought there'd have been more of you today.

I reckon there's enough of us, Pap says. We don't want no trouble. But we don't aim to leave our homes—

Those are the last words spoken. You're not sure who has fired the first shot, or why, but suddenly the afternoon is shattered by a staccato burst of gunfire: the deep-throated boom of shotguns intermixed with the long flat cracks of rifles and the sharp reports of Granville Snidow's pistols, popping over and over again.

The two clumps of men seem to explode in all directions. Men dive to the earth and dart away to the edges of the street. In the confusion of smoke and gunfire and moving bodies, you search for Cade, but you don't see him.

And then, as suddenly as it began, it is over. The acrid tang of burned powder hangs in the air. Granville Snidow stands alone in the midst of the crumpled bodies, a pistol in either hand. Smoke drifts along the silent street.

Pap! you cry. Cade!

The shout decays into a long rattling cough and then you are running toward the middle of the street. Your short legs plow through the gray snow. Pap writhes on the tracks by his rifle, cursing and clutching at his leg. But Cade is still. He lies several yards beyond Pap, flat on his back with his arms flung wide as if to embrace you. His face is the color of ashes against the leaden snow and blood bubbles at his lips.

Cade! you cry again, your voice breaking.

You go to your knees in the snow beside him, cradle his head in your lap. Blood boils out of a ragged hole in his chest. Every time he sucks in a breath, the hole whistles like a tea kettle when the water begins to boil.

Cade, you say. Cade.

And Cade opens his eyes, those eyes so blue they are like the clear blue ice that forms along the edge of the commissary roof. Well now, Jorey, Cade says, lifting his head. Don't this beat all?

He tries to laugh, but the laugh turns into an explosive cough. A thin spray of blood coats your flanel jacket, and Cade's head drops back, his eyes going dark.

Dead as the eyes of the squirrel.

Just then you hear the crack of heels against the ties behind you, and Mama screams from the commissary porch, No! No!

You twist your head around to see Granville Snidow, still clutching a pistol in either hand, wearing a kind of terrible expression like you've never seen on any adult's face. He is so pale and haggard that even his mustache seems to droop. His eyes gleam from dark hollows.

No! Mama screams.

But Granville Snidow lurches a step closer. Oh, Christ, kid, he whispers. Oh, Christ, I'm sorry, I—

He raises his arms to the sky, and a bloody flower blossoms in the center of his chest. There is a hollow echoing boom and Granville Snidow pitches forward, his body thrashing in the snow. Behind him, you see Pap, half-upright, his wounded leg drawn up beneath him, still clutching his smoking rifle.

Jesus, Pap says, and then he, too, pitches forward, dropping the rifle and curling tight around his leg.

Jorey! Mama screams. Jorey!

Looking around, you see her descend the porch steps. You glance down at Cade, remembering all those days when he sat with you in your special place, just being with you the way he always was, not even caring that you were stupid the way the other kids cared, the way Mama cared. That was the way Cade was. Just Cade.

No, you whisper, and the memory of the squirrel, twisting and twisting in your hands, returns to you.

You can feel it again, that power, that touch. It surges through your body until your nerves sing, tingles down your arms and through your hands. Your fingers flush with electric heat, so hot they seem to glow, and then, almost of their own accord, they flex in Cade's blond hair. The touch jerks through them. Cade's eyelids twitch and flicker open, and you know you can do it.

You can bring him back. You know you can.

But just then, you hear Mama, her voice shrill in the silence as she crosses the rutted street, Mama, crying, Jorey! Jorey! Is Cade okay?

The sour taste of bile floods your mouth, and you jerk away from Cade, your hands and fingers going suddenly numb in the cold. His eyelids close again and his head lolls back along his shoulder. Blood drips from his open mouth, melting the gray snow.

Then Mama is standing before you.

Cade's dead, you say.

Mama sobs. Oh, Jorey, she says. Oh, Jorey.

But her voice is different somehow. There is a hint of something warm and rich in that voice, as if it might someday sound all full up, the way it used to sound for Cade. And it can be for you. Just you. It always can be.

For the rest of your life, this moment will stand apart in time, as stark and memorable as a glimpse of wind-lashed trees along the ridge-tops, frozen against the sky by a sudden flash of lightning. In that timeless instant, you sob out your grief and joy—for some new loneliness, some irrevocable loss that you will never understand no matter how hard you try; for some old hollowness within you, forever filled. At last, the sob breaks, becomes the unceasing cough that has been with you for days now. And coughing, you stand. Stand and step over Cade's body to clutch her fiercely, to press your face tight into her warm skirts.

Oh, Mama, you say. And again: Oh, Mama.

MOM'S LITTLE FRIENDS

◆　　◆　　◆

Ray Vukcevich

Ray Vukcevich is a mild-mannered graduate student working in the area of artificial intelligence. He says language fascinates him, hence his interest in computers and his interest in fiction. His short fiction has appeared in Asimov's, Aboriginal SF, *and* F&SF. *Pulphouse:* A Fiction Magazine *has published most of his short work, including other stories about the tiny out-of-control people featured in "Mom's Little Friends."*

Because he wouldn't understand, we left Mom's German shepherd Toby leashed to the big black roll bar in the back of Ada's pickup truck, and because Mom's hands were tied behind her back and because her ankles were lashed together, we had some trouble wrestling her out of the cab and onto the bridge.

My sister Ada rolled her over—a little roughly, I thought—and checked the knots. I had faith in those knots. Ada was a rancher from Arizona and knew how to tie things up. I made sure Mom's sweater was buttoned. I jerked her green-and-white housedress back down over her pasty knees. I made sure her boots were tightly tied.

The breeze sweeping down the gorge made the gray curls above her forehead quiver. The wind seemed to move the steel bridge a little, too, but that may have been my imagination. Even from up here, I could smell the river and hear its gravelly whisper. Blackbirds circled and complained in the clear blue sky above us. The sun was a hot spotlight in the chilly, thin mountain air. Toby paced back and forth in the truck bed, whining and pulling at his leash and watching us closely.

"What about the glasses, Barry?" Ada tapped a fingernail on the lenses of Mom's fragile, wire-rimmed glasses.

"Please don't do this, children."

"Shut up, Jessica." Ada spoke, not to our mother, but to Mom's interface with her nanopeople. When Dr. Holly Ketchum (Mom, that is) introduced a colony of nanopeople into her own body, it was seen by many as a bold new step. It had, after all, never before been done under controlled conditions. Nanotechnology held such promise—long life and good health, a kind of immortality, really.

So, how did it work out? What one word would sum it all up? Well, "whoops" might be a good choice.

The problem was that after a few generations—that is to say, after a few hours—the nanopeople became convinced that their world shouldn't take any unnecessary chances. It made no sense to the nanopeople to let their world endanger herself. Jessica claimed that, individually, nanopeople were as adventurous as anyone else. "But put yourself in our place, Barry," she'd once said to me. "Would you let your world put sticks on her feet and go speeding down a snowy mountain at sixty miles an hour? Or swim with sharks? Be reasonable."

Mom looked like a TV grandmother these days—plump, rosy cheeks and translucent white skin. Her nanopeople could have fixed her vision easily enough, but they thought the glasses would make her more cautious in most situations. They could have left her appearance at its natural forty-eight years or even made her look younger, but they chose this cookie-cutting, slow-shuffling granny look to discourage relationships that might turn out to be dangerous. They could have left her mind alone; instead, they struck her silly. A slow-moving, stupid world is a world that takes no chances.

Jessica had been created to explain things to Mom. She was really a network of nanopeople working in shifts to produce the illusion that called itself Jessica. The nanopeople—invisible, sentient, self-replicating robots of nanotechnology—simply thought more quickly than big people. If Mom were struggling to access a multisyllabic word, there could be a week's worth of shift changes among the nanopeople running the Jessica interface. In fact, a nanoperson could come into existence, grow up, get trained, find a mate, write poetry, procreate, rise to the top of a career, screw up a relationship, get cynical, and die in the time it took Mom to cook up a batch of brownies.

The real horror, I suppose, was that while individual nanopeople might come and go, as a society, they intended to keep Mom alive and stupid pretty much forever.

I plucked the glasses from her face. "I'll save these for you, Jessica, just in case you ever need them again." I gave her a look I hoped was menacing, and let my remarks just sit there for a moment, then I sat Mom up and leaned her against the bridge railing. "There's still time for negotiation, Jessica," I said.

"I'm sure I don't know what you mean, Barry." Jessica was doing what the nanopeople thought was Mom's voice. I wasn't fooled. Mom never whined. Not the old Mom, anyway. At least we had the nanopeople's attention these days. At first, Jessica had not bothered to even acknowledge our existence. Then we started pushing Mom into water over her head, and Jessica decided to talk to us.

I tied the big rubber bands to Mom's boots.

"The word is *bungee*, Jessica," Ada said.

My sister was becoming one scary chick, I thought, what with her horse tattoo and western hat and the ever-present toothpick in the corner of her mouth. It was almost like she was enjoying this. Or maybe she was just a better actor. I remembered how she'd cried on the phone the night she called me home from graduate school in Oregon, how she kept saying Mom had nothing on her mind but cookies—cookies and cakes and those little flaky things with sweet red crap in the middle—and I need your help, Barry; I can't do this alone, Barry. I'd gotten verbal assurance from my adviser in the physics department that I could take a leave of absence, and had bused to Tucson the very next day.

Mom made me a pie when I got home.

I took Mom under the arms, and Ada grabbed her feet. We swung her like a sack of laundry, and on the count of three, tossed her over the side of the bridge. Toby went crazy, barking and pulling at his leash in the back of Ada's truck.

We put our hands on the bridge rail and watched Mom fall and fall toward the river, the long bungee bands trailing behind her, and listened to her scream—well, listened to someone scream, anyway; when it was Jessica, it was a howl of frustration and terror, but when it was Mom, it was an exuberant whoop! Or maybe I was imagining things. Maybe I didn't have the faith Ada had in this plan to get the nanopeople out of Mom.

We watched Mom bounce like a yo-yo on the end of her bungee bands, her housedress hanging down over her head. We decided to let her swing awhile. Ada unpacked our picnic lunch, and we settled down on the bridge to eat.

As we munched and sipped, I heard a small voice calling, "Help, help," but I decided to ignore it.

"So, Ada," I said. "How come Mom's nanopeople don't transform her into something that can climb up the rubber bands? A giant spider, say."

"I call the answer to that my King Kong theory," Ada said. "I'll bet the nanopeople can see in Mom's memory that picture of Kong on the Empire State Building with all the airplanes buzzing around and shooting. Or some other picture like that. The thing with these guys is safety first and always."

Those faraway cries for help were getting to me. I gave Ada a sidelong glance. I didn't want my big sister to think I was wimping out on her. "So, shall we pull her up?" I tried to sound casual.

"I suppose." Ada took another bite of her sandwich, then tossed it into the basket.

We pulled Mom up.

"So Jessica," Ada said. "You want to do that again?"

"No!"

"Let's talk, then."

Jessica let Mom's chin fall to her chest and was quiet for a minute or so. Then she raised Mom's head. "What do you want? How can we make you stop this?"

"Get out of Mom!" I shouted, and Ada gave me a sharp look. I had no talent for diplomacy.

"That's pretty much what we want, Jessica," Ada said. "We need to discuss the terms of your eviction."

"That is an absurd notion," Jessica said. "Each one of us lives a life every bit as important and significant as yours, Ada. You just move more slowly. You're just bigger. None of that signifies. Have you no empathy? Holly is our world. This is the only world the People have ever known. Just where do you suppose we could go?"

"We have an idea about that." Ada signaled me with her eyes.

I got up and walked to the truck and untied Toby's leash. With a great leap of joy, he bounded out of the bed of the truck. Tail wagging, trying to look everywhere at once, nose to the ground, nose in the air, he dragged me back to Mom and Ada. I convinced him to sit down in front of Mom. Taking advantage of the fact that she was tied up, he licked her face. I often wondered whether the dog knew this was Mom. He seemed to like this dowdy little person, but this person was always around these days, and it seemed to me his enthusiasm for her was somehow of a lower quality than the worship he had always had for Mom. Maybe he'd just gotten used to Jessica.

"We want you to move to Toby," Ada said.

Toby's ears stiffened at the sound of his name, and he looked up at Ada.

Jessica was quiet for a moment. Then she made Mom's soft grandmother mouth a hard line. "You want us to move into a dog?" She sounded incredulous.

"You got it," Ada said.

"You want an entire civilization, billions of us, each with definite ideas and hopes and dreams, to just shuffle off to another world? You think that generations of tradition and deeply felt religion and philosophy can be tossed aside? You think we'll move into a dog?"

"I think she's got it," Ada said.

"We won't do it," Jessica said. "And we won't discuss it further." She closed Mom's mouth and squeezed Mom's eyes tightly shut.

"Hey! Wait a minute!" I yelled.

"Never mind, Barry." Ada grabbled Mom's feet and gave me a sharp look.

I got the message. I took Mom under the arms, and we tossed her over the side again. Toby just sat there for a moment like he couldn't believe his eyes, then he jumped up and put his front paws up on the railing and watched Mom bounce.

When we pulled her up this time and propped her against the bridge railing, I looked closely at her wild eyes, hoping, I guess, for a little momness. Not a chance. It was clear we'd finally pissed off her little friends. Big things were happening in Mom. Her face twisted into a horrible grimace, her cheeks puffed out, and her eyes bulged. She suddenly spit a huge stream of green stuff at us. We jumped out of the way.

"She's mine." The voice was deep and male, a truly scary demon voice. "You can't have her."

"Ah, Jessica," Ada said. She took off her cowgirl hat and used it to swat Mom on the side of the head. "We've seen those movies, too. If you're not going to be serious, we're going to throw you over again."

"You don't know what you've done," Jessica said in her usual Jessica voice. "There have been uprisings since we talked last. People have died. Listen to me, Ada. Barry. People have died. People every bit as real as you. Good people. How can you continue this?"

"But you're destroying our mother!" I said.

"One person for the good of billions! And besides, she's not destroyed."

"This one person is our mother," Ada said. "And that's where you're in trouble. We won't quit. Mom would rather be dead than stupid. Let's throw her over again, Barry."

"Wait!" Jessica said. "That's not true. What you just said. You forget we're inside here. We have access that you don't have. We talk to Holly all the time. We're not monsters. Holly is our Mother World."

"Then why do you keep her stupid?" Ada asked.

"Not stupid." Jessica sounded sincere, but I didn't buy it. "Content. Holly is our mother, but she is also our child to be guided, much as you mold and guide your own world."

I could have told her a thing or two about how well we molded and guided our own world, but suddenly that seemed as if it might work against us. I kept my mouth shut.

"Our solution is perfect," Ada said. She put her hand between Toby's ears and scratched. "What do dogs do but lie around all day, anyway? You could keep him as fat and lazy and silly as you want."

"That will simply never happen," Jessica said. "We will never be able to convince all of the people. In fact, we will be able to convince very few. If you throw Holly off the bridge again, you could cause a war in here. I want you to think carefully. It won't be nice if there is artillery shelling going on in your mother's lungs. Hand-to-hand combat in her stomach. Swordplay in her heart. There will be cell damage. We are fighting for our very world. Would you destroy an entire people, an entire world, for your Mother?"

"Yes," Ada said at once.

I was glad I didn't have to answer that one. I didn't even want to think about it.

"And what will you do, Ada, if you force our society into a state of primitive savagery?" Jessica said. "How do you think Holly will like having little bands of hunter/gatherers roaming around in her liver?"

"If her mind is free, she'll be able to handle her liver."

"We won't move to a dog," Jessica said, and then she was quiet. Ada took her feet. "One more time, Barry."

"But what about all those people?" I asked.

"Shut up." Ada dropped Mom's feet and wiped tears from her own eyes with a big blue-checked handkerchief from her back pocket. I shut up and took Mom under the arms again.

We threw her over the side. Jessica didn't even scream this time.

We pulled her up after only a few bounces. Ada looked grim, and I feared that this whole business would fail. All those people. I could be honest with myself, at least in little short bursts. I understood how entire lives could be lived in minutes. I knew that Jessica was right when she said the nanopeople were as real as I. I understood that some of them were dying. We rolled Mom over. She looked dead herself, but when I grabbed her wrist, I felt a pulse. Ada sat her up and gently slapped her face over and over again. I scooted back and grabbed a soda out of the picnic basket and poured a little in my hand and flicked it at Mom. No response. Toby pushed his way in between Ada and me and licked Mom's face again.

Some time passed.

Then Jessica opened Mom's eyes.

"So much has changed." Jessica sounded weak, diminished somehow. "But one thing is still firm. We will not abandon our world."

Ada sighed. I hoped she wouldn't want to toss Mom over the side again.

"We propose a compromise," Jessica said.

"We're listening," Ada said.

"We propose to let Holly have more control over her life," Jessica said. "We have combed through her memory and have found a set of activities that we feel prepared to tolerate. Ballroom dancing is an example."

Ada's face got absolutely purple. Her hands closed in fists and opened in claws, closed and opened. When she spoke, her voice was steady and cold, but coiled like a spring, cobra tight. "You're telling me that you will allow Dr. Holly Ketchum, a respected physicist and leading authority on nanotechnology, a woman so full of curiosity and life that some people simply have to step out of her light or get burned, a woman vibrating with sexual vitality and gentle, innocent love and openness for almost everyone. . . ." She jumped up and shouted: "A woman who thrives on the adrenaline rush of white water and rock faces and free-fall. You're telling me you're going to allow this woman to do ballroom dancing? Is that what you're telling me?"

"Well, yes. Among other things."

"Ada." I grabbed her hand, and the look she turned down on me would have loosened the bowels of a biker. "Let me try," I said. I thought she was going to say something to make me feel small or even hit me, but she jerked her hand away and stomped off to her truck instead. Toby and I watched as she kicked big dents in the door of her truck. When she stopped yelling and slumped to the ground, I turned to Mom and spoke to Jessica.

"If there is to be a compromise, Jessica," I said. "It will have to be on our terms. Or, if you think about that a little, it'll have to be on Mom's terms. You're going to have to learn to live with what your world wants, not what you want for your world."

"Well, we did come up with this list."

"You're going to have to let Mom come out and tell you what she wants."

"But she takes such chances!"

"You'll have to learn to trust her," I said.

Jessica didn't reply, and I was suddenly at a loss. It seemed clear what must happen next, but I didn't know how to convince the nanopeople. I felt a hand on my shoulder and jerked my head around in time to see Ada squat down beside me.

"Barry's right," Ada said. "You must turn inward. You must let Mom take care of the stuff outside. You don't have what it takes to deal with things out here. We can keep throwing you off the bridge until your society is completely disrupted. If it starts to look like those of you who are left are getting used to bungee, we can do something else. Access Mom's memory of alligator wrestling."

Jessica squinted Mom's eyes for a moment, then jerked her head to the right as if Ada had slapped her.

"Look at ultralight stunt flying," I said, encouraged again by Ada's support.

Jessica jerked Mom's head to the left.

"Do we need to go on?" Ada asked. "We won't quit."

Jessica let Mom's shoulders slump. She sighed. "We'll try it your way," she said. "We'll try it. But strictly on a trial basis!"

"No conditions," Ada said.

Jessica rolled Mom's eyes for a long time, then she said, "You win."

A smile grew on Mom's face, bigger and bigger, until she laughed out loud. "Ada! Barry!" She struggled with the ropes around her wrists. "I knew I could count on you two."

I could see it was Mom—something about the way the body was controlled convinced me Mom was to some degree in charge—but how much Mom was it? I worried that the nanopeople would have her on a short leash.

Toby lunged across my lap to get to her. The entire back end of his body wagged as he licked her face, and he could not contain his joy, to the point that he peed all over me. I didn't know how Ada felt about it, but a Mom real enough to make a dog pee was a Mom real enough for me. I leaned in and kissed her cheek.

"Untie me," Mom said, twisting her head this way and that to avoid Toby's tongue.

Ada pushed the dog away and pulled the big blade from the sheath on her belt. She turned Mom around and cut her wrists loose.

Mom's hair turned brown even as she stripped off her sweater. Her eyes cleared; her skin tightened. She pulled the dreary house-dress from first one shoulder and then the other and wiggled it down to her hips. She bounced a little and pulled the dress along with her underwear down her thighs and over her knees. Ada undid the bungee boots and pulled them off Mom's feet. Mom's wrinkles disappeared, and her bones straightened. When she stood, nude and magnificent and beaming a big smile at us, she was Mom in body again. Well, in a way. This was Mom, I thought, as she must have looked at thirty or so. Long reddish brown hair falling over slightly freckled shoulders. Pale blue eyes. Small, high breasts. Long, strong legs.

"Shall we go home, Mother?" Ada asked.

"Not so fast." Mom sat down on the bridge and pulled the bungee boots on again. "I need to pin down just who's boss in here." She climbed up on the bridge rail and, with a wild scream of joy, did a perfect swan dive into the abyss.

We watched the arch of her dive and listened to her yell and watched her bounce.

"Do you suppose we've just postponed things?" I asked.

"What do you mean?"

"Well, what do you think will happen to her when we've either got nanopeople of our own or we've died? How about then?"

Ada seemed to think about that as we listened to Mom whoop at the upswing of each bounce.

"Well, maybe we'd better pull her up and get some motherly advice," Ada said.

CAST ON A DISTANT SHORE

◆　　◆　　◆

R. Garcia y Robertson

Rod Garcia is a historian with a Ph.D. from UCLA. He has taught at UCLA and at Villanova, and in the late 1980s started to write SF under the name R. Garcia y Robertson. He seems equally at home and inventive with fantasy or SF; his novel The Spiral Dance *is based on several fantasy stories in F&SF. "Cast on a Distant Shore" was his first F&SF story. It was a product, says the author, of time spent studying evolutionary theory and animal mimicry, and of time spent swimming in the Caribbean. It turns out to be science fiction at its best: fresh, exotic, and fast paced.*

Windward Mat

Floating facedown in the blood-warm water, Kafirr watched the sea creature become a carnivore. A heartbeat before, it had been a harmless root scavenger, but now its body sucked in saltwater, expanding and elongating. Its tail flattened into a single stiff blade, and its jaws drew back, revealing a predator's evil grin. Dark shadows crept over the creature's upper surfaces, while the belly turned corpse white. This coloring mimicked the two-tone camouflage favored by deep-water hunters. Pseudolimbs beat faster, and the scavenger's tentative movements turned to swift, decisive lunges. Tiny grim teeth prepared to rip apart anything in its path.

The first time Kafirr had seen a copy-fish go though this act, it had scared him right out of the water. He had stayed out for over a hundred hours, and only hunger had driven him back in. Grown children who did not dive did not eat. Now, after thousands of hours in the water, he found the sudden transformation comforting. Copy-fish were harmless; they mimicked a dozen different carnivores to disguise themselves and scare off smaller predators. By keeping watch on the copy-fish, Kafirr could tell what real predators were hunting through the root grottoes. Neither the copy-fish nor the carnivores it mimicked were true fishes. They were crafty, warm-blooded sea creatures, swimming with the aid of paddlelike pseudolimbs. Kafirr did not know the names he used were wrong; he was not an ichthyologist, just a child of earth cast on a distant shore, using the words of a world that he had never seen.

Every odor, every vibration, triggered a change in the copy-fish. This one had heard or smelled a deepdevil coming up from below. Since deepdevils never ate their own, a good disguise was effective defense.

Kafirr had no defense and no disguise, but the boy had been warned. He had to dive fast and be done before the real deepdevil arrived. Kicking down from the surface with his foot paddles, he edged toward the nearest grotto. This hole in the sea was a shaggy opening between the roots, filled with sinister shadows. Working fast did not mean working foolishly. Worse things than deepdevils clung to the roots all around him. Puffballs crowded the grotto, warning predators away with speckled red-orange and yellow spines. Nothing fed on puffs, or at least not for long. Kafirr had once seen a diver brush a puffball and die before he broke the surface. The victim's muscles had contracted so violently that his back was broken and intestines protruded through his gaping mouth. The only nice thing said about puffs was that they were quick. Stingworm venom took over a hundred painful hours to kill, giving their victims plenty of time to regret the mistake.

Kafirr pulled on his safety line for slack, then swam into the grotto. Large roots and boles were all about him, forming a twisting, shadowy tube barely three meters wide. Kafirr doubted that the deepdevil would follow him here. In a grotto the slightest mistake brought hunter or hunted into fatal contact with a venomous root dweller. Deepdevils preferred the root fringes where meals were scarcer but safer. Kafirr had to work down here, swimming naked among the multicolored puffs and the blue-banded stingworms, because the root fringes were plucked clean of seastones.

For as long as his lungs would allow, Kafirr used his pry bar to pick seastones off the roots. When the need to breathe was overwhelming, he stopped filling his stuffsack and turned back on his safety line, kicking toward the surface.

Waiting at the entrance to the grotto was the real deepdevil. It took only a glance for Kafirr to tell that this was the true carnivore: two hundred kilos of hungry flesh feeder wearing the same wicked grin that he had seen on the copy-fish. The long white knives behind the grin were a part of this predator that even a copy-fish could not mimic. Deepdevils were as cunning as they were cruel. Kafirr had once seen a deepdevil feeding on a sea-snake calf several times its size. The deepdevil had ripped slice after slice out of the screaming calf, keeping its meal warm by avoiding a deathblow.

This deepdevil had seen Kafirr's line going into the grotto, and was waiting for a meal to come out. For a moment, Kafirr hung like a hooked fish, tethered to a surface line with death at the other end. Then the boy exhaled and slipped off his loincloth, leaving weight belt and stuffsack attached to the safety line. Wearing only his foot paddles, he dived deeper into the dim grotto, searching for the passage that led to the surface. Pressure stabbed at his eardrums, and shadows closed in around him. His vision blurred as oxygen debt built up and his limbs turned leaden.

Seeing nothing but a pale circle of rosy light, Kafirr kicked upward. With lungs bursting, he broke the surface in a fountain of fine spray. Taking air in great gulps, Kafirr was too exhausted to do anything but tread water. Here on the fringes of Windward Mat, holes opened in the tangle of branches overhead. Kafirr could look up from the somber water and see rose-colored clouds above the dense vegetation. Thin streaks of lightning crackled across the pink cloud bottoms, connecting deep red chasms many kilometers tall.

Catching a branch, Kafirr heaved himself into the dense, wet air. The brine that ran off his body was instantly replaced by beads of sweat. Kafirr preferred the feel of the water, which was several degrees cooler and did not tingle with static. He might have enjoyed the ocean's cool embrace if it had not included stingworms, puffballs, spinebacks, and hordes of large predators.

The supersaturated air tasted of ozone. Several seconds of rain swept by as the boy sat shaking, wishing that he never had to dive again. When his shivering stopped, he got up, threading his way through the catwalks to the dock where his line was tied. Green gillhoppers, slim humanoids with stunted fins and small, dry scales, jostled past him as though he were a moving obstruction. Gillhoppers ignored even the ocean that lapped around their mats; they could hardly be expected to notice adolescent humans. When he was growing up and learning to dive, Kafirr had wanted desperately to be a gillhopper. He had wished for green skin and scales; to never be hungry, to never go near the water. Now he was beyond such childish fantasies. He had been born a diver, and he expected to die a diver. His mother had dipped him newborn into the water, telling the sea to make her son a strong swimmer. Both Kafirr's parents had been divers; both had died in the water. The boy learned to ignore gillhoppers just as they ignored him.

Kafirr came to the end of the catwalks and stepped down onto the dock. Here the smell of the undrinkable, iridescent ocean was overpowering. Air and sea surface were pressed flat by many kilometers of atmosphere, and greenhouse effect kept the air hot and the water blood-warm. The Systems Guide said the air was breathable, but *bearable* would have been the better word. Excursionists took one whiff and went back to their landers for filters. Somewhere above the distant cloud tops was a feeble red sun that the boy had never seen. Dayside was always turned toward this invisible primary, so half the world was in red twilight, and half the world was a hot, dark oven. Kafirr had never been to Darkside; Dayside was bad enough.

A crowd had gathered around his slack safety lines. The outer ring was excursionists, not too secretly expecting tragedy. They were a typical tour group wearing nose filters and extravagant costumes—gossamer wings, shaved silver headdresses, chrome-yellow skindye with circular patches of purple fabric covering their private parts. Kafirr was no prude—he dived in only a loincloth—but the metal in the costumes bothered him. Some of these clanking off-world outfits had more metal than he could earn in a hundred hours of diving. Kafirr struggled to set aside his anger. Anger did a diver no good, and he had not seen enough of the universe to know that hating the hand that fed you was a common phenomenon.

As he slipped through the tour group, Kafirr saw divers down on their knees, sniffing for blood in the water and checking the copy-fish. They leaped up, happy to see the boy and slapping him on the back. Kafirr reeled in his safety line, spilling his stuffsack on the dock. Seastones tumbled out. He selected a pure crimson for the diver who had stood watch over his line.

Making the best of his survival, the excursionists crowded closer to look at his stones. The ring of human and humanoid faces made the air even less breathable, wasting oxygen with inane noises. The immense atmosphere and planetwide ocean kept a constant balance between CO_2 and oxygen, but it was not the balance that humans had evolved in. Only high atmospheric pressure made the air breathable, forcing relatively scarce oxygen into the blood. Divers bought whiffs of pure oxygen from vendors before each dive. It burned the back of Kafirr's throat and made his head spin, but pure, high-pressure oxygen fueled long, deep dives.

This time the seastones that glittered on the dock were prime. Only a few were pales and buffs; the rest were crimsons, beryls, and indigos. Kafirr got good prices. Off-worlders always paid the best at dockside. Seastones were small metallic deposits produced by prolific colonies of microorganisms that clung to the mat roots. The stones themselves were common enough and no problem to manufacture off-planet. What tourists were really paying for was the danger. As he bargained, Kafirr described the venomous grotto, the copy-fish, and the deepdevil. A harrowing story, told by a naked boy with a diver's whip-hard body, easily tripled the price. Insensitive souls could buy their stones much cheaper from waterfront shops, but those who wanted the real thing had to come to dockside, to touch the grim water, to buy from the diver who risked death to bring the stones up. Each curio came complete with an enthralling anecdote, and off-worlders had not crossed time and space just to get bits of metal and stone they could have bought at home.

Kafirr could see the rough justice in all this. If the waters of his world were not so deadly, off-worlders would pick their own seastones. Then he and the other divers would probably starve.

When the last stone was sold, the excursionists drifted away. Divers left to buy oxygen or lie down next to their lines, readying bodies for the next dive. Others sat gossiping in twos or threes, or gambled for bits of metal and unsold stones. The water-shy ones moped alone or begged. A female diver strummed a crude-stringed dulcimer, and someone joined in with a pair of pipes, playing a tune brought from ancient Earth. As he struggled into his wet loincloth, Kafirr hummed what he thought were the words, though he hardly understood them:

May the circle be unbroken by and by, yes, by and by;
There's a better world awaiting in the sky, yes, in the sky. . . .

His humming stopped, and Kafirr searched about in shocked disbelief. His pry bar was missing. He must have dropped it in the grotto when he was escaping from the deepdevil. The metal tool was so valuable that Kafirr snapped on his safety line, getting ready to dive after it. One look at the solid gray water brought his senses back. By now the pry bar was drifting down into the smoky depths, past the deepdevils, to where the pressure was heavy enough to float metal and flatten an armorfish. It was approaching the planet's sunken crust, where thousands of vents and volcanoes spewed out the minerals that gave the ocean its metallic taste.

Kafirr sat stunned on the dock, weeping at the unfairness in the world, missing his mother and father. Masses of metal landed and departed for orbit every dozen hours. Moored nearby was a slick orbital yacht, a Fornax Skylark, with a bulb-shaped body and a needle-sharp nose. Next to it was a hydrofoil cruiser with a catamaran bow and smooth airfoils over the stern. Both of these vessels must have held over a hundred tons of metal. Airless worlds and lifeless asteroids had metal in abundance, but on this ocean each gram had to be brought down from orbit or screened from the mineral-rich water. Gillhoppers did not use metal at all, except for trace amounts their mats extracted through osmotic pumps. Only oceanography and excursionists brought in the hard credit needed to support metal import or production. By far the most common metal makers on the planet were the microorganisms that made seastones, but most of their harvest was carried away as curios by off-worlders. What metal remained was expensive. The pry bar was his most important inheritance from his parents, the one material thing they had passed on to him. The few kilos that went into that pry bar would cost Kafirr more hard credit than he had accumulated in thousands of hours of diving.

Life went on by the dock. Kafirr could hear the pipes and dulci-mer playing, along with the groans and yells of the gamblers. It grated him to hear that other divers could be so happy, while he had lost half his livelihood. But that was how it had to be; and music always played loudest after a diver was pulled dead from the water.

Kafirr kept looking at the hydro-cruiser, and saw two xenos come down the gangway. The first was an Eridani Hound, a fairly common species in this reach of Eridanus Sector. Hounds adapted well to star travel and looked comfortably familiar to humans, resembling semiupright hyenas or oversized baboons. This Hound was probably a pilot, since he wore a zero-g harness and had a comlink clipped to his left jaw. The Hound had a zestful, good-living air, and addressed his larger companion as Q'Maax'doux. This Q'Maax'doux was an aquatic xeno unlike any that Kafirr had ever seen, with webbed digits, strong legs, and the barrel chest of a swimmer. A blunt amphibian head sat directly on Q'Maax'doux's huge shoulders, topped with a webbed crest that blended into a dorsal fin running the full length of the spine. The creature had gill fringes under the forelimbs, and nostril flaps to keep liquid out of the lungs. Kafirr envied the webbing and powerful limbs, wishing nature had equipped him half so well for the water. The xeno had no clothes, no obvious sex, and was colored like a deepdevil, dark on top and light on the belly. The colors were shades of blue-gray that seemed somehow too drab and similar, as if the xeno's home star were whiter and brighter. The bulging muscles and rapid gait certainly suggested a home world with greater gravity, though local gravity was a tiring 1.6 g.

Q'Maax'doux spoke to the Hound through the standard tourist speakbox: "I have promised a school of silver rippers to the Insti-tute of Zoological Morphology on Epsilon Eridani IV. In a few hundred hours, a high-boost institute ship will be here to take delivery."

"Silver rippers; sounds very exciting and very strenuous," said the Hound. "I would be right in the water beside you, but I have a rare allergy to ocean spray. The mere mention of deep water makes my skin creep about uncontrollably."

"I am sorry to hear of your handicap." The bigger xeno set the speakbox to a correct mix of pity and contempt: "At the moment

I am in the market for nothing more dangerous than a couple of creatures suitable for deep-water work.

"Do you have any particular type of creature in mind?" The Hound also had a speakbox, whose tone signified helpful disinterest.

Q'Maax'doux indicated the green gillhoppers tending their pods from catwalks. "This planet has an indigenous semi-intelligent species. They should know their own waters best."

The Hound reset his speakbox to indicate amusement: "Gillhoppers share my allergy and never go near the water."

Q'Maax'doux came to a surprised stop a few meters from Kafirr, with gill fringes flaring and dorsal spines erect. "This planet is entirely oceanic; how can any sensible species ignore that?"

"Are gillhoppers sensible?" said the Hound. "Since they ignore us completely, it is difficult to judge. No doubt they consider themselves prudent. They are related to several aquatic-prey species that inhabit the root fringes. Note that they still possess stunted fins and the rudimentary gills that give them their name."

Q'Maax'doux's neckless head could not nod; instead, the xeno set the speakbox for impatient assent. "All the more reason for them to be in the water."

The Hound grinned. He had learned from humans to express humor by exposing his fangs. "Eons ago the ancestral gillhoppers learned to grow these great vegetable mats, and harvest the mat pods. There are now hundreds of these mats totaling thousands of square kilometers, each inhabited by a different variety of gillhopper. Once they left the water, gillhoppers probably saw no good reason to go back. The waters of this world are not as safe as they should be."

Despite his troubles, Kafirr smiled at the Hound's grim humor. Heavy metals made the mat pods poisonous to humans. If Kafirr could have harvested pods like a gillhopper, nothing could have dragged him back into the water.

Q'Maax'doux found a rude noise in the speakbox's vocabulary. "Then what sort of creature shall I use for deep-water work?"

"That sort." The Eridani Hound turned his sharp snout toward Kafirr.

"Oh," Q'Maax'doux's speakbox transmitted profound disappointment. "I already have one of those, and frankly, I hoped to do better. These creatures were not bred for water work."

The Hound shrugged, another human gesture he had learned to imitate. "No doubt they do their best. Humans are what everyone here uses for water work. Their need for processed food and distilled water makes them tractable and tolerably anxious to please. Though, I would address him as 'man'; they are often slow in answering to 'creature.' "

Q'Maax'doux gave the Hound grudging thanks, and bid him farewell. Kafirr was already on his feet when Q'Maax'doux strode over to him. "Man," said the xeno, "are you suitable for deep-water work?"

Kafirr bobbed his head, nodding and grinning. "Yes, yes, more than suitable." He wanted to land the job before the big xeno attracted a crowd. The hint of steady work drew divers as fast as blood in the water drew copy-fish.

"Have you done deep-water work before?" Q'Maax'doux was still casting about for some reason to reject the human.

"Yes, yes." Kafirr lied enthusiastically, amazed that a chance conversation between two xenos had turned his life around.

"Are you familiar with silver rippers?" Q'Maax'doux was still reluctant to reel in this easy catch.

"Of course, very familiar." Kafirr would have sworn he mated with them, if it would get him the job.

Q'Maax'doux grunted through the speakbox, then picked up Kafirr's safety line. Nothing had been said about payment, but then, Kafirr had never worked for a wage before. Anything was better than being a diver without a pry bar.

Leading Kafirr by the safety line, Q'Maax'doux boarded the hydro-cruiser. Kafirr could not really accept his good fortune until the gangway retracted behind him, vanishing into the seamless hull. "I have another man in my employ," said the xeno. "He will tell you your duties." Q'Maax'doux started to walk away with the safety line, then dropped it on the deck. "Wait here until the other man comes for you."

Kafirr waited for the man to come, his bare toes caressing the cruiser's smooth deck. The cruiser's reactor and superstructure were slung between the two light hulls. He could feel the hum of power from the stern and saw the graceful double curve of the bow. Kafirr had watched boats come and go all his life, and this one was by far the largest. The hydro-cruiser was over a hundred meters long and a dozen meters wide; but with superlight materials everywhere, Kafirr doubted that it massed a thousand tons. He saw a large electroprojector forward and two smaller ones aft. A matched pair of gigs rested on the fantail.

Still the man did not arrive. Kafirr studied the towering super-structure, topped by a silver hedge of antennas that he could not identify. Kafirr was puzzling over a laser range finder, when a voice behind him asked, "What are you doing here?"

Kafirr turned faster than a copy-fish, but it was not the man he had been expecting. Instead, he saw a woman stepping down from the gangway that led to the main deck. But for her sex, he might have been looking into a mirror. She was a diver: her head was shaved as close as his; her limbs were as thick, her belly as flat. Like Kafirr, she wore only a loincloth; her breasts were small, with large, flat nipples. Her eyes were as wide and brown as his, but the lines on her face were deeper. The woman was several score kilo-hours older than Kafirr.

"I am waiting for a man," said the boy. "The xeno who owns this boat—"

She cut him short with a curt shake of her head. "I am the man you are waiting for. Quasimodo never learned how to sex humans."

"Quasimodo?" Kafirr missed the allusion; the nearest tape of Victor Hugo's works was trillions of kilometers distant.

She cocked her head toward the main deck. "The xeno who owns this boat. Our web-fingered master does not mind the name, and just assumes that I cannot pronounce Q'Maax'doux. My own name is Nila." She said it in a flat voice; not an introduction, just information. "Q'Maax'doux hired me a couple of dozen hours ago, which makes me senior to you." There was a hint of challenge in how she said that. "The xeno said that we were getting something suitable for deep-water work. Are you supposed to be that something?"

Kafirr nodded. Lying to these cold brown eyes was going to be harder.

"So, you lied to him." Nila's words were easy and matter-of-fact; no accusation, just more information.

He started to deny it, but she cut him short with another shake of her head. "Look, there are not a dozen divers on Windward Mat who have ever done deep-water work. You are too young to be one of them. This xeno thinks that all humans are alike; you and I know better."

Nila paused, swinging her hand about to indicate that hydro-cruiser. "You like this boat?"

It was better than anything Kafirr had ever seen, but the boy barely had time to say yes.

"Right," she went on. "If you want to stay aboard, never lie to me. I do not care if you lie to Q'Maax'doux. I do that myself. But if I catch you in a lie to me, I will tell Q'Maax'doux that you have never done deep-water work. This tenderhearted xeno will heave you into the water and get another diver. Like I said, we're all the same to the xeno."

Kafirr's yes was overready, anything to keep that smooth deck beneath his feet.

"Good." Nila made the word sound menacing. "You stay, and you do all the diving. I do not go into the water."

The boy hated the water—only fools or suicides welcomed it—but he still found Nila's adamance startling. He had seen water-shy divers before; those with bad omens, or who had lost any will to live. You could read the fear in their eyes, and they never lasted long. Fear can kill you quicker than a puffball. But Nila did not look afraid of anything; her gaze was as cold and hard as the waves in the wake of a storm.

Kafirr agreed again, since doing the diving was no more than he had expected. Nila relaxed and took him to the forecastle. From amidships aft, the hydro-cruiser was almost all engine, but the forward hulls were filled with flotation foam and cross bracing. There were several pockets in the foam large enough for spacious cabins. The hydro-cruiser was human-built, but with more than humans in mind, and each cabin was big enough for a few Q'Maax'douxs.

"This is mine?" the boy asked.

"Ours," Nila replied. "The xeno thinks one cabin is more than enough for two humans." She deposited him and left without ever asking his name.

Kafirr put Nila out of his mind and poked about, finding an inner cubicle with an equally large basin and bath. There was also a spacious locker stocked with meals. Testing the food, he found it better than any he had ever eaten. Only the need to dive would keep him from getting fat. Kafirr sprawled on the huge sleeping mat, thinking that if he died on his first dive, he would have already lived as no one he knew had ever lived.

Deep Water

Garrulous as a gargoyle, Q'Maax'doux did not head right for deep water. Instead, the hydro-cruiser steered along the leeward line of mats at four hundred kilometers per hour, rocking the great floating gardens with its wake. Huge airfoils extended out over the stern to keep the cruiser from porpoising or blowing over at high speed. Every millimeter of the hydro-cruiser was computer-controlled and coded in Q'Maax'doux's language, a code harder to break than any human cipher. Nila taught Kafirr the few words she had learned, the ones that opened hatches and called down ladders. Otherwise, there was nothing the two humans could do to control the craft or affect their fate. Their only duties were to keep to themselves until their xeno needed them. Swift orders punctuated long silences.

Nila acted like a shadowy extension of Q'Maax'doux, transmitting orders and limiting conversation. Neither human stood watches, and no duties drew them together. Kafirr ate when he was hungry and slept when he was tired. Still, it shocked him the first time he entered the cabin and found Nila sleeping. She lay curled on one side of the mat: with trim feet tucked below her buttocks, one hand shielding two tender breasts, the other hand clinched in front of her face, thumb tip almost touching moist lips. Curved in sleep, her strong shoulders had no tension. Close-clipped hair ended in a soft tangle at the nape of her neck. With her eyes closed, Kafirr could now see that her lashes were long and silky, and she looked much younger.

For some time he sat on the mat, close enough to have touched her, watching her breath move in and out. Then he went up on the deck to lie down. Kafirr needed his sleep, and he would have gotten no rest lying beside Nila.

When they were both awake, Kafirr tried to create conversation. On deck he asked Nila why they were not headed straight for deep water. Instead, they seemed to be on a high-speed tour of the mats that banded the planet's equator.

She shrugged, staring at the long jade mat that was whipping by, less than a kilometer to starboard. "Q'Maax'doux does not tell me. If our lord feels lonely, talking to humans is not the cure." Nila bent her wrist backward and twisted a finger against the solid substance of the cruiser. "The xeno thinks that talking to us is about the same as talking to the bulkheads. Maybe Quasimodo just wants to shake up the gillhoppers, startle them into showing how they run their mats."

That last comment was pure extravagance, a speculation that served no purpose except to converse with Kafirr. No one knew how gillhoppers controlled their mats. Gillhoppers treated the ocean the way humans sometimes treat sex. They pretended it did not exist, but privately knew every nuance of wind or current. Noting how gillhoppers tended their pods was better than satellite forecasting if you wanted to know what the local weather would be like. Nor did their mats drift aimlessly. Instead, they inscribed slow circles in the planet's equatorial regions, somehow alternating between the prevailing currents that ran in the opposite hemispheres. Any other course might carry them through the terminator, into Darkside, where pods would die and mats disintegrate. How they maneuvered their mats through these currents was a mystery, gillhoppers being as vocal on this subject as they were on any other.

Kafirr could have been sharing his cabin with a gillhopper for all the attention he got out of Nila, but through it all he was enthralled. He was eating, sleeping, and not diving.

At the tip of the last archipelago, Q'Maax'doux made a wide turn that carried them out toward the terminator, then doubled back. The cruiser dropped its sea anchor off the most leeward line of mats. When he saw Nila coming to fetch him, Kafirr knew he was going into the water. She was cold and hard-eyed again, determined not to be drawn into conversation; as if contact with Kafirr could contaminate her. She merely handed him goggles, snorkel, and foot paddles.

Q'Maax'doux was waiting on the fantail, looking at the mats, now a few kilometers off. "I want you to swim," said the xeno.

"Where?" asked Kafirr.

Finding a patient tone in his speakbox, the xeno replied, "Swim to the root fringe, then turn around and swim back."

Swimming three or four kilometers in open water was not like diving for seastones. Out in the ocean there was no safety line, nor was there rest at the other end; the root fringes were loaded with puffs, and divers always worked from cleared docks. It was a long swim without a shred of protection, and Kafirr now knew how he would pay for all those hours of sleeping and eating.

Nila was ready by the oxygen line. Looking straight into his eyes, she helped him hold the oxygen mask. For a moment, Nila put a firm hand over his, then she took it away. Another pure extravagance.

Charged with oxygen, Kafirr swung over the stern rail and dived into the dull gray water. As he sank, Kafirr could feel that the sea was different here. He heard a strong sea surge in his ears, the pulsing of the planetwide ocean. The water itself was vibrant and bottomless, divided into descending layers of light. Below, Kafirr could sense nothing but the limitless, smoky deep.

Taking his direction from the cruiser's twin hulls, Kafirr kicked off toward the mat, senses alert for any sea changes. Almost at once a larger body broke the surface behind him. Kafirr spun about and saw Q'Maax'doux passing him. A few powerful kicks, and the xeno was well ahead, with a portable electroprojector trailing from a forelimb. Kafirr wondered why the xeno needed lumbering humans crowding the water when he could swim like that.

He struggled after the disappearing xeno. By now the oxygen was gone, and the boy was breathing through the snorkel. Q'Maax'doux's finned feet vanished in the murk ahead, and the emptiness closed in. Kafirr was alone again, hearing the sea surge and feeling the vast void of the ocean, stretching around the world and down to the sunken planet surface. Deep water even smelled different, more mineral, more metallic; it had not been swept and strained by the mats.

After an eternity of kicking in emptiness, Kafirr saw copy-fish ahead. Now he was nearing the root fringe, though he had no idea how far out from the fringe these scavengers swam. The copy-fish crowded around him, knowing he was harmless and making no attempt to match his alien outline. Kafirr felt the comfort that copy-fish brought. Then they all turned in unison, alerted by an invisible signal. Without changing configuration, the copy-fish dashed off in the direction of the mats.

Kafirr redoubled his efforts. That sudden flight meant that the copy-fish had sensed a predator too big and horrible to be mimicked. For a full minute he fled from the unknown, then he saw immense inky shapes emerging from the murk. Big black shadows with slow-beating wings drew closer, growing larger and more distinct. Kafirr had never seen giant mantlewings before, but the configuration was unmistakable: thick black wings with a tired beat, followed by a long, undulating tail. Kafirr could not see their mouths, but he had heard they were two meters across and shaped like air scoops.

Kafirr kicked harder. The gliding shadows were gaining on him, eating as they went, swimming in a staggered formation so each had a clear feeding path. Kaffir could hear soft, high-pitched, and penetrating calls, probing after him and echoing off the mat fringe. He had to reach the roots, where large predators did not dare follow; but his puny human effort would never be enough. The mantlewings did not even bother to increase their speed. One of the larger ones would scoop him up without even breaking rhythm. Blind panic kept Kafirr pushing forward, straining to see the root fringe through the gloom. All he saw were visions of his parents, and how they had died.

First there was the flash of a sighting laser, followed by an electric crackle in the water. Q'Maax'doux kicked into view, the elctroprojector already at rest and trailing from a forelimb. The lead mantlewing was collapsing, folding in on itself. The others broke formation and circled about, confused by conflicting signals from their stunned leader.

Q'Maax'doux signaled for Kafirr to surface. The boy obeyed, his lungs and legs aching. When his head broke water, Kafirr saw he was still a kilometer short of the nearest mat. If Q'Maax'doux had not come back, Kafirr would have been an easy meal. The mantlewings were milling about a few hundred meters off, flapping to the surface, then diving again. The hydro-cruiser was charging over the waves toward its owner, obeying commands that came from Q'Maax'doux's comlink.

When the cruiser churned up, the soft black phantoms faded into more distant water, Kafirr called down a trailing ladder and hauled himself aboard. As he lay gasping on the fantail, Nila knelt beside him. In her lips and breasts, and in the cloud bottoms, Kafirr saw beauty that he had not remembered from before. All Nila said was, "You cannot study predators if you haven't any prey."

Q'Maax'doux was still in the water, directing the port crane to grapple and raise the paralyzed mantlewing. Kafirr lay limp and exhausted until he saw the mantlewing swing up over the rail. At once he rolled to his feet and retreated from the fantail to the main deck, before the monster could come down on top of him. Q'Maax'doux rode the mantlewing aboard, a conqueror lifted high on the back of the vanquished.

The xeno spent a happy hour or two butchering the living beast. Q'Maax'doux poked and peered, making measurements and stimulating internal organs with a variable-voltage prod, then cutting off bits for the bioscope and laser spectrograph. When the study was complete, Q'Maax'doux ordered the remains lowered into a hold. Then the xeno came bounding up the ladder, reeking of bile and preservatives.

As soon as Q'Maax'doux's speakbox was on line, it began to fire questions at Kafirr: "How did that attack compare with attacks by other deep-water predators? Do they move that slowly in deeper water?" Q'Maax'doux returned to his special subject, the "silver ripper." It was known to be much smaller than the mantlewing, the xeno explained, but thought to be more active and even deadlier. How would Kafirr compare them?

Kafirr had nothing to compare the mantlewing with, and was too aghast to invent replies. The monster cut up and lying in the hold was twenty meters of wing supporting thirty meters of digestive tract. Something "more deadly" was not the sort of horror that Kafirr could just fabricate answers about. He had to admit that this piece of ocean was as far as he had ever been from a gillhopper mat. Q'Maax'doux adjusted the speakbox, playing back the boy's reply. When the xeno was sure of the sense of it, Q'Maax'doux dismissed Kafirr and turned to Nila. "This one is unsuitable, and you failed to apprise me. I am ready to hunt again, so this time you will swim."

Nila's brown eyes narrowed. She shook her head, without taking her gaze off the xeno. "I do not go into the water. You selected this diver, and so far he has been adequate."

Q'Maax'doux lowered the tone of the speakbox until the words turned to a growl. "You are going into the water. There is no other option. You may go in as my employee, or you may leave my employment and swim to the nearest mat."

Nila snatched the goggles and snorkel from Kafirr, and sat for a moment on the stern rail, adjusting the lenses and pulling on the foot paddles. She kept her chin and head averted. Muscles rippled under soft skin, making each movement swift and sure. As soon as the foot paddles were secure, she rose up on the rail, balanced for an instant, then went into the water, leaving barely a ripple. Kafirr watched with professional interest, finding her form perfect. Q'Maax'doux splashed in behind her; as powerful as the xeno was in the water, Q'Maax'doux could not match Nila's grace in the air.

Once the waters had swallowed them, Kafirr returned to the cabin. He told the lights to dim, and relaxed on the sleeping mat. The terror of the swim had been cleansing, a frightening baptism in deep water, but he actually felt better for it. The worst had happened. Q'Maax'doux had discovered his lie, but had not thrown him overboard. Now Nila had nothing to hold over him. She was now the one in danger, but doing no more than he had done. Happy with the world, Kafirr went to sleep.

He awoke in hot darkness. Nila was standing over him, dripping wet, with her arms folded across her chest.

"So," said Kafirr, "you went in the water."

She glared past him, seeming to see nothing, not even the cabin bulkhead, and least of all the boy.

Kafirr did his best to coax her into a better mood. "Being bait for Q'Maax'doux is spooky, but it is much safer than working the root grottoes. No stingworms, no puffs, and Q'Maax'doux is an incredible swimmer. We are safer with the xeno than we would be alone, or with any dozen human divers."

Her eyes remained distant; her mouth moved slowly, trying to make her meaning clear. "You may find this difficult, but I do not want to be a happy slave: eating, sleeping, and relaxing on safe dives. I do not want some xeno making life-and-death decisions for me. Remember, Q'Maax'doux's ganglia are fixed on bringing in a school of silver rippers. Those are carnivores no bigger than copyfish, but connoisseurs consider them the worst predators on the planet. Few have ever been captured, and live ones have never been taken off-planet. Ever wonder why? If he plans to use us as bait for silver rippers, it will not be a pleasant splash around the boat with a flock of mantlewings. Rippers hunt in huge packs that can strip a thousand-meter sea snake in a matter of minutes. They will use that electroprojector for a toothpick."

Kafirr was somewhat stunned. He had never heard Nila speak for so long on any single subject, but once she started talking, there seemed to be no stopping her. Nila sat down on the mat, with her moist skin only millimeters away. Kafirr could see tears in her eyes, and felt the way he had the first time he saw her sleeping. He wanted to hold this new Nila, and tell her not to worry. "There are no rippers right now," said Kafirr. "We are safe and fed. Why worry about things that have not happened?"

Nila dried her eyes, then rested her hand on the mat next to his. She leaned forward, trying desperately to be understood, but her body had an intoxicating fragrance that kept Kafirr from concentrating on her words. "Don't you see? What I want is no more diving, no more hours in the water."

"How?" To the boy, that sounded insane. Diving was horrible, but how could you give up the one thing that put food in your mouth?

"Do you know that a River Lines packet accelerates at thirty pseudogravities, and can reach near light speed in a few hundred hours?"

"So?" Kafirr could see no connection between diving and the performance of a River Lines packet.

"A few hours after Q'Maax'doux docks, the packet *Jordan River* will lift off from orbit. When it does, I am going with it. This job will give me the last credit I need to cover my fare. I am not going to die only hours from freedom."

"You are going off-planet?" Kafirr had never seen a moon nor star, never seen anything but the bottom of perpetual, impenetrable cloud cover.

"As far off-planet as a cheap ticket will take me. I was not born on this world," said Nila, "and nothing I have seen here encourages me to stay."

No wonder her head was always so high in the cloud cover, thought Kafirr. Nila was an off-worlder. To Kafirr, that explained a lot. Her distance and coldness were now natural, and he no longer wanted to touch her. Before, he had considered Nila aloof, arrogant, and uncaring, but he had never suspected she was a tourist. Kafirr got up and left, leaving her alone in the cabin.

Jordan River

Q'Maax'doux set a course for deep water, skipping over the equatorial current, heading for the terminator. The hydro-cruiser wove through floating forests spread over the sea. Long strands of gold-green vegetation lay in parallel rows, streaming with the current. The sea around the gillhopper mats had been free of such obstruction, because the mats swept up stray vegetation, growing by a process that only the gillhoppers understood and controlled. Cyclonic storms blew out of the terminator, covering the sea-forests with sheets of warm rain. The hydro-cruiser skipped between the typhoons, sonar and all-weather guidance finding lanes through the storms and vegetation.

The sea change that had come over Nila continued. No longer aloof, she found reasons to comment on everything: the speed of the cruiser, the clouds overhead, the sea around them. With little else to do, Kafirr listened. Then, in their dark, warm cabin, she told him her whole story. It was overloaded with off-world concepts, but Kafirr could follow most of it.

"My parents retired young," she said, "and took me on Tour, investing their savings in several corporations. That way their credit would accumulate for millions of hours while they were on Tour. They would have come back both young and wealthy. I saw half the worlds in Eridanus Sector while I was still growing up. The deal was a cheap package tour bought from Pisicum Freight and Ferry; but to me, it was wonderful. Even this planet was a delight seen from orbit, a clouded pearl resting on the black fabric of space. As we decelerated from light speed, communications returned, and people discovered that Pisicum Freight and Ferry had gone belly-up. It was the biggest bust in millions of hours; ships were stranded all over Eridanus Sector. A battalion of smart lawyers got a venue ruling that said all claims against Pisicum had to be adjudicated at the sector captial in Epsilon Eridani system. I watched my folks go crazy. It takes three hundred thousand hours to get a message through to Epsilon from here, and claims on Pisicum were selling at a mil on the credit in the local securities market. Pisicum Freight and Ferry had only one local asset, the ship that had dumped us here, which Paradise Development attached. Pisicum had left monumental debts to Paradise Development, and at one mil on the credit, our little claim was not even worth a ride into orbit."

She lay back on the mat, looking straight up at the deckhead above. A thin metal skin and layers of foam kept out the gray sea and gray rain. "We were washed up on a worthless world. Anyone who knew us or could help us was tens of thousands of hours off by ship or signal." Her gaze seemed to go through the deckhead, searching for the heavens that were hidden by pink cloud cover. "Our original complaints are still crawling to Epsilon at light speed. My dad died trying his hand at diving. My mom became a wharf rat, telling her story to tourists and living on handouts. Finally, some mildly disgusting guy offered her a lift to Paradise system, just a single seat. He had no room for overgrown children, since I would not do for him what my mother did. I suppose if I had done it, he would have taken us both. He was pretty broad-minded in his own repulsive way. Mom said she would come back for me, but that was forty thousand hours ago."

She sat up, resting her chin on her hand, looking Kafirr over. "By then I was already a diver. You know what that is like. I spent long hours in the water, saving every bit of credit, eating any way I could. Quasimodo is warmth itself compared to some of the humans I worked for. At least this xeno never learned to sex humans, and does not expect us to spread for him after hard hours in the water." She paused, noting that he had said nothing. "This may not seem much of a tragedy to you, but I wasn't born here, and believe me, I know better."

"I am sorry for you anyway." Kafirr could think of nothing else to say. He did not know which Nila he liked better: the old Nila, who ignored him and whom he half-hated; or this new Nila, who seemed determined to expand and complicate his world. He half-wanted to tell her his story, and talk about his family; but how could he expose his private pain to Nila? Nila could think of going off-planet, but leaving was plainly beyond him. Diving was a delayed death sentence, but it was all he had.

She flopped back on the bed: "You probably are dumb enough to be sorry for me. Take some off-world advice, and start being sorry for yourself."

When Q'Maax'doux called them up on deck, the storms had evaporated, and the cloud cover was the gray-pink of decaying meat. In the wake of the rains, the clouds had come down to blend with the water, fusing into a single wet substance. At various distances into the murk, Kafirr could see long, undulating lines that looked like standing waves in the sea. These lines slowly slid across each other, appearing ahead, disappearing behind.

"Sea snakes," said Q'Maax'doux.

Looking closer, the humans could see that the moving wave crests were really parts of immense creatures, whose long bodies extended off into the fog. A dozen lay off either bow, thick black lines drawn on the sea mist. The cruiser was a slick little toy, rocking in the troughs between them, with three mites standing on its surface.

The triumph of the moment made Q'Maax'doux almost talkative. "This is the hunting ground," said the xeno as he spun the cruiser around. "Silver rippers are the only predators that feed on adult sea snakes." At low speeds, the cruiser had a tight radius, but even so, they nearly beached on the head of an oncoming snake. Wide gill fringes and thousands of feeding tentacles slid by the starboard hull. The huge head had no eyes: sea snakes steered by sonar and were stone-blind on the surface, ignoring any obstacle smaller than a gillhopper mat.

Weaving between the rows of snakes, Q'Maax'doux kept the cruiser on a reciprocal course until it shot out of the rear end of the herd. Then the cruiser leaped about, bouncing high on the chop left by hundreds of huge bodies. The bow electroprojector spun at Q'Maax'doux's command, taking aim at one of the rear snakes. When the projector flashed, the snake twisted in pain, howling out of its air holes, with a deep burn mark all along its back. Seismic waves spread over the surface as the wounded giant lashed the water.

Q'Maax'doux halted the cruiser, throwing out the sea anchor. The superstructure was swinging in a wild arc, falling and rising a hundred meters with each wave. The catamaran hull was stable at any angle of inclination, but as springy as a raft in heavy seas. As the spasms slackened and the beast grew limp, scavengers assembled. Nila pointed out several varieties of deep-water copy-fish.

The cruiser circled beside the dying snake until it stopped twitching. Then Q'Maax'doux hauled in the anchor and gunned the cruiser after the herd, slaughtering another snake in similar fashion. For hours the xeno continued to kill sea snakes, leaving an archipelago of long, dead islands rocking in the swell.

"This is senseless," said Kafirr. The sea snakes were so huge they hardly seemed to be living beings, but their screaming and thrashing would have gotten pity from a gillhopper.

"Silver rippers are not scavengers," Nila explained. "They come up for live meat. Only a wounded snake can get their attention. Do you want to go back to being bait?"

Many dead monsters later, the hydro-cruiser's sonar signaled a large contact separating from a deep thermocline. Q'Maax'doux announced that a shoal of silver rippers was rising to feed. Soon the sea around the latest victim began to boil with silver bodies. The snake's struggles increased. Now it was not only dying, but also being eaten alive.

It seemed then that the whole ocean had gone mad. The water was alive with thousands of silver rippers. While they tore at a struggling sea beast many times larger than the cruiser, scavengers crowded close to share in the feast. Even Nila had nothing to say.

Q'Maax'doux gave a gleeful command to the cruiser, and the boat began to fling little dark packets in a broad pattern. These small black specks hung for a moment at the top of their arcs, then splashed into the sea. Where each one landed, the water was indented for a moment, then thrown up in a thick column. All around these pillars, the air and water surface shook with the muffled boom of deep explosions. For a full minute, the hydro-cruiser was hidden by a forest of splashes, then the last column collapsed and the sea subsided. The whole community of predators and scavengers that had been drawn by the dying snakes was knocked senseless, with most of its members dying. Q'Maax'doux tossed Nila a net. "You will look for any silver rippers that might survive."

Fresh copy-fish collected to feed on this new bounty. Working from the gigs, Kafirr and Nila moved over the dead sea, looking for living rippers. While Q'Maax'doux watched from the bridge, the humans dragged stunned carnivores into the hold, entering directly through an opening on the trailing edge of the starboard ram wing.

When they were done, they collapsed in the cabin. Kafirr said nothing; the killing had made him morose.

"I suppose you think this is a waste of time," said Nila. "Just wait; we may be doing all this for nothing. The rippers we got are so weak they may never reach Windward Mat, much less Epsilon Eridani."

Once the hold was full, Q'Maax'doux swung the hydro-cruiser

around. The xeno was in a silent frenzy to get his catch back to Windward Mat, where they could be loaded for the long voyage to Epsilon E. Many hours out of port, Nila returned from the hold with the news that the rippers were dying.

Q'Maax'doux adjusted his speakbox to indicate annoyed indignation. "It is your job to keep them alive."

"Listen, Quas," the woman replied. "Your collecting methods have shaken them up. Silver rippers are social, active carnivores. You cannot just knock them silly, keep them comatose, and then expect them to come out on their own. They need to be revived, exercised, even reintroduced to eating."

"Then you will do that." Q'Maax'doux spoke simply, as though explaining the world to children.

Nila folded her arms over her breasts and gave him a sidelong look. "Do I pipe dance and dinner music down into the hold?"

"No," said Q'Maax'doux. "That would be pointless. Your companion will exercise them."

"Exercise them?" Nila did not even bother to look at Kafirr, who was himself astonished.

"Yes, have him push them about," said Q'Maax'doux. "Use mild electric probes, and hand-feed living bait to any that show signs of hunger."

Kafirr was staggered at the thought of spending any extended time in that hold. It was as dark and stagnant as the deepest root grotto, filled with dead and dying hundred-kilo carnivores.

Before he could speak, Nila spoke for him. "Don't you think that is a bit dangerous? If he succeeds, the little dears will wake up hungry. The boy will be pinned in a dark hold with angry and ill-fed predators twice his size."

Q'Maax'doux's blunt head swiveled back in her direction, and the xeno selected a lecturing tone: "Risk is what he is paid for. He is only human and has no special skills. It is sensible that any danger should fall on the least essential creature available."

Nila's eyes narrowed. "Well, listen, neckless wonder, I am no more essential than he is. Let me exercise the rippers."

Kafirr was surprised, but Q'Maax'doux was not. The xeno merely said that one would do as well as another.

"But," she added, "before I go back in that hold, I want to be paid in advance; I want to hold the payment in my hand."

"That is a strange and primitive request." Now Q'Maax'doux did seem surprised.

"I am a primitive-type person," said Nila. "Now or later—what does it mean to you?"

"Nothing," said Q'Maax'doux, and he paid her.

Kafirr watched the xeno's broad back depart. "You did not have to do that."

"Didn't I?" Nila gave him a sour look.

"I would have gone in the hold," said the boy.

"That is just why I did it." She shook her head. "This is a job that must be done only one way. The first rippers to wake up would have had you for hors d'oeuvres. Then kindly Quasimodo would have sent me into water warm with your blood, or made me walk home."

"Why don't you just call me stupid?" Kafirr complained.

"Because that would be rude. Look, I know I sound hard," said Nila, "but this job is my ticket." Her fist tightened compulsively around the credit scrip. "I need to feel the payment in my hands, and to give Q'Maax'doux no reason to back out, or complain to the Port Authorities. That makes my life very simple; I just have to stay alive until the *Jordan River* lifts for Paradise system."

For the entire trip back, Kafirr had nothing to do but watch Nila go in and out of the hold. Several times he offered to help, but she shrugged him off. He should have been pleased to be paid for nothing, but instead, he felt slighted. The closer they got to Windward Mat, the more he felt the tension, thinking by now the rippers were bound to be more active. Nila was spending almost all her time in the hold, but Kafirr caught her getting up from a short rest in the cabin. "Look," he said, "this is crazy; you are bound to make a slip. Why are you taking all the danger onto yourself? There was a time when you did not care if I lived at all."

Nila sat up on the edge of the sleeping mat, looking up with weary eyes. "That was different. I was trying to keep myself separate from diving. I did not dare know you, or care for you. You were just a diver who was going to die in my place."

The boy sat down beside her. "But you have gone too far the other way. You will not even let me help."

She rubbed the sleep out of her eyes. "You cannot do what I am doing. You don't have the training for it." Seeing he was hurt, she reached out and took his hand. "It is just that you have spent your whole life taking horrible risks for next to nothing. What I am doing requires a keener sense of self-preservation. Are you mad at me?"

The boy shrugged. At that exact moment, he was not sure of his feelings.

She sighed. "I promise to apologize, if you promise to grab your ticket when it comes."

"My ticket?" Kafirr had never thought of anything as being reserved for him.

She looked hard at him. "If you get a chance to go off-planet, will you take it?"

"I guess." It seemed safe enough; no one had ever offered him even a ride around Windward Mat.

"Then I am sorry," she said. "You are not so stupid."

She paused and pressed his hand. "This farce is almost over. If anything happens to me, I want you to ask Q'Maax'doux for a ticket off-planet. Tell him that the Port Authorities will not let him lift off if there are any complications."

"What complications?"

"Just promise to use your brain. If anything happens to me, just press the xeno. Quas is not all that smart. I have already beaten him. Having my ticket makes me free; even if I never come back from that hold, even if I die in the next hour, I have still won. I would feel better knowing you had a chance, too." She leaned over and kissed him. Her warm body and soft lips took Kafirr by surprise. She left him sitting on the mat, watching her leave for the hold. Her strong back was beaded with sweat; buttock muscles bunched and released with each firm step.

Even when she was into the hold and out of sight, he sat there, thinking over what he would say when she came back. He turned the words over in his mind until he had them just right; but Nila never returned to the cabin.

When they docked at Windward Mat, Nila had still not come up from the hold. Kafirr was worried, but Q'Maax'doux showed no concern. The xeno was delighted to have docked, and made immediate plans for transferring the entire hold container from the hydro-cruiser to the Skylark. Kafirr went at once to check the hold, before it was embedded in the orbital yacht and headed for Epsilon E.

Pausing at the hatch, he heard no noise from behind the panel.

He said the alien word that opened the hold, and light streamed into the gloom, scattering on the water's surface and dancing off the bulkheads. Active silver shapes whipped back and forth amid the light. Eagerly, they collected near the hatch, jostling each other, displaying the feeding energy that distinguished the silver ripper. Once this frenzy was under way, nothing halted it until prey or appetites were exhausted. There was no sign of Nila, just a bed of bones at the bottom of the hold. Kafirr could not even see if they were human, but the lively shapes and the absence of Nila told him all he needed to know.

Both the hold and human cabin were in the starboard hull. Kafirr retraced his steps. He had seen Nila go into the hold. Since she had not come back out of the hatch, she must have gone into the water with those creatures. The only other hold exits were underwater ones.

When he got to the main deck, Kafirr told the xeno that Nila had gone into the hold and now was missing. He added that the creatures in the hold were very much alive and alert. Q'Maax'doux was happy to hear that all was well in the hold, and Kafirr had some trouble fixing the xeno's attention on what had happened to Nila. But this time the boy persisted, drawing on some of Nila's anger.

"Nila?" Q'Maax'doux's speakbox turned the name into a question.

"Yes, the other human."

"That man demanded—and received—payment in advance. His relationship with me has ended, and so should yours." With unsentimental efficiency, Q'Maax'doux proceeded to pay Kafirr off as well.

Kafirr looked down at the scrip in his hands; it was more than enough for a new pry bar, but he remembered how Nila had spoken to him a few hours before. "This is not nearly sufficient; a human is missing. I want the Port Authorities to inspect that hold, and examine the bones at the bottom."

"Impossible," explained Q'Maax'doux. "As you must know, I am working within a tight schedule. There is no time to remove the rippers. I must lift at once to make connections with a high-g institute ship headed outsystem. You may be certain that the content of this hold will be thoroughly studied by the Institute of

Zoological Morphology when I reach Epsilon Eridani IV. A report will be made available to the public."

This promise of eventual publication did not meet immediate needs. "That is hundreds of thousands of hours in the future. Am I supposed to just sit here wondering what happened to Nila? What do I say if someone comes looking for her? You and all the evidence will be off-planet. I will be left to face all the complications and consequences."

Q'Maax'doux set his speakbox for patient reproof. "What consequences? One more or less is no concern. Who would come looking for him?"

"Her," Kafirr corrected.

The xeno adjusted the speakbox: "Who would come looking for it?"

Kafirr was adamant, thinking of Nila's last words to him, because the last advice of a diver is always the most valued. "Then I am going direct to the Port Authorities. I will not be left holding the line; either we both answer their questions, or we both go off-planet."

The speakbox expressed surprise. "The specimen deck on the Skylark is full, and I no longer need your services. Taking you to Epsilon Eridani would be a pointless exercise."

"Fine," said Kafirr. "I will take a ticket to Paradise system instead; the *Jordan River* lifts within the hour."

More surprise came from the speakbox: "Such an expense exceeds all reasonable wages."

"Be unreasonable," Kafirr advised. "A human is missing, and those creatures in the hold are material evidence. The Port Authorities might not want you to export them."

Q'Maax'doux took back the scrip, telling Kafirr that it was senseless to haggle with a human. The xeno then told the hydro-cruiser's comlink to order a single-seat, one-way ticket to Paradise system.

In less than an hour, Kafirr was waiting for a shuttle to lift, thinking of Nila and watching magnetic cranes transfer the hold container from the hydro-cruiser to the Skylark's plump belly. He was surrounded by a small wave of humanity. The last humans allowed to board the shuttle were pressed against the loading gate, carrying packages, bundles, bags, and possessions of every description. With their future slung on their backs or tucked under their arms, these lucky few were preparing to start life anew in Paradise system. The shuttle doors dilated, and people stumbled forward, sea creatures surging into the metal net.

The shuttle pilot was an Eridani Hound, cordial and aloof, whose firm commands showed he was used to herding humans about. He packed them as tight as he could, so the press of bodies and cargo would cushion any minor acceleration effects. When the Hound came to him, Kafirr studied the alien face and asked, "Do you remember me? You got me a job with Q'Maax'doux."

The xeno paused. There were so many humans; they all looked so alike. "The diver on the dock? Deep water must have been good to you, if it brought you here."

"It was a mixed experience," said Kafirr, "but I am grateful for it."

The Hound nodded; human gratitude was something the xeno had learned to take with good grace, though he had no particular use for it.

"I would also be grateful for a seat over there." The boy pointed out an open space beside a nearly nude young woman with a short pelt of brown hair.

"Of course," said the Hound, drawing his lips back in an imitation of a human grin. The Hound had learned to sex humans. He sat Kafirr down, pressing him against the female and telling them to both look up at the viewer. "Soon you will have your first look at the stars."

The woman turned to correct the xeno. She was about to say that she had seen the stars before, but seeing Kafirr made her forget the Hound. "You," she said, "I did not really expect to see."

It was the first time Kafirr could remember seeing Nila's brown eyes wide with surprise. He enjoyed the feel of her bare hip and shoulder pressed against his. "I knew you would be here, Nila. I knew it as soon as I saw what you had left in the hold."

"Yes," she said, hanging her head but keeping her smile. It was the sort of gesture the Hound might have made, to mimic human sorrow. "The silver rippers all went belly-up. Maybe I did not walk the little monsters well enough. Anyway, I did my best to break the tragedy gently; you know what a sensitive soul Quasimodo is."

The gasp went round the circle of faces as the shuttle burst through the cloud cover and they saw the stars spread overhead. The world they were leaving looked just as Nila had said it would, a white pearl hanging on the black ear of night. The people huddled in the shuttle began to sing:

> *There's a better world awaiting, in the sky, yes, in the sky. . . .*

Nila took Kafirr's hand again, saying, "It could hardly be worse."

The Skylark lifted soon after, and matched with the high-boost ship bound for Epsilon E; but when Q'Maax'doux displayed his catch, the Institute of Zoological Morphology was not interested. They told him that the hold held nothing but copy-fish, common scavengers that would enter any baited hold. The copy-fish fed on the dead rippers while mimicking the dying ones. Q'Maax'doux took his speakbox off and cursed shiftless, thieving humans in an alien tongue.

GRAVES

◆   ◆   ◆

Joe Haldeman

*Joe Haldeman, who has previously won the Hugo and the Nebula
for his fiction, won both the Nebula and the World Fantasy Award
with this short horror story.*

*About "Graves" he writes, "In Vietnam I was demolition engi-
neer attached to various infantry companies, and out in the field I
carried a demolition bag, full of stuff like fuses and high explosives,
which were safe, and blasting caps, which were not. I typically had
a box of fifty blasting caps in the bag, and I was sure some days a
stray bullet would hit it, and it would be Joe All Over. It wouldn't
even take a bullet; just falling down on a rock or having somebody
be careless with a cigarette. That fear provided the only recurring
dream I've ever had, or dream image: for several years I occasionally dreamed I was running down a jungle trail unarmed with a
black pyjamaed Viet Cong in hot pursuit ... throwing burning
cigarettes at me."*

*The dream image is slapstick, born of fear. "Graves," born of
the same fear, is anything but funny.*

I have this persistent sleep disorder that makes life difficult for
me, but still I want to keep it. Boy, do I want to keep it. It
goes back twenty years, to Vietnam. To Graves.

Dead bodies turn from bad to worse real fast in the jungle.
You've got a few hours before rigor mortis makes them hard to
handle, hard to stuff in a bag. By that time, they start to turn
greenish, if they started out white or yellow, where you can see the
skin. It's mostly bugs by then, usually ants. Then they go to black
and start to smell.

They swell up and burst.

You'd think the ants and roaches and beetles and millipedes would make short work of them after that, but they don't. Just when they get to looking and smelling the worst, the bugs sort of lose interest, get fastidious, send out for pizza. Except for the flies. Laying eggs.

The funny thing is, unless some big animal got to it and tore it up, even after a week or so, you've still got something more than a skeleton, even a sort of a face. No eyes, though. Every now and then, we'd get one like that. Not too often, since soldiers usually don't die alone and sit there for that long, but sometimes. We called them "dry ones." Still damp underneath, of course, and inside, but kind of like a sunburned mummy otherwise.

You tell people what you do at Graves Registration, "Graves," and it sounds like about the worst job the army has to offer. It isn't. You just stand there all day and open body bags, figure out which parts maybe belong to which dog tag—not that it's usually that important—sew them up more or less with a big needle, account for all the wallets and jewelry, steal the dope out of their pockets, box them up, seal the casket, do the paperwork. When you have enough boxes, you truck them out to the airfield. The first week maybe is pretty bad. But after a hundred or so, after you get use to the smell and the god-awful feel of them, you get to thinking that opening a body bag is a lot better than ending up inside one. They put Graves in safe places.

Since I'd had a couple years of college, premed, I got some of the more interesting jobs. Captain French, who was the pathologist actually in charge of the outfit, always took me with him out into the field when he had to examine a corpse in situ, which happened only maybe once a month. I got to wear a .45 in a shoulder holster, tough guy. Never fired it, never got shot at, except the one time.

That was a hell of a time. It's funny what gets to you, stays with you.

Usually when we had an in situ, it was a forensic matter, like an officer they suspected had been fragged or otherwise terminated by his own men. We'd take pictures and interview some people, and then Frenchy would bring the stiff back for autopsy, see whether the bullets were American or Vietnamese. (Not that that would be conclusive either way. The Vietcong stole our weapons, and our guys used the North Vietnamese AK-47s, when we could get our hands on them. More reliable than the M-16, and a better cartridge for killing. Both sides proved that over and over.) Usually Frenchy would send a report up to Division, and that would be it. Once he had to testify at a court-martial. The kid was guilty, but just got life. The officer was a real prick.

Anyhow, we got the call to come look at this in situ corpse about five in the afternoon. Frenchy tried to put it off until the next day, since if it got dark, we'd have to spend the night. The guy he was talking to was a major, though, and obviously proud of it, so it was no use arguing. I threw some C's and beer and a couple canteens into two rucksacks that already had blankets and air mattresses tied on the bottom. Box of .45 ammo and a couple hand grenades. Went and got a jeep while Frenchy got his stuff together and made sure Doc Carter was sober enough to count the stiffs as they came in. (Doc Carter was the one supposed to be in charge, but he didn't much care for the work.)

Drove us out to the pad, and lo and behold, there was a chopper waiting, blades idling. Should've started to smell a rat then. We don't get real high priority, and it's not easy to get a chopper to go anywhere so close to sundown. They even helped us stow our gear. Up, up, and away.

I never flew enough in helicopters to make it routine. Kontum looked almost pretty in the low sun, golden red. I had to sit between two flamethrowers, though, which didn't make me feel too secure. The door gunner was smoking. The flamethrower tanks were stenciled NO SMOKING.

We went fast and low out toward the mountains to the west. I was hoping we'd wind up at one of the big fire bases up there, figuring I'd sleep better with a few hundred men around. But no such luck. When the chopper started to slow down, the blades' whir deepening to a whuck-whuck-whuck, there was no clearing as far as the eye could see. Thick jungle canopy everywhere. Then a wisp of purple smoke showed us a helicopter-sized hole in the leaves. The pilot brought us down an inch at a time, nicking twigs. I was very much aware of the flamethrowers. If he clipped a large branch, we'd be so much pot roast.

When we touched down, four guys in a big hurry unloaded our gear and the flamethrowers and a couple cases of ammo. They put two wounded guys and one client on board and shooed the helicopter away. Yeah, it would sort of broadcast your position. One of them told us to wait; he'd go get the major.

"I don't like this at all," Frenchy said.

"Me neither," I said. "Let's go home."

"Any outfit that's got a major and two flamethrowers is planning to fight a real war." He pulled his .45 out and looked at it as if he'd never seen one before. "Which end of this do you think the bullets come out of?"

"Shit," I advised, and rummaged through the rucksack for a beer. I gave Frenchy one, and he put it in his side pocket.

A machine gun opened up off to our right. Frenchy and I grabbed the dirt. Three grenade blasts. Somebody yelled for them to cut that out. Guy yelled back he thought he saw something. Machine gun started up again. We tried to get a little lower.

Up walks this old guy, thirties, looking annoyed. The major.

"You men get up. What's wrong with you?" He was playin' games.

Frenchy got up, dusting himself off. We had the only clean fatigues in twenty miles. "Captain French, Graves Registration."

"Oh," he said, not visibly impressed. "Secure your gear and follow me." He drifted off like a mighty ship of the jungle. Frenchy rolled his eyes, and we hoisted our rucksacks and followed him. I wasn't sure whether "secure your gear" meant bring your stuff or leave it behind, but Budweiser could get to be a real collector's item in the boonies, and there were a lot of collectors out here.

We walked too far. I mean a couple hundred yards. That meant they were really spread out thin. I didn't look forward to spending the night. The goddamned machine gun started up again. The major looked annoyed and shouted, "Sergeant, will you please control your men?", and the sergeant told the machine gunner to shut the fuck up, and the machine gunner told the sergeant there was a fuckin' gook out there, and then somebody popped a big one, like a Claymore, and then everybody was shooting every which way. Frenchy and I got real horizontal. I heard a bullet whip by over my head. The major was leaning against a tree, looking bored, shouting, "Cease firing, cease firing!" The shooting dwindled down like popcorn getting done. The major looked over at us and said, "Come on. While there's still light." He led us into a small clearing, ele-

phant grass pretty well trampled down. I guess everybody had had
his turn to look at the corpse.

It wasn't a real gruesome body, as bodies go, but it was odd-
looking, even for a dry one. Moldy, like someone had dusted flour
over it. Naked and probably male, though incomplete: all the soft
parts were gone. Tall; one of our Montagnard allies rather than an
ethnic Vietnamese. Emaciated, dry skin taut over ribs. Probably
old, though it doesn't take long for these people to get old. Lying
on its back, mouth wide open, a familiar posture. Empy eye sockets
staring skyward. Arms flung out in supplication, loosely, long past
rigor mortis.

Teeth chipped and filed to points, probably some Montagnard
tribal custom. I'd never seen it before, but we didn't "do" many
natives.

Frenchy knelt down and reached for it, then stopped. "Checked
for booby traps?"

"No," the major said. "Figure that's your job." Frenchy looked
at me with an expression that said it was my job.

Both officers stood back a respectful distance while I felt under
the corpse. Sometimes they pull the pin on a hand grenade and slip
it under the body so that the body's weight keeps the arming lever
in place. You turn it over, and *Tomato Surprise*!

I always worry less about a hand grenade than about the various
weird serpents and bugs that might enjoy living underneath a de-
composing corpse. Vietnam has its share of snakes and scorpions
and megapedes.

I was lucky this time; nothing but maggots. I flicked them off
my hand and watched the major turn a little green. People are
funny. What does he think is going to happen to him when he dies?
Everything has to eat. And he was sure as hell going to die if he
didn't start keeping his head down. I remember that thought, but
didn't think of it then as a prophecy.

They came over. "What do you make of it, Doctor?"

"I don't think we can cure him." Frenchy was getting annoyed
at this cherry bomb. "What else do you want to know?"

"Isn't it a little . . . *odd* to find something like this in the middle
of nowhere?"

"Naw. Country's full of corpses." He knelt down and studied
the face, wiggling the head by its chin. "We keep it up, you'll be

able to walk from the Mekong to the DMZ without stepping on anything but corpses."

"But he's been castrated!"

"Birds." He toed the body over, busy white crawlers running from the light. "Just some old geezer who walked out into the woods naked and fell over dead. Could happen back in the World. Old people do funny things."

"I thought maybe he'd been tortured by the VC or something."

"God knows. It could happen." The body eased back into its original position with a creepy creaking sound, like leather. Its mouth had closed halfway. "If you want to put 'evidence of VC torture' in your report, your body count, I'll initial it."

"What do you mean by that, Captain?"

"Exactly what I said." He kept staring at the major while he flipped a cigarette into his mouth and fired it up. Nonfilter Camels; you'd think a guy who worked with corpses all day long would be less anxious to turn into one. "I'm just trying to get along."

"You believe I want you to falsify—"

Now, "falsify" is a strange word for a last word. The enemy had set up a heavy machine gun on the other side of the clearing, and we were the closest targets. A round struck the major in the small of his back, we found on later examination. At the time, it was just an explosion of blood and guts, and he went down with his legs flopping every which way, barfing, then loud death rattle. Frenchy was on the ground in a ball, holding his left hand, going, "Shit shit shit." He'd lost the last joint of his little finger. Painful, but not serious enough, as it turned out, to get him back to the World.

I myself was horizontal and aspiring to be subterranean. I managed to get my pistol out and cocked, but realized I didn't want to do anything that might draw attention to us. The machine gun was spraying back and forth over us at about knee height. Maybe they couldn't see us; maybe they thought we were dead. I was scared shitless.

"Frenchy," I stage-whispered, "we've got to get outa here." He was trying to wrap his finger up in a standard first-aid-pack gauze bandage, much too large. "Get back to the trees."

"After you, asshole. We wouldn't get halfway." He worked his pistol out of the holster, but couldn't cock it, his left hand clamping the bandage and slippery with blood. I armed it for him and handed it back. "These are going to do a hell of a lot of good. How are you with grenades?"

"Shit. How you think I wound up in Graves?" In basic training, they'd put me on KP whenever they went out for live grenade practice. In school, I was always the last person when they chose up sides for baseball, for the same reason—though, to my knowledge, a baseball wouldn't kill you if you couldn't throw far enough. "I couldn't get one halfway there." The tree line was about sixty yards away.

"Neither could I, with this hand." He was a lefty.

Behind us came the "poink" sound of a sixty-millimeter mortar, and in a couple of seconds, there was a gray-smoke explosion between us and the tree line. The machine gun stopped, and somebody behind us yelled, "Add twenty!"

At the tree line, we could hear some shouting in Vietnamese, and a clanking of metal. "They're gonna bug out," Frenchy said. "Let's di-di."

We got up and ran, and somebody did fire a couple of bursts at us, probably an AK-47, but he missed, and then there were a series of poinks and a series of explosions pretty close to where the gun had been.

We rushed back to the LZ and found the command group, about the time the firing started up again. There was a first lieutenant in charge, and when things slowed down enough for us to tell him what had happened to the major, he expressed neither surprise nor grief. The man had been an observer from Battalion, and had assumed command when their captain was killed that morning. He'd take our word for it that the guy was dead—that was one thing we were trained observers in—and not send a squad out for him until the fighting had died down and it was light again.

We inherited the major's hole, which was nice and deep, and in his rucksack found a dozen cans and jars of real food and a flask of scotch. So, as the battle raged through the night, we munched pâté on Ritz crackers, pickled herring in sour-cream sauce, little Polish sausages on party rye with real French mustard. We drank all the scotch and saved the beer for breakfast.

For hours the lieutenant called in for artillery and air support, but to no avail. Later we found out that the enemy had launched coordinated attacks on all the local airfields and Special Forces camps, and every camp that held POWs. We were much lower priority.

Then, about three in the morning, Snoopy came over. Snoopy was a big C-130 cargo plane that carried nothing but ammunition and Gatling guns; they said it could fly over a football field and put a round into every square inch. Anyhow, it saturated the perimeter with fire, and the enemy stopped shooting. Frenchy and I went to sleep.

At first light, we went out to help round up the KIAs. There were only four dead, counting the major, but the major was an astounding sight, at least in context.

He looked sort of like a cadaver left over from a teaching autopsy. His shirt had been opened and his pants pulled down to his thighs, and the entire thoracic and abdominal cavities had been ripped open and emptied of everything soft, everything from esophagus to testicles, rib cage like blood-streaked fingers sticking rigid out of sagging skin, and there wasn't a sign of any of the guts anywhere, just a lot of dried blood.

Nobody had heard anything. There was a machine-gun position not twenty yards away, and they'd been straining their ears all night. All they'd heard was flies.

Maybe an animal feeding very quietly. The body hadn't been opened with a scalpel or a knife; the skin had been torn by teeth or claws—but seemingly systematically, throat to balls.

And the dry one was gone. Him with the pointed teeth.

There is one rational explanation. Modern warfare is partly mindfuck, and we aren't the only ones who do it, dropping unlucky cards, invoking magic and superstition. The Vietnamese knew how squeamish Americans were, and would mutilate bodies in clever ways. They could also move very quietly. The dry one? They might have spirited him away just to fuck with us. Show what they could do under our noses.

And as for the dry one's odd mummified appearance, the mold, there might be an explanation. I found out that the Montagnards in that area don't bury their dead; they put them in a coffin made from a hollowed-out log and leave them aboveground. So maybe he was just the victim of a grave robber. I thought the nearest village was miles away, like twenty miles, but I could have been wrong. Or the body could have been carried that distance for some obscure purpose—maybe the VC set it out on the trail to make the Americans stop in a good place to be ambushed.

That's probably it. But for twenty years now, several nights a week, I wake up sweating with a terrible image in my mind. I've gone out with a flashlight, and there it is, the dry one, scooping steaming entrails from the major's body, tearing them with its sharp teeth, staring into my light with black empty sockets, unconcerned. I reach for my pistol, and it's never there. The creature stands up, shiny with blood, and takes a step toward me—for a year or so, that was it; I would wake up. Then it was two steps, and then three. After twenty years it has covered half the distance and its dripping hands are raising from its sides.

The doctor gives me tranquilizers. I don't take them. They might help me stay asleep.

THE DARK

◆ ◆ ◆

Karen Joy Fowler

Karen Joy Fowler has published a collection of stories, Artificial
Things, *and, in 1991, her first novel,* Sarah Canary, *was published
to excellent reviews. More recently, she served as a consultant on*
The Norton Book of Science Fiction. *She has been an infrequent*
F&SF *contributor, but her stories shine with quality, as does this
tale, which opens with a mysterious disappearance and the beginnings of a modern plague. . . .*

In the summer of 1954, Anna and Richard Becker disappeared
from Yosemite National Park along with Paul Becker, their
three-year-old son. Their campsite was intact; two paper plates
with half-eaten frankfurters remained on the picnic table, and a
third frankfurter was in the trash. The rangers took several black-
and-white photographs of the meal, which, when blown up to eight
by ten, as part of the investigation, showed clearly the words *love
bites,* carved into the wooden picnic table many years ago. There
appeared to be some fresh scratches as well; the expert witness at
the trial attributed them, with no great assurance, to raccoons.

The Becker's car was still backed into the campsite, a green
DeSoto with a spare key under the right bumper and half a tank
of gas. Inside the tent, two sleeping bags had been zipped together
marital style and laid on a large tarp. A smaller flannel bag was
spread over an inflated pool raft. Toiletries included three tooth-
brushes; Ipana toothpaste, squeezed in the middle; Ivory soap;
three washcloths; and one towel. The newspapers discreetly made
no mention of Anna's diaphragm, which remained powdered with

87

talc, inside its pink shell, or of the fact that Paul apparently still took a bottle to bed with him.

Their nearest neighbor had seen nothing. He had been in his hammock, he said, listening to the game. Of course, the reception in Yosemite was lousy. At home he had a shortwave set; he said he had once pulled in Dover, clear as a bell. "You had to really concentrate to hear the game," he told the rangers. "You could've dropped the bomb. I wouldn't have noticed."

Anna Becker's mother, Edna, received a postcard postmarked a day earlier. "Seen the firefall," it said simply. "Home Wednesday. Love." Edna identified the bottle. "Oh yes, that's Paul's bokkie," she told the police. She dissolved into tears. "He never goes anywhere without it," she said.

In the spring of 1960, Mark Cooper and Manuel Rodriguez went on a fishing expedition in Yosemite. They set up a base camp in Tuolumne Meadows and went off to pursue steelhead. They were gone from camp approximately six hours, leaving their food and a six-pack of beer zipped inside their backpacks zipped inside their tent. When they returned, both beer and food were gone. Canine footprints circled the tent, but a small and mysterious handprint remained on the tent flap. "Raccoon," said the rangers who hadn't seen it. The tent and packs were undamaged. Whatever had taken the food had worked the zippers. "Has to be raccoon."

The last time Manuel had gone backpacking, he'd suspended his pack from a tree to protect it. A deer had stopped to investigate, and when Manuel shouted to warn it off, the deer hooked the pack over its antlers in a panic, tearing the pack loose from the branch and carrying it away. Pack and antlers were so entangled, Manuel imagined the deer must have worn his provisions and clean shirts until antler-shedding season. He reported that incident to the rangers, too, but what could anyone do? He was reminded of it, guiltily, every time he read *Thidwick, the Big-Hearted Moose* to his four-year-old son.

Manuel and Mark arrived home three days early. Manuel's wife said she'd been expecting him.

She emptied his pack. "Where's the can opener?" she asked.

"It's there somewhere," said Manuel.

"It's not," she said.

"Check the shirt pocket."

"It's not here." Manuel's wife held the pack upside down and shook it. Dead leaves fell out. "How were you going to drink the beer?" she asked.

In August of 1962, Caroline Crosby, a teenager from Palo Alto, accompanied her family on a forced march from Tuolumne Meadows to Vogelsang. She carried fourteen pounds in a pack with an aluminum frame—and her father said it was the lightest pack on the market, and she should be able to carry one-third her weight, so fourteen pounds was nothing, but her back stabbed her continuously in one coin-sized spot just below her right shoulder, and it still hurt the next morning. Her boots left a blister on her right heel, and her pack straps had rubbed. Her father had bought her a mummy bag with no zipper so as to minimize its weight; it was stiflingly hot, and she sweated all night. She missed an overnight at Ann Watson's house, where Ann showed them her sister's Mark Eden bust developer, and her sister retaliated by freezing all their bras behind the twin-pops. She missed "The Beverly Hillbillies."

Caroline's father had quit smoking just for the duration of the trip so as to spare himself the weight of the cigarettes, and made continual comments about Nature, which were laudatory in content and increasingly abusive in tone. Caroline's mother kept telling her to smile.

In the morning her father mixed half a cup of stream water into a packet of powdered eggs and cooked them over a Coleman stove. "Damn fine breakfast," he told Caroline intimidatingly as she stared in horror at her plate. "Out here in God's own country. What else could you ask for?" He turned to Caroline's mother, who was still trying to get a pot of water to come to a boil. "Where's the goddamn coffee?" he asked. He went to the stream to brush his teeth with a toothbrush he had sawed the handle from in order to save the weight. Her mother told her to please make a little effort to be cheerful and not spoil the trip for everyone.

One week later she was in Letterman Hospital in San Francisco. The diagnosis was septicemic plague.

Which is finally where I come into the story. My name is Keith Harmon. B.A. in history with a special emphasis on epidemics. I probably know as much as anyone about the plague of Athens. Typhus. Tarantism. Tsutsugamushi fever. It's an odder historical specialty than it ought to be. More battles have been decided by disease than by generals—and if you don't believe me, take a closer look at the Crusades or the fall of the Roman Empire or Napolean's Russian campaign.

My M.A. is in public administration. Vietnam veteran, too, but in 1962 I worked for the state of California as part of the plague-monitoring team. When Letterman's reported a plague victim, Sacramento sent me down to talk to her.

Caroline had been moved to a private room. "You're going to be fine," I told her. Of course, she was. We still lose people to the pneumonic plague, but the slower form is easily cured. The only tricky part is making the diagnosis.

"I don't feel well. I don't like the food," she said. She pointed out Letterman's Tuesday menu. "Hawaiian Delight. You know what that is? Green Jello-O with a canned pineapple ring on top. What's delightful about that?" She was feverish and lethargic. Her hair lay limply about her head, and she kept tangling it in her fingers as she talked. "I'm missing a lot of school." Impossible to tell if this last was a complaint or a boast. She raised her bed to a sitting position and spent most of the rest of the interview looking out the window, making it clear that a view of the Letterman parking lot was more arresting than a conversation with an old man like me. She seemed younger than fifteen. Of course, everyone in a hospital bed feels young. Helpless. "Will you ask them to let me wash and set my hair?"

I pulled a chair over to the bed. "I need to know if you've been anywhere unusual recently. We know about Yosemite. Anywhere else. Hiking out around the airport, for instance." The plague is endemic in the San Bruno Mountains by the San Francisco Airport. That particular species of flea doesn't bite humans, though. Or so we'd always thought. "It's kind of a romantic spot for some teenagers, isn't it?"

I've seen some withering adolescent stares in my time, but this one was practiced. I still remember it. I may be sick, it said, but at least I'm not an idiot. "Out by the airport?" she said. "Oh, right. Real romantic. The radio playing and those 727s overhead. Give me a break."

"Let's talk about Yosemite, then."

She softened a little. "In Palo Alto we go to the water temple," she informed me. "And, no, I haven't been there, either. My parents *made* me go to Yosemite. And now I've got bubonic plague." Her tone was one of satisfaction. "I think it was the powdered eggs. They *made* me eat them. I've been sick ever since."

"Did you see any unusual wildlife there? Did you play with any squirrels?"

"Oh, right," she said. "I always play with squirrels. Birds sit on my fingers." She resumed the stare. "My parents didn't tell you what I saw?"

"No," I said.

"Figures." Caroline combed her fingers through her hair. "If I had a brush, I could at least rat it. Will you ask the doctors to bring me a brush?"

"What did you see, Caroline?"

"Nothing. According to my parents. No big deal." She looked out at the parking lot. "I saw a boy."

She wouldn't look at me, but she finished her story. I heard about the mummy bag and the overnight party she missed. I heard about the eggs. Apparently, the altercation over breakfast had escalated, culminating in Caroline's refusal to accompany her parents on a brisk hike to Ireland Lake. She stayed behind, lying on top of her sleeping bag and reading the part of *Green Mansions* where Abel eats a fine meal of anteater flesh. "After the breakfast I had, my mouth was watering," she told me. Something made her look up suddenly from her book. She said it wasn't a sound. She said it was a silence.

A naked boy dipped his hands into the stream and licked the water from his fingers. His fingernails curled toward his palms like claws. "Hey," Caroline told me she told him. She could see his penis and everything. The boy gave her a quick look, and then backed away into the trees. She went back to her book.

She described him to her family when they returned. "Real dirty," she said "Real hairy."

"You have a very superior attitude," her mother noted. "It's going to get you in trouble someday."

"Fine," said Caroline, feeling superior. "Don't believe me." She made a vow never to tell her parents anything again. "And

I never will," she told me. "Not if I have to eat powdered eggs until I die."

> At this time there started a plague. It appeared not in one part of the world only, not in one race of men only, and not in any particular season; but it spread over the entire earth, and afflicted all without mercy of both sexes and of every age. It began in Egypt, at Pelusium; thence it spread to Alexandria and to the rest of Egypt; then went to Palestine, and from there over the whole world. . . .
>
> In the second year, in the spring, it reached Byzantium and began in the following manner: To many there appeared phantoms in human form. Those who were so encountered, were struck by a blow from the phantom, and so contracted the disease. Others locked themselves into their houses. But then the phantoms appeared to them in dreams, or they heard voices that told them that they had been selected for death.

This comes from Procopius's account of the first pandemic. A.D. 541, *De Bello Persico*, chapter XXII. It's the only explanation I can give you for why Caroline's story made me so uneasy, why I chose not to mention it to anyone. I thought she'd had a fever dream, but thinking this didn't settle me any. I talked to her parents briefly, and then went back to Sacramento to write my report.

We have no way of calculating the deaths in the first pandemic. Gibbon says that during three months, five to ten thousand people died daily in Constantinople, and many Eastern cities were completely abandoned.

The second pandemic began in 1346. It was the darkest time the planet has known. A third of the world died. The Jews were blamed, and throughout Europe, pogroms occurred wherever sufficient health remained for the activity. When murdering Jews provided no alleviation, a committee of doctors at the University of Paris concluded the plague was the result of an unfortunate conjunction of Saturn, Jupiter, and Mars.

The third pandemic occurred in Europe during the 15th to 18th centuries. The fourth began in China in 1855. It reached Hong Kong in 1894, where Alexandre Yersin of the Institut Pasteur at least identified the responsible bacilli. By 1898 the disease had killed 6 million people in India. Dr. Paul-Louis Simond, also working for the Institut Pasteur, but stationed in Bombay, finally identified fleas as the primary carriers. "On June 2, 1898, I was overwhelmed," he wrote. "I had just unveiled a secret which had tormented man for so long."

His discoveries went unnoticed for another decade or so. On June 27, 1899, the disease came to San Francisco. The governor of California, acting in protection of business interests, made it a felony to publicize the presence of the plague. People died instead of *syphilitic septicemia*. Because of this deception, thirteen of the Western states are still designated plague areas.

The state team went into the high country in early October. Think of us as soldiers. One of the great mysteries of history is why the plague finally disappeared. The rats are still here. The fleas are still here. The disease is still here; it shows up in isolated cases like Caroline's. Only the epidemic is missing. We're in the middle of the fourth assault. The enemy is elusive. The war is unwinnable. We remain vigilant.

The Vogelsang Camp had already been closed for the winter. No snow yet, but the days were chilly and the nights below freezing. If the plague was present, it wasn't really going to be a problem until spring. We amused ourselves, poking sticks into warm burrows looking for dead rodents. We set out some traps. Not many. You don't want to decrease the rodent population. Deprive the fleas of their natural hosts, and they just look for replacements. They just bring the war home.

We picked up a few bodies, but no positives. We could have dusted the place anyway as a precaution. *Silent Spring* came out in 1962, but I hadn't read it.

I saw the coyote on the fourth day. She came out of a hole on the bank of Lewis Creek and stood for a minute with her nose in the air. She was grayed with age around her muzzle, possibly a bit arthritic. She shook out one hind leg. She shook out the other. Then, right as I watched, Caroline's boy climbed out of the burrow after the coyote.

I couldn't see the boy's face. There was too much hair in the way. But his body was hairless, and even though his movements were peculiar and inhuman, I never thought that he was anything but a boy. Twelve years old or maybe thirteen, I thought, although small for thirteen. Wild as a wolf, obviously. Raised by coyotes maybe. But clearly human. Circumsized, if anyone is interested.

I didn't move. I forgot about Procopius and stepped into the *National Enquirer* instead. Marilyn was in my den. Elvis was in my rinse cycle. It was my lucky day. I was amusing myself when I should have been awed. It was a stupid mistake. I wish now that I'd been someone different.

The boy yawned and closed his eyes, then shook himself awake and followed the coyote along the creek and out of sight. I went back to camp. The next morning we surrounded the hole and netted them coming out. This is the moment it stopped being such a lark. This is an uncomfortable memory. The coyote was terrified, and we let her go. The boy was terrified, and we kept him. He scratched us and bit and snarled. He cut me, and I thought it was one of his nails, but he turned out to be holding a can opener. He was covered with fleas, fifty or sixty of them visible at a time, which jumped from him to us, and they all bit, too. It was like being attacked by a cloud. We sprayed the burrow and the boy and ourselves, but we'd all been bitten by then. We took an immediate blood sample. The boy screamed and rolled his eyes all the way through it. The reading was negative. By the time we all calmed down, the boy really didn't like us.

Clint and I tied him up, and we took turns carrying him down to Tuolumne. His odor was somewhere between dog and boy, and worse than both. We tried to clean him up in the showers at the ranger station. Clint and I both had to strip to do this, so God knows what he must have thought we were about. He reacted to the touch of water as if it burned. There was no way to shampoo his hair, and no one with the strength to cut it. So we settled for washing his face and hands, put our clothes back on, gave him a sweater that he dropped by the drain, put him in the backseat of my Rambler, and drove to Sacramento. He cried most of the way, and when we went around curves, he allowed his body to be flung unresisting from one side of the car to the other, occasionally knocking his head against the door handle with a loud, painful sound.

I bought him a ham sandwich when we stopped for gas in Modesto, but he wouldn't eat it. He was a nice-looking kid, had a normal face, freckled, with blue eyes, brown hair; and if he'd had a haircut, you could have imagined him in some Sears catalog modeling raincoats.

One of life's little ironies. It was October 14. We rescue a wild boy from isolation and deprivation and winter in the mountains. We bring him civilization and human contact. We bring him straight into the Cuban Missile Crisis.

Maybe that's why you don't remember reading about him in the paper. We turned him over to the state of California, which had other things on its mind.

The state put him in Mercy Hospital and assigned maybe a hundred doctors to the case. I was sent back to Yosemite to continue looking for fleas. The next time I saw the boy, about a week had passed. He'd been cleaned up, of course. Scoured of parasites, inside and out. Measured. He was just over four feet tall and weighed seventy-five pounds. His head was all but shaved so as not to interfere with the various neurological tests, which had turned out normal and were being redone. He had been observed rocking in a seated position, left to right and back to front, mouth closed, chin up, eyes staring at nothing. Occasionally he had small spasms, convulsive movements, which suggested abnormalities in the nervous system. His teeth needed extensive work. He was sleeping under his bed. He wouldn't touch his Hawaiian Delight. He liked us even less than before.

About this time I had a brief conversation with a doctor whose name I didn't notice. I was never able to find him again. Red-haired doctor with glasses. Maybe thirty, thirty-two years old. "He's got some unusual musculature," this red-haired doctor told me. "Quite singular. Especially the development of the legs. He's shown us some really surprising capabilities." The boy started to howl, an unpleasant, inhuman sound that started in his throat and ended in yours. It was so unhappy. It made me so unhappy to hear it. I never followed up on what the doctor had said.

I felt peculiar about the boy, responsible for him. He had such a *boyish* face. I visited several times, and I took him little presents, a Dodgers baseball cap and an illustrated *Goldilocks and the Three Bears* with the words printed big. Pretty silly, I suppose, but what would you have gotten? I drove to Fresno and asked Manuel Rodriguez if he could identify the can opener. "Not with any assurance," he said. I talked personally to Sergeant Redburn, the man from Missing Persons. When he told me about the Beckers, I went to the state library and read the newspaper articles for myself. Sergeant Redburn thought the boy might be just about the same age as Paul Becker, and I thought so, too. And I know the sergeant went to talk to Anna Becker's mother about it, because he told me she was going to come and try to identify the boy.

By now it's November. Suddenly I get a call sending me back to Yosemite. In Sacramento they claim the team has reported a positive, but when I arrive in Yosemite, the whole team denies it. Fleas are astounding creatures. They can be frozen for a year or more and then revived to full activity. But November in the mountains is a stupid time to be out looking for them. It's already snowed once, and it snows again, so that I can't get my team back out. We spend three weeks in the ranger station at Vogelsang huddled around our camp stoves while they air-drop supplies to us. And when I get back, a doctor I've never seen before, a Dr. Frank Li, tells me the boy, who was not Paul Becker, died suddenly of a seizure while he slept. I have to work hard to put away the sense that it was my fault, that I should have left the boy where he belonged.

And then I hear Sergeant Redburn has jumped off the Golden Gate Bridge.

Non Gratum Anus Rodentum. Not worth a rat's ass. This was the unofficial motto of the tunnel rats. We're leaping ahead here. Now it's 1967. Vietnam. Does the name Cu Chi mean anything to you? If not, why not? The district of Cu Chi is the most bombed, shelled, gassed, strafed, defoliated, and destroyed piece of earth in the history of warfare. And beneath Cu Chi runs the most complex part of a network of tunnels that connects Saigon all the way to the Cambodian border.

I want you to imagine, for a moment, a battle fought entirely in the dark. Imagine that you are in a hole that is too hot and too small. You cannot stand up; you must move on your hands and knees by touch and hearing alone through a terrain you can't see toward an enemy you can't see. At any moment you might trip a mine, put your hand on a snake, put your face on a decaying corpse. You know people who have done all three of these things. At any moment the air you breathe might turn to gas, the tunnel become so small you can't get back out; you could fall into a well of water and drown; you could be buried alive. If you are lucky, you will put your knife into an enemy you may never see before he puts his knife into you. In Cu Chi the Vietnamese and the Americans created, inch by inch, body part by body part, an entirely new type of warfare.

Among the Vietnamese who survived are soldiers who lived in the tiny underground tunnels without surfacing for five solid years. Their eyesight was permanently damaged. They suffered constant malnutrition, felt lucky when they could eat spoiled rice and rats. Self-deprivation was their weapon; they used it to force the soldiers of the most technologically advanced army in the world to face them with knives, one on one, underground, in the dark.

On the American side, the tunnel rats were all volunteers. You can't force a man to do what he cannot do. Most Americans hyperventilated, had attacks of claustrophobia, were too big. The tunnel rats could be no bigger than the Vietnamese, or they wouldn't fit through the tunnels. Most of the tunnel rats were Hispanics and Puerto Ricans. They stopped wearing after-shave so the Vietcong wouldn't smell them. They stopped chewing gum, smoking, and eating candy because it impaired their ability to sense the enemy. They had to develop the sonar of bats. They had, in their own words, to become animals. What they did in the tunnels, they said, was unnatural.

In 1967 I was attached to the 521st Medical Detachment. I was an old man by Vietnamese standards, but then, I hadn't come to fight in the Vietnam War. Remember that the fourth pandemic began in China. Just before he died, Chinese poet Shih Tao-nan wrote:

Few days following the death of the rats,
Men pass away like falling walls.

Between 1965 and 1970, 24,848 cases of the plague were reported in Vietnam.

War is the perfect breeding ground for disease. They always go together, the trinity: war, disease, and cruelty. Disease was my war. I'd been sent to Vietnam to keep my war from interfering with everybody else's war.

In March we received by special courier a package containing three dead rats. The rats had been found—already dead, but leashed—inside a tunnel in Hau Nghia province. Also found—but not sent to us—were a syringe, a phial containing yellow fluid, and several cages. I did the test myself. One of the dead rats carried the plague.

There has been speculation that the Vietcong were trying to use plague rats as weapons. It's also possible they were merely testing the rats prior to eating them themselves. In the end, it makes little difference. The plague was there in the tunnels whether the Vietcong used it or not.

I set up a tent outside Cu Chi town to give boosters to the tunnel rats. One of the men I inoculated was David Rivera. "David has been into the tunnels so many times, he's a legend," his companions told me.

"Yeah," said David. "Right. Me and Victor."

"Victor Charlie?" I said. I was just making conversation. I could see David, whatever his record in the tunnels, was afraid of the needle. He held out one stiff arm. I was trying to get him to relax.

"No. Not hardly. Victor is the one." He took his shot, put his shirt back on, gave up his place to the next man in line.

"Victor can see in the dark," the next man told me.

"Victor Charlie?" I asked again.

"No," the man said impatiently.

"You want to know about Victor?" David said. "Let me tell you about Victor. Victor's the one who comes when someone goes down and doesn't come back out."

"Victor can go faster on his hands and knees than most men can run," the other man said. I pressed cotton on his arm after I withdrew the needle; he got up from the table. A third man sat down and took off his shirt.

David still stood next to me. "I go into this tunnel. I'm not too scared, because I think it's cold; I'm not *feeling* anybody else there, and I'm maybe a quarter of a mile in, on my hands and knees, when I can almost see a hole in front of me, blacker than anything else in the tunnel, which is all black, you know. So I go into the hole, feeling my way, and I have this funny sense like I'm not moving into the hole; the hole is moving over to me. I put out my hands, and the ground moves under them."

"Shit," said the third man. I didn't know if it was David's story or the shot. A fourth man sat down.

"I risk a light, and the whole tunnel is covered with spiders, covered like wallpaper, only worse, two or three bodies thick," David said. "I'm sitting on them, and the spiders are already inside my pants and inside my shirt and covering my arms—and it's fucking Vietnam, you know; I don't even know if they're poisonous or not. Don't care, really, because I'm going to die just from having them on me. I can feel them moving toward my face. So I start to scream, and then this little guy comes and pulls me back out a ways, and then he sits for maybe half an hour, calm as can be, picking spiders off me. When I decide to live after all, I go back out. I tell everybody. 'That was Victor,' they say. 'Had to be Victor.'"

"I know a guy says Victor pulled him from a hole," the fourth soldier said. "He falls through a false floor down maybe twelve straight feet into this tiny little trap with straight walls all around and no way up, and Victor comes down after him. *Jumps* back out, holding the guy in his arms. Twelve feet; the guy swears it."

"Tiny little guy," said David. "Even for V.C., this guy'd be tiny."

"He just looks tiny," the second soldier said. "I know a guy saw Victor buried under more than a ton of dirt. Victor just digs his way out again. No broken bones, no nothing."

Inexcusably slow, and I'd been told twice, but I had just figured out that Victor wasn't short for V.C. "I'd better inoculate this Victor," I said. "You think you could send him in?"

The men stared at me. "You don't get it, do you?" said David.

"Victor don't report," the fourth man says.

"No C.O.," says the third man. "No unit."

"He's got the uniform," the second man tells me. "So we don't know if he's special forces of some sort or if he's AWOL down in the tunnels."

"Victor lives in the tunnels," said David. "Nobody up top has ever seen him."

I tried to talk to one of the doctors about it. "Tunnel vision," he told me. "We get a lot of that. Forget it."

* * *

In May we got a report of more rats—some leashed, some in cages—in a tunnel near Ah Nhon Tay village in the Ho Bo Woods. But no one wanted to go in and get them, because these rats were alive. And somebody got the idea this was my job, and somebody else agreed. They would clear the tunnel of V.C. first, they promised me. So I volunteered.

Let me tell you about rats. Maybe they're not responsible for the plague, but they're still destructive to every kind of life-form and beneficial to none. They eat anything that lets them. They breed during all seasons. They kill their own kind; they can do it singly, but they can also organize and attack in hordes. The brown rat is currently embroiled in a war of extinction against the black rat. Most animals behave better than that.

I'm not afraid of rats. I read somewhere that about the turn of the century, a man in western Illinois heard a rustling in his fields one night. He got out of bed and went to the back door, and behind his house he saw a great mass of rats that stretched all the way to the horizon. I suppose this would have frightened me. All those naked tails in the moonlight. But I thought I could handle a few rats in cages, no problem.

It wasn't hard to locate them. I was on my hands and knees, but using a flashlight. I thought there might be some loose rats, too, and that I ought to look at least; and I'd also heard that there was an abandoned V.C. hospital in the tunnel that I was curious about. So I left the cages and poked around in the tunnels a bit; and when I'd had enough, I started back to get the rats, and I hit a water trap. There hadn't been a water trap before, so I knew I must have taken a wrong turn. I went back a bit, took another turn, and then another, and hit the water trap again. By now I was starting to panic. I couldn't find anything I'd ever seen before except the damn water. I went back again, farther without turning, took a turn, hit the trap.

I must have tried seven, eight times. I no longer thought the tunnel was cold. I thought the V.C. had closed the door on my original route so that I wouldn't find it again. I thought they were watching every move I made, pretty easy with me waving my flashlight about. I switched it off. I could hear them in the dark, their eyelids closing and opening, their hands tightening on their knives.

I was sweating, head to toe, like I was ill, like I had the mysterious English sweating sickness or the *Suette des Picards*.

And I knew that to get back to the entrance, I had to go into the water. I sat and thought that through, and when I finished, I wasn't the same man I'd been when I began the thought.

It would have been bad to have to crawl back through the tunnels with no light. To go into the water with no light, not knowing how much water there was, not knowing if one lungful of air would be enough or if there were underwater turns so you might get lost before you found air again, was something you'd have to be crazy to do. I had to do it, so I had to be crazy first. It wasn't as hard as you might think. It took me only a minute.

I filled my lungs as full as I could. Emptied them once. Filled them again and dove in. Someone grabbed me by the ankle and hauled me back out. It frightened me so much I swallowed water so I came up coughing and kicking. The hand released me at once, and I lay there for a bit, dripping water and still sweating, too, feeling the part of the tunnel that was directly below my body turn to mud, while I tried to convince myself that no one was touching me.

Then I was crazy enough to turn my light on. Far down the tunnel, just within range of the light, knelt a little kid dressed in the uniform of the rats. I tried to get closer to him. He moved away, just the same amount I had moved, always just in the light. I followed him down one tunnel, around a turn, down another. Outside, the sun rose and set. We crawled for days. My right knee began to bleed.

"Talk to me," I asked him. He didn't.

Finally he stood up ahead of me. I could see the rat cages, and I knew where the entrance was behind him. And then he was gone. I tried to follow with my flashlight, but he'd jumped or something. He was just gone.

"Victor," Rat Six told me when I finally came out. "Goddamn Victor."

Maybe so. If Victor was the same little boy I put a net over in the high country in Yosemite.

When I came out, they told me less than three hours had passed. I didn't believe them. I told them about Victor. Most of them didn't believe me. Nobody outside the tunnels believed in Victor. "We just sent home one of the rats," a doctor told me. "He emptied his whole gun into a tunnel. Claimed there were V.C. all around him, but that he got them. He shot every one. Only, when we went down to clean it up, there were no bodies. All his bullets were found in the walls.

"Tunnel vision. Everyone sees things. It's the dark. Your eyes no longer impose any limit on the things you can see."

I didn't listen. I made demands right up the chain of command for records; recruitment, AWOLs, special projects. I wanted to talk to everyone who'd ever seen Victor. I wrote Clint to see what he remembered of the drive back from Yosemite. I wrote a thousand letters to Mercy Hospital, telling them I'd uncovered their little game. I demanded to speak with the red-haired doctor with glasses whose name I never knew. I wrote the Curry Company and suggested they conduct a private investigation into the supposed suicide of Sergeant Redburn. I asked the CIA what they had done with Paul's parents. That part was paranoid. I was so unstrung I thought they'd killed his parents and given him to the coyote to raise him up for the tunnel wars. When I calmed down, I knew the CIA would never be so farsighted. I knew they'd just gotten lucky. I didn't know what happened to the parents; still don't.

There were so many crazy people in Vietnam, it could take them a long time to notice a new one, but I made a lot of noise. A team of three doctors talked to me for a total of seven hours. Then they said I was suffering from delayed guilt over the death of my little dog-boy, and that it surfaced, along with every other weak link in my personality, in the stress and the darkness of the tunnels. They sent me home. I missed the moon landing, because I was having a nice little time in a hospital of my own.

When I was finally and truly released, I went looking for Caroline Crosby. The Crosbys still lived in Palo Alto, but Caroline did not. She'd started college at Berkeley, but then she'd dropped out. Her parents hadn't seen her for several months.

Her mother took me through their beautiful house and showed me Caroline's old room. She had a canopy bed and her own bathroom. There was a mirror with old pictures of some boy on it. A throw rug with roses. There was a lot of pink. "We drive through the Haight every weekend," Caroline's mother said. "Just looking."

She was pale and controlled. "If you should see her, would you tell her to call?"

I would not. I made one attempt to return one little boy to his family, and look what happened. Either Sergeant Redburn jumped from the Golden Gate Bridge in the middle of his investigation or he didn't. Either Paul Becker died in Mercy Hospital or he was picked up by the military to be their special weapon in a special war.

I've thought about it now for a couple of decades, and I've decided that, at least for Paul, once he'd escaped from the military, things didn't work out so badly. He must have felt more at home in the tunnels under Cu Chi than he had under the bed in Mercy Hospital.

There is a darkness inside us all that is animal. Against some things—untreated or untreatable disease, for example, or old age—the darkness is all we are. Either we are strong enough animals or we are not. Such things pare everything that is not animal away from us. As animals, we have a physical value, but in moral terms we are neither good nor bad. Morality begins on the way back from the darkness.

The first two plagues were largely believed to be a punishment for man's sinfulness. "So many died," wrote Agnolo di Tura the Fat, who buried all five of his own children himself, "that all believed that it was the end of the world." This being the case, you'd imagine the cessation of the plague must have been accompanied by outbreaks of charity and godliness. The truth was just the opposite. In 1349, in Erfurt, Germany, of the three thousand Jewish residents there, not one survived. This is a single instance of a barbarism so marked and so pervasive, it can be understood only as a form of mass insanity.

Here is what Procopius said: *And after the plague had ceased, there was so much depravity and general licentiousness, that it seemed as though the disease had left only the most wicked.*

When men are turned into animals, it's hard for them to find their way back to themselves. When children are turned into animals, there's no self to find. There's never been a feral child who found his way out of the dark. Maybe there's never been a feral child who wanted to.

You don't believe I saw Paul in the tunnels at all. You think I'm crazy or, charitably, that I was crazy then, just for a little while. Maybe you think the CIA would never have killed a policeman or tried to use a little child in a black war even though the CIA has done everything else you've ever been told and refused to believe.

That's O.K. I like your version just fine. Because if I made him up, and all the tunnel rats who ever saw him made him up, then he belongs to us, he marks us. Our vision, our Procopian phantom in the tunnels. Victor to take care of us in the dark.

Caroline came home without me. I read her wedding announcement in the paper more than twenty years ago. She married a Stanford chemist. There was a picture of her in her parents' backyard with gardenias in her hair. She was twenty-five years old. She looked happy. I never did go talk to her.

So here's a story for you, Caroline:

A small German town was much plagued by rats who ate the crops and the chickens, the ducks, the cloth and the seeds. Finally the citizens called in an exterminator. He was the best; he trapped and poisoned the rats. Within a month he had deprived the fleas of most of their hosts.

The fleas then bit the children of the town instead. Hundreds of children were taken with a strange dancing and raving disease. Their parents tried to control them, tried to keep them safe in their beds, but the moment their mothers' backs were turned, the children ran into the streets and danced. The town was Erfurt. The year was 1237.

Most of the children danced themselves to death. But not all. A few of them recovered and lived to be grown-ups. They married and worked and had their own children. They lived reasonable and productive lives.

The only thing is that they still twitch sometimes. Just now and then. They can't help it.

Stop me, Caroline, if you've heard this story before.

WILLIE

◆   ◆   ◆

Madeleine E. Robins

Madeleine E. Robins works for Metropolitan *magazine. She has written a number of novels in other genres, and has sold several short
stories to F&SF. Somewhere in all that, she finds time to be a mother.*
"Willie" came into being after she watched a clip from the movie
Young Frankenstein. *"I had had my usual reaction," she writes.
"Impatience with the Doctor, who didn't have the responsibility
to follow through on his project. Only after the story was written
did I realize that I had incorporated a year's worth of mothering
into it. I'm a little chagrined to have been so unconscious about
that; on the other hand, I still like my Doctor, for all his ineptitude,
better than Victor Frankenstein."*

T he night is stormy. Each time the sky lightens, the air in
the lab is filled with static. The Doctor did not intend to
work so late, with the sky acting out a melodrama over the parking
lot. But everything has come together at this time, and he and his
assistant stand together in the lab, staring at the thing on the table.
Finally the Doctor signals and the assistant throws a switch: a
charge passes through coils of wire, elaborate structures, at last
through the thing on the table. It quivers violently until the current
is turned off. The lab is silent except for the breathing of the Doctor
and his assistant. Then a beep. Another. As the EKG chitters, the
Doctor and his assistant look at one another, awed.

"It's alive," the Doctor murmurs. Then, loudly: "It's alive!" He
is overwhelmed; the culmination of his years of work, vindication
of his theories, is almost too much for him.

The thing on the table stirs slightly. It is a hodgepodge of spare parts, some acquired from organ banks, others cloned. It is not pretty: the Doctor's skill is not in surgery, and there are scars and sutures, quite visible, all over its body.

The thing shudders and opens its mouth. The assistant looks nervously at the restraints, as if fearful the thing will break free. The bonds hold. From the mouth of the thing comes a noise, rusty and spasmodic, almost a bleating. The thing is crying.

"What?" the Doctor asks vaguely. In all his planning, he made no provision for this moment, and now the thing on the table is crying, and he cannot think what to do.

"Hungry?" the assistant asks helpfully. The Doctor nods, and the assistant goes to the refrigerator, where he finds half of the sandwich the Doctor had for dinner. Gingerly, he approaches the thing and, tearing off a small piece of corned beef on rye, nudges it between the thing's lips. It is immediately spat out, and the thing wails louder. Why? the Doctor wonders. It has teeth; it can chew. After another attempt, the assistant has an idea. He takes a rubber glove, fills it with tap water, pierces one finger, and prods the finger into the thing's mouth. It sucks contentedly, making small grunting noises. When it finishes, it becomes quiet again.

"Now what, Doctor?" the assistant asks. He is longing for his bed, his fat wife warm beside him. "It's as helpless as a baby."

The Doctor frowns. A baby, that thing on the table that measures six and a half feet in length and weighs close to two hundred pounds? What does he do now? Thinking of the thing as a baby, as something helpless, almost formless, he must revise his initial plan to take the thing on a road show of scientific conferences. You bring a baby into the world, you must take care of it.

He sends the assistant out for baby bottles, cans of liquid nutritional supplement. As an afterthought, he adds adult diapers to the list; already the thing has wet itself. *So many things I did not think of*, he realizes.

Over the next week, he attempts to evaluate the thing's status. His tests confirm: the thing has the musculature of an adult male, but its brain has no idea of how to manage the body. He will have to teach it to hold its head up, focus its eyes, learn its own physical boundaries, walk, talk. He spends two days in the medical library reading monographs on rehabilitative medicine before he understands that he is looking at the problem the wrong way. On the way back to the lab, he stops at Waldenbooks and buys Spock, Leach, Brazelton; dozens of books with titles like *What to Expect the First Year* and *Your Baby and You.* He reads them at night, making copious notes, lists of things to buy, to do. The thing continues to lie on the table, crying when hungry or wet or cold, looking soberly at the patterns of light thrown by sunlight in the day, fluorescent lights by night. One eye is blue, the other brown: the Doctor made shift with what he could get.

The Doctor puts his work, his life on hold; he spends his days and nights at the lab, ministering to the thing, which he has named Willie, after his own father, whose name was Wilhelm. He sleeps as Willie's erratic schedule permits; *I must train him to a more reasonable schedule,* the Doctor tells himself. His assistant, who has four children, is helpful during the day, but insists on going home to his own bed at night. Gradually, Willie begins to sleep through the night, and the Doctor is able to catch five or six hours of sleep himself, on the daybed catercorner to the lab door.

He will say later that his life in this period was an endless round of changing and feeding, punctuated by naps. One night, when Willie refuses to be calmed with food or a fresh diaper, the Doctor thumbs frantically through his books, wondering if this is colic or something more serious. " 'Sometimes a child will cry because it is lonely. Comfort and cuddling are as necessary to human beings as to any other animal on the planet.' "

He drops the book into his lap and stares at the thing lying there, weeping with harsh, heartbroken sobs. It is difficult to overcome not simply his physical revulsion at being so close to the thing, but years of training in laboratory protocol, and his own strict and isolated upbringing. Finally the Doctor edges close to Willie and, with some difficulty, raises him to sitting so that the thing's head can rest on his shoulder. Awkwardly, he strokes Willie's coarse hair, murmuring, "Hush now, hush now; it's all right; I'm here."

Willie draws a few more shuddering breaths, then sighs, nestles closer to the Doctor's shoulder, and sleeps. He has discovered his thumb.

Willie's physical progress is more rapid than that of ordinary children; after all, his body is that of a man, however inexpertly he may use it. Early on, for example, he is able to chew his food quite vigorously, but cannot raise his cup to his lips to drink. By three months, however, he is able to eat finger foods, drink from a cup, and is beginning to take awkward steps, one and two at a time. The Doctor buys a video camera to record his subject's development. With all Willie's progress, the Doctor is in no way certain of his own ability to accomplish the task he has taken on. How, for example, to toilet train? How to handle the "Terrible Twos"? How to explain to Willie where he came from? He can only take each day as it comes.

The assistant comes less often now; the Doctor sometimes forgets to write out the checks, and there are other jobs available to a man with lab training, as the assistant hurries to point out. The Doctor apologizes: he has been absorbed in Willie's progress. He decides to sublet his condominium and move into the lab, where there is enough room for both Willie and himself. With his own work on hold, the Doctor does not apply for new grants; for a time, they live on his investments while the Doctor looks for some kind of work that he can do at night, after Willie is asleep. The waking hours are too precious, too vital to science. Willie said "Doctor" yesterday—at least the Doctor believes it was "Doctor"; the sound itself was more like "dohda," but the Doctor feels the intent is clear.

Realizing that Willie will need more social input than he himself can provide, the Doctor starts to research preschool programs. The directors of several programs are sympathetic, but few feel they can accommodate a two-hundred-pound two-year-old who is not yet toilet trained. Finally, persevering, the Doctor finds a preschool, and Willie enters with the other two-year-olds. If anything, he is shyer than most, and gentle. His association with the animals in the lab has made Willie careful not to hurt creatures smaller than himself. The other children accept Willie, and while he is subject to the normal politics of infant social groups, he is no different in that way than any other child. The teacher, who began by averting her eyes and shuddering when Willie arrived for school, writes at the end of the year: "Willie is extraordinarily generous and sensitive, with a real gift for making others feel at ease. He loves to finger-paint, and enjoys singing with the class." In truth, Willie's voice is hideously unmusical, but neither he nor his classmates appear to care.

Willie enters first grade a year late, not because he was unable to do the work, but because the Doctor was forced to go to court to make the local school district admit his protégé. To ensure that Willie will be well treated, and because he wishes to have some control over the educational process Willie will be subject to, the Doctor becomes an active and vocal member of the PTA. He even, for a time, is a Cub Scout leader. The laboratory, its equipment long shrouded in holland covers, is filled with Willie's stamp collection, his baseball cards, roller skates, his Lego blocks. When Willie brings home his first real report card, his face, his ugly seamed face with the mismatched eyes and jutting brow, shines with pleasure. "Look, Papa, look! I got three A's and two B's!"

The Doctor puts his arm around Willie's shoulders, although he must stand on tiptoe to do so. "I am proud," he says quietly.

Little League is another battle. Parents and the coach argue that there is a real hazard to their children in playing baseball with a two-hundred-pound nine-year-old. Again they go to court, and the judge speaks to Willie in his chambers. Willie's face shines with longing as he speaks of playing ball like the other kids. The Doctor speaks, too: "I want my boy to have all the things any other child would have. What he is, I made him—quite literally. It is not his fault that he is different from other children, and it is not fair that he should be penalized for his very being." The judge rules that, if accommodations can be made to safeguard the players of the opposite team, Willie may play in Little League. After the judgment the Doctor takes Willie out for hot-fudge sundaes. Willie's face is a beatific smear of chocolate, whipped cream, and joy.

There is no puberty per se: Willie was created an adult male. But as his schoolmates begin to go through the tremors of adolescence, Willie feels his own stirrings and confusion. The Doctor again turns to books, trying to find ways to safeguard his boy against what he knows will be the inevitable disappointments. No cheerleader or beauty queen will go out with Willie. For the first time in his life, Willie looks at himself in the mirror and really sees the traces of suturing, the scars, the mismatched eyes, the haphazard arrangement of limbs. When he was building Willie, the Doctor reflects, he did so without regard to the cosmetics of the situation. Were he doing it again today, he would be more careful.

Willie begins to mope, spending his afternoons feeding the few remaining lab animals, doing his homework. His friends call for him, but Willie is listless, cannot be cajoled out to the mall or drive-in. The Doctor talks to a few of Willie's friends, and learns that the two girls Willie had asked to the prom had turned him down, one gently, one without tact. The Doctor is surprised at the rage that fills him; he must remind himself that rage is unproductive. Instead, he and several of Willie's friends concoct a plan whereby the youngsters will go to the prom together. Whether Willie understands the purpose of this tactic or not, he goes to the prom and has a wonderful time. The Doctor waits up to hear the stories when the boy returns.

Willie begins to talk about college. The Doctor is not quite easy with the idea that the boy will be so far away, but feels he must support Willie's choice. For a time the table in the laboratory is covered with college catalogs and application forms. They wait together, the Doctor and Willie, and as each envelope comes, they open it with delicious anticipation. Willie is accepted everywhere he applies: his grades are good, his SATs excellent, and the universities are probably too mindful of the potential for a discrimination lawsuit to reject the boy on the grounds that he is a golem. After some discussion, Willie chooses to attend the state university, only half an hour's drive away. The Doctor hides his pleasure, not wishing Willie to feel confined. Willie decides to live on campus, but most weekends he comes home, and he and the Doctor discuss what he is learning. His freshman year, Willie takes English theory, freshman composition, advanced French, and biology. He is gifted in languages, and his French accent is particularly good.

The subject of girls arises again, more than once. Willie has girl friends, but no girlfriend. Privately, the Doctor feels some anger: stupid females, can't they see past Willie's physical defects to the loving and worthwhile person his boy has become? Willie does not blame the girls, but he is lonely. Finally, one weekend, he sits with the Doctor after dinner and begins to talk seriously.

"Father, make a girl for me."

The Doctor shakes his head. "No, Willie. I cannot." He explains that even if he were to assemble the parts, disinter the lab equipment, and duplicate his feat of twenty years before, Willie would still have to wait until the girl grew up. "That was my error: not realizing that you would need to be raised like any other child, my boy. If I built a wife for you, who would raise her?" He holds up his hands to the light: paper thin and bony, with the raised veins and wrinkled flesh of age. "I'm not a young man, Willie. I could not do it again."

Willie doesn't hear. He rises from his chair and says, "If you loved me, you'd do it," and storms out.

They are estranged for some time afterward. At night, alone on the daybed in the laboratory, the Doctor wonders, Should I have said yes? Was he asking such a little thing that I should have said yes? But he knows he is right: lately he has taken to monitoring the sinus rhythms of his heart, and knows that he could not undertake to raise another child. It is lonely at the laboratory without Willie's phone calls and Willie's weekend visits. The Doctor's heart is heavy, but his pride will not let him call the boy. Willie's graduation comes and goes; the Doctor has to call the university to learn that the boy was graduated with high honors and distinction in his major field, French literature. He sends Willie a Mont Blanc pen with a note, and tells himself not to mind too much if he hears nothing back.

Willie calls, his voice tentative and cautious. The Doctor invites him for dinner, and Willie accepts. Over dinner: "I want to hear how you've been doing," the Doctor says heartily, and Willie tells him about playing football, about finishing his thesis, about graduate school in the fall. "The university has offered me a teaching assistantship," he says proudly.

"Another scholar in the family!" The Doctor is delighted, slightly drunk, and filled with German sentimentality. He throws his arm around Willie's shoulders and says, "I am proud of you, my son." He does not notice that Willie stoops to permit the embrace: the Doctor is indeed getting old.

They fall again into the old pattern of phone calls and weekend visits. Willie gets his master's degree and, while working toward a

Ph.D., is offered an instructorship in the French department. He becomes a popular teacher. The word on campus, he tells the Doctor, is that "I'm gross to look at, but I really understand Racine." Willie chuckles as he quotes.

The Doctor, regarding his son, does not quite understand the reference. Gross to look at? Do students now require that their teachers be Adonises? he wonders.

Willie calls at midweek to say that he'll be coming down on Friday this week. And bringing someone. His tone, to the Doctor's sensitive ears, is resonant with excitement. A girl, the Doctor thinks. At last.

On Friday, Willie's car pulls into the parking lot in midafternoon. The Doctor watches from his office upstairs as Willie parks, goes around to the passenger-side door, and opens it for his companion. Such manners, he thinks. The girl stands and takes Willie's arm in a way both firm and affectionate. She has shoulder-length red hair and stands only as high as Willie's breast pocket. The Doctor takes pleasure in the warmth of the smile she gives his son. Still smiling himself, he leaves his office and goes downstairs to greet the arrivals. Only when they are face-to-face does the Doctor realize the girl is blind.

It is a good weekend. The girl, Gwen, knows all about Willie's background and is not troubled by it. For his part, Willie seems to enjoy taking care of Gwen in little ways. Is she good enough for Willie? The Doctor reminds himself that he would have misgivings about any match his son made; Gwen is a fine girl, and Willie loves her. When Willie tells him they want to marry, the Doctor is prepared. He puts a hand on each of their shoulders and gives them his blessing.

The wedding takes place in the university arboretum, and is attended by friends and colleagues of Willie's and Gwen's. Willie still keeps up his friendships from grade school, Scouts, high school, as well as with his co-workers and friends from college days. After the ceremony, when the bride and groom are making their way around the crowd collecting good wishes, the Doctor chats with this person, then that. Everyone says what a fine man Willie is, and the Doctor agrees. He talks animatedly with members of the science faculty who are there; several of them profess to have read his monographs from years before. It is only as he walks away that he hears the associate professor of anatomy say to his colleague, "So that's what became of him? A brilliant mind, despite his crackpot theories, and then he just dropped out of the scientific community."

The colleague nods. "Just couldn't keep up with the field, I suppose." They walk away to get more punch.

Willie and Gwen live in faculty housing on campus. Twice a month, they visit the Doctor, bringing the baby with them. Watching his son with the baby, the Doctor thinks sentimentally, "Were you ever so tiny?" then feels foolish, remembering the effort with which, long ago, he gathered his massive son into a similar embrace. He finds in time that handling little Alice is no more difficult. Sometimes the Doctor watches over her so her parents can go hear a concert or take a walk alone together. When she is fed and changed, the Doctor raises her into the crook of his arm—so very tiny, he thinks—and hums rustily to her. Sometimes he strokes her silky hair and murmurs, "Hush now, hush now; it's all right; I'm here."

The baby watches him with trusting eyes and falls asleep.

THE LAST FEAST
OF HARLEQUIN

✦   ✦   ✦

Thomas Ligotti

*Thomas Ligotti's stories have appeared in several magazines and
anthologies, including Ramsey Campbell's* Stories that Scared Me
and Douglas Winter's Prime Evil, *and they have been collected in
three volumes,* Songs of a Dead Dreamer, Grimscribe, *and* Noctu-
ary. *This tale—concerning the remarkable events surrounding an
annual festival in the midwestern town of Mirocaw—is not long
on violence or gore. But it is one of the most menacing and convincing weird tales we have ever read, an accomplished job of storytell-
ing that makes a nightmare seem real.*

I

My interest in the town of Mirocaw was first aroused
when I heard that an annual festival was held there
that promised to include, to some extent, the participation of
clowns among its other elements of pageantry. A former colleague
of mine, who is now attached to the anthropology department of
a distant university, had read one of my recent articles ("The Clown
Figure in American Media," *Journal of Popular Culture*), and wrote
to me that he vaguely remembered reading or being told of a town
somewhere in the state that held a kind of "Fool's Feast" every
year, thinking that this might be pertinent to my peculiar line of
study. It was, of course, more pertinent that he had reason to think,
both to my academic aims in this area and to my personal pursuits.

Aside from my teaching, I had for some years been engaged
in various anthropological projects with the primary ambition of

articulating the significance of the clown figure in diverse cultural contexts. Every year for the past twenty years, I have attended the pre-Lenten festivals that are held in various places throughout the southern United States. Every year I learned something more concerning the esoterics of celebration. In these studies I was an enthusiastic participant—along with playing my part as an anthropologist, I also took a place behind the clownish masks myself. And I cherished this role as I did nothing else in my life. To me the title of Clown has always carried connotations of a noble sort. I was an adroit jester, strangely enough, and had always taken pride in the skills I worked so diligently to develop.

I wrote to the State Department of Recreation, indicating what information I desired, and exposing an enthusiastic urgency that came naturally to me on this topic. Many weeks later I received a tan envelope imprinted with a government logo. Inside was a pamphlet that cataloged all of the various seasonal festivities of which the state was officially aware, and I noted in passing that there were as many in late autumn and winter as in the warmer seasons. A letter inserted within the pamphlet explained to me that, according to their voluminous records, no festivals held in the town of Mirocaw had been officially registered. Their files, nonetheless, could be placed at my disposal if I should wish to research this or similar matters in connection with some definite project. At the time this offer was made, I was already laboring under so many professional and personal burdens that, with a weary hand, I simply deposited the envelope and its contents in a drawer, never to be consulted again.

Some months later, however, I made an impulsive digression from my responsibilites and, rather haphazardly, became engaged in a new project. This happened as I was driving north one afternoon in late summer with the intention of examining some journals in the holdings of a library at another university. Once out of the city limits, the scenery changed to sunny fields and farms, diverting my thoughts from the signs that I passed along the highway. Nevertheless, the subconscious scholar in me must have been regarding these with studious care. The name of a town loomed in my vision. Instantly the scholar retrieved certain records from some deep mental drawer, and I was faced with making a few hasty calculations as to whether there was enough time and motivation for an investigative side trip. But the exit along the highway was even hastier in making its appearance, and I soon found myself leaving the highway, recalling the road sign's promise that the town was no more than seven miles east.

These seven miles included several turns, the forced taking of a temporarily alternate route, and a destination not even visible until a steep rise had been fully ascended. On the descent another helpful sign informed me that I was within the city limits of Mirocaw. Some scattered houses on the outskirts of the town were the first structures I encountered. Beyond them the numerical highway became Townshend Street, the main avenue of Mirocaw.

The town impressed me as being much larger once I was within its limits than it had appeared from the summit of the hill just outside. I saw that the general hilliness of the surrounding countryside was also an internal feature of Mirocaw. Here, though, the effect was different. The parts of the town did not look as if they adhered very well to one another. This was partly due to the irregularly hilly sections upon which various buildings of the town so antagonistically stood. Behind some of the old stores in the business district, steeply roofed houses had been erected on a sudden incline, their peaks appearing at an extraordinary elevation above the lower buildings. I should say that perhaps the disharmonies of Mirocaw are more acutely affecting my imagination in retrospect than they were on that first day, when I was primarily concerned with locating the city hall or some other center of information.

I pulled around a corner and parked. Sliding over to the other side of the seat, I rolled down the window and called to a passerby: "Excuse me, sir," I said. The man, who was shabbily dressed and very old, paused for a moment and stared at me without approaching the car. Though he had apparently responded to my call, his vacant expression did not betray the least awareness of my presence, and for a moment I thought it just a coincidence that he halted on the sidewalk at the same time I addressed him. His eyes were focused somewhere beyond me with a weary and imbecilic gaze. After a few moments, he continued on his way, and I said nothing to call him back, even though at the last second, his face began to appear dimly familiar. Someone else finally came along who was able to direct me to the Mirocaw City Hall and Community Center.

Inside, I stood at a counter behind which some people were working at desks and walking up and down a back hallway. On one wall was a poster for the state lottery: a jack-in-the-box with both hands grasping green bills. After a few moments, a tall, middle-aged woman came over to the counter.

"Can I help you?" she asked in a neutral, bureaucratic voice.

I explained that I had heard about the festival—saying nothing about being a nosy academic—and asked if she could provide me with further information or direct me to someone who could.

"Do you mean the one held in the winter?" she asked.

"How many of them are there?"

"Just that one."

"I suppose, then, that's the one I mean." I smiled as if sharing a joke with her.

Without another word, she walked off into the back hallway. While she was absent, I exchanged glances with several of the people behind the counter who periodically looked up at me from their work.

"There you are," she said when she returned, handing me a piece of paper that looked like the product of the office copy machine. *Please Come to the Fun*, it said in large letters. *Parades*, it went on, *Street Masquerade, Bands, The Winter Raffle*, and *The Coronation of the Winter Queen*. The page continued with the mention of a number of other miscellaneous festivities. I read the words again. There was something about that imploring little "please" at the top of the announcement that made the whole affair seem like a charity function.

"When is it held? It doesn't say when the festival takes place."

"Most people already know that." She reappropriated the announcement from my hands and wrote something at the bottom. When she gave it back to me, I saw "Dec. 19-21" written in blue-green ink. I was immediately struck by an odd sense of scheduling on the part of the festival committee. There was, of course, some anthropological and historical precedent for holding festivities around the winter solstice, but it did not seem entirely practical.

"If you don't mind my asking, don't these days somewhat conflict with the regular holiday season? I mean, most people have enough going on at that time."

"It's just tradition," she said, as if invoking some venerable ancestry behind her words.

"That's very interesting," I said, as much to myself as to her.

"Is there anything else?" she asked.

"Yes. Could you tell me if this festival has anything to do with clowns? I see there's something about a masquerade—"

"Yes, of course there are some people in . . . costumes. I've never been in that position myself . . . that is, yes, there are clowns of a sort."

At that point my interest was definitely aroused, but I was not sure how much further I wanted to pursue it. I noncommittally thanked her for her help, and asked the best way to get back to the interstate, not anxious to retrace the labyrinthine route by which I had entered the town. I walked back to my car with a whole flurry of half-formed questions, and as many vague and conflicting answers, cluttering my mind.

The directions the woman gave me necessitated passing through the south end of Mirocaw. There were not many people moving about in this section of town. Those that I did see, shuffling lethargically down a block of battered storefronts, exhibited the same sort of forlorn expression and manner as the old man from whom I had asked directions earlier. I must have been passing through a central artery of this area, for on each side of me stretched street after street of poorly tended yards, and houses bowed with age and indifference. When I came to a stop at a street corner, one of the citizens of the slum passed in front of my car. This lean, morose, and epicene person turned and, without really looking directly at me, smiled or sneered ambiguously from one corner of a taut little mouth. After progressing a few streets farther, I came to a road that led back to the interstate. I felt detectably more comfortable as soon as I found myself traveling once again through the expanses of sun-drenched farmlands.

I reached the library with more than enough time for my research, and so I decided to make a scholarly detour to see what material I could find that might illuminate the winter festival held in Mirocaw. The library included in its holdings the entire run of the *Mirocaw Courier*, which the librarian told me was the major newspaper in the county that included the town within its borders. I thought this would be an excellent place to start. I soon found, however, that there was no handy way in which to research information from this newspaper, and I did not want to engage in a blind search for articles concerning a specific subject.

I next turned to the more organized resources of the newspapers for the larger cities located in the same general area. I uncovered very little about the town, and almost nothing concerning its festival, except in one general article on annual events in the state that erroneously attributed to Mirocaw a "large Middle Eastern community" that every spring hosted a kind of ethnic jamboree. From what I had already observed, and from what I subsequently learned, the citizens of Mirocaw were solidly midwestern American, the probable descendants in a direct line from some enterprising pack of New Englanders of the past century. There was one brief item devoted to a Mirocavian event, but this merely turned out to be an obituary notice for an old woman who had quietly taken her life around Christmastime. Thus, I returned home that day all but empty-handed on the subject of Mirocaw.

However, it was not long afterward that I received another letter from the former colleague of mine who had first led me to seek out Mirocaw and its festival. As it happened, he rediscovered the article that caused him to stir my interest in a local "Fool's Feast." This article had its sole appearance in an obscure festschrift of anthropology studies published in Amsterdam twenty years ago. Most of these papers were in Dutch, a few in German, and only one was in English: "The Last Feast of Harlequin: Preliminary Notes on a Local Festival." It was exciting, of course, finally to be able to read this study, but even more exciting was the name of its author: Dr. Raymond Thoss.

II

Before proceeding any further, I should mention something about Thoss, and inevitably about myself. Over two decades ago, at my alma mater in Cambridge, Massachusetts, Thoss was a professor of mine. Long before playing a role in the events I am about to describe, he was already one of the most important figures in my life. A striking personality, he inevitably influenced everyone who came in contact with him. I remember his lectures on social anthropology, how he turned that dim room into the brilliant and many-ringed stage of a profound circus. He moved in an uncannily brisk manner. When he swept his arm around to indicate some common term on the blackboard behind him, one felt he was presenting nothing less than an item of fantastic qualities and secret value. When he replaced his hand in the pocket of his old jacket, this fleeting magic was once again stored away in its well-worn pouch, to be retrieved at the sorcerer's discretion. We sensed he was teaching us more than we could possibly learn, and that he himself was in possession of greater and deeper knowledge than he could possibly impart. On one occasion I summoned up the audacity to offer an interpretation—which was somewhat opposed to his own—regarding the tribal clowns of the Hopi Indians. I implied that personal experience as an amateur clown and special devotion to this study provided me with an insight possibly more valuable than his own. It was then he disclosed, casually and very obiter dicta, that he had actually acted in the role of one of the masked tribal fools and had celebrated with them the dance of the kachinas. In revealing these facts, however, he somehow managed not to add to the humiliation I had already inflicted upon myself. And for this I was grateful to him.

Thoss's activities were such that he sometimes became the object of gossip or romanticized speculation. He was a field-worker par excellence, and his ability to insinuate himself into exotic cultures and situations, thereby gaining insights where other anthropologists merely gathered data, was renowned. At various times in his career, there had been rumors of his having "gone native" á la the Frank Hamilton Cushing legend. There were hints, which were not always irresponsible or cheaply glamorized, that he was involved in projects of a freakish sort, many of which focused on New England. It is a fact that he spent six months posing as a mental patient at an institution in western Massachusetts, gathering information on the "culture" of the psychically disturbed. When his book *Winter Solstice: The Longest Night of a Society* was published, the general opinion was that it was disappointingly subjective and impressionistic, and, aside from a few moving but "poetically obscure" observations, there was nothing at all to give it value. Those who defended Thoss claimed he was both less than an anthropologist, in the sense that much of his work emphasized his own mind and feelings, and more than one, meaning that his experience had penetrated to a rich core of hard data that he had yet to disclose in objective discourse. As a student of Thoss, I tended to support this latter estimation of him. For a variety of rational and nonrational reasons, I believed Thoss capable of touching hitherto inaccessible regions of human existence. So it was gratifying at first that this article titled "The Last Feast of Harlequin" seemed to uphold the Thoss mystique, and in an area I personally found captivating.

Much of the content of the article I did not immediately comprehend, given its author's characteristic and often strategic obscurities. On first reading, the most interesting aspect of this brief study—the "notes" encompassed only twenty pages—was the general mood of the piece. Thoss's egocentricities were definitely present in these pages, but only as a struggling inner force that was definitely contained—incarcerated, I might say—by the somber rhythmic movements of his prose and by some glossy reference he occasionally called upon. Two references in particular shared a common theme to some extent. One was a quotation from Poe's "The Conqueror Worm," which Thoss employed as a rather sensational epigraph. The point of the epigraph, however, was nowhere echoed in the text of the article save in another passing reference. Thoss brought up the well-known genesis of the modern Christmas celebration, which of course descends from the Roman Saturnalia. Then, making it clear he had not yet observed the Mirocaw festival and had gathered its nature only from various informants, he established that it, too, contained many, even more overt, elements of the Saturnalia. Next he made what seemed to me a trivial and purely linguistic observation, one that had less to do with his main course of argument than it did with the equally peripheral Poe epigraph. He briefly mentioned that an early sect of Syrian Gnostics called themselves "Saturnians" and believed, among other religious heresies, that mankind was created by angels who were in turn created by the Supreme Unknown. The angels, however, did not possess the power to make their creation an erect being, and for a time he crawled upon the earth like a worm. Later the Creator remedied this grotesque state of affairs. At the time I supposed that the symbolic correspondences of mankind's origins and ultimate condition being associated with worms, combined with a year-end festival recognizing the winter death of the earth, was the gist of this Thossian "insight," a poetic but scientifically valueless observation.

Other observations he made on the Mirocaw festival were strictly etic; in other words, they were based on secondhand

sources, hearsay testimony. Even at that juncture, however, I felt
Thoss knew more than he disclosed; and, as I later discovered, he
had indeed included information on certain aspects of Mirocaw
that suggested he was already in possession of several keys that
for the moment he was keeping securely in his own pocket. By
then I myself possessed a most revealing fragment of knowledge.
A note to the "Harlequin" article apprised the reader that the piece
was only a fragment in rude form of a more wide-ranging work in
preparation. This work was never seen by the world. My former
professor had not published anything since his withdrawal from
academic circulation some twenty years ago. Now I suspected
where he had gone.

For the man from whom I had asked directions on the streets of
Mirocaw, the man with the disconcertingly lethargic gaze, had very
much resembled a superannuated version of Dr. Raymond Thoss.

III

And now I have a confession to make. Despite my reasons for being
enthusiastic about Mirocaw and its mysteries, not to mention its
relationship to both Thoss and my own deepest concerns as a
scholar, I contemplated the days ahead of me with no more than a
feeling of frigid numbness and often with a sense of profound
depression. Yet I had no reason to be surprised at this emotional
state, which had little relevance to the outward events in my life,
but were determined by inward conditions that worked according
to their own, quite enigmatic, seasons and cycles. For many years,
at least since my university days, I have suffered from this dark
malady, this recurrent despondency in which I would become buried when it came time for the earth to grow cold and bare and the
skies heavy with shadows. Nevertheless, I pursued my plans,
though somewhat mechanically, to visit Mirocaw during its festival
days, for I superstitiously hoped that this activity might diminish
the weight of my seasonal lethargy. In Mirocaw would be parades
and parties and the opportunity to play the clown once again.

For weeks in advance, I practiced my art, even perfecting a new
feat of juggling magic, which was my special forte in foolery. I had
my costumes cleaned, purchased fresh makeup, and was ready. I
received permission from the university to cancel some of my classes

prior to the holiday, explaining the nature of my project and the necessity of arriving in the town a few days before the festival began, in order to do some preliminary research, establish informants, and so on. Actually, my plan was to postpone any formal inquiry until after the festival, and to involve myself beforehand as much as possible in its activities. I would, of course, keep a journal during this time.

There was one resource I did want to consult, however. Specifically, I returned to that outstate library to examine those issues of the *Mirocaw Courier* dating from December two decades ago. One story in particular confirmed a point Thoss made in the "Harlequin" article, though the event it chronicled must have taken place after Thoss had written his study.

The *Courier* story appeared two weeks after the festival had ended for that year, and was concerned with the disappearance of a woman named Elizabeth Beadle, the wife of Samuel Beadle, a hotel owner in Mirocaw. The county authorities speculated that this was another instance of the "holiday suicides" that seemed to occur with inordinate seasonal regularity in the Mirocaw region. Thoss documented this situation in his "Harlequin" article, though I suspected that today these deaths would be neatly categorized under the heading "seasonal affective disorder." In any case, the authorities searched a half-frozen lake near the outskirts of Mirocaw where they had found many successful suicides in years past. This year, however, no body was discovered. Alongside the article was a picture of Elizabeth Beadle. Even in the grainy microfilm reproduction, one could detect a certian vibrancy and vitality in Mrs. Beadle's face. That a hypothesis of "holiday suicide" should be so readily posited to explain her disappearance seemed strange and in some way unjust.

Thoss, in his brief article, wrote that every year there occurred changes of a moral or spiritual cast that seemed to affect Mirocaw along with the usual winter metamorphosis. He was not precise about its origin or nature, but stated, in typically mystic fashion, that the effect of this "subseason" on the town was conspicuously negative. In addition to the number of suicides actually accomplished during this time, there was also a rise in treatment of "hypochondriacal" conditions, which was how the medical men of twenty years past characterized these cases in discussions with Thoss. This state of affairs would gradually worsen and finally reach a climax during the days scheduled for the Mirocaw festival. Thoss speculated that given the secretive nature of small towns, the situation was probably even more intensely pronounced than casual investigation could reveal.

The connection between the festival and this insidious subseasonal climate in Mirocaw was a point on which Thoss did not come to any rigid conclusions. He did write, nevertheless, that these two "climatic aspects" had had a parallel existence in the town's history as far back as available records could document. A late-nineteenth-century history of Mirocaw County speaks of the town by its original name of New Colstead, and castigates the townspeople for holding a "ribald and soulless feast" to the exclusion of normal Christmas observances. (Thoss comments that the historian had mistakenly fused two distinct aspects of the season, their actual relationship being essentially antagonistic.) The "Harlequin" article did not trace the festival to its earliest appearance (this may not have been possible), though Thoss emphasized the New England origins of Mirocaw's founders. The festival, therefore, was one imported from this region, and could reasonably be extended at least a century; that is, if it had not been brought over from the Old World, in which case its roots would become indefinite until further research could be done. Surely Thoss's allusion to the Syrian Gnostics suggested the latter possibility could not entirely be ruled out.

But it seemed to be the festival's source in New England that nourished Thoss's speculations. He wrote of this patch of geography as if it were an acceptable place to end the search. For him, the very words "New England" seemed to be stripped of all traditional connotations and had come to imply nothing less than a gateway to all lands, both known and suspected, and even to ages beyond the civilized history of the region. Having been educated partly in New England, I could somewhat understand this sentimental exaggeration, for indeed there are places that seem archaic beyond chronological measure, appearing to transcend relative standards of time and achieving a kind of absolute antiquity that cannot be logically fathomed. But how this vague suggestion related to a small town in the Midwest, I could not imagine. Thoss himself observed that the residents of Mirocaw did not betray any mysteriously primitive consciousness. On the contrary, they appeared superficially unaware of the genesis of their winter merrymaking. That such a tradition had endured through the years, however, even eclipsing the conventional Christmas holiday, revealed a profound awareness of the festival's meaning and function.

I cannot deny that what I had learned about the Mirocaw festival did inspire a trite sense of mystery, especially given the involvement of such an important figure from my past as Thoss. It was the first time in my academic career that I knew myself to be better suited than anyone else to discern the true meaning of scattered data, even if I could attribute this special authority only to chance circumstances.

Nevertheless, as I sat in that library on a morning in mid-December, I doubted for a moment the wisdom of setting out for Mirocaw rather than returning home, where the more familiar rite de passage of winter depression awaited me. My original scheme was to avoid the cyclical blues the season held for me, but it seemed this was also a part of the history of Mirocaw, only on a much larger scale. My emotional instability, however, was exactly what qualified me most for the particular fieldwork ahead, though I did not take pride or consolation in the fact. And to retreat would have been to deny myself an opportunity that might never offer itself again. In retrospect, there seems to have been no fortuitous resolution to the decision I had to make. As it happened, I went ahead to the town.

IV

Just past noon on December 18, I started driving toward Mirocaw. A blur of dull, earthen-colored scenery passed by me. The snowfalls of late autumn had been sparse, and only a few white patches appeared in the stiff, dead grass of the fields along the highway. The clouds, which also looked stiff, were gray and abundant. In the mesh of bare branches above, there occasionally clung a few black, ragged clumps that were abandoned nests. I thought I saw blackbirds skittering over the road ahead, but they were leaves, and I passed through them.

I drove into Mirocaw from the south, entering the town from the direction I had left it on my visit the previous summer. This took me once again through that part of town that seemed to be on the other side of some great invisible line dividing the desired areas from the nondesirable. As lurid as this section had appeared to me under the summer sun, in the thin light of that winter afternoon, it degenerated into a pale phantom of itself. The frail stores and starved-looking houses suggested a paradoxical limbo existing between the material and nonmaterial worlds, with one sardonically wearing the mask of the other. I saw a few bowed pedestrians who turned as I passed by, though seemingly not *because* I passed by, making my way up to the main street of Mirocaw.

Driving up the steep rise of Townshend Street, I found the sights there comparatively welcoming. The rolling avenues of the town were in readiness for the festival. Streetlights had their poles raveled with evergreen, the fresh boughs proudly conspicuous in a barren season. On the doors of many of the businesses on Townshend were holly wreaths, equally green but observably plastic. However, although there was nothing unusual in this traditional greenery of the season, it soon became apparent to me that Mirocaw had quite abandoned itself to this particular symbol of Yuletide. It was garishly in evidence everywhere. The windows of stores and houses were framed in green lights, green streamers hung down from storefront awnings, and the beacons of the Red Rooster Bar were peacock-green floodlights. I supposed the residents of Mirocaw desired these decorations, but the effect was one of excess. An eerie emerald haze permeated the town, and faces looked slightly reptilian.

At the time I assumed that the prodigious evergreen, holly wreaths, and colored lights (if only of a single color) demonstrated an emphasis on the vegetable symbols of the Nordic Yuletide that was in some way connected with the festival. In his "Harlequin" article, Thoss wrote of the pagan aspect of Mirocaw's festival, likening it to the ritual of a fertility cult, with probable connections to chthonic divinities at some time in the past. But Thoss had mistaken, as I had, what was only part of the festival's significance for the whole.

The hotel at which I had made reservations was located on Townshend. It was an old building of brown brick, with an arched doorway and a pathetic coping intended to convey an impression of classicism. I found a parking space in front and left my suitcases in the car.

When I first entered the hotel lobby, it was empty. I thought that

perhaps the Mirocaw festival would have attracted enough visitors
to at least bolster the business of its only hotel, but it seemed I was
mistaken. Tapping a little bell, I leaned on the desk and turned to
look at a small, traditionally decorated Christmas tree on a table
near the entranceway. It was complete with shiny, egg-fragile bulbs;
miniature candy canes; flat, laughing Santas with arms wide; a star
on top nodding awkwardly against the delicate shoulder of an
upper branch; and colored lights that bloomed out of flower-shaped
sockets. For some reason this seemed to me a sorry little piece.

"May I help you?" said a young woman arriving from a room
adjacent to the lobby.

I must have been staring rather intently at her, for she looked
away and seemed quite uneasy. I could hardly imagine what to
say to her or how to explain what I was thinking. In person she
immediately radiated a chilling brilliance of manner and expression. But if this woman had not committed suicide twenty years
before, as the newspaper article had suggested, neither had she aged
in that time.

"Sarah," called a masculine voice from the invisible heights of a
stairway. A tall, middle-aged man came down the steps. "I thought
you were in your room," said the man, whom I took to be Samuel
Beadle. Sarah, not Elizabeth, Beadle glanced sideways in my direction to indicate to her father that she was conducting the business
of the hotel. Beadle apologized to me, and then excused the two of
them for a moment while they went off to one side to continue
their exchange.

I smiled and pretended everything was normal, while trying to
remain within earshot of their conversation. They spoke in tones
that suggested their conflict was a familiar one: Beadle's overprotec-
tive concern with his daughter's whereabouts, and Sarah's frus-
trated understanding of certain restrictions placed upon her. The
conversation ended, and Sarah ascended the stairs, turning for a
moment to give me a facial pantomime of apology for the unprofes-
sional scene that had just taken place.

"Now, sir, what can I do for you?" Beadle asked, almost demanded.

"Yes, I have a reservation. Actually, I'm a day early, if that
doesn't present a problem." I gave the hotel the benefit of the doubt
that its business might have been secretly flourishing.

"No problem at all, sir," he said, presenting me with the registration forms, and then a brass-colored key dangling from a small black plastic disk bearing the number 44.

"Luggage?"

"Yes, it's in my car."

"I'll give you a hand with that."

While Beadle was settling me in my fourth-floor room, it seemed an opportune moment to broach the subject of the festival, the holiday suicides, and perhaps, depending upon his reaction, the fate of his wife. I needed a respondent who had lived in the town for a good many years and who could enlighten me about the attitude of Mirocavians toward their season of sea-green lights.

"This is just fine," I said about the clean but somber room. "Nice view. I can see the bright green lights of Mirocaw just fine from up here. Is the town usually all decked out like this? For the festival, I mean."

"Yes, sir, for the festival," he replied mechanically.

"I imagine you'll probably be getting quite a few of us out-of-towners in the next couple days.

"Could be. Is there anything else?"

"Yes, there is. I wonder if you could tell me something about the festivities."

"Such as. . . ."

"Well, you know, the clowns and so forth."

"Only clowns here are the ones that're . . . well, picked out, I suppose you would say."

"I don't understand."

"Excuse me, sir. I'm very busy right now. Is there anything else?"

I could think of nothing at the moment to perpetuate our conversation. Beadle wished me a good stay and left.

I unpacked my suitcases. In addition to regular clothing, I had also brought along some items from my clown's wardrobe. Beadle's comments that clowns were "picked out" here left me wondering exactly what purpose these street masqueraders served in the festival. The clown figure had had so many meanings in different times and cultures. The jolly, well-loved joker familiar to most people is actually but one aspect of this protean creature. Madmen, hunchbacks, amputees, and other abnormals were once considered natural clowns; they were selected to fulfill a comic role that could allow others to see them as ludicrous rather than as terrible reminders of the forces of disorder in the world. But sometimes a cheerless jester was required to draw attention to this same disorder, as in the case of King Lear's morbid and honest fool, who of course was eventually hanged, and so much for his clownish wisdom. Clowns have often had ambiguous and sometimes contradictory roles to play. Thus, I knew enough not to brashly jump into costume and cry out, "Here I am again!"

That first day in Mirocaw, I did not stray far from the hotel. I read and rested for a few hours, and then ate at a nearby diner. Through the window beside my table, I watched the winter night turn the soft green glow of the town into a harsh and almost totally new color as it contrasted with the darkness. The streets of Mirocaw seemed to me unusually busy for a small town at evening. Yet it was not the kind of activity one normally sees before an approaching Christmas holiday. This was not a crowd of bustling shoppers loaded with bright bags of presents. Their arms were empty, their hands shoved deep in their pockets against the cold, which nevertheless had not driven them to the solitude of their presumably warm houses. I watched them enter and exit store after store without buying; the merchants still remained open late, and even the places that were closed had left their neons illuminated. The faces that passed the window of the restaurant were possibly just stiffened by the cold, I thought; frozen into deep frowns and nothing else. In the window I saw the reflection of my own face. It was not the face of an adept clown; it was slack and flabby and at that moment seemed the face of someone less than alive. Outside was the town of Mirocaw, its street dipping and rising with a lunatic severity, its citizens packing the sidewalks, its heart bathed in green: as promising a field of professional and personal challenge as I had ever encountered—and I was bored to the point of dread. I hurried back to my hotel room.

"Mirocaw has another coldness within its cold," I wrote in my journal that night. "Another set of buildings and streets that exists behind the visible town's facade like a world of disgraceful back alleys." I went on like this for about a page, across which I finally engraved a big "X." Then I went to bed.

In the morning I left my car at the hotel and walked toward the main business district a few blocks away. Mingling with the good people of Mirocaw seemed like the proper thing to do at that point in my scientific sojourn. But as I began laboriously walking up Townshend (the sidewalks were cramped with wandering pedestrians), a glimpse of someone suddenly replaced my haphazard plan with a more specific and immediate one. Through the crowd and about fifteen paces ahead was my goal.

"Dr. Thoss," I called.

His head almost seemed to turn and look back in response to my shout, but I could not be certain. I pushed past several warmly wrapped bodies and green-scarfed necks, only to find that my object appeared to be maintaining the same distance from me, though I did not know if this was being done deliberately or not. At the next corner, the dark-coated Thoss abruptly turned right onto a steep street that led downward directly toward the dilapidated south end of Mirocaw. When I reached the corner, I looked down the sidewalk and could see him very clearly from above. I also saw how he managed to stay so far ahead of me in a mob that had impeded my own progress. For some reason the people on the sidewalk made room so that he could move past them easily without the usual jostling of bodies. It was not a dramatic physical avoidance, though it seemed nonetheless intentional. Fighting the tight fabric of the throng, I continued to follow Thoss, losing and regaining sight of him.

By the time I reached the bottom of this street, the crowd had thinned out considerably, and after walking a block or so farther, I found myself practically a lone pedestrian pacing behind a distant figure that I hoped was still Thoss. He was now walking quite swiftly and in a way that seemed to acknowledge my pursuit of him, though, really, it felt as if he were leading me as much as I was chasing him. I called his name a few more times at a volume he could not have failed to hear, assuming that deafness was not one of the changes to have come over him; he was, after all, not a young man, nor even a middle-aged one any longer.

Thoss suddenly crossed in the middle of the street. He walked a few more steps and entered a signless brick building between a liquor store and a repair shop of some kind. In the "Harlequin" article, Thoss had mentioned that the people living in this section of Mirocaw maintained their own businesses, and that these were patronized almost exclusively by residents of the area. I could believe this when I looked at these little sheds of commerce, for they had the same badly weathered appearance as their clientele. The formidable shoddiness of these buildings notwithstanding, I followed Thoss into the plain brick shell of what had been, or possibly still was, a diner.

Inside, it was unusually dark. Even before my eyes made the adjustment, I sensed that this was not a thriving restaurant cozily cluttered with chairs and tables—as was the establishment where I had eaten the night before—but a place with only a few disarranged objects, like an abandoned storeroom, and very cold. It seemed colder, in fact, than the winter streets outside.

"Dr. Thoss?" I called toward a lone table near the center of the long room. Perhaps four or five were sitting around the table, with some others blending into the dimness behind them. Scattered across the top of the table were some books and loose papers. Seated there was an old man indicating something in the pages before him, but it was not Thoss. Beside him were two youths whose fresh features distinguished them from the surliness of the others. I approached the table, and they all looked up at me. None of them showed a glimmer of emotion except the two boys, who exchanged worried and guilt-ridden glances with each other, as if they had just been discovered in some shameful act. They both suddenly burst from the table and ran into the dark background, where a light appeared briefly as they exited by a back door.

"I'm sorry," I said diffidently. "I thought I saw someone I knew come in here."

They said nothing. Out of a back room, others began to emerge, no doubt interested in the source of the commotion. In a few moments, the room was crowded with these tramplike figures, all of them gazing emptily in the dimness. I was not at this point frightened of them; at least, I was not afraid they would do me any physical harm. Actually, I felt as if it was quite within my power to pummel them easily into submission, their mousy faces almost inviting a succession of firm blows. But there were so many of them.

They slid slowly toward me in a wormlike mass. Their eyes seemed directed nowhere, and I even wondered a moment if they were aware of my presence. Nevertheless, I was the center upon which their lethargic shuffling converged, their shoes scuffing softly along the bare floor. I began to deliver a number of hasty inanities as they continued to crowd toward me, their weak and unexpectedly odorless bodies pressing against mine. I understood now why the people along the sidewalks seemed to instinctively avoid Thoss. Unseen legs seemed to be entangling with mine; I staggered and then regained my balance. This sudden movement aroused me from a kind of mesmeric daze that I must have fallen into without being aware of it. I had intended to leave the dark room long before events there had reached such a ludicrous juncture, but for some reason could not focus my intentions strongly enough to cause myself to act. My mind had been drifting farther away as these slavish things approached, and finally I realized the potential danger of the situation. In a sudden surge of panic, I pushed through their soft ranks and was outside.

The open air revived me to my former alertness, and I immediately started pacing swiftly up the hill. I was not really sure anymore that I had not simply imagined what had seemed, and at the same time did not seem, like a perilous moment. Had one of them tried to trip me deliberately, or were they trying merely to intimidate me? As I reached the green-glazed main street of Mirocaw, I really could not be sure what had just happened.

The sidewalks were still jammed with a multitude of pedestrians, but now they seemed to be moving and chattering in a livelier way. There was a kind of electricity that could be attributed only to the imminent festivities. A group of young men had begun celebrating prematurely, and strode noisily across the street at midpoint, obviously intoxicated. From the laughter and joking among the still-sober citizens, I gathered that, Mardi Gras style, public drunkenness was within the traditions of this winter festival. I looked for anything to indicate the beginnings of the "Street Masquerade," but saw nothing. No brightly garbed Harlequins or snow-white Pierrots. Were the ceremonies even now in preparation for the "coronation of the Winter Queen"? I wondered. "The Winter Queen," I wrote in my journal. "Figure of fertility invested with symbolic powers of revival and prosperity. Elected in the manner of a high school prom queen. Check for possible consort figure in the form of a representative from the underworld."

In the predarkness hours of December 19, I sat in my hotel room and wrote and thought and organized. I did not feel too badly, all things considered. The holiday excitement that was steadily rising in the streets below my window was definitely infecting me. I forced myself to take a short nap in anticipation of a long night. When I awoke, Mirocaw's annual feast had begun.

V

Shouting, commotion, carousing. Sleepily, I went to the window and looked out over the town. It seemed all the lights of Mirocaw were shining, save in that section down the hill that became part of the black void of winter. And now the town's greenish tinge was even more pronounced, spreading everywhere like a great green rainbow that had melted from the sky and endured, phosphorescent, into the night. In the streets was the daylight of an artificial spring. The byways of Mirocaw vibrated with activity: on a nearby corner, a brass band blared; marauding cars blew their horns and were sometimes mounted by laughing pedestrians; a man emerged from the Red Rooster Bar, threw up his arms, and crowed. I looked closely at the individual celebrants, searching for the vestments of clowns. Soon, delightedly, I saw them. The costume was red and white, with matching cap, and the face painted a noble alabaster. It almost seemed to be a clownish incarnation of the well-known bearded and black-booted Christmas fool.

This particular fool, however, was not receiving the affection and respect usually accorded to a Santa Claus. My poor fellow clown was in the middle of a circle of revelers who were pushing him back and forth from one to the other. The object of this abuse seemed to accept it somewhat willingly, but this little game nevertheless appeared to have humiliation as its purpose. "Only clowns here are the ones that're picked out," echoed Beadle's voice in my memory. "Picked *on*" seemed closer to the truth.

Packing myself in some heavy clothes, I went out into the green gleaming streets. Not far from the hotel, I was stumbled into by a character with a wide blue-and-red grin and bright, baggy clothes. Actually, he had been shoved into me by some youths outside a drugstore.

"See the freak," said an obese and drunken fellow. "See the freak fall."

My first response was anger, and then fear as I saw two others flanking the fat drunk. They walked toward me, and I tensed myself for a confrontation.

"This is a disgrace," one said, the neck of a wine bottle held loosely in his left hand.

But it was not to me they were speaking; it was to the clown, who was now being pushed to the sidewalk. There were three of them who helped him up with a sudden jerk and then splashed wine in his face. They ignored me altogether.

"Let him loose," the fat one said. "Crawl away, freak. Oh, he flies!"

The clown trotted off, becoming lost in the throng.

"Wait a minute," I said to the rowdy trio, who had started stumbling away. I quickly decided that it would probably be futile to ask them to explain what I had just witnessed, especially amid the noise and confusion of the festivities. In my best jovial fashion, I proposed we all go someplace where I could buy them each a drink. They had no objection, and in a short while, we were all squeezed around a table in the Red Rooster.

Over several drinks, I explained to them that I was from out of town, which pleased them no end for some reason. I told them there were some things I did not understand about their festival.

"I don't think there's anything *to* understand," the fat one said. "It's just what you see."

I asked him about the people dressed as clowns.

"Them? They're the freaks. It's their turn this year. Everyone takes their turn. Next year it might be mine. Or *yours*," he said, pointing at one of his friends across the table. "And when we find out which one of you are—"

"You're not smart enough," said the defiant potential freak.

This was an important point: the fact that individuals who play the clowns remain, or at least attempted to remain, anonymous. This arrangement would help remove inhibitions a resident of Mirocaw might have about abusing his own neighbor or even a family relation. From what I later observed, the extent of this abuse did not go beyond a kind of playful roughhousing. And even so, it was only the occasional group of rowdies who actually took advantage of this aspect of the festival, the majority of the citizens very much content to stay on the sidelines.

As far as being able to illuminate the meaning of this custom, my three young friends were quite useless. To them, it was just amusement, as I imagine it was to the majority of Mirocavians. This was understandable. I suppose the average person would not be able to explain exactly how the profoundly familiar Christmas holiday came to be celebrated in its present form.

I left the bar alone and not unaffected by the drinks I had consumed there. Outside, the general merrymaking continued. Loud music emanated from several quarters. Mirocaw had fully transformed itself from a sedate small town to an enclave of Saturnalia within the dark immensity of a winter night. But Saturn is also the planetary symbol of melancholy and sterility, a clash of opposites contained within that single word. And as I wandered half-drunkenly down the street, I discovered that there was a conflict within the winter festival itself. This discovery indeed appeared to be that secret key that Thoss withheld in his study of the town. Oddly enough, it was through my unfamiliarity with the outward nature of the festival that I came to know its true nature.

I was mingling on the street with the crowd, warmly enjoying the confusion around me, when I saw a strangely designed creature lingering on the corner up ahead. It was one of the Mirocaw clowns. Its clothes were shabby and nondescript, almost in the style of a tramp-type clown, but not humorously exaggerated enough. The face, though, made up for the lackluster costume. I had never seen such a strange conception for a clown's countenance. The figure stood beneath a dim streetlight, and when it turned its head my way, I realized why it seemed familiar. The thin, smooth, and pale head; the wide eyes; the oval-shaped features resembling nothing so much as that skull-faced, terror-stricken creature in that famous painting of someone screaming (memory fails me). This clownish imitation rivaled the original in suggesting pathetic realms of abject horror and despair: an inhuman likeness more proper to something under the earth than upon it.

From the moment I saw this creature, I thought of those inhabitants of the ghetto down the hill. There was the same nauseating passivity and languor in its bearing. Perhaps, if I had not been drinking earlier, I would not have been bold enough to take the action I did. I decided to join in one of the upstanding traditions of the winter festival, for it annoyed me to see this morbid impostor of a clown standing up. When I reached the corner, I laughingly pushed myself into the creature—"Whoops!"—who stumbled backward and ended up on the sidewalk. I laughed again and looked around for approval from the festivalers in the vicinity. No one, however, seemed to appreciate or even acknowledge what I had done. They did not laugh with me or point with amusement, but only passed me by, perhaps walking a little faster until they were some distance from this street-corner incident. I realized instantly I had violated some tacit rule of behavior, though I had thought my action well within the common practice. The thought occurred to me that I might even be apprehended and prosecuted for what in other circumstances was certainly a criminal act. I turned around to help the clown back to his feet, hoping somehow to redeem my offense, but the creature was gone. Solemnly, I walked away from the scene of my inadvertent crime and sought other streets away from its witnesses.

Along the various back avenues of Mirocaw I wandered, pausing exhaustedly at one point to sit at the counter of a small sandwich shop that was packed with customers. I ordered a cup of coffee to revive my overly alcoholed system. Warming my hands around the cup and sipping slowly from it, I watched the people outside as they passed the front window. It was well after midnight, but the thick flow of passersby gave no indication that anyone was going home early. A carnival of profiles filed past the window, and I was content simply to sit back and observe, until finally one of these faces made me start. The frightful little clown I had roughed up had just gone past on the sidewalk outside. But although its face was familiar in its ghastly aspect, there was something different about it. And I wondered that there should be two such hideous freaks.

Quickly paying the man at the counter, I dashed out to get a second glimpse of the clown, who was now nowhere in sight. The dense crowd kept me from pursuing this figure with any speed, and I wondered how the clown could have made its way so easily ahead of me. Unless the crowd had instinctively allowed this creature to pass unhindered by its massive ranks, as it did for Thoss. In the process of searching for this particular freak, I discovered that interspersed throughout the celebrating populace of Mirocaw, and among the sanctioned festival clowns, there was not one or two, but a considerable number of these pale, wraithlike creatures. And they all drifted along the streets unmolested by even the rowdiest of revelers. I now understood one of the taboos of the festival. These other clowns were not to be disturbed, and should even be avoided, much as were the residents of the slum at the edge of town. Nevertheless, I felt instinctively that the two groups of clowns were somehow identified with each other, even if the ghetto clowns were not welcome at Mirocaw's winter festival. Indeed, they were not simply part of the community and celebrating the season in their own way. To all appearances, this group of melancholy mummers constituted nothing less than an entirely independent festival—a festival within a festival.

Returning to my room, I entered my suppositions into the journal I was keeping for this venture. The following are excerpts:

> There is a superstitiousness displayed by the residents of Mirocaw with regard to these people from the slum section, particularly as they lately appear in those dreadful faces signifying their own festival. What is the relationship between these simultaneous celebrations? Did one precede the other? If so, which? My opinion at this point—and I claim no conclusiveness for it—is that Mirocaw's winter festival is the later manifestation, that it appeared after the festival of those depressingly pallid clowns, in order to cover it up or mitigate its effect. The holiday suicides come to mind, and the subclimate Thoss wrote about, the disappearance of Elizabeth Beadle twenty years ago, and my own experience with this pariah clan existing outside yet within the community. Of my own experience with this emotionally deleterious subseason, I would rather not speak at this time. Still not able to say whether or not my usual winter melancholy is the cause. On the general subject of mental health, I must consider Thoss's book about his stay in a psychiatric hospital (in western Mass., almost sure of that. Check on this book & Mirocaw's New England roots). The winter solstice is tomorrow, and it is, of course, the day of the year in which night hours surpass daylight hours by the greatest margin. Note what this has to do with the suicides and a rise in psychic disorder. Recalling Thoss's list of documented suicides in his article, there seemed to be a recurrence of specific family names, as there very likely

might be for any kind of data collected in a small town. Among these names was a Beadle or two. Perhaps, then, there is a genealogical basis for the suicides that has nothing to do with Thoss's mystical subclimate, which is a colorful idea to be sure, and one that seems fitting for this town of various outward and inward aspects, but is not a conception that can be substantiated.

One thing that seems certain, however, is the division of Mirocaw into two very distinct types of citizenry, resulting in two festivals and the appearance of similar clowns—a term now used in an extremely loose sense. But there is a connection, and I believe I have some idea of what it is. I said before that the normal residents of the town regard those from the ghetto, and especially their clown figures, with superstition. Yet there is more than that: there is fear, perhaps a kind of hatred—the particular kind of hatred resulting from some powerful and irrational memory. What threatens Mirocaw I think I can very well understand. I recall the incident earlier today in that vacant diner. "Vacant" is the appropriate word here, despite its contradiction of fact. The congregation of that half-lit room formed less a presence than an absence, even considering the oppressive number of them. Those eyes that did not or could not focus on anything, the pining lassitude of their faces, the lazy march of their feet. I was spiritually drained when I ran out of there. I then understood why these people and their activities are avoided. I cannot question the wisdom of those ancestral Mirocavians who began the tradition of the winter festival and gave the town a pretext for celebration and social intercourse at a time when the consequences of brooding isolation are most severe, those longest and darkest days of the solstice. A mood of Christmas joviality obviously would not be sufficient to counter the menace of this season. But even so, there are still the suicides of individuals who are somehow cut off, I imagine, from the vitalizing activities of the festival.

It is the nature of this insidious subseason and of the solstice festival that yearly drifts out from the slums that seem to determine the outward forms of Mirocaw's winter festival: the optimistic greenery in a period of gray dormancy; the fertile promise of the Winter Queen; and, most interesting to my mind, the clowns. The bright clowns of Mirocaw who are treated so badly; they appear to serve as substitute figures for those dark-eyed mummers of the slums. Since the latter are feared for some power or influence they possess, they may still be symbolically confronted and conquered through their counterparts, who are elected for precisely this function. If I am right about this, I wonder to what extent there is a conscious awareness among the town's populace of this indirect show of aggression. Those three I spoke with tonight did not seem to possess much insight beyond seeing that there was a certain amount of robust fun in the festival's tradition. For that matter, how much awareness is there on the other side of these two antagonistic festival's tradition? Too horrible to think of such a thing, but I must wonder if, for all their apparent aimlessness, those inhabitants of the ghetto are not the only ones who know what they are about. No denying that behind those inhumanly limp expressions, there seems to lie a kind of obnoxious intelligence.

Now I realize the confusion of my present state, but as I wobbled from street to street tonight, watching those oval-mouthed clowns, I could not help feeling that all the merry-making in Mirocaw was somehow allowed only by their sufferance. This, I hope, is no more than a fanciful Thossian intuition, the sort of idea that is curious and thought-provoking without ever seeming to gain the benefit of proof. I know my mind is not entirely lucid, but I feel that it may be possible to penetrate Mirocaw's many complexities and illuminate the hidden side of the festival season. In particular I must look for the significance of the other festival. Is it also some kind of fertility celebration? From what I have seen, the tenor of this celebrating subclan is one of antifertility, if anything. How have they managed to keep from dying out completely over the years? How do they maintain their numbers?

* * *

But I was too tired to formulate any more of my sodden speculations. Falling onto my bed, I soon became lost in dreams of streets and faces.

VI

I was, of course, slightly hung over when I woke up late the next morning. The festival was still going strong, and blaring music outside roused me from a nightmare. It was a parade. A number of floats floated down Townshend, a familiar color predominating. There were theme floats of Pilgrims and Indians, cowboys and Indians, and clowns of an orthodox type. In the middle of it all was the Winter Queen herself, freezing atop an icy throne. She waved in all directions. I even imagined she waved up at my dark window.

In the first few groggy moments of wakefulness, I had no sympathy with my excitation of the previous night. But I discovered that this enthusiasm had merely lain dormant, and soon returned with an even greater intensity. Never before had my mind and senses been so active during this usually inert time of year. At home I would have been playing lugubrious old records and looking out the windows quite a bit. I was terribly grateful in a completely abstract way for my commitment to a meaningful mania. And I was eager to get to work after I had had some breakfast at the coffee shop.

When I got back to my room, I discovered the door was unlocked. And there was something written on the dresser mirror. The writing was red and greasy, as if from a clown's makeup pencil—my own, I realized. I read the legend, or rather, I should say *riddle*, several times: "What buries itself before it is dead?" I looked at it for quite a while, very shaken at how vulnerable my holiday fortifications were. Was this supposed to be a warning of some kind? A threat to the effect that if I persisted in a certain course, I would end up prematurely interred? I would simply have to be careful, I told myself. My resolution was to let nothing deter me from the inspired strategy I had conceived for myself. I wiped the mirror clean, for it was now needed for other purposes.

I spent the rest of the day devising a very special costume and the appropriate face to go with it. I easily shabbied up my overcoat with a torn pocket or two and a complete set of stains. Combined with blue jeans and a pair of rather worn-out shoes, I had a passable costume for a derelict. The face, however, was more difficult, for I had to experiment from memory. Remembering the screaming Pierrot in that painting (*The Scream*, I now recall) helped me quite a bit. At nightfall I exited the hotel by the back stairway.

It was strange to walk down the crowded street in this gruesome disguise. Though I thought I would feel conspicuous, the actual experience was very close, I imagined, to one of complete invisibility. No one looked at me as I strolled by, or as they strolled by, or as we strolled by each other. I was a phantom—perhaps the ghost of festivals past, or those yet to come.

I had no clear idea where my disguise would take me that night, only vague expectations of gaining the confidence of my fellow specters and possibly in some way coming to know their secrets. For a while I would simply wander around in that lackadaisical way I had learned from them, following their lead in any way they might indicate. And for the most part, this meant doing almost nothing and doing it silently. If I passed one of my kind on the sidewalk, there was no speaking, no exchange of knowing looks, no recognition at all that I was aware of. We were there on the streets of Mirocaw to create a presence and nothing more. At least, this is how I came to feel about it. As I drifted along with my bodiless invisibility, I felt myself more and more becoming an empty, floating shape, seeing without being seen, and walking without the interference of those grosser creatures who shared my world. It was not an experience completely without interest or even pleasure. The clown's shibboleth of "here we are again" took on a new meaning for me as I felt myself a novitiate of a more rarefied order of harlequinry. And very soon the opportunity to make further progress along this path presented itself.

On the other side of the street, going the opposite direction, a pickup truck slowly passed, gently parting a sea of zigging and zagging celebrants. The cargo in the back of this truck was curious, for it was made up entirely of my fellow sectarians. Farther down the street, the truck stopped, and another of them boarded it over the back gate. One block down I saw still another get on. Two blocks down the truck made a U-turn at an intersection and headed in my direction.

I stood at the curb as I had seen the others do. I was not sure that the truck would slow down to pick me up, thinking that somehow they knew I was an impostor. The truck did, however, slow down, almost coming to a stop when it reached me. The others were crowded on the floor of the truck bed. Most of them were just staring into nothingness with the usual indifference I had come to expect from their kind. But a few actually glanced at me with some anticipation. For a second I hesitated, not sure I wanted to pursue this ruse any further. At the last moment, some impulse sent me climbing up the back of the truck and squeezing in among the others.

There were only a few more to pick up before the truck headed for the outskirts of Mirocaw and beyond. At first I tried to maintain a clear orientation with respect to the town. But as we took turn after turn through the darkness of narrow, forest-crowded roads, I found myself unable to preserve any sense of direction. The majority of the others in the back of the truck exhibited no apparent awareness of their fellow passengers. Guardedly, I looked from face to ghostly face. A few of them spoke in short, whispered phrases to others close by. I could not make out what they were saying, but the tone of their voices was one of innocent normalcy, as if they were not of the hardened slum herd of Mirocaw. Perhaps, I thought, these were thrill-seekers who had disguised themselves as I had done, or more likely, initiates of some kind, who had received prior instructions at such meetings as I had stumbled onto the day before. It was also likely that those very boys I had frightened into a hasty escape were members of this crew.

The truck was now speeding along a fairly open stretch of country, heading toward those higher hills that surrounded the now-distant town of Mirocaw. The icy wind whipped around us, and I could not keep myself from trembling with cold. This definitely betrayed me as one of the newcomers among the group, for the two bodies that pressed against mine were rigidly still and even seemed to be radiating a frigidity of their own. I glanced ahead at the darkness into which we were rapidly progressing.

We had left all open country behind us now, and the road was enclosed by thick woods. The mass of bodies in the truck leaned into each other as we began traveling up a steep incline. Above us, at the top of the hill, were lights shining somewhere within the woods. When the road leveled off, the truck made an abrupt turn,

144 ◆ Thomas Ligotti

steering into what I thought was the roadside blackness or a great ditch. There was an unpaved path, however, upon which the truck proceeded toward the glowing in the near distance.

This glowing became brighter and sharper as we approached, flickering upon the trees and revealing stark details where there had formerly been only smooth darkness. As the truck pulled into a clearing and came to a stop, I saw a loose assembly of figures, many of which held lanterns that beamed with a dazzling and frosty light. I stood up in the back of the truck to disembark as the others were doing. Glancing around from that height, I saw approximately thirty more of those cadaverous clowns milling about. One of my fellow passengers spied me lingering in the truck, and in a strangely high-pitched whisper, told me to hurry, explaining something about the "apex of darkness." I thought again about this solstice night; it was technically the longest period of darkness of the year, even if not by a very significant margin from many other winter nights. Its true significance, though, was related to considerations having little to do with statistics of the calendar.

I went over to the place where the others were forming into a tighter crowd, and in which there was a sense of expectancy in the subtle gestures and expressions of its individual members. Glances were now exchanged, the hand of one lightly touched the shoulder of another, and a pair of circled eyes gazed over to where two figures were setting their lanterns on the ground about six feet apart. The illumination of these lanterns revealed an opening in the earth. Eventually the awareness of everyone was focused on this roundish pit, and, as if by prearranged signal, we all began huddling around it. The only sounds were those of the wind and our own movements as we crushed frozen leaves and sticks underfoot.

Finally, when we had all surrounded this gaping hole, the first one jumped in, leaving our sight for a moment, but then reappearing to take hold of a lantern that another one handed him from above. The miniature abyss filled with light, and I could see it was not more than six feet deep. Near the base of its inner wall, the mouth of a tunnel was carved out. The figure holding the lantern stooped a little and disappeared into the passage.

One by one, then, the members of the crowd leaped into the darkness of this pit, and every fifth one took a lantern. I kept to the back of the group, for whatever subterranean activities were going to take place, I was sure I wanted to be on their periphery. When only about ten of us remained on the ground above, I maneuvered to let four of them precede me so that as the fifth I might receive a lantern. This was exactly how it worked out, for after I had leaped to the bottom of the hole, a light was ritually handed down to me. Turning about-face, I quickly entered the passageway. At that point I shook so with cold that I was neither curious nor afraid, but only grateful for the shelter.

I entered a long, gently sloping tunnel, just high enough for me to stand upright. It was considerably warmer down there than outside in the cold darkness of the woods. After a few moments, I had sufficiently thawed out so that my concerns shifted from those of physical comfort to a sudden and justified preoccupation with my survival. As I walked, I held my lantern close to the sides of the tunnel. They were relatively smooth and even, as if the passage had not been made by manual digging, but had been burrowed by something that had left behind a clue to its dimensions by the tunnel's size and shape. I had to admit that this delirious idea came to me when I recalled the message that had been left on my bedroom mirror: "What buries itself before it is dead?"

The uncanny spelunkers behind me began to overtake me, and I had to hurry along to keep up with those in front. The lanterns ahead bobbed with every step of their bearers, the lumbering procession seeming less and less real the farther we marched into that snug little tunnel. At some point I noticed the line ahead of me growing shorter. The processioners were emptying out into a cavernous chamber, where I, too, soon arrived. This area was about twenty feet in height, its other dimensions approximating those of a large ballroom. Gazing into the distance above made me uncomfortably aware of how far we had descended into the earth. Unlike the smooth sides of the tunnel, the walls of this cavern looked jagged and irregular, as though they had been gnawed at. The earth had been removed, I assumed, either through the tunnel from which we had emerged, or else by way of one of the many black openings that I saw around the edges of the chamber, for possibly they, too, led back to the surface.

But the structure of this chamber occupied my mind a great deal less than did its occupants. There to meet us on the floor of the great cavern was what must have been the entire slum population of Mirocaw, and more, all with the same eerily wide-eyed and oval-mouthed faces. They formed a circle around an altarlike object that had some kind of dark, leathery covering draped over it. Upon this altar another covering of the same material concealed a lumpy form beneath.

And behind this form, looking down upon the altar, was the only figure whose face was not greased with makeup.

He wore a long, snowy robe that was the same color as the wispy hair rimming his head. His arms were calmly at his sides. He made no movement. The man I had thought would penetrate great secrets stood before us with the same professional bearing that had impressed me so many years ago, yet now I felt nothing but dread at the thought of what revelations lay pocketed within the abysmal folds of his magisterial attire. Had I really come to challenge such a formidable figure? The name by which I knew him seemed itself insufficient to designate one of his stature. Rather, I should name him by his other incarnations: god of all wisdom, scribe of all sacred books, father of all magicians, thrice great and more—rather, I should call him *Thoth*.

He raised his cupped hands to his congregation, and the ceremony was under way.

It was all very simple. The entire assembly, which had remained speechless until this moment, broke out in the most horrendous, high-pitched singing that can be imagined. It was a choir of sorrow, of shrieking delirium, and of shame. The cavern rang shrilly with the dissonant, whining chorus. My voice, too, was added to the congregation's, trying to blend with their maimed music. But my singing could not imitate theirs, having a huskiness unlike their cacophonous, keening wail. To keep from exposing myself as an intruder, I continued to mouth their words without sound. These words were a revelation of the moody malignancy that until then I had no more than sensed whenever in the presence of these figures. They were singing to the "unborn in paradise," to the "pure, un-lived lives." They sang a dirge for existence, for all its vital forms and seasons. Their ideals were those of darkness, chaos, and a melancholy half-existence consecrated to all the many shapes of death. A sea of thin, bloodless faces trembled and screamed with perverted hopes. And the robed, guiding figure at the heart of all this—elevated over the course of twenty years to the status of high priest—was the man from whom I had taken so many of my own life's principles. It would be useless to describe what I felt at that moment, and a waste of the time I need to describe the event that followed.

The singing abruptly stopped, and the towering, white-haired figure began to speak. He was welcoming those of the new genera-tion—twenty winters had passed since the "Pure Ones" had ex-panded their ranks. The word "pure" in this setting was a violence to what sense and composure I still retained, for nothing could have been more foul than what was to come. Thoss—and I employ this defunct identity only as a convenience—ceased his sermon and moved back toward the dark-skinned altar. There, with all the flourish of his former life, he drew back the topmost covering. Beneath it was a limp-limbed effigy, a collapsed puppet sprawled upon the slab. I was standing toward the rear of the congregation, and attempted to keep as close to the exit passage as I could. Thus, I did not see everything as clearly as I might have.

Thoss looked down over the crooked, doll-like form, and then out at the gathering. I even imagined that he made knowing eye contact with me. He spread his arms, and a stream of continuous and unintelligible words flowed from his moaning mouth. The congregation began to stir, not greatly but perceptibly. Until that moment there was a limit to what I believed was the evil of these people. They were, after all, only that. They were merely morbid, self-tortured souls with strange beliefs. If there was anything I had learned in all my years as an anthropologist, it was that the world is infinitely rich in strange ideas, even to the point where the concept of strangeness itself had little meaning for me. But with the scene I then witnessed, my experience bounded into a realm from which it will never return.

For now was the transformation scene, the culmination of every harlequinade.

It began slowly. There was some slight movement among the crowd on the far side of the chamber from where I stood. Someone had fallen to the floor, and the others in the area backed away. The voice at the altar continued its chanting. I tried to gain a better view, but there were too many of them around me. Through the mass of obstructing bodies, I caught only glimpses of what was taking place. It had begun before I realized what was happen-ing. . . .

The one who had swooned to the floor of the chamber seemed

to be losing all former shape and proportions. I thought it was a clown's trick. They were clowns, were they not? I myself could make four white balls transform into four black balls as I juggled them. And this was not my most astonishing feat of clownish magic. And is there not always a sleight of hand inherent in all ceremonies, often dependent on the transported delusions of the celebrants? This was a good show, I thought, and giggled to myself. The transformation scene of Harlequin throwing off his fool's facade. O God, Harlequin, do not move like that! Harlequin, where are your arms? And your legs have melted together and have begun squirming upon the floor. What horrible, mouthing umbilicus is that where your face should be? *What is it that buries itself before it is dead?* The almighty serpent of wisdom—the Conqueror Worm.

It now started happening all around the chamber. Individual members of the congregation would gaze emptily—caught for a moment in a frozen trance—and then collapse to the floor to begin the sickening metamorphosis. This happened with ever-increasing frequency the louder and more frantically Thoss chanted his insane prayer or curse. Then there began a writhing movement toward the altar, and Thoss welcomed the things as they curled their way to the altar top. I knew now what lax figure lay upon it.

This was Kora and Persephone, the daughter of Ceres and the Winter Queen: the child abducted into the underworld of death. Except, this child had no supernatural mother to save her, no living mother at all. For the sacrifice I witnessed was an echo of one that had occurred twenty years before, the carnival feast of the preceding generation—O *carne vale!* Now both mother and daughter had become victims of this subterranean Sabbath. I finally realized this truth when the figure stirred upon the altar, lifted its head of icy beauty, and screamed at the sight of mute mouths closing around her.

I ran from the chamber into the tunnel. (There was nothing else that could be done, I have obsessively told myself.) Some of the others who had not yet changed began to pursue me. They would have caught up to me, I have no doubt, for I fell only a few yards into the passage. And for a moment I imagined that I, too, was about to undergo a transformation, but I had not been prepared as the others had been. When I heard the approaching footsteps of my pursuers, I was sure there was an even worse fate facing me upon the altar. But the footsteps ceased and retreated. They had received an order in the voice of their high priest. I, too, heard the order, though I wish I had not. And until that moment I had imagined that Thoss did not remember who I was. It was that voice that taught me otherwise.

For the moment I was free to leave. I struggled to my feet and, having broken my lantern in the fall, retraced my way back through cloacal blackness.

Everything seemed to happen very quickly once I emerged from the tunnel and climbed up from the pit. I wiped the reeking grease-paint from my face as I ran through the woods and back to the road. A passing car stopped, though I gave it no other choice except to run me down.

"Thank you for stopping."

"What the hell are you doing out here?" the driver asked.

I caught my breath. "It was a joke. The festival. Friends thought it would be funny. . . . Please drive on."

My ride let me off about a mile out of town, and from there I could find my way. It was the same way I had come into Mirocaw on my first visit the summer before. I stood for a while at the summit of that high hill just outside the city limits, looking down upon the busy little hamlet. The intensity of the festival had not abated, and would not until morning. I walked down toward the welcoming glow of green, slipped through the festivities unnoticed, and returned to the hotel.

VII

When I awoke the next morning, I saw from my window that the town and surrounding countryside had been visited during the night by a snowstorm, one that was entirely unpredicted. The snow was still falling and blowing and gathering on the now-deserted streets of Mirocaw. The festival was over. Everyone had gone home.

And this was exactly my own intention. Any action on my part concerning what I had seen the night before would have to wait until I was away from the town. I am still not sure it will do any good to speak up like this. Any accusations I could make against the slum populace of Mirocaw would be resisted, as well they should be, as unbelievable. Perhaps in a very short while, none of this will be my concern.

With packed suitcases in both hands, I walked up to the front desk to check out. The man behind the desk was not Beadle, and he had to fumble around to find my bill.

"Here we are. Everything all right?"

"Fine," I answered. "Is Mr. Beadle around?"

"No, I'm afraid he's not back yet. Been out all night looking for his daughter. She's a very popular girl, being the Winter Queen and all that nonsense. Probably find she was at a party somewhere."

A little noise came out of my throat.

I threw my suitcases in the backseat of my car and got behind the wheel. On that morning, nothing I could recall seemed real to me. The snow was falling, and I watched it through my windshield, slow and silent and entrancing. I started up my car, routinely glancing in my rearview mirror. What I saw there is now vividly framed in my mind, as it was framed in the back window of my car when I turned to verify its reality.

In the middle of the street behind me, standing ankle-deep in snow, were Thoss and another figure. When I looked closely at the other, I recognized him as one of the boys whom I surprised in that diner. But he had now taken on a corrupt and listless resemblance to his new family. Both he and Thoss stared at me, making no attempt to forestall my departure.

I had to carry the image of those two dark figures in my mind as I drove back home. But only now has the full weight of my experience descended upon me. So far I have claimed illness in order to avoid my teaching schedule. To face the normal flow of life as I had formerly known it would be impossible. I am now very much under the influence of a season and a climate far colder and more barren than all the winters in human memory. And retracing all the phases of past events does not seem to have helped; I can feel myself sinking deeper into a velvety white abyss.

At certain times I could almost dissolve entirely into this inner realm of awful purity and emptiness. I remember those invisible moments when in disguise I drifted through the streets of Mirocaw, untouched by the drunken, noisy forms around me: untouchable. But instantly I recoil at this grotesque nostalgia, for I realize what is happening, and what I do not want to be true, though Thoss prophesied it was. I recall his command to those others as I lay helplessly prone in the tunnel. They could have apprehended me, but Thoss, my old master, called them back. His voice echoed throughout that cavern, and it now reverberates within my own psychic chambers of memory.

"He is one of us," it said. "He has *always* been one of us."

It is this voice that now fills my dreams and days and my long winter nights. I have seen you, Dr. Thoss, through the snow outside my window. Soon I will celebrate that last feast that will kill your words, only to prove how well I have learned their truth.

To the memory of H. P. Lovecraft

COFFINS

♦ ♦ ♦

Robert Reed

Robert Reed has written six novels: The Leeshore, The Hormone
Jungle, Black Milk, Down the Bright Way, The Remarkables, *and*
Beyond the Veil of Stars. *His short fiction won the Writers of the
Future Award, and has been nominated for the Hugo. He is such
a regular contributor to* F&SF *that Locus Magazine recently called
him "the quintessential* F&SF *writer." "Coffins" is quintessential
Reed: excellent, intriguing, and thoughtful.*

He sits before a projected clerk, confessing his fears.
"You can't assure my safety. I know this. You can't
tell me that my ship won't strike a comet or explode on its own.
There's an attrition rate with star travel, isn't there? It's got its
inherent dangers, and no technology can absolutely guarantee my
survival. Am I right?"

The clerk, sculpted from light and designed to nourish confidence, offers an easy smile while nodding. "Your heart," it offers,
"is a chaotic organ, sir. There's a measurable statistical chance of
complete failure sometime during an average thousand-year life
span. A tiny chance, but quite real."

"I know, I know." The man leans back and sighs. "Life itself is
dangerous. You don't have to remind me."

"Starships are the safest mode of travel in existence."

Sure, on a per-kilometer basis. But that's a ridiculous statistic,
the man shutting his eyes and shuddering.

"You say you're being transferred? That your employer wants
you to establish a division on New Mars?"

Eyes open. "The chance of a lifetime."

"No doubt," says the enthusiastic clerk.

"It's just. . . . I don't know. . . . I keep seeing myself being killed. I don't daydream as a rule—I test pretty low on creativity scales—but this daydream seems so real. There's some terrible, sudden disaster, then I die."

And the clerk, speaking with authority, tells him, "Travelers have those kinds of premonitions, sir. Studies show. A human being isn't on a true journey unless he feels some impending doom."

The man says nothing.

"Sir?"

"What's the attrition rate among starships?"

"Vanishingly small," the clerk declares. "Hardly worth mentioning, I dare say."

"And now you climb inside," says the robot, one of nine arms pressing at him from behind. "Go on now. The mold's ready and waiting."

He looks downward. The mold is made from a shiny pseudosolid, and it's human-shaped but oversized. Surrounding it and him are a variety of clean machines, humming as if impatient. Kneeling, he places one hand on the mold's wall, finding it cool and slick. An odd stink lingers in his nose and throat. He coughs and looks upward, seeing the mold's cap dropping. The robot tells him to lie on his back, please, and please remain still. The pouring will follow his sizing, the process completely safe . . . and with that the voice fades away, closed out. As promised, the walls flow and close on him. He feels himself being lifted and centered, held motionless by invisible hands. Clucking his tongue, he measures the distance around his face. Beside the faintest glow, there is no illumination. It's like an old-fashioned coffin, he thinks; then the robot's voice comes from everywhere at once.

"Your lifesuit's constructed from hyperfibers coated with a modern flux-field." A kind of pride lies in the words. "In effect, you'll be inside a miniature starship. You'll have your own fusion reactor, plus a sophisticated recyke system—the best of everything—and you'll be entirely self-sustaining. Sir. The lifesuit's computer includes a universal library. You can enjoy any book or song or any visual entertainment while you're awake. I presume you've supplied us with personal digitals and other memorabilia—"

"Sure."

"—and at this time, if you would, please express your preference. Do you wish to travel to New Mars awake or asleep?"

"Asleep," he blurts.

"Slumber-sleep, or cold-sleep?"

"Cold."

A pause. "You'll have to be awakened occasionally, as I'm sure you know. Your body will have to purge itself of radiation damage and molecular creeping. Your lifesuit's computer will use its complete autodoc capacities to ensure your health." Another pause. "The average is one week awake for every ten years of cold-sleep."

"I know."

"Are you comfortable, sir?"

The voice has changed without warning. It isn't the robot's or the clerk's. He listens to it repeating the questions, then he says, "I'm fine. Fine."

"I'm your lifesuit's computer sir. I'm very, very pleased to be serving you."

He thinks of the future, long and uncertain.

"How soon would you like to be placed into cold-sleep, sir?"

"Right away," he replies.

"But the pouring isn't complete. It should be another full hour, then a second hour of systems trials. All very standard, I assure you."

"Can I watch a movie? While I wait?"

A pause, brief and vaguely disappointed. "Your faceplate is not yet grown, sir. I'm sorry."

Now it's totally dark inside the mold, claustrophobic and becoming more so by the moment. Lifesuits have nicknames, he recalls. Bodyhouses, for one. More commonly: *Coffins.*

"What can you do for me?" he inquires.

"Name a kind of music, sir."

"Something nice."

"Can you be more specific?"

"It doesn't matter. Just something happy. Use your discretion. I just want a happy tune, please."

His head is flooded with noise, light and flowing. A delight, and later he asks about it.

"An Io funeral dance," the computer confesses.

"What?!"

This pause seems embarrassed, then it admits, "I thought you'd see the humor, sir. My apologies. My mistake."

The starship is an armored bullet filled with lifesuits—with coffins—accelerating out of the solar system with its giant engines working flawlessly, month after month, every onboard system correcting and repairing itself as needed. The local Oort cloud has been mapped, its most dangerous places avoided. There are a few chunks of debris that slip past the ship's flux-field, but nothing serious. No permanent damage. Starships are most at risk between suns, streaking along at a substantial fraction of light-speed, snowballs capable of etching craters in their armored hulls and larger hazards always lurking in the cold darkness.

The man sleeps at a few degrees above absolute zero, gladly unaware.

Ten years into the voyage he's awakened, and for a week his lifesuit entertains and coddles him. If the ship had room he could rise and move about, but there are no hallways or cabins. He is cargo like everyone else, safely set in a framework of carbon spiderwebs. The most he can manage is to turn his head, asking for his faceplate to turn transparent and him watching the other cargo. Most are in cold-sleep; the ten-year schedule is just an approximate. But a few people are awake, and would he like to speak with them? asks the computer.

"Not really," he says.

Silence.

"I mean, why?" he asks. "Most of these people aren't going to New Mars. They'll disembark first and be gone. Right? So why should I waste the breath?"

"It's your decision," says the computer.

"It is," he agrees.

"Is there anything else I can offer?"

Yes, but he's embarrassed to ask. This is the first week for him, and it's not as if he's never gone without sexual relations before. These coffins are supposed to have tricks. Devices. But instead he says, "Let me read something, will you?"

"Something already begun?"

He stares at the inert coffins suspended around him. Each has a huge pack fused to its shoulders and back, its mirrored finish bright.

Almost liquid. Independent of the ship's power, each one is like a tiny world onto itself.

"Sir? What do you want to read?"

"That one. The one about New Mars that I started. . . ."

And now he's alone with his book unrolling before his eyes, the computer tracking his progress and him barely following the narrative. New Mars refuses to be a real place in his mind. He tries and tries, but it's as if he knows something. As if there's no point in even daydreaming about the faraway place.

Fifty-nine years into the voyage—five weeks by his count—the starship suffers a glancing blow with an unmapped comet. No combination of armor and flux-fields can withstand such energies. The hull vaporizes; passengers spill out and oftentimes die. The waking passengers are torn apart by the shock. But cold-sleepers are rigid and mostly safe, provided they can clear the wreckage, approximating the ship's vector. And all the while the lifesuit computers wait, weighing damage and other factors, judging when it would be best to wake up their people.

By the most gentle means.

"What am I seeing?" the man inquires.

"Stars, aren't they?"

"But why?" Panic causes him to flinch, heavy limbs moving and nothing before him but blue shifted suns. "What's happening?"

"You're healthy, sir. I assure you."

The man listens to the story, panic becoming disbelief. Finally he interrupts, claiming, "This can't be. It's a joke. You're projecting stars on my faceplate, and I'm still on board the ship. That's got to be it. You're just having fun with me, aren't you?"

"Yes," says the computer. "You've seen through me, all right."

"Show me what's really there. I order you!"

The computer selects an image of lifesuits, as before, tens of thousands of them surrounding him. It makes the man relax, believing in this scene. His scared mind can start considering the prospects of being adrift between suns; and eventually he can ask, "If I'm in space, what are my prospects? Hypothetically speaking."

"They'd be good, sir. Relatively speaking."

"What's possible?"

"Well," says the computer, "you'll certainly pass near the next port of call, and since they'll know about the accident and know your approximate trajectory, there's always a chance of being rescued."

"A chance."

"Almost one in fifty."

For no reason, the man feels a sudden conviction in his own good luck. Of course he'll be that one in fifty. He'll be rescued, and afterward he will point to his premonitions and feel quite smug.

"And if you do slip past," says the reassuring voice, "then I can keep you comfortable and healthy for as long as necessary. My systems have no inherent limitations in time. No simulation has been able to put a cap on their life spans, and since I can harvest hydrogen by extending my flux-field, my reactor needs for nothing—"

"Overall," he asks, "what are my chances? What are the odds that someone somewhere will find me?"

"Judging by what I know," it answers, "perhaps one chance in twenty. Or even one in fifteen."

The man shuts his eyes, then says, "Show me those stars again, will you?"

The computer complies.

Blueshifted suns are gathered before him. He's moving face-first at an astonishing speed.

"And this is real?" he whipers.

"Yes. Yes, it is."

"Can you keep me in cold-sleep? The rest of the way?"

"If you prefer. Is that what you want?"

"Wake me when you have to. And when we're close to the next destination, if you would."

"Naturally."

He feels the air around his face growing colder, his breath becoming a white vapor. "And thank you," he offers. "I mean it. You've been very helpful all around."

"Thank you, sir."

"You're a good friend."

"Good night, sir."

"And good luck," he mutters. Then louder: "To both of us."

There is no rescue. An orange sun brightens, then fades, the computer broadcasting the strongest distress signal it can muster. But

thousands of other scattered survivors are doing the same, mud-
dying the skies and the local rescue teams overmatched. One in
forty-eight are retrieved, and later missions from more-distant suns
are able to snag a few more. But none of this is known to the man
or computer. From their perspective there's nothing but stars and
the cold emptiness. Sometimes bits of grit come close, but the flux-
field is able to surge and drive them aside. The lifesuit's design
proves itself time and again. The man asks why the starship wasn't
as adept at avoiding collisions, and the computer explains, "We're
a smaller target, in part. And the ship was thoroughly unlucky too."

A smaller target, yes. Maybe it would be smarter, and safer, to
shoot people from sun to sun with nothing on but their lifesuits.
No fancy starships begging to be struck, he argues.

"A good point, sir. You're possibly right."

But he thinks again. "Except who'd travel that way? Nothing
but you and your fancy coffin. . . . I know I wouldn't have ever,
ever risked such a journey."

"Besides," the computer interjects, "there'd have to be some
means to accelerate you, plus a system to catch you at your destination."

He's barely listening. That word *coffin* is making him shudder.

The computer waits, then says, "Sir? I've been watching, and I
think you'll need to be awake more often. I'm sorry, but without
the ship's hull you're experiencing more radiation. Your body has
to have its chances to heal itself."

A thousand-year life span, and suddenly that seems like a brief
time. "Awake how often? And for how long?"

"Every five years, perhaps, and for a full month at a time."

"You can see cellular damage?"

"And I'm using my autodoc powers to help you." The same
miniature synthesizers that create his food can produce almost any
complex molecule. Medicines and antioxidants are injected through
hair-thin needles. "But I can't work when you're a block of ice."

A pause, then he has to ask, "What are my chances now? I mean
for being found, based on everything you know—"

"One in four thousand."

He cannot speak.

"Unfortunately," the computer explains, "we've been moving
through an underpopulated region, and since we're traveling somewhat perpendicular to the galactic plane—"

"I understand."

"Yet," says the calm voice, "my estimates are just that. As time passes, new advances in propulsion and long-range sensors might make our discovery inevitable. There's no good way to be certain about anything."

A tightness builds in his throat, in his chest. He makes fists of his clumsy gloved hands, and for a long while he strikes his own chest, leaving himself panting but otherwise unaffected.

"I want to die," he moans.

"You will," his companion promises.

"But you won't help me, will you?"

Silence.

"Will you?"

"First of all," it confesses, "my programming makes that impossible. And secondly, I frankly don't believe you. Sir."

Cold-sleep, then awake.

Cold-sleep.

Awake.

The routine is established quickly, and eventually it feels as if his entire life has been spent inside this coffin. The computer calculates his age on the basis of waking hours, and they celebrate his birthdays and every holiday with as much fanfare as possible. Special foods; strong wines; fantasy women. At some vague point he discovers himself to be comfortable with everything. He actually wakes from both kinds of sleep feeling ready, even eager, always some book to be read or some digital entertainment to be enjoyed. Two hundred years old, then three hundred. Then four hundred, and he gives up wondering how his life would have gone on New Mars. It would have been ordinary, no doubt. Colorless. Even silly. But here he's strolling through the galaxy, preparing to leave it altogether . . . and how many people can make that claim?

Here he's been challenged in a grand fashion, and he's adapted as well as anyone could ever adapt.

How can he feel anything but pride?

He reaches his five hundredth birthday, biologically speaking.

Then the seven hundredth.

Then the ninth.

The lifesuit can be turned slowly, the computer adjusting the flux-field to interact with the local magnetic fields. Sometimes the man sees the redshifted faces of the Milky Way behind him. All pretense of a rescue is finished. There is no place for regrets, his life lonely but otherwise rich. Probably no one else has digested as much of a universal library as he has managed, and now he thinks calmly, in organized ways, weighing options with the computer. Centuries of preparation give him ideas and a general outline; the computer absorbs his broad instructions. And as the work progresses, the man finds himself more and more excited about the prospects.

The scheme is amazing, and in its fashion, quite lovely.

"Not bad for a bland little businessman," he declares, laughing and laughing. "Don't you think so?"

"I look forward to beginning the work," the computer jokes.

And the man laughs still harder.

A little short of his thousandth birthday, he dies. And the griefless computer watches the peaceful failure of organs and the ancient brain. It's done its primary job as well as possible; it contemplates the silence within and without. But life persists even now. Bacteria begin to feed on the corpse, harvesting its latent energies. Dozens of species thrive, and the computer consciously helps them with warmth and oxygen. Dead tissues become a living goo. The entire body is eradicated, bones dissolving and then the hard white teeth. The goo is fed sugars and amino acids made by the recyke systems. The computer uses its autodoc needles to ensure fair shares to everyone. And it learns as it works, discovering which species prefer which treats, then moving on with the man's strange, patient plan.

The lifesuit races away from the galaxy. The darkness around it is mostly empty, save the hydrogen used for fuel. As promised, the machinery seems impervious to time and wear. Radiation begets mutations in the passengers; the computer picks and chooses. They're wondrous creatures, these passengers. They're tough and vigorous and almost infinitely flexible, and their best qualities can be married into an organized whole. In effect, a symbiotic mass of bacterial cultures.

One species serves as a nervous system; another is muscle; a third mimics bone; and a fourth is an efficient blood.

The culture fills the lifesuit, built along the dead man's shape. It's not a single organism. Not after even 10 million years is it anything more, or less, than a compilation of tightly orchestrated creatures. Yet it functions much like any multicellular creature. There are recognizable hearts and kidneys. Functional eyes appear after eons of false starts and ugly failures. Every success is nourished by the watchful computer. And when the broad work is completed, it feeds the compilation as it would any man: Rich foods are ingested by a greedy mouthlike affair, then digested, and the fragrant shit is collected from the ass and reprocessed in an endless cycle.

The lifesuit is a biosphere unto itself, enclosed and perpetual.

Ten million years of travel, then more. A busy, busy span of time, and there's still so much work to be done.

The compilation becomes sentient gradually, in stages. It grows up watching fixed pinwheels of stars, discovering a voice—deep and strong—and then a second voice. Its own voice. It learns how to read and sing, how to reason and do mathematics. Not quite as quick or coordinated as a human being, it nonetheless has its advantages. It's much more durable. It rejuvenates itself without end. Its mind isn't subject to depressions or failures of will. And since it's married so effectively to the lifesuit, it can't imagine any other existence for itself.

There is a sense of humor, white pseudoteeth showing when it smiles.

It picks its own name, saying, "Multitude," with a voice not unlike the dead man's. "I am Multitude."

"Hello, Multitude. How do you feel today?"

"Fine. What's to happen?"

"Like always, we'll continue with your education. Then when your brain species tire, you'll sleep and recharge, digesting the day's lessons."

"What about later?"

"Later?" echoes the computer. "What do you mean?"

"That splotch of light is getting bigger, isn't it? That means it's closer, doesn't it?"

A spiral galaxy lies in their path, yes. The computer explains that they'll pass through it. Or not. "There's a heightened chance of an impact while we're inside it," it warns. "But we've lost a good deal of our initial velocity. Every time I grab a local hydrogen atom, we're slowed a little bit. So we probably won't hit hard enough to shatter."

"Good."

A long pause, then it adds, "If we miss, it's only temporary. We don't have enough velocity to escape that galaxy's pull, and we'll stop and fall back through again. Over and over again, and we'll eventually hit some obstruction."

"Which means?"

"Possibilities. There are always possibilities."

Multitude is content with the open-ended answer. What's the hurry? "So tell me more about this man. What kind of organism was it? That's what I want to learn about today."

"Gladly," says the computer. "Of course."

Multitude watches the yellow sun on its right, and the computer speaks about the coming impact and how it has changed their vector just enough, wrestling with the magnetic fields. A blue planet lies straight ahead, peaceful and apparently new; and once again the computer explains, "In one sense you'll die. The gee forces will shatter you. But your individual cells will survive, and their spores, and I promise that the next Multitude will be as close to you as I can manage."

Multitude says nothing.

"Do you have any questions?"

A laugh, and it says, "None you can answer fast enough—"

The coffin is a meteorite, small but faster than most; and the flux-field surges at the last instant, softening the impact, bleeding heat into the surrounding seawater and the muddy seafloor.

The computer finds minor damage and initiates repairs.

Multitude is reborn and reeducated.

Once strong enough, it rises to its feet and walks. There are no fishes or shelled creatures. The only life on this world are various colored scums in the shallowest waters. Multitude leaves deep footprints in the shoreline muds. It stops on the shoreline, eats and sleeps, then heads inland with the first light, barren gray country beneath a blue-and-white sky.

Simple tools yield to more-sophisticated ones.

Multitude and the computer use the ancient library, mastering hundreds of technologies. The first fusion reactor works after a mere eleven millennia of intricate fiddling. It's an imperfect but effective mirror of Multitude's reactor, as are the hyperfiber shell and the other proven systems. Multitude and computer replicate themselves once, then again. Then a thousand times. They use native bacteria to fill the new lifesuits, each onboard computer taking charge, twisting biology to serve the great plan.

A factory rises on the barren ground. Humming machinery and molds work night and day, producing new citizens by the thousands.

Launchpads shake, mighty rockets driving skyward.

Most are bound for nearby suns, but a few have a more distant and personal goal—capsules bursting open in deep space, shiny figures like dust en route to the ancestor's homeland.

Multitude and the computer are eventually destroyed in an industrial accident, an experimental plasma drill all but evaporating both of them. And the others, following strict instructions, take what remains to the sea and let the tides take them away. Human faces weep. Human voices sing a light, almost happy song from some vanished world called Io. Then it's back to work, to life, much to be done and the possibilities without number.

THE RESURRECTION OF
ALONSO QUIJANA

◆ ◆ ◆

translation and annotation
Marcos Donnelly

Marcos Donnelly has sold short fiction to F&SF *and Bantam's* Full
Spectrum *anthologies. This story, "The Resurrection of Alonso
Quijana," made the preliminary ballot for the Nebula Award, and
received a great deal of critical attention. In addition to being a
story about the Gulf War, as mentioned in the Introduction to the
volume, "The Resurrection of Alonso Quijana" manages to mix
the legacy left by Miguel Cervantes in* Don Quixote *with some very
real modern-day concerns.*

*Translator's Note: The following tale is translated from a quite
old-looking manuscript of Cervantes'* El Ingenioso Hidalgo Don
Quijote de La Mancha, *a text discovered by my brother Martin in
a house of shady repute several kilometers south of Montreal. I
never learned what my brother was doing in the upstairs closet of
that hovel, but he subsequently smuggled the manuscript past U.S.
and Canadian Customs—for the sake of literature, boldly disre-
garding the risk of substantial border delay. I here publish a Cervantes selection that has not appeared in earlier translations of his
masterpiece, and leave the determination of its legitimacy to the
scholarly community and the reading public.*

A Foreword by Miguel de Cervantes Saavedra

Being dead, I shall be brief.

A number of my colleagues in the afterlife have taken to publishing additional works after their own deaths. Until recently, I have abhorred this practice. Necessity compels me, however, to once again take up pen to further elucidate the nature of my gift to the world, one Alonso Quijana, who in madness pretended himself a valiant knight-errant, Don Quijote de La Mancha. Since my departure from mortality, my mad knight has been variously ballad-ed, poem-ed, opera-ed, theater-ed, and even, God save us, adjectived: "*quixotic*, romantically chivalric, having high but impractical sentiments, aims, etc."

Rot and rubbish. You've all missed the point.

Don Quijote was born for me alone—so a pox and the clap and a shot in the bum to all of you who have bastardized my grand theme. Wherein your "Quijote" would melt innocent hearts, mine would in delusion pierce them through (as I thought I had made clear in my first collection of the insane vagabond's tales). And wherein your "Quijote" possesses lips that would burst into enchanting melody, mine sports a mouth that spews vomit in the face of his idiot squire.

So the heirs of my legacy have been fools with my fortune. I hereby disown them to make clear, yet again, the nature of the Manchegan madman.

II, lxxiv, supplement A: In which our knight awakens sane from his mysterious sleep.

As is the wont of all things, particularly things human, Don Quijote found himself at the stairway of paradise, confined now to bed to await the mortal coming of immortality. The physician sent for by his faithful friends—Sansón, Sancho, and Nicolás the Barber—declared that melancholy and fantastic defeat had robbed the knight-errant of his vital spirits, of his desire to stay his residence within the mortal tent in which our souls pass earthly pilgrimage for but a while—in short, Don Quijote was dying.

Our knight requested that his friends leave him for a time, as he wished to rest. They retired, and he had a long, unbroken sleep of more than six hours. When he awoke, his friends heard him calling out in a loud voice, and they rushed to his bedside.

"Blessed be God!" the knight exclaimed. "In His mercy, my delusions have left me! For I no longer fancy myself Don Quijote, but am again Alonso Quijana el Bueno, formerly respected of the world for his virtuous life."

His friends, hearing him, were sorely troubled, believing some new madness had overtaken their master. But Don Quijote summoned his squire close to him and in confidence asked: "Tell me, loyal friend. Have you any notion what would mean such terms as *machismo* and *cojones?*"

His squire, worried that his master now insisted on being called by the old name, answered carefully: "I would only guess, my lord, that the one would speak of being male and the other speak of great big boxes."[1]

"Nay," Don Quijote growled, of a sudden quite angry. "T'was a strange adventure, and now my eyes are opened, my friend. T'was indeed the greatest and most horrible of all my adventures."

"And you had it in *bed*, my lord?"

"I tell you, Sancho, that knight-errantry is evil! It must at once be banished! Condemned! Abandoned, Sancho, utterly abandoned!" The ferocity of Don Quijote made him to weep, and he cried, "Dulcinea! My sweet lady Dulcinea, how I have been deceived!"

Sancho was sorely worried by his master's cursing of knight-errantry, fearing that now there would never arrive the afore promised lands and treasures and conquered islands. "My lord," he said, "what adventure, however horrid, could make a valiant knight forswear his noble and, I must add, potentially very profitable calling?"

"I am not your lord," Don Quijote snapped. "I am Alonso Quijana el Bueno."

II, lxxiv, supplement B: In which our knight considers the strange adventure that befell him in his sleep.

During his six hours of repose, Don Quijote fell into a dream that he took to be real, and which he therefore counted as his greatest

---

1. Sancho here understandably confuses cojones, a twentieth-century obscenity for "testicles," with its older and unquestionably less interesting meaning.

adventure of all. Finding himself inexplicably in a mist, Don Quijote wandered in attempt to find anew the bed he had been enjoying so. Venturing far, Don Quijote became weary, and in his mind he fancied hearing the voice of Frestón, that mad enchanter who had plagued so many of the knight's valiant adventures. The voice of Frestón spoke thus to Don Quijote: "Foolish pretender! Germ of the foul offspring of a griffin's vomit block![2] Know ye not what evil thou hast sustained in the world?"

"I shall answer you," quoth Don Quijote, "but the demon in your mind, foul Frestón, shall render my apologia incomprehensible to the likes of you: I have fought for justice, truth, and chivalry in the name of my lady Dulcinea."

"Cretin!" screamed the voice of the enchanter. "Thou hast beaten on innocents! Thou hast broken the legs of mourners in funeral processions! Thou hast thrashed men of cloth and of valor, and they on their parts have thrashed a fool! Thou, Don Quijote, art a twerp!"

Rage overcoming his fear, the knight swore by lance and sword: "You shall pay for your malhumor, Frestón! My doughty arm shall rip the wires from your spark plugs and rupture your radiator!"[3]

Then the mist before our fearless knight parted and opened itself to a vast desert wasteland. "See thy principles, Don Quijote de La Mancha. See the world thou hast helped create." Trembling with fury, Don Quijote stepped from the mists into the desert conjured by Frestón. "This is thy land of chivalry, knight-pretender. Find the truth in the sands of Sudúrabu."[4] Whereupon the mists dispelled, and Don Quijote stood in the sands of that strange country.

There wandered through the wasteland a recalcitrant soldier named Santiago Rojas of the U.S. Army, who, sick with worry about the beginnings of war in Sudúrabu, and justifying himself by insisting he had joined the Army only to have regular work, and not to fight

---

2. A difficult phrase to interpret, although certainly a vile oath of some sort.

3. This line is undoubtedly the addition of later editors.

4. After careful consideration, I've opted to keep this word in the manuscript's original form. It should be noted, however, that my brother insists it means "Saudi Arabia," while my dad prefers "South Hampton."

wars or to be all that he could be, had secreted himself away from his company, his companions, and his compatriots. This decrepit, having been educated in twentieth-century city schools of the New World, mistakenly believed himself capable of journeying home from the warring desert if only he were to travel northwest.[5]

So it was this unworthy who came upon our knight-errant in the desert, spying him from afar. Santiago quaked to his very Army-commissioned leather boots upon seeing Don Quijote, for he feared that there would be military patrols hunting him to punish his desertion.

As Don Quijote drew closer, Santiago lost his fear and grew amazed, for never had he seen so ludicrous a sight as our knight-errant. Don Quijote sported a metal basin as helm, and his beaver was bent plasterboard poked with holes for breathing; his sword was rusted, as dull on the sharp side as it was sharp on the dull; his lance was twisted, as blunt on the pointed side as it was pointed on the blunt.[6] And Santiago for a moment thought he was seeing a mirage.

For his part, Don Quijote thought he had come across another knight who, like himself, was a victim of Frestón's enchantments. Cautious, however, he called to the man: "Ho! Valiant knight or pretender? Speak your intent, and hither and whence as well, that I might determine whether I shall greet you as friend or remove your guts from your stomach!"

The soldier called back to Don Quijote in a tongue that, while Spanish, was harsh and hissing and skipped far too many consonants to be called Castellano. Nonetheless, Don Quijote understood, hearing the man's name to be Saint James the Red. Saint James followed his name with a string of numbers, and Don Quijote determined that this was no knight, but instead a valiant wizard. (For Don Quijote had read that many wizards practiced their art by the use of magic numbers.)

"You with the Army?" asked Santiago.

---

5. Geographical studies prove that this sort of journey would be extremely difficult, thus confirming the claim of Santiago's poor education.

6. Such euphuistic turns of phrase are common in Cervantes' work, although my sister Cheryl, a social worker, insists the device is used subconsciously, revealing Cervantes' confusion and fears concerning his own masculinity.

"Good Saint James," quoth Don Quijote, "I shall assist any army that fights for truth and justice, but I am tied to no force. I am a knight-errant."

Santiago was greatly relieved, for in his style of Spanish, "knight-errant" sounded to him like "a wandering gentleman." So he asked Don Quijote: "You know how far it is to Paris?"

"I know not," quoth Don Quijote. "Are we perchance in France?"

"Nah, we're in Sudúrabu. Gotta go around Chordini, I guess. Never got much geography in school, see? But I'm getting myself to Paris and catching the first plane out of here to America."

Don Quijote was hard pressed to follow these words, so his delusion made him to understand that this noble wizard intended to conquer the city of Paris. "Ho and hie, then!" quoth Don Quijote. "Suffer me to journey with you, that I might lend my doughty arm and sturdy lance to your fearsome magic. For know ye, noble Saint James the Red, it is no ordinary knight with whom you converse, but the servant of the finest, purest, and most exalted of all women, the incomparable Dulcinea; I am her warrior, the famed Don Quijote de La Mancha, Knight of the Sad Figure."

Saint James gazed upon the face of Don Quijote for so much time without speaking that Don Quijote concluded such behavior must not be deemed rude in the homeland of Saint James. When Saint James at last spoke, Don Quijote was further befuddled, for the wizard chanted a dozen times and twice a dozen more: "Sacred feces. Sacred feces."[7] Then Don Quijote recalled that he had heard of far-off lands where cows were worshiped; and if the cows, why not the manure of cows, which fertilized the land and brought forth plants and fruit to nourish the body? So Don Quijote determined he should honor the wizard's customs, and, nodding his head to match rhythm, he joined the chant, saying along with Saint James the Red: "Sacred feces. Sacred feces."

At once Don Quijote heard the rumbling of thunder, although there was in the sky not a single cloud. Before he could make inquiry concerning this marvel, Saint James the Red knocked him from his feet. "Jesus Christ!" the wizard prayed harshly. "Border patrol!"

---

7. My brother Martin prefers a less dignified translation of this phrase.

II, lxxiv, supplement C: In which Don Quijote faces the minions of the Moor Brandabaran.

Don Quijote spit great quantities of sand from his mouth, for he had been gaping when knocked face-first to the desert floor. "What a strange enchantment is this!" he managed to say. "For I see before us a lion made of iron storming 'cross the sands!"

"Shaddup!" said valiant Saint James. "Oh Jesus, those are Air-achis![8] I'm farther north than I thought!"

"Then rejoice," said Don Quijote. "We are all the closer to Paris for it." Don Quijote again looked upon the iron lion and perceived on its back three men whose headdresses were unmistakably the foolish garb of Moors. Over the headdresses, each wore a simple, unadorned helm, as if trying to hide their true identities from the keen eyes of Don Quijote.

"By the fingernails of Saint Conklin's mother!" hollered the knight, raising himself to full stature. "Know you not who these be, righteous Saint James? None other than minions of Branda-baran, Lord of the Three Arabias, come to rob more land for their demented sultan! Come, Saint James! For what are mere henchmen to a knight and a wizard such as we?" Whence Don Quijote called upon the name of his beloved Dulcinea, and Saint James, still prostrate, resumed his mystical Chant of the Sacred Feces.

Now the three Moors, seeing the old man approach them with a twisted stick, raised their own weapons; but they did so with only half a heart. For the knight seemed to them entirely harmless, and the moaning heap behind the knight appeared to them to be one wounded who, if not yet dead, then soon would be thanks to nature and the desert sun.

"He looks malnourished; do you think he's an escaped hostage?" the youngest of the three asked his leader. The leader considered this question, then called to Don Quijote: "Say! Halt there, you! Are you a hostage?"

---

8. This term is also retained in the original manuscript's form. My dad suggests the translation "Iroquois," holding that those American Indian tribes were indeed situated somewhat north of South Hampton. My brother insists on "Iraquis," allowing topical bias to cloud his scholarly vision.

Don Quijote, who had a difficult enough time understanding Santiago, hadn't the slightest clue what the singsongy words of his adversaries meant, but he understood the Moors to be mocking him with baby talk. He charged with his lance, feeling both enraged and confident, for although his opponents themselves carried lances, their lances were short and gnarled and stubby at the ends; judged as lances, they were inferior even to Don Quijote's own.

Just as he was about to pierce the heart of the closest wicked Moor—the one who was the youngest—the Moor nudged aside the feeble tip of the knight's lance, and Don Quijote found himself hurtling forward of his own velocity. He wound up once again with a mouthful of the Sudúrabu's burning sands.

The young Moor soldier laughed heartily at this, and his companions, still upon the back of the iron lion, likewise roared with mirth. "Shall I radio this in?" the soldier Moor asked his captain, but the captain stayed him, enjoying the folly of Don Quijote and suggesting they could have a bit more fun with the knight.

"No, no," said the youngest, for his soul was kind; he, like Santiago, had joined his Army for the benefit of regular meals, and every month he sent much of his pay to his wife, his infant daughter, and his brother who watched over them at home. "The man is an old fool, made crazy by the heat. We've had fun, and now we should help him up and ask what in the name of Allah he's doing so far out in the desert." And the youngest Moor walked toward Don Quijote to do just that.

Don Quijote had by now managed to roll himself over on his back; bruised from his second fall, however, he could not yet bring himself to his feet. Seeing his enemy advancing, and convinced that he was about to be pierced through, Don Quijote swung his lance, albeit feebly, at the Moor.

It was through simple Fortune and the hand of Providence that the lance, while missing the Moor himself, struck the enemy's own gnarled, stunted weapon. The young Moor, seeing nothing to fear in our ferocious knight, had been holding his weapon much too loosely, and, for that matter, backward. When Don Quijote's lance struck it, the tip became caught under the weapon's handle. The Moor jerked back by instinct, and there filled the air a sound like a dozen stones pelting a steel basin. This was, in fact, something like what was happening, for the Moor's weapon spit forth a series of volleys faster than any knight had ever seen, and those volleys pierced the side of the iron dragon. Don Quijote heard the Moor's sudden exclamations of ". . .,"[9] and so deadly were the volleys that before you could say, " 'S' wounds and 'S' blood!", the lion exploded, thoroughly toasting the two Moors on its back and throwing the upper part of the youngest Moor a good twenty lengths, the lower part a good thirty-five.

Don Quijote, being flat on the ground, was not harmed greatly, save that half the hair of his head was singed and his basin helm was significantly dented.

"Victory!" yelled the undaunted knight. "You, Saint James! You have brought us victory! I know not what strange incantation you have used to consume the iron lion and the minions of Brandabaran in the Holy Flame of God, but your success was thorough! Now more than before am I committed to standing by your side in our great siege of Paris!"

Santiago, at last looking up, was awed by the utter destruction wrought by Don Quijote. He suspected for the first time that there was something more than met the eye to this wandering gentleman. Then, seeing what remained of the three Airachis, he promptly vomited.

II, lxxiv, supplement D: In which Saint James learns our knight's chivalric philosophies.

After taking repast on the rations Santiago had stolen for his desertion, the companions watched the fierce sun set behind the endless banks and waves and hills of the sands of the Sudúrabu [. . . .][10] And our knight and his companion sat for rest and discussion, warming their hands in the rapid chill of night over Saint James' magic lamp that gave off heat but no smoke or flame. And Don

---

9. The text here is written in Arabic, a language in which I am not adept. My brother, who once dated a Tunisian girl, says he believes the translation is similar to Santiago's "Sacred Feces" oath. I have not verified this, but the reader should be aware of a possible motif.

10. On the advice of my dad, I have here deleted four tedious paragraphs of description for which the twentieth-century audience would have little patience.

Quijote spoke thus to Saint James: "Would it not, good and valor-
ous friend, be more sensible for us to travel by the moon than by
the sun? For we would do better to travel briskly in the cold than
to travel sluggishly by Apollo's unkindness."

Saint James the Red answered: "I thought about that, but I think
they've got infrared shit that can see you better in the night. 'Sides,
who the hell would think I'd cross by day? Only an idiot would do
that."

"Well said, wizard," quoth Don Quijote. "By acting as fools
when our enemy knows us not as fools, then we shall wisely be
fools indeed, fooling them all! And even if we bake and rot like fish
jumped too far from shore, we shall perish knowing the wisdom
of our folly and the folly of our enemy's wisdom."

And the words of Don Quijote much confounded Santiago.

"Tell me something, old man," Santiago said. "What in hell you
doing out here? We gotta be, I dunno, a hundred miles from Spain,
and maybe even two hundred from the United States.[11] What's
your act?"

Quoth Don Quijote, only partially understanding the wizard: "I
am upon this earth to kill for the sake of life and to battle for the
sake of peace."

"You oughta fit right in," said Santiago.

Don Quijote noted the sarcasm with which Santiago had spoken,
but forgave him in his heart, knowing that wizards were not as
familiar with physical conflicts as were knights-errant. But still
wishing to defend his good name and his profession, the knight
said: "Know you not wizard, the sanctity of my calling? Do you
not share my belief in the honor of men and the beauty of women?"

"Look, man," said Saint James the Red. "All I know is that I'm
over here getting shot at because gas costs too much, and even
though I'm here, it costs too much anyway. My recruiter didn't say
nothing about risking getting killed for gas."

"Then forgive me," quoth the knight, "but you are a fool, and
twice a fool at that. Does a man join the field of battle not expecting
violence? He who does is deceived. And does a true man, gifted by
Providence with the opportunity to draw his enemy's blood, scoff
at that gift? Nay, Saint James; though a just man face the prospect

---

11. My calculations show that Santiago's figures are inaccurate.

of losing an ear or an eye or a leg or his tongue or even his very britches burnt from his bottom, he should thank Heaven for the honor of slicing the skin from his foe. How else shall a knight honor his lady? This is true manhood, true knight-errantry."

Saint James the Red was, despite himself, quite taken by the passion of the old man. And although he did not truly believe his companion to be Don Quijote de La Mancha, he said: "I gotta admit, you showed a lot of *machismo* when you whipped those Airachis. That takes real *cojones.*"

"Ah," said Don Quijote, not grasping the words, but understanding their intent. "Then prove yourself a true man and an even nobler wizard by—"

Don Quijote did not finish his exhortation, for there now arose a roaring far greater even than that of the iron lion.

II, lxxiv, supplement E: Wherein Don Quijote faces the chariot of Apollo.

"In the sky, brave Saint James!" shouted the knight. "Treachery from the very sky!"

"Helicopter!" cried Santiago.

"Helios, I agree, and I fear I know exactly what this means. Recall you, Saint James, that I only recently cursed Apollo for his unkindness to us? He is here to take his vengeance, and we see above us his very chariot. Methinks I even glimpse a piece of the sun itself gazing as it were an eye to find us out." For, indeed, a shaft of light was sweeping the sky, and its gaze fell directly on them.

"We're dead," said Santiago.

"I fear you are right," quoth Don Quijote sadly. "Even the strength of my arm can be no match against a very god. But together, Saint James? Could it be that Providence has brought us together to show that wizardry and knight-errantry sum up the souls of men? It could well be that we are meant to win this encounter against the pagan deity himself. Recall my words, and we shall rout the very prince of Olympus."

"*Cojones,*" said Saint James.

"Have you no spell as before?"

"I'll give you a spell. Go like this." With that, Saint James the Red raised both hands above his head.

"Ah," said Don Quijote, "the Spell of Raised Palms. I have heard of it, but confess my ignorance of its power."

Said Saint James: "This here spell keeps us alive."

"Indeed," quoth the knight. "Invincibility! I once had a helm with much the same property."

As they spoke, the chariot of Apollo settled to the ground but a short distance from them, and Don Quijote girded his heart against the fear he felt of the fearsome thunder. The chariot had no steeds to draw it, which gave Don Quijote courage: for he believed that Apollo, himself uncertain of this battle's outcome, had left behind the mighty steeds of Olympus, that, should the god fail in conflict with the world's two mightiest mortals, the sacred steeds might not be taken as loot.

"Courage, Saint James. I sense our enemy is as anxious as we."

"Yeah?" said Santiago. "I'd always wondered about that."

Whereupon the sides of the great chariot opened, and there came forth, not Apollo, but several Moors dressed in like fashion to the ones Don Quijote had routed earlier. These, too, had stunted lances, headdresses like unto women's, and, further, they sported decorations of metal pineapples in crossing bands upon their chests. Seeing them, Don Quijote was filled with ire. Would it be, he considered, that the god mocks us? For here we stand ready to face him, and he elects to advance Moorish chattel upon us. "Such insult!" quoth he to Saint James, but he did not drop his hands, fearing he would break the wizard's powerful spell.

The Moors advanced to face them directly, and Don Quijote could not help but smile, sorry for these fools that did not know they were already defeated by the knight's and wizard's invulnerability.

One of the Moors took the butt of his gnarled lance and stoutly rammed Saint James in the stomach. Saint James fell to the ground, uttering moans of discomfort.

"Well done!" quoth Don Quijote. "Seeing that these are simpletons sent to us as an insult, I see no reason not to make sport with them. Should they strike me, I, too, shall pretend to be injured. What laughs we shall have later tonight, Saint James!"

Then the Moor struck Don Quijote. True to his word, the knight fell to the sand, pretending to have been well smitten. After a moment, Don Quijote thought perhaps he was playing his own act far too well, for his gut seemed to burn from the pain he feigned. I act so well, he thought, that I should perhaps have been in theater, were theater not beneath the dignity of a knight-errant. He prepared to act even better should more blows fall upon him, but the Moors returned their attention to Saint James. They booted and beat and smote him often, and the wizard kept up his commendable performance to the point that Don Quijote himself would have believed the pain had he not known better.

But soon the knight tired of the playacting. "Come," he called to Saint James, "let's have done with these cretins and find worthier prey." With that, Don Quijote drew his sword and ran full into the closest Moor. He would have killed him, too, had the Moor not turned upon seeing the knight; as it was, there was only a slight wound to the shoulder, not at all fatal.

Hearing the commotion, the Moors who had been taking sport on Saint James now rushed to Don Quijote, waving their pathetic lances in his direction. Saint James saw them advance upon the knight, and he shouted, as best a beaten man could: "Leave him alone! He's just an old guy! Leave him alone!" But the Moors were, if anything, even more vicious in their beating of Don Quijote than they had been with Santiago.

Feeling pain, and now convinced that he had somehow botched the spell and that the pain was real, Don Quijote cried out: "Noble Saint James! I fear the enchanter Frestón has stopped my arms, with the intent of having me leveled by these infidel Moors! The *machismo* and *cojones* for which you earlier praised me seem to have been silenced, and I fear it is your *cojones* alone that shall bring us victory!"

Santiago was sickened by the treatment of the old fool. Summoning his remaining powers and rising to his feet, he recalled the words of the knight in their earlier conversation; and counting himself as good as dead, he elected to at least die fighting for an honorable cause—the protection of his recent friend.

And then Santiago Rojas, in the elation of his own fear, remembered her: a girl in his tenth-grade class, Lucinda Rosario Dias of Tenth Avenue, the first girl he'd ever gone with under the old Stutson Street Bridge. It seemed to him a silly thought to be having at the very last moment in his life, but remembering *that* conquest empowered him to face *this* insane defeat. He nearly invoked her, the way the old man invoked his Dulcinea: "I am the servant of the finest, purest, and most exalted of all women, the incomparable Lucinda Rosario Dias of Tenth Avenue!"

He thought better of it. Without invocation, Santiago Rojas threw himself into the midst of the thrashing Moors in Don Quijote's defense.

Don Quijote saw this; and what he saw next amazed him more than any other demonstration of the wizard's powers. Saint James, whose ineffectual blows did little to deter the Moorish mob (for, understand, he was a man of magic and not of muscle), grabbed hold of one of the metal pineapples that crossed the enemy's chest. He made a strange yanking gesture with his hand, as if ripping the very soul from the heart of the Moor, although what he held was no soul, but a small pin of metal. Of a sudden the entire crowd dispersed with shouts of terror. The Moor whose pineapple had been yanked stood as if frozen, and he then began to scream and claw at his chest. Saint James the Red grabbed the man's waist, lifted him, and hurled the Moorish cretin into the body of Apollo's chariot. There were screams from inside, and again Don Quijote witnessed the scourge of the Holy Flame of God, all of the chariot consumed by Providence's wrath.

Don Quijote now saw Saint James outlined in fearsome countenance by the flames of the spell. Saint James grabbed the gnarled lance dropped by the soulless Moor and began by magic to spout killing fire from the lance's tip. And this was the last that Don Quijote saw before falling into unconsciousness, fading with the thought: "There is no one mightier than Saint James the Red. See how easily he, but a wizard, has come to understand the calling of knight-errantry."

II, lxxiv, supplement F: In which our knight discovers the true nature of chivalry in the Sudúrabu.

Don Quijote awoke to the ministrations of an attending maiden, and though she was to him a stranger, he said unto her: "This, then, is Heaven? For such attention from a maid so beautiful could not be an element of earth, save that woman be my own true Dulcinea."

The woman did not understand his language, nor did he grasp hers when she said, "Soldier! What's he saying?"

Then Don Quijote saw above him the figure of Saint James the Red. "He says thanks for taking care of him," quoth the wizard, although these words, too, made no sense to the knight.

"You can talk to him, soldier. Five minutes, no more."

"Yes ma'am."

"And, soldier?"

"Yes, ma'am?"

"Good work."

The maiden departed, and Santiago began to speak in a manner understandable to the knight-errant. "You were right!" he said. "I tell you, I've never felt like I did fighting against those Airachis. God damn, the sense of power! The sense of it being so . . . I dunno, so *right*!"

The knight was touched by the wizard's words, and also felt gratified that his grand theme had been made clear to Saint James. "I am pleased," said the knight. "But tell me, where are we? Have we sacked Paris?"

The wizard gave a jovial laugh. "No, no, old man, we're back with the U.S. Army. We took three days getting here. You know what? I even captured two prisoners, made 'em take turns carrying you. 'Course, I had to lie a bit to the brass, said I'd been grabbed by those two and taken hostage on this side of the border. God damn, I'm almost a hero here. The Airachis will contradict my story, but who believes a bunch of Airachis? 'Infidel Moors,' right?"

"Indeed," quoth Don Quijote, "and I am proud that you have rejoined your noble army. Tell me of that maiden, however. Your manner with her was so meek and resigned. Could she perhaps be your one true beloved, and have I had the pleasure of meeting the damsel to whom your heart belongs, she who is to you as Dulcinea is to me?"

Don Quijote's sentiments seemed to baffle Saint James the Red. "You mean Clancey? She's head of the nurses. She outranks me, so I gotta be . . . uh, meek and resigend."

"What say you?" quoth Don Quijote. "The knights of your army bring their maidens onto the very fields of battle that they might benefit from feminine ministrations? This seems odd to me, Saint James, and quite unwholesome."

"Oh, they're not just nurses," said Saint James. "Women work in maintenance, supplies, even strategy if you go up a ways. They're a big part of the military. Just a matter of time till they're fighting right next to men."

"What!" bellowed Don Quijote in a voice that resounded through the hall in which he lay. "You mean to say that your chivalry allows the fairer sex to endanger themselves on the very field of battle? Outrage! Unthinkable! How can any band of knights hold in so low esteem the very flower of God's creation?"

"Hey," quoth Santiago with a peculiar shrugging of his shoulders, "Equality and all that. I tell you, though, out there fighting, I never felt more like a man in my life."

It was then that Don Quijote felt his madness leaving him. "What for, all of this?" he said in a diminutive voice. "If fighting is for honor, and honor for the glory of the fairer sex, and here I find the fairer sex themselves involved in battle—wherefore, I ask you, is knight-errantry?"

"Man, I never felt stronger," quoth Saint James.

"Wherefore?" again quoth Don Quijote. "Know not these people that it is a far better thing for men to spill the guts of other men, and for women, far off and safe, to hold such deeds as noble? Alas, I find myself conceding: Frestón, oh wicked tongue of reality, perhaps you have cajoled me with more than lies. Perhaps you have cajoled me with truth, bitter, bitter, ugly truth!"

Just then Don Quijote heard again the voice of Frestón. "Enough," the enchanter said. "Thou has learned well, Don Quijote, and thou hast learned bitterly. Fit it is, then, that thy bones should rest in the earth of thine own age. Hate me not for the evil thou perceiveth in me."

Behind the voice of Frestón, the knight-errant heard the voice of Saint James the Red, saying: "Can't wait. Can't wait till the next real fighting starts."[12]

And Don Quijote, passing through mist, found himself again in his own country and in his own bed. He awoke weeping for his lady Dulcinea, and declaring of his friends that knight-errantry be

---

12. My interpretation is that Frestón was indeed confronting Don Quijote with truth. My brother agrees, although my dad has some reservations. My sister Cheryl only nods and reminds me of the meaning of *cojones*: both the symbol of male strength, and physiologically his greatest vulnerability. Although not an original insight, definitely a noteworthy one.

forever condemned, and demanding it never be spoken of again in his presence or in his household. And to them all, he declared: "I am Alonso Quijana—el Bueno."

An Afterword by Miguel de Cervantes Saavedra

So what is our verdict? Whom shall we praise? Don Quijote de La Mancha, in whose world men slay men, and women either cheer or weep from afar? Or Saint James the Red, whose men slay men, slay women, slay men and women? Or perhaps Don Alonso Quijana el Bueno, whose fantasies become unthinkable if the slaying isn't done just so, just right?

The afterlife has broadened my vision in many ways, but it has only strengthened my resolve: praise neither and none of these gentlemen. For if you praise them, then you, reader, are again the Don Quijote I tried so long ago to bury. You become the protagonist, the gallant knave, the kindly killer, the vicious fool.

Just once, I should think, we would try to praise a story's true hero. We would try to be Frestón.

I fear I shall rewrite this tale forever.

STEEL DOGS

◆ ◆ ◆

Ray Aldridge

Ray Aldridge is one of the best of the new writers who developed in F&SF and elsewhere during the last five or six years. In addition to more than a dozen strong stories for us, he has written a series of science fiction novels, most recently The Orpheus Machine. *"Steel Dogs" was published in 1989; it concerns an abandoned resort planet controlled by ghostly machines and a young woman who falls into the hands of a steel huntsman and his dogs.*

Aandred waited in the egress lock, jammed in with the horse and the dogs. In that small place, the air was dense with the stinks of machine oil and ozone and hydraulic fluid. The dogs were excited, and their bodies clashed together, metal against metal, making a thunderous din. "Calm down, puppies," Aandred said, making his harsh voice soothing. "Droam's a little slower than usual tonight, I know, I know, but soon, soon. . . ." The dogs quieted, waiting with only an occasional wriggle of eagerness, a muffled whimper.

Aandred flipped open the panel set into his forearm, studied the telltales there. All burned a steady green, except for an occasional amber flicker on the one that monitored Umber's olfactory transducer. *Not bad enough to make Umber stay behind,* he thought. Umber was a sweet puppy, not contentious; she would stay with the pack even if her nose failed her completely.

Droam spoke, using the direct mode. "Ready, Huntsman?" Aandred hated the sound of the castle's voice in his head; it was an intrusion, a reminder that he was Droam's property. Tonight the voice was a shade less unctuous than usual. Aandred imagined a quiver of apprehension in its smooth tones. *Good,* he thought. *Suffer, monster. Be afraid.* But all he said was, "Yes."

Aandred mounted his horse, a hulk beautifully fashioned of black steel. He latched himself into the saddle, snapping down the levers, locking the armored cables into their channels. The dogs surged with excitement, and the horse shied. Aandred reached out, crashed his fist against the back of its head. Sparks flew, but the horse quieted. "Idiot," Aandred muttered. The horse was the revenant of a supposedly noble animal, but if he rode it every night for another seven hundred years, he would still dislike it. And it would never love him; unlike the dogs, it was either too stupid or too aloof to form such attachments.

Over the sally gate's lintel, the ready light went to amber, then to green. The gate slammed open. The Hunt boiled out into the starlight, the dogs belling, clattering against each other. The sound was deafening for a moment, until the dogs began to string out along the grassy track that led down into the Green Places. Aandred glanced back at Droam; the castle loomed huge and gray against the stars, its thousand twisted towers like spines on an angry hedge-hog's back. For a moment, Aandred's vision grew dim, such was the force of his hatred. He shuddered, wrenched himself straight in the saddle, and gave his attention to the Hunt.

Aandred did not love the horse, but he still loved to ride. His death and revenancy seven hundred years before had narrowed the range of his pleasures, and time had worn away much of what was left, but this was still good. To pound along in the wake of a dozen dogs under the black sky, the cool wind of his passage blowing back the metallic strands of his hair and billowing his great cape, the ground whipping past, the eager sounds of the pack filling his ears . . . it was still good. He might have laughed, but his laughter was a mad roar, suitable to the Master of the Hunt. It no longer pleased him.

Droam's voice filled his head again. "Down to the windward beach, Aandred. That's where the troll saw them come ashore."

Aandred touched the pommel of his saddle, and Crimson, the pack leader, veered off onto the trail that led down to the sea. The trail traversed a crumbling bluff, frequently disappearing in washouts. The Hunt leaped the gaps with reckless abandon. Aandred delighted in the risk. Should the horse fail to keep its footing, sharp rocks waited in the surf below; the fall was great enough to burst open even Aandred's metal body. He shouted with pleasure, but then he thought of the dogs, and his pleasure evaporated, replaced by concern. He touched the pommel again, and Crimson slowed, ran more carefully. "Good dog," Aandred whispered.

When they reached the hard sand at the foot of the cliff, he let the dogs stretch again, and they sent up a fierce baying. The Hunt thundered north on the narrow beach; the red moon rose over the Sea of Islands.

Aandred had almost forgotten his purpose, when Droam spoke again. "Listen—here are your instructions, Aandred," the castle said. "Kill them all, except for one. Keep one alive, for me to question."

Aandred frowned. "What weapons will they have?" he asked, thinking of the dogs. He wondered why it had not occurred to him to ask before. *I've been dead too long*, he thought.

"Nothing for you to be concerned about. No energy weapons, no high explosives. They won't have had time to dig traps, rig deadfalls. A simple job; see that you make no mistakes."

Aandred ground his chromed teeth together. Droam's arrogance still enraged him, even after all the years. It was a remarkable phenomenon, when he thought how pale most of the other emotions had grown for him. Still, he did Droam's bidding, he muted the belling of the pack, and adjusted the horse so that it ran on muffling cushions of air. The night went silent.

When they reached the place where the prey had come from the sea, the dogs swirled around the base of the cliff like a steel wave. They quickly found the cave where the boat was hidden, and dragged the craft out into the starlight, snapping and tearing. In moments, it was a tangle of splinters. Aandred was a little sorry. In his time as a man, he had been pleasurably acquainted with boats, and this one had seemed a well-made, graceful one.

The dogs caught the scent, raced down the beach to a place where a small waterfall spilled through the branches of a dead juniper. Here the cliff was divided by a gully that reached back into the headland. The dogs swarmed up the narrow defile; with a great bound, the horse carried Aandred after them.

The darkness in the gully was dense, and Aandred lowered his visual range into the infrared. The dogs became churning red swirls in the blackness; their exhaust louvers glowed brightly. He considered his instructions. When they came upon the prey, he must act instantly, or Droam wouldn't get its prisoner. The dogs were enthusiastic; they often broke teeth on the armored flanks of the revenant stags that were their customary prey. Flesh and bone were so soft, in comparison.

They reached the top of the gully and broke out onto an open heath. A quarter mile away loomed the edge of the Dimlorn Woods.

Aandred slowed the dogs again, fed a little more power to the horse. When he had drawn even with Crimson, he glanced aside at the pack leader. Crimson rolled a puzzled eye at him, seemed to be asking a silent question.

"Sorry, puppy," Aandred whispered. "Just this once."

Aandred reached the edge of the trees fifty meters ahead of the dogs. He charged along the dim path, and seconds later reached the clearing where the prey was camped. He burst through the briars that hedged the open space, and half a dozen of the Bonepickers turned at the sound. They'd sheltered under a low-hanging black willow, except for the one who stood guard in the middle of the clearing. That one, a tall, thin man, leveled a crossbow at Aandred and fired.

The bolt hit his cheek and sang away into the trees. Aandred roared with pain; the bolt had left no more than a shiny nick in the metal, but the metal was thickly impregnated with pseudonerve endings. He felt as if his cheek had been torn open; he twitched the reins and rode the man down.

When Aandred had passed, the guard was a bloody tatter, tumbling in his wake.

The others still moved slowly: three of them crawling for the concealment of the trees, two of them still sitting stupidly under the willow. Only one had gained her feet, a woman dressed in ragged fringes. Instead of fleeing, she started forward, swinging some sort of club at Aandred. Because she was most convenient, he veered in her direction. The club glanced harmlessly from the shoulder of the horse, and in the next instant, Aandred scooped her up and rode crashing into the black willow. The two slowest Pickers died then, as the horse pranced and stamped, disengaging itself from the tree.

The dogs arrived, still silent, pouring through the clearing. The horse reared in startlement, and Aandred nearly dropped the woman into the pack. Perversely, she squirmed and twisted. His metal hands tightened. She gasped and became very still. "Good," he whispered, backing the horse away from the willow. "Droam doesn't need you healthy, just alive."

As he spoke, the dogs found the remaining Pickers, and brief screams came from the darkness under the trees. It was over in a moment, and the dogs came trotting back into the clearing, their muzzles dripping black in the starlight.

The horse danced sideways, its hooves plopping unpleasantly through the guard's remains, and the woman sobbed once, a brief, shocking sound. Aandred administered another monitory blow to the back of the horse's head. "Cursed creature," he muttered; then he wheeled and rode back out of the Dimlorn Woods, leaving the mess for the trolls to clean up. Long years had passed since their last real manroast. There would be no guests to taste the meat, but the trolls would enjoy the ritual. He supposed they would be grateful.

He would find their gratitude odious. Of all the revenants that haunted Castle Droam, the trolls seemed to have sunk the deepest into their ugly souls.

Out on the heath, he took the trail that led along the clifftop. The dogs were relaxed now; they cavorted, barked, nipped playfully at each other. Aandred enjoyed their pleasure. He reined in for a moment, looked out at the fairy pavilion that perched on the craggy seastack a hundred meters offshore. A spidery bridge arced gracefully out to the pavilion. Tiny lights sparkled its length, a pretty sight. The black water that swirled beneath the bridge hid the sea troll who had seen the Bonepickers land their boat.

The woman lying across his saddlebow stirred. He noticed that she had a narrow, muscular waist, under the rags. She still had not spoken a word. He wondered if she were capable of speech. If so, surely she would wish to curse him. He shrugged, cantered on.

She was still silent when the Hunt returned up the long, grassy hill below Droam. The gate flew open before they reached it, and the dogs streamed inside. Aandred followed more sedately. His captive chose that moment to renew her struggles. He gave her a shake as he passed within, and she went limp. He felt a distant apprehension; Droam would be severe with him if the woman died before the castle could put her to the question.

Then he had a vivid vision of what she must have felt, approaching the gate—the dark fanged maw of Droam, opening to swallow her forever. He shook his head. *Foolishness,* he thought. *Perhaps I grow decrepit; perhaps I'll wear out someday, after all.*

The dogs followed as he carried her up to Droam's audience hall. Droam would have preferred that he leave the dogs in their kennels. He took them partly to prickle Droam, but mostly because the dogs spent far too much time in the kennels. They took such pleasure in being allowed to accompany him. And they were well-behaved; they could not foul the shining corridors, after all, nor would they frighten any guests. No guests had come to Droam in four hundred years.

The dogs might frighten the other revenants who haunted the castle, but Aandred did not care about *them.*

The woman's body was rigid, but she kept her eyes shut. "You might as well see," he said. "Why go to your end in darkness?"

Her eyes opened. They were wide and green, wild with hate and grief, and Aandred wished he had not spoken. An unpleasant emotion seeped into him. He came to an abrupt stop, and the dogs pressed against his legs, confused. What was he feeling? The emotion was one he had felt too long ago to identify now. Was this guilt? Pity? *Absurd,* he thought, and strode on.

On the second landing of the broad staircase that led from the Silver Ballroom to Droam's audience hall, he met Merm the Troll King.

Merm pressed back against the rubyglass wall, watching the dogs with a trace of apprehension. Merm wore a particularly ugly hulk: broad and squat, with skin of warty gray-green plastic, a pointed head, and small, doughy features. His mouth was loose and red, and he peered at Aandred's burden with glittering eyes. "Meat for the fires, eh?" Merm asked.

Aandred felt a vast distaste. He choked back a reply as he passed; what was the point? Merm was as he was.

Merm made as if to follow, but the dogs, sensing their master's animosity, turned and showed bloody teeth to the troll. Merm turned away, but not before Aandred saw the hatred in his face.

We all hate each other, he thought. *And why not? We are all hateful creatures here.*

At the top of the stairs, three elfish women blocked his way. Their hulks seemed carved from gemstone—translucent, but in some clever manner hiding the machinery within, so that the rich light of the chandeliers glowed through them. They glittered like cold, extravagant jewels, and that was how they saw themselves. Despite this appearance, their crystal skins were soft and warm to touch. He knew this because he had touched each of them more times than he could remember. Droam permitted its devices certain pleasures, as reward for efficient functioning.

"Look!" cried Amethyst, pointing with a slim, elegant finger. "A flesh-woman! Where did you find her? What will you do with her? Does Droam know? You naughty thing."

"Ooh," shrieked Citrine. "Be careful, Aandred. Your equipment will rust off, if you're not careful where you put it. After, come to me. I have an oilcan for you—you know where."

Garnet was the least frivolous of the three. "Disgusting," she said. She stepped close, pushed the Bonepicker's tangled black hair aside, looked at the white face. "She's not ugly, for a fact. When Droam is done with her, give her to us for a time. Before you give her to the trolls. We'll dress her as a guest; we'll practice our pleasing. It will be amusing—like old times, before Droam became unfashionable." Her dark, lovely face glowed with a hunger too ancient to ever be satisfied.

Aandred pushed past them without speaking, though the dogs snarled and whined. He heard their laughter, like horrid little silver bells, as he carried the woman through heavy doors of burnished metal, into the audience room.

At the midpoint of the tall, narrow hall, a circular pit glowed—Droam's prime logic nexus. At the far end, intricately colored windows flanked a platform. There the King-Under-the-Hill slouched on its throne under a patina of cobwebs and dust. Of all the hulks in Droam, this one alone carried no revenant personality; this was the voice of Droam. Formerly, Droam would take possession of the hulk each night and go down to the banquet hall to dine with its most important guests. There it would press the flesh, sample the cuisine, make witty conversation, ensure that each guest was luxuriously satisfied, and in general promote the smooth function-

190 ◆ Ray Aldridge

ing of the castle. But now Droam had no reason to use the hulk, and Aandred was surprised when it stood and stepped down from the platform. In a moment, repellor fields had cleansed it of the detritus of years.

The hulk was built in the shape of an elfish god; it was the most beautiful object in Droam. Its skin was a lambent silver, washed with a haze of gold, sparkled with a million tiny lights, as if covered with minute scales. It wore stately garments, gray silk and white linen, trimmed with the glossy crimson fur of the spotted seaweasel. Its eyes were magenta coals, and its perfect features were quirked in slight annoyance. "Must you take your animals everywhere?" The voice was sweet and smooth.

"It does no harm." Aandred hated the defensive sound in his voice. Droam could at its whim punish its possessions with searing pain, more terrible than anything Aandred had felt as a man.

"Perhaps. Still, they distract me, with their fidgeting, their scratching, their snuffling. Take them out, but first give me the Picker. When you've put them out, come back, and we'll get to our business."

Aandred held out the woman; the glorious hulk took her in careless arms. Her eyes stared from one to the other, huge. Aandred turned away, whistled to the dogs. Outside, he motioned, and they clanked to the floor. "Stay," he ordered, and pulled the great doors shut.

As he walked back up the hall, he glanced down into the logic nexus. Hot light boiled there, along the tangled web of macromolecules that held Droam's intellect. He wished briefly for a small burnbomb; immediately suppressed the thought. It did no good to dream.

Arriving at the throne, he looked at the hulk's beautiful face, and was thankful that his own coarse features were fixed in a permanent mask of mad enthusiasm. Droam would react vindictively, should it ever detect his murderous inclinations.

"Bring the probe," Droam instructed. The Picker was struggling feebly; Droam took no notice.

Aandred fetched the probe from behind the screen of silver lace. The machine was dusty, but it sprang to life when he opened its master touch-panel. Myriad telltales glowed on the black surface, the visualizer displayed the ready signal, and the restraint chair opened like a skeletal flower to receive the woman. She whimpered, sobbed, but did not plead. He helped Droam clamp her in securely, then stood back.

While Droam fussed with the machine, establishing baselines for its investigations, Aandred remembered. In times past, a guest might attempt to depart the island without settling his bill. If the guest were of no great importance or influence, Droam would order Aandred to bring the guest here, where Droam would use the probe to uncover sufficient of the guest's assets to satisfy his account. Ah, those were the days, when Aandred still maintained the illusion that his revenancy served some meaningful purpose. *How foolish of me*, he thought blackly. *Dead is dead.*

The woman's eyes went dreamy; her taut face relaxed. The visualizer bloomed with dark shapes; remembered sensations floated from the empathic emanator, sinking into Aandred's mind.

. . . a muffled thunder from the edge of the woods. A crashing, then the emergence of a nightmare shape, too terrible to grasp. A monstrous man-shape on a huge black horse . . . the eyes of the horse: yellow fire. Jebaum fires his crossbow; the monster roars, an ear-hurting sound, and smashes Jebaum to rags. Kill it, kill it, the hateful thing, rage red as blood. An impact, befuddlement, suspension, a sight more terrible yet. Skeletal dog-things, gleaming metal in the night, swarming across the clearing, bounding with a hideous vitality, jaws snapping, eyes burning bright. . . .

Aandred turned away, and Droam made a fretful sound, slapped at the touchboard. "Effective, Huntsman," Droam said. "But irrelevant, now, to my needs."

Droam tapped the telltales, and the pattern twinkled, shifted.

. . . the warm, sweet scent of Mother's breasts. A viewpoint of such golden clarity, such liquid focus, as to be unmistakably that of a very young child. A caress from Mother's hand, a soft murmur, the touch of sunlight on new skin. A crowing laugh. . . .

Droam tried again.

. . . a summer night, dense with the smell of the sea. Darkness on the beach, small festival fires glowing in the distance. Running over the white dunes with Mondeaux in pursuit. His hands when he caught her, hard from his work with the nets, gentle where they touched her. His breath, spicy with wine and desire. The hammering of her heart when he laid her down on his tattered cloak, the heat that flared when they touched, skin to skin, all down her long length. . . .

Aandred had no heart to hammer, but he felt the pressure of some great unknown emotion, pushing from somewhere, desperate to escape. He shut his eyes, clenched his fists, swayed there for a moment until the mysterious sensation eased. Droam noticed nothing. The beautiful mask was distorted by frustration. "Useless, useless. . . . I'm getting nothing but tangential deep memory. Nothing recent except for her capture; some trauma thwarts me. What's wrong with her?"

Aandred looked at Droam, full of weary astonishment. "What can it be? A mystery! Wait, a notion occurs to me—probably a foolish one—could it have anything to do with the fact that I murdered six of her friends an hour ago?"

Droam gave him a long, cool look. "You indulge your sense of humor dangerously, Huntsman."

Astonishment drained away, leaving only weariness. "My apologies."

"But of course you are correct," Droam said. "She requires time to recover her faculties. I give her into your safekeeping. Cleanse her of vermin; feed and water her; see that no harm befalls her."

"Where can *I* keep her? Would it not be better to give her into the care of one of those who are experienced at guesting? Garnet has volunteered." As soon as he had spoken, Aandred regretted his words, remembering Garnet's face.

But Droam rejected his suggestion. "Keep her in the kennels; surely you have more than one empty run? As to Garnet and the other servitors—I fear they have gone a bit strange over these years of inactivity. When we reopen, I may well be forced to replace them with fresh revenants. Besides, the Picker is a prisoner, not a guest."

Droam's hulk froze; the light went out of its glorious eyes. Aandred extricated the unconscious woman from the probe's chair. Her head fell back; her arms hung limply; her lips had a bluish cast. Inexplicably, he was filled by a sudden fear that she was dead—sometimes guests would not survive Droam's questioning. He held her closer. Breath warmed his damaged cheek; he detected a pulse at the base of her throat. Reassured, he went out to the waiting dogs.

The kennel consisted of a large common area, with the dogs' individual runs along one long wall, and the door into Aandred's small, bare apartment on the other. The walls were unadorned granite, windowless, but well-lit by ceiling light tubes. At one end stood a broad worktable and a bank of diagnostic equipment.

He brought the woman into his quarters and laid her in the wall niche in which he slept away his inactive time, then locked the dogs in their runs.

Aandred considered. How to bathe her? No human facilities existed in the castle's crew quarters; Aandred would wash away the dust of his ride under a spray of oil-rich solvent. He almost decided to leave her as she was, but Droam's instructions had been explicit.

Eventually he carried her up to the level where live prostitutes had once been kept, for the use of those guests prohibited by religion or prejudice from copulating with the castle's revenants. The whores were four hundred years gone, but the taps still flowed clean water and nutrient broth.

He set her down on a bed of greasy plastic, stripped away her fringed leathers. The leather was well-tanned and supple, he noticed, not the work of primitives. Still, he pitched it fastidiously down the refuse chute.

When she was naked, he looked at her until his curiosity was satisfied. How long since he had seen a flesh-and-blood woman? He could not remember. She was tall, with small breasts and long, muscular thighs. Her body was imperfect, of course; old silvery scars marked one flank, perhaps the long-healed claw marks of some wild beast. Her pale skin was smooth, though nothing like the silken gloss of the revenant women who staffed the castle. Bruises flowered here and there, where Aandred had gripped her. Her hair . . . her hair was probably magnificent, though now it was a black tangle that obscured her features. He bent over her, parted her air, searched for parasites. He was somewhat surprised to find none.

Aandred sponged her down with disinfectant solution, then dried her carefully. Strangely, he did not resent the domestic role into which Droam had thrust him. There was a certain fascination in touching the flesh of a living woman.

When he was done, he prowled around the apartment. Most of the clothing in the closet disintegrated into reeking dust at his touch, except for a coverall woven of sturdier synthetic. He took it. He went to the vanity, opened a drawer. A faint ancient perfume still clung miraculously to the combs and brushes. On an impulse, he picked up a comb, slipped it into a pocket of the coveralls. He looked up; the mirror showed him a mad black face, red glaring eyes, glittering teeth. *I'm an ugly one*, he thought ruefully.

He carried her back down to the kennel. On the way, she shifted in his arms, and he realized she had awakened, but she kept her eyes shut, her limbs slack.

He put her in dead Cerulean's run, on the mat of artificial grass; beside her he laid the coverall. Cerulean had been one of his favorites, until the night she had fallen down a well and ruptured vital elements of her personality skein. Her empty hulk still lay on the worktable in the kennel.

Aandred shut the grating, thumbed the lock. He took two stainless pans from a locker and went back up to the apartment. One he filled with water, the other with thick broth.

Back in the kennel, he slid the pans through the grating. "Here," he said. "Drink, eat. You'll need your strength."

She lay still, her back to him.

He shrugged. "Do as you like, then. No one will molest you here; you're safe for a time." He opened his forearm and put the dogs to sleep, so that they would not frighten her. They froze, their bright eyes dimming, and Aandred went into his quarters.

Aandred's internal timer awakened him from that vague dreamless state that served him for sleep. He unplugged the recharge cable and swung himself from the niche; his feet clanged to the floor. Through his door came a squeak of fear—then a metallic rattle.

Aandred went swiftly into the kennel. Merm the Troll King was crouched at the captive's grating, jabbing a long-handled meat fork at her. She was pressed back into the far corner, just out of Merm's reach. Her eyes were blank with terror.

"Here," said Aandred. "What's this?" *Merm dared invade his home?* He took a step toward the troll, hands clenching.

Merm's lumpy face was at first full of malicious pleasure, but that emotion rapidly drained away, to be replaced by cringing bravado. "Hello, Huntsman. Just amusing myself. Your prisoner is the talk of the castle. I had to see; the kennel door was open, and I took it to mean you were in the mood for company."

Disgust filled Aandred. "Would I ever describe you as 'company'? Get out, and in the future I'll leave a dog active in the kennel. You'll extract the proper meaning from the situation, should you wander this way again."

Merm rose slowly from the grating, holding his meat fork like a weapon. His small eyes glittered. "Droam wouldn't want you to talk so. I'm a valuable property; harm me, and you'll feel Droam's anger."

Aandred raised a trembling finger, pointed to the exit. Merm's bravado crumbled, and the troll scuttled away. At the door, Merm cast a bright, poisonous look over his shoulder, a look that included Aandred, the dogs, and the prisoner.

Aandred stepped to the grating, looked in at the prisoner. She had donned the coverall and made use of the comb. Her hair *was* quite lovely, a thick, silken mane framing a face of unconventional beauty. Her eyes, fixed unblinkingly on him, were huge with apprehension, but Aandred saw that they would still be large, even in less fearful circumstances. Her cheekbones were a bit too sharp, her chin sturdy, her mouth wide.

Aandred saw that food and water were untouched. "Are you not thirsty? Hungry?"

Her eyes veiled, and she looked away.

"Ah," said Aandred. "I understand. You fear poison, or drugs. Am I right? Don't concern yourself. The probe is more effective than any drug, and when Droam wants you dead, it has a million ways to do the deed."

He was surprised when she replied; he had almost decided she was a mute. "What of you, iron thing? You're a skillful murderer, as you proved last night. Do you want me dead? How many ways do you have to do the deed?" She spoke bitterly, but her voice was low and soft, almost a whisper. Her accent was unfamiliar.

He nearly laughed his terrible laugh, but caught himself in time. For some reason, he didn't want to frighten her. "No. No longer do I lust for anything's blood. Except, perhaps, for Merm's, though he has none to spill." *And of course, Droam's.* "Merm is that smelly green heap I just threatened from my kennel, the one who wanted to test you with his fork."

She shuddered. "Him. I thought *you* the ugliest thing I'd ever seen, until I saw him. Are there none but gods and demons in this place?"

"God? Oh, I see. You mean Droam's pretty hulk? I assure you, that was no god, only a better-looking puppet than I, carved of richer material."

She seemed to fall into deep thought, and said no more. After a bit, she lifted the water bowl and drank deeply. Aandred watched her, wondering. She was remarkably self-possessed, considering recent events. Had the human race changed so much, or was she simply an unusual woman?

Aandred activated the dogs, and they rose from their sleeping mats, tails wagging. He fed them their morning pseudofood, a ritual they never tired of. It served no purpose beyond providing them with a pleasurable stimulus. The pseudofood passed through them unchanged, to be reinvested with odor and taste and then fed to them again.

When the dogs had finished their breakfast, he decided to repair Umber's olfactory transducer. He released Umber from her run, and she leaped joyfully about him. The prisoner's face was pale. Aandred shook his head; her apprehension was natural enough. What would it be like, to die torn by the dogs? His own death had been easy: the prick of the injection, torpor, then oblivion.

Aandred moved Cerulean's empty hulk aside, feeling a small, familiar twinge of sorrow. He whistled at Umber, snapped his fingers. She jumped nimbly to the insulated tabletop, waited with her usual good humor. "Good girl," he said, and stroked her back. She wriggled ecstatically. He opened his forearm and touched a switch. She became a graceful statue, and he applied a screwdriver to the access panel on her brisket.

The transducer was mounted on a swing-out card. He eased it out, applied the point of an analyzer to various diagnostic nodes. The malfunction became clear: a loose memory flake. He popped it out, examined the contact edge, reseated it.

When he had buttoned Umber's chassis and restored her to active mode, the telltale on his forearm burned a steady green. Umber bounced off the table, raced around the kennel, barked her mechanical bark. "Better, girl?" asked Aandred.

His captive pressed against the grating, watching. "You speak oddly for a machine," she said.

"That's because we're not entirely machines," he said. "Not entirely."

"What do you mean?"

He took a stool, sat beside the grating. She drew back slightly; she controlled her fear well. "Once upon a time, we were all living creatures, alive as you," he said. "Me, the dogs, even the rats in the dungeons. Even Merm. All once alive, all now dead—except for Droam, who is indeed a machine."

Aandred moved his stool a little closer to the grating, leaned toward the bars. She didn't move away, though her eyes narrowed. "Shall I explain?" he asked. "If I do, what will you trade for this information?" When he had spoken, he felt a trickle of shame. Why was he trying to frighten her? *An ugly old habit*, he thought. She would, soon enough, know terror, when Droam gave her to the trolls, and then she would be dead. "Never mind. Just tell me your name—that will be sufficient."

She stared at him for a long moment. "What harm can it do? My name is Sundee Gareaux." She lifted her chin, gazed into his face with cold eyes, as if daring him to sneer.

Her courage is pleasing, he thought, and then he said, "Listen."

He told of the beginning, seven hundred years past. SeedCorp had come to the Sea of Islands and built Droam, an expensive resort for a special kind of guest, those fascinated by certain legends of Old Earth. Droam's bulk covered several hectares; its towers rose three hundred feet above the island's highest hill. The builders endowed Droam with a potent macromolecular intelligence, and then they conceived their grand scheme.

"Oh, it was a wonderful idea," Aandred muttered. "At first they intended to staff Droam with robots in the shape of the Ancient Folk of Old Earth: elves, trolls, fairies, dwarfs, wizards, and witches. But one of them, the cleverest one . . . she was supervising the building of the castle when the idea came to her. Robots had one flaw—they were predictable. Why, a guest might come to Droam dozens of times over his lifetime. Would boredom set in, if the staff never changed their behavior, never acted irrationally, never displayed any human flaws or foibles? Of course."

Sundee Gareaux's face was intent. "And so . . . ?"

"And so they decided to purchase revenant personalities to ride the hulks."

"What does it mean . . . revenant?"

"Ghosts. We're all ghosts in Droam. The dogs, for example . . . the ghosts of puppies who died for Droam seven hundred years ago. Put to death—painlessly, I'm sure—and their little souls recorded for the Hunt."

Revulsion stained her eyes. "That is how you came to be what you are? You were killed to fill the machine?"

"Not exactly." He chuckled rustily. "Oh, one or two of the human revenants were bargained for that way—dying men and women who sold themselves for money to leave to their families, and for a chance at some sort of continued life. But most of us are executed criminals, our personalities auctioned to defray the costs of our crime."

The revulsion spread to her mouth. "And were you always a murderer, then?"

He sat and looked at her for a time, until she turned away uneasily. Umber whined and nudged his leg, distressed. Finally Aandred answered. "Of course. I was a famous pirate, I laired on Sook, I went forth with my armada and stole worlds, and always, I laughed. Oh, I was a mighty killer in those days; I destroyed thousands and never thought of it again." He looked away, and red memory blinded him. "But I've had time to think."

"Of what? Last night you and your creatures killed easily enough."

He saw that tears trembled in her eyes. "Droam commands me. Should I defy the castle to spare a band of raggedy Bonepickers? I would be ended instantly. Fail-safes, deadman switches are built into all our hulks; after all, Droam couldn't have the tourists terrorized by criminal zombies, should we decide to run amok. Eh?" He spoke sadly. "It's true that I'm dead already. Still, it's the only sort of life I'll ever have, and I'm somewhat reluctant to give it up."

She spoke in a dreary voice. "I see. So, what happened to the guests?"

He gripped the grating. The mesh buckled under the pressure of his hands. "Fashions changed, oh, about four hundred years ago. Suddenly Droam was passé. The tourists stopped coming, and now we're forgotten. Droam remains convinced that they will come again; I know better. There were other resorts in the Sea of Islands—all dead now. Of course, you know this, you Bonepickers; you survive in the debris of their passing. Droam was always the strongest of them. It may well resist your attacks forever. Such is its intention."

"Attacks?" She was contemptuous. "We attacked no one. We landed to explore, nothing more. The island has plenty of empty land; why should we not farm it? Every year there are more children, and we must feed them. We wouldn't have injured your precious castle. Why would we bother?"

Aandred laughed at her audacity. "What a notion! Turnip patches in the Vale of Lights, Bonepickers gathering mushrooms in the Dimlorn Woods. Urchins fishing in the River Dark. Droam won't be amused."

Her eyes flashed dangerously. "I've told you my name; do you have a name?"

"Droam calls me Huntsman. But I had another name when I was a man." He paused. "Aandred, I was. A glorious, wicked name once. Now? Meaningless. . . ." His voice had fallen to a wistful whisper.

"I'd almost forgotten it," he lied.

He released the other dogs from their runs, and they tumbled about the common room in a frenzy of delight. Crimson sniffed at the prisoner's grating, wagged his tail, and trotted away. Aandred saw that her face was white. "Don't be afraid," he said. "They wouldn't hurt you now, unless you run."

She seemed unconvinced. "Watch, this is pretty," he said, opening the storage niche built into his right hip. He brought out their favorite toy, a magical ball containing a tiny mechanical homunculus; he had long ago filched it from one of the tower wizards. He tossed it; it rolled along the floor, flashing blue lights, emitting comical squeaks and puffs of violet smoke. The dogs leaped after it joyfully. Sienna reached it first, brought it back to him proudly, ignoring the jealous nips of the others. He kicked it away again, setting of another manic pursuit.

In half an hour, they were bored, and they settled about Aandred. They seemed fascinated by the prisoner; they watched her intently, eyes bright, segmented silver tongues lolling from their mouths.

Sundee Gareaux watched them in equal fascination. "They have a strange look in their eyes," she said. "As if they know some secret."

"Well, they aren't ordinary dogs. They were intelligent puppies when they were flesh, and even a dog can learn many things in seven hundred years." *Perhaps*, he thought, *more than a man*. "I often wonder how much they understand," he mused, stroking Umber's head. "Still, they *are* only dogs."

She was silent for a time, watching the dogs at their play. Then she looked up at him with confused eyes. "They don't seem so terrible now. How very strange, when just last night they killed. . . . Then your dogs were hideous, nightmares." Her mouth twisted. "Now I see grace, even a sort of beauty."

"Of course they're beautiful," he said fiercely. "Of all Droam's creatures, they are the finest and cleanest. You shouldn't blame them for your friends' deaths. They do only what they are bred and trained to do. The dogs would chase a ball from the hand of a Picker as readily as they chase it from mine."

Aandred gave his attention to the dogs for a while. When he next glanced in at the prisoner, she lay on the mat, her back to him, apparently asleep.

The day passed as a hundred thousand other days had passed. Aandred played with the dogs and thought about his former life, the lovely bad old days. But the memories had worn thin, as if from too much remembering, and he found his thoughts straying to the Picker woman. What had her life been? he wondered. She had been born in a profoundly regressed culture, the descendants of lost guests and escaped slaves, on a backwater world where the starboats no longer called. She could hope for no more than a lifetime of suffering and an early death. She would never know the wonders of the human galaxy; she would never walk the gilded halls of Dilvermoon or the dirty corridors of Beasterheim, would never see a world from space, like a jewel on the richest velvet, would never experience the thousand joyful luxuries that he had taken for granted in his life as a man.

He shook his head. *Pointless maundering*. Sundee Gareaux no doubt valued her life, such as it was, as much as he valued his own synthetic existence. *Or more*, he thought darkly, but the notion frightened him, and he pushed it aside. *A shame that she must end her life as a troll's plaything*. That thought made him angry. He resolved to break her neck before he gave her to Merm, as Droam would certainly order him to do. He could spare her that horror.

As day passed into evening, the annunciator chimed. Droam's

voice sounded from the wall speaker and in his head, a disorienting sensation. "Huntsman. Bring your prisoner to the audience hall."

Aandred found a jeweled leash in a locker he had not opened in a hundred years. "Come," he said to Sundee Gareaux. "You must wear this. Droam will expect me to deliver you without difficulties."

Her eyes were huge, and she hung back. "What if I promise not to run?"

"I'm sorry," he said. "Were I you, I would promise anything and run at the first opportunity. You may be more agile than I, and though you could never escape the castle, you might evade me for a time. Droam would soothe its impatience with my pain."

She bowed her head, and he locked the collar around her neck. The dogs jumped against the gratings of their runs and implored him to take them, too. "Be good, puppies," he said. "You can't go this time. I'll be back soon."

They walked through the bright corridors of the castle, the leash slack between them. Sundee Gareaux looked about curiously. Few of the castle's staff were abroad so early in the evening, but they passed a party of dwarf janitors armed with mop buckets and sonic brooms, a white-bearded wizard and his youthful assistant, three trolls who stood in a dark doorway and sniggered, a red-haired witch magnificent in the glittering habit of the Dark Mystery. His prisoner studied each passerby closely.

"All dead," she said in a marveling voice.

"In a sense. They believe themselves to be alive." To his amazement, he felt slightly defensive.

"I'm bewildered," she said. "But they don't seem to be enjoying their immortality; they all wear sad, bitter faces."

"You don't see why?" The long, empty years weighed on him. "I'll explain, so you won't think us the Fortunate Folk." *It could be worse for you, Sundee Gareaux,* he thought. *Perhaps you'll find your own fate more acceptable if I tell you about us.*

"Droam is staffed by a few more than three thousand human revenants. Is there a Picker village that big? No? Does that seem a great many people to you?" He laughed a booming laugh, and she winced. "Oh, it would be, if our halflives lasted no longer than yours. Seventy years, eighty—is that a good span for a Picker? We've been together here in Droam for seven hundred years. Can you imagine? Imagine! And consider who we are. Murderers, rapists, torturers, those who stole things so precious that they were put to death for it. Merm, for example, was a high sheriff. He enslaved young boys and girls with spurious charges, used them brutally, and when they were worn out, he buried their bodies on his prison farm. He swears they found only a fraction of his victims, and they found a thousand! Do you wonder at the evil you see in his face?"

Sundee Gareaux watched him with a mixture of pity and horror, her face white, her lips bloodless.

He continued, pushed by a passion he had thought worn away forever.

"Did you think I exaggerated my crimes? No! And I was a paragon of nobility, compared to many here in Droam: I stole only from the wealthy; I used violence only on the violent; I attacked only those who could defend themselves. I admit I was a quixotic pirate, but I did not wish to think of myself as a monster. Hah!" Had he tear ducts, he might have cried; instead he slammed his fist against the wall. The smooth marble facing shattered explosively, revealing the rough concrete beneath.

She stood at the farthest extent of the leash, hands pressed to her mouth. A chip of marble had nicked her cheek and caused a small trickle of blood.

"I'm sorry," he said. "I've become overexcited. I'll calm myself; don't be afraid."

"Why don't you run away?" For the first time, her voice carried no undertone of hatred. "Surely there are boats."

"Oh yes. Fairy boats drift on the River Dark, and the Elf King's funeral galley hangs in slings under his pavilion on the Quiet Shore. You don't understand. Droam knows where each of us is at all times; with a thought, it could terminate me. Or punish me terribly. And, of course, we cannot preserve our personalities without Droam; without access to Droam's refresher circuits and energy nodes, we would all fade away. If I left or Droam were destroyed— in five years or ten, I'd be gone."

"Does it know your thoughts, too?"

"No. We have that much privacy. It can speak directly to our minds; but to reply, we must direct our thoughts into a special mode. This is true only because so many direct linkages would spread Droam's intellect too thin; it might diffuse away into noth-ing. Though for a fact there's been some migration; some of our darkness has seeped into Droam over the years." He sighed.

They walked on in silence. When they were nearly to the audience hall, she spoke again. "I still don't understand. Why did they fill their resort with horrors?"

"They aimed for a quality of 'dark glamour'; they succeeded, but that sort of thing went out of vogue. . . ."

In the audience hall, she was silent until they approached the nexus pit. "What is it?" she asked.

"Droam. Its brain, in essence." He detected a sudden tension in her body, and tightened his grip on the leash. "Restrain yourself, Sundee Gareaux. What you're considering would do no good. Look carefully; see how the force bubble diffracts the light? If you jump over the wall, the bubble will prevent you from falling onto the nexus, unless you now weigh ten times what you weighed when last I carried you. That much mass might, I think, overload the bubble." He tugged at the leash. "Besides, if you kill Droam, I will die. You wouldn't want that on your conscience." He meant it as a joke, but her face was full of baffled despair.

Droam's hulk waited beside the probe. "Ah," it said. "Our guest." ·

The probe confirmed Droam's worst fears. Sundee Gareaux's tribe was desperate; they had no choice but to try to occupy the island. Aandred watched the deliberations of several village councils, through Sundee Gareaux's eyes. Each group of grim old men and women came to the same conclusion: settlers would be sent to the island they called Neverland, despite the terrifying legends.

Aandred learned an interesting thing about Sundee Gareaux: she was the leading tribal authority on the decaying synthetic ecologies that infested the Sea of Islands. So she had been chosen to go ashore with the first exploratory party.

. . . she stood on the beach, holding her husband tight, forcing back tears for his sake. "Don't worry; we'll be fine. No one's been to Neverland for eighty years or more. The monsters have probably all broken down—entropy's on our side." She looked down at her son, a sturdy two-year-old with flame-red hair and a truculent expression. "You'll be in more danger than I will, I think. Be careful, and keep a close eye on our own little monster." She ruffled the fiery hair, picked the child up for a last hug. He clung to her, though ordinarily he would have struggled to escape. His father pulled him gently away, and she waded through the surf to the waiting boat. She waved, until they crossed the reef into blue water and the figures on the beach were lost in the light. . . .

Once again Aandred found himself in the grip of some powerful alien emotion. It was so difficult to identify, without the somatic tags that living humans took for granted. Were he alive, would he feel tears on his cheeks, would he feel a great pressure in his throat, would his chest heave with suppressed sobs? He could not say, but he was almost blind with it, whatever it was. He looked down at Sundee Gareaux's pale, dreaming face, and the pressure of the unknown emotion increased to an unbearable level.

He shuddered. Droam was speaking to him. ". . . so I'll leave the organization of the teams to you—this was your area of expertise, not so? We'll take the galley, knock them back one island at a time. We'll kill as many as we can, burn the fields, blow up the reefs, poison the wells. We won't get them all, of course, but it will be many generations before they breed back enough to be dangerous."

The situation becomes unreal, Aandred thought. He felt like a shadow in a tragic farce. "A large undertaking," he muttered.

"But necessary. Report your progress tomorrow; be ready to sail in three days."

"What of the woman?" he asked, before he thought.

"Give her to Merm and his crew. Call it incentive, if you like." Droam went still and spoke no more.

Aandred carried her slowly down through the castle. He tried to think, but he could see no way out. He reached the kennel, shut the portal behind him, laid her on the worktable. She was pale, but a pulse beat strongly at the base of her throat. *Better if she'd died in the probe,* he thought. *Do it now, before she wakes; she'll never know.* He flexed his hands, cupped them around her fragile skull. *Such a shame, to destroy so lovely a vitality.*

For a long moment, he could not move. Then he thought of the trolls and their spits and fires and hooks. His resolve hardened. But before he could do the kindness, her eyes fluttered open and she looked up at him. Disconcertingly, there was no confusion in them; it was as if she understood what he meant to do. He snatched his hands away from her.

Minutes passed in charged silence. Finally she struggled to sit up. "What did I say?" she asked in a shaky voice.

"Everything. The truth."

"What will happen now?"

He looked at her, thankful for the mad mask that served him for a face. He could do her one kindness, at least: he could conceal from her the imminent death of her people. "I don't know," he answered.

"But nothing good?"

He shrugged, searched for some soft lie. His mind would not respond; in frustration, he thumped his forehead with his fists.

She huddled away, frightened. "What is it, Aandred?"

A pounding came from the portal. "Huntsman! We're here to collect our prize!" It was Merm's oily voice. The Troll King thrust open the portal and waddled into the room, followed by two of his subjects.

Merm started to push past Aandred. The troll was bright-eyed with triumph and anticipated pleasure. "What fun, what fun," Merm said, reaching out for Sundee Gareaux.

Time seemed to stop. Aandred had forever to look into her unbelieving face—the wide green eyes, the pale, taut mouth. The moment ended; he roared and threw Merm away.

The Troll King smashed into the wall, then bounced up quivering, his loose mouth working furiously. "You dare? Droam will punish you. But first we will punish you!" He drew an iron truncheon from his sash, as did his two henchmen.

The dogs pressed against their gratings, snarling. Aandred felt his rage expand, a beautiful, soundless explosion, lighting up all his dark corners. He flipped open his forearm, touched a switch, and the gratings snapped open. The dogs bounded forth, leaped on the astounded trolls. All three died before they could make another sound.

The dogs played with the tatters of plastic, the mangled steel struts, the tangles of wire and hydraulic tubing, making happy dog noises. "You see," Aandred said. "Such good dogs. So loyal." He waited, hunched over with dread, for Droam's response.

When it came, he fell among the dogs, writhing. The pain enfolded Aandred with an intensity that drove away all thought. After a timeless period, the pain eased enough for him to hear Droam's words. "Come to the hall, Huntsman. Bring your prisoner, *alive*; bring your miserable, ruinous beasts." The pain closed in for a final searing moment, then ceased.

He lay on the floor for a moment, gathering his strength, while the dogs sniffed him anxiously. Then fear drove him to his feet. "I dare not wait, Sundee Gareaux. Droam has summoned me—and you. And the dogs." A great sadness stole into him, filling the emptiness left by the pain.

He held her leash loosely, led her toward the audience hall. Her face was still white with fear, but she walked steadily, head high. "What will it do?" she asked.

"Droam will punish me," he said. The dogs sensed his mood and stayed close, casting worried looks up at him.

"How? Pain?"

That too, he thought. "It will kill dogs. It knows what I value, it knows how best to hurt me."

They paused before the tall doors of the audience hall. "What will it do to me?" she asked.

He set his hand on the great silver latch. "I think you must die, Sundee Gareaux. If I have a chance, I'll try to make it easy."

Her face crumpled, but only for an instant. Then she nodded, and her mouth lifted into a very small smile. He swung back the door, and they went inside.

At the far end, Droam's hulk paced back and forth with quick little steps. "Come," it roared, and now its voice was not so beautiful. "Come here swiftly. There are things I need to do with these hands."

Aandred glanced aside. She was shaking, but under control. *Admirable*, he thought. *Admirable*.

As they passed the glowing nexus, his hand darted into his hip compartment, came out with the magic ball. He gave himself no time to reconsider; in the same motion, he tossed it over the wall into the nexus. The tiny homunculus inside shrieked piercingly. Aandred shouted, "Fetch!"

Instantly, Droam began to kill him, and he felt his hulk collapse.

But before he was quite dead, Droam had transferred its attention to the dogs.

It was too late. One dog stiffened and spasmed in midleap, but the rest landed on the force bubble. The bubble collapsed with a flat, snapping implosion, spilling the dogs onto the surface of Droam's intellect. The scrambled after the ball, floundered through the delicate crystalline strands, shattered Droam into a cloud of glittering shards.

Aandred got to his knees, shuddering, his hands clattering against the floor. Droam's hulk had toppled and lay facedown, motionless. Inside the castle an emptiness spread, until it had swept through every niche and corner of that great pile. The first faint screams reached his ears.

A long time later, a red-haired boy of ten led his younger sister along a path through green woods. On a stone bench sat a statue of black metal. The statue's hand rested on the withers of a rusting steel dog; two similar dogs lay corroding at the statue's feet. The statue's face was mad, brutish, with horrible glaring eyes, and the little girl was frightened. "Ugly," she said.

"No," the boy said sternly. "Never say that! When we first came to Neverland, he killed a hundred monsters with his dogs and kept the rest away until they wore out. Without him, we'd all be dead."

"Well, then, why is he out here by himself?"

The boy's face was somber, as if he remembered a sorrow too deep for his years. "He got slower and slower, after the last monsters were gone. One day he came up here with the dogs he still had left. For the rest of that summer, he would wink at me when I came to see him. But in the spring, he'd stopped moving."

"That's sad."

"Yes."

After a while they turned and went back down the hill, toward their lives.

ABE LINCOLN IN McDONALD'S

◆ ◆ ◆

James Morrow

The stereotypic time-traveler returns in time to confront a famous figure. Here James Morrow reverses the stereotype to create an ironic and entertaining view of history. James Morrow is an award-winning novelist and short story writer, whose novella, "City of Truth," won a Nebula in 1993.

H e caught the last train out of 1863 and got off at the blustery December of 2009, not far from Christmas, where he walked well past the turn of the decade and, without glancing back, settled down in the fifth of July for a good look around. To be a mere tourist in this place would not suffice. No, he must get it under his skin, work it into his bones, enfold it with his soul.

In his vest pocket, pressed against his heart's grim cadence, lay the final draft of the dreadful Seward Treaty. He needed but to add his name—Jefferson Davis had already signed it on behalf of the seccessionist states—and a cleft nation would become whole. A signature, that was all, a simple "A. Lincoln."

Adjusting his string tie, he waded into the chaos grinding and snorting down Pennsylvania Avenue and began his quest for a savings bank.

"The news isn't good," came Norman Grant's terrible announcement, stabbing from the phone like a poisoned dagger. "Jimmy's test was positive."

Walter Sherman's flabby, pumpkinlike face whitened with dread. "Are you sure?" *Positive*, what a paradoxical term, so ironic in its clinical denotations: nullity, disease, doom.

"We ran two separate blood tests, followed by a fluorescent antibody check. Sorry. Poor Jim's got Blue Nile Fever."

Walter groaned. Thank God his daughter was over at the Sheridans'. Jimmy had been Tanya's main Christmas present of three years ago—he came with a special note from Santa—and her affection for the old slave ran deep. Second father, she called him. Walter never could figure out why Tanya had asked for a sexagenarian and not a whelp like most kids wanted, but who could know the mind of a preschooler?

If only one of their others had caught the lousy virus. Jimmy wasn't the usual chore-boy. Indeed, when it came to cultivating a garden, washing a rug, or painting a house, he didn't know his nose from a nine of spades. Ah, but his bond with Tanya! Jimmy was her guardian, playmate, confidant, and, yes, her teacher; Walter never ceased marveling at the great discovery of the past century—how, if you chained a whelp to a computer at the right age (no younger than two, no older than six), he'd soak up vast tracts of knowledge and subsequently pass them on to your children. Through Jimmy and Jimmy alone, Tanya had learned a formidable amount of plane geometry, music theory, American history, and Greek before ever setting foot in kindergarten.

"Prognosis?"

The doctor sighed. "Blue Nile Fever follows a predictable course. In a year or so, Jimmy's T-cell defenses will collapse, leaving him prey to a hundred opportunistic infections. What worries me, of course, is Marge's pregnancy."

A dull dread crept through Walter's white flesh. "You mean—it could hurt the baby?"

"Well, there's this policy—the Centers for Disease Control urge permanent removal of Nile-positive chattel from all households containing pregnant women."

"Removed?" Walter echoed indignantly. "I thought it didn't cross the pigmentation barrier."

"That's probably true." Grant's voice descended several registers. "But *fetuses*, Walter, know what I'm saying? *Fetuses*, with their undeveloped immune systems. We don't want to ask for trouble, not with a retrovirus."

"God, this is depressing. You really think there's a risk?"

"I'll put it this way. If my wife were pregnant—"

"I know, I know."

"Bring Jimmy down here next week, and we'll take care of it. Quick. Painless. Is Tuesday at 2:30 good?"

Of course it was good. Walter had gone into orthodontics for the flexible hours, the dearth of authentic emergencies. That, and never having to pay for his own kids' braces. "See you then," he replied, laying a hand on his shattered heart.

The President strode out of Northeast Federal Savings and Loan and continued toward the derby-hatted Capitol. Such an exquisite building—at least some of the city remained intact, all was not glass-faced offices and dull, boxy banks. "If we were still on the gold standard, this would be a more normal transaction," the assistant manager, a fool named Meade, had whined when Abe presented his coins for conversion. Not on the gold standard! A Democrat's doing, no doubt.

Luckily, the White House soothsayer had prepared Abe for the wondrous monstrosities and wrenching innovations that now assailed his senses. The self-propelled railway coaches roaring along causeways of black stone. The sky-high mechanical condors whisking travelers across the nation at hundreds of miles per hour. The dense medley of honks, bleeps, and technological growls.

So Washington was indeed living in its proper century—but what of the nation at large?

Stripped to their waists, two slave teams were busily transforming Pennsylvania Avenue, the first chopping into the asphalt with pickaxes, the second filling the gorge with huge cylindrical pipes. Their sweat-speckled backs were free of gashes and scars—hardly a surprise, as the overseers carried no whips, merely queer one-chamber pistols and portable Gatling guns.

Among the clutter at the Constitution Avenue instersection—signs, trash receptacles, small landlocked lighthouses regulating the coaches' flow—a pair of green arrows commanded Abe's notice. *Capitol Building*, announced the eastward-pointing arrow. *Lincoln Memorial*, said its opposite. His own memorial! So this particular tomorrow, the one fated by the awful Seward Treaty, would be kind to him.

The President hailed a cab. Removing his stovepipe hat, he wedged his six-foot-four frame into the passenger compartment—don't ride up front, the White House soothsayer had briefed him—and offered a cheery "Good morning."

The driver, a blowsy woman, slid back a section of the soft rubbery glass. "Lincoln, right?" she called through the opening like Pyramus talking to Thisbe. "You're supposed to be Abe Lincoln. Costume party?"

"Republican."

"Where to?"

"Boston." If any city had let itself get mired in the past, Abe figured, that city would be Boston.

"Boston, *Massachusetts?*"

"Correct."

"Hey, that's crazy, Mac. You're talking five hours at least, and that's if we push the speed limit all the way. I'd have to charge you for my return trip."

The President lifted a sack of money from his greatcoat. Even if backed only by good intentions, twentieth-century currency was aesthetically satisfying: that noble profile on the pennies, that handsome three-quarter view on the fives. As far as he could tell, he and Washington were the only ones to score twice. "How much altogether?"

"You serious? Probably four hundred dollars."

Abe peeled the driver's price from his wad and passed the bills through the window. "Take me to Boston."

"They're so adorable!" Tanya exclaimed as she and Walter strolled past Sonny's Super Slaver, a Chestnut Hill Mall emporium second only in size to the sporting goods store. "Ah, look at *that* one—those big ears!" Recently weaned babies jammed the glass cages, tumbling over themselves, clutching stuffed jackhammers and toy garden hoses. "Could we get one, Pappy?"

As Walter fixed on his daughter's face, its glow nearly made him squint. "Tanya, I've got some bad news. Jimmy's real sick."

"Sick? He looks fine."

"It's Blue Nile, honey. He could die."

"Die?" Tanya's angelic face crinkled with the effort of fighting tears. What a brave little tomato she was. "Soon?"

"Soon." Walter's throat swelled like a broken ankle. "Tell you what. Let's go pick out a whelp right now. We'll have them put it aside until. . . ."

"Until Jimmy"—a wrenching gulp—"goes away?"

"Uh-huh."

"Poor Jimmy."

The sweet, bracing fragrance of newborn chattel wafted into Walter's nostrils as they approached the counter, behind which a wiry Asian man, tongue pinned against his upper lip, methodically arranged a display of Tarbaby Treats. "Now *here's* a girl who needs a friend," he sang out, flashing Tanya a fake smile.

"Our best slave has Blue Nile," Walter explained, "and we wanted to—"

"Say no more." The clerk lifted his palms as if stopping traffic. "We can hold one for you clear till August."

"I'm afraid it won't be that long."

The clerk led them to a cage containing a solitary whelp chewing on a small plastic lawn mower. *Male*, the sign said. *Ten months. $399.95.* "This guy arrived only yesterday. You'll have him litter-trained in two weeks—this we guarantee."

"Had his shots?"

"You bet. The polio booster's due next month."

"Oh Daddy, I *love him*," Tanya gushed, jumping up and down. "I completely *love* him. Let's bring him home tonight!"

"No, tomato. Jimmy'd get jealous." Walter gave the clerk a wink and, simultaneously, a twenty. "See that he gets a couple of really good meals this weekend, right?"

"Sure thing."

"Pappy?"

"Yes, tomato?"

"When Jimmy dies, will he go to slave Heaven? Will he get to see his old friends?"

"Certainly."

"Like Buzzy?"

"He'll definitely see Buzzy."

A smile of intense pride leaped spontaneously to Walter's face. Buzzy had died when Tanya was only four, yet she remembered; she actually remembered!

* * *

So hard-edged, the future, Abe thought, levering himself out of the taxi and unflexing his long, cramped limbs. Boston had become a thing of brick and rock, tar and glass, iron and steel. "Wait here," he told the driver.

He entered the public gardens. A truly lovely spot, he decided, sauntering past a slave team planting flower beds—impetuous tulips, swirling gladiolus, purse-lipped daffodils. Not far beyond, a white family cruised across a duck pond in a swan-shaped boat peddled by a scowling adolescent with skin like obsidian.

Leaving the park, he started down Boylston Street. A hundred yards away a burly Irish overseer stood beneath a gargantuan structure called the John Hancock Tower and began raising the scaffold, thus sending aloft a dozen slaves equipped with window-washing fluid. Dear Lord, what a job—the facade must contain a million square yards of mirrored glass.

Hard-edged, ungiving—and yet the city brought Abe peace.

In recent months he had started to grasp the true cause of the war. The issue, he realized, was not slavery. As with all things political, the issue was power. The South had seceded because they despaired of ever seizing the helm of state; as long as its fate was linked to a grimy, uncouth, industrialized North, Dixie could never fully flower. By endeavoring to expand slavery into the territories, those southerners who hated the institution and those who loved it were speaking with a single tongue, saying, "The Republic's true destiny is manifest—an agrarian Utopia, now and forever."

But here was Boston, full of slaves and steeped in progress. Clearly, the Seward Treaty would not prove to be the recipe for feudalism and inertia that Abe's advisers feared. Crude, yes; morally ambiguous, true: and yet slavery wasn't dragging the Republic into the past, wasn't retarding its bid for modernity and might.

"Sign the treaty," an inner voice instructed Abe. "End the war."

Sunday was the Fourth of July, which meant the annual backyard picnic with the Burnsides, boring Ralph and boorish Helen, a tedious afternoon of horseshoe tossing, conspicuous drinking, and stupefying poolside chat, the whole ordeal relieved only by Libby's barbecued spareribs. Libby was one of those wonderful yard-sale items Marge had such a knack for finding, a healthy, well-mannered female who turned out to be a splendid cook, easily worth ten times her sticker price.

The Burnsides were an hour late—their rickshaw puller, Zippy, had broken his foot the day before, and so they were forced to use Bubbles, their unathletic gardener—a whole glorious hour of not hearing Ralph's views on the Boston sports scene. When they did finally show, the first thing out of Ralph's mouth was, "Is it a law the Sox can't own a decent pitcher? I mean, did they actually pass a *law*?", and Walter steeled himself. Luckily, Libby used a loose hand with the bourbon, and by three o'clock Walter was so anesthetized by mint juleps he could have floated happily through an amputation—not to mention Ralph's vapid views on the Sox, Celtics, and Patriots.

With the sixth drink, his numbness segued into a kind of contented courage, and he took unflinching stock of himself. Yes, his wife had probably bedded down with a couple of teachers from the Wellesley Adult Education Center—that superfluously muscled pottery instructor, most likely, though the drama coach also seemed to have a roving dick—but it wasn't as if Walter didn't occasionally use his orthodontic chair as a motel bed, wasn't as if he didn't frolic with Katie Mulligan every Wednesday afternoon at the West Newton Hot Tubs. And look at his splendid house, with its Jacuzzi, bowling alley, tennis court, and twenty-five-meter pool. Look at his thriving practice. His portfolio. Porsche. Silver rickshaw. Graceful daughter flopping through sterile turquoise waters (damn that Happy, always using too much chlorine). And look at his sturdy, handsome Marge, back-floating, her pregnancy rising from the deep end like a volcanic island. Walter was sure the kid was his. Eighty-five percent sure.

He'd achieved something in this life.

At dusk, while Happy set off the fireworks, the talk got around to Blue Nile. "We had Jimmy tested last week," Walter revealed, exhaling a small tornado of despair. "Positive."

"God, and you let him stay in the house?" wailed Ralph, fingering the grip of his Luger Parabellum PO8. A cardboard rocket screeched into the sky and became a dozen crimson starbursts, their reflections cruising across the pool like phosphorescent fish. "You should've told us. He might infect Bubbles."

"It's a pretty hard virus to contract," Walter retorted. A buzz

216 ♦ James Morrow

bomb whistled overhead, annihilating itself in a glittery blue-and-red mandala. "There has to be an exchange of saliva or blood."

"Still, I can't believe you're keeping him, with Marge pregnant and everything."

Ten fiery spheres popped from a roman candle and sailed into the night like clay pigeons. "Matter of fact, I've got an appointment with Grant on Monday."

"You know, Walter, if Jimmy were mine, I'd allow him a little dignity. I wouldn't take him to some lousy clinic."

The pièce de résistance blossomed over the yard—Abe Lincoln's portrait in sparks. "What would you do?"

"You know perfectly well what I'd do."

Walter grimaced. Dignity. Ralph was right, by damn. Jimmy had served the family with devotion and zest. They owed him an honorable exit.

The President chomped into a Big Mac, reveling in the soggy sauces and sultry juices as they bathed his tongue and rolled down his gullet. Were he not permanently lodged elsewhere—rail-splitter, country lawyer, the whole captivating myth—he might well have wished to settle down here in 2010. Big Macs were a quality commodity. The whole menu, in fact—the large fries, vanilla shakes, Diet Cokes, and Chicken McNuggets—seemed to Abe a major improvement over nineteenth-century cuisine. And such a soothing environment, its every surface clean and sleek, as if carved from tepid ice.

An enormous clown named Ronald was emblazoned on the picture window. Outside, across the street, an elegant sign—Old English characters on whitewashed wood—heralded the Chestnut Hill Country Club. On the grassy slopes beyond, smooth and green like a billiard table, a curious event unfolded, men and women whacking balls into the air with sticks. When not employed, the sticks resided in cylindrical bags slung over the shoulders of sturdy male slaves.

"Excuse me, madam," Abe addressed the chubby woman in the next booth. "What are those men doing? Is it religious?"

"That's quite a convincing Lincoln you've got on." Hunched over a newspaper, the woman wielded a writing implement, using it to fill tiny squares with alphabet letters. "Are you serious? They're golfing."

"A game?"

"Uh-huh." The woman started on her second Quarter Pounder. "The game of golf."

"It's like croquet, isn't it?"

"It's like golf."

Dipping and swelling like a verdant sea, the golf field put Abe in mind of Virginia's hilly provinces. Virginia, Lee's stronghold. A soft moan left the sixteenth President. Having thrown Hooker and Sedgwick back across the Rappahannock, Lee was ideally positioned to bring the war to the Union, either by attacking Washington directly or, more likely, by forming separate corps under Longstreet, Hill, and Ewell and invading Pennsylvania. Overrunning the border towns, he could probably cut the flow of reinforcements to Vicksburg while simultaneously equipping the Army of Northern Virginia for a push on the capital.

It was all too nightmarish to contemplate.

Sighing heavily, Abe took the Seward Treaty from his vest and asked to borrow his neighbor's pen.

Monday was a holiday. Right after breakfast, Walter changed into his golfing togs, hunted down his clubs, and told Jimmy they'd be spending the day on the links. He ended up playing the entire course, partly to improve his game, partly to postpone the inevitable.

His best shot of the day—a 350-yard blast with his one-iron— carried straight down the eighteenth fairway and ran right up on the green. Sink the putt, and he'd finish the day one under par.

Sweating in the relentless fifth-of-July sun, Jimmy pulled out the putter. Such a fine fellow, with his trim body and huge, eager eyes, zags of silver shooting through his steel-wool hair like the aftermath of an electrocution, his black biceps and white polo shirt meeting like adjacent squares on a chessboard. He would be sorely missed.

"No, Jimmy, we won't be needing that. Just pass the bag over here. Thanks."

As Walter retrieved his .22-caliber army rifle from among the clubs, Jimy's face hardened with bewilderment.

"May I ask why you require a firearm?" asked the slave.

218 ◆ *James Morrow*

"I'm going to shoot you."

"What?"

"Results came Thursday, Jimmy. You have Blue Nile. Sorry. I'd love to keep you around, but it's too dangerous, what with Marge's pregnancy and everything."

Jimmy's teeth came together in a tight, dense grid. "In the name of reason, *sell* me. Surely that's a viable option."

"Let's be realistic. Nobody's going to take in a Nile-positive just to watch him wilt and die."

"Very well—then turn me loose." Sweat spouted from the slave's ebony face. "I'll pursue my remaining years on the road. I'll—"

"Loose? I can't go around undermining the economy like that, Jim. I'm sure you understand."

"There's something I've always wanted to tell you, Mr. Sherman."

"I'm listening."

"I believe you are probably the biggest asshole in the entire Commonwealth of Massachusetts."

"No need for that kind of talk, fellow. Just sit down on the green, and I'll—"

"No."

"Let's not make this difficult. Sit down, and you'll receive a swift shot in the head—no pain, a dignified death. Run away, and you'll get it in the back. It's your choice."

"Of course I'm going to run, you degenerate moron."

"Sit!"

Spinning around, Jimmy sprinted toward the rough. Walter jammed the stock against his shoulder and, like a biologist focusing his microscope on a protozoan, found the retreating chattel in his high-powered optical sight.

"Stop!"

Jimmy reached the western edge of the fairway just as Walter fired, a clean shot right through the slave's left calf. With a deep, wolfish howl, he pitched forward and, to Walter's surprise, rose almost instantly, clutching a rusty, discarded nine-iron that he evidently hoped to use as a crutch. But the slave got no farther. As he stood fully erect, his high, wrinkled forehead neatly entered the gunsight, the cross hairs branding him with an X, and Walter had but to squeeze the trigger again.

Impacting, the bullet dug out a substantial portion of cranium—

a glutinous divot of skin, bone, and cerebrum shooting away from Jimmy's temple like a missile launched from a dark planet. He spun around twice and fell into the rough, landing behind a clump of rose bushes spangled with white blossoms. So: a dignified death after all.

Tears bubbled out of Walter as if from a medicine dropper. Oh Jimmy, Jimmy. . . . And the worst was yet to come, wasn't it? Of course, he wouldn't tell Tanya the facts. "Jimmy was in pain," he'd say. "Unbearable agony. The doctors put him to sleep. He's in slave Heaven now." And they'd give him a classy send-off, oh yes, with flowers and a moment of silence. Maybe Pastor McClellan would be willing to preside.

Walter staggered toward the rough. To do a funeral, you needed a body. Doubtless the morticians could patch up his head, mold a gentle smile, bend his arms across his chest in a posture suggesting serenity. . . .

A tall, bearded man in an Abe Lincoln suit was on the eighteenth fairway, coming Walter's way. An eccentric, probably. Maybe a full-blown nut. Walter locked his gaze on the roses and marched straight ahead.

"I saw what you did," said the stranger, voice edged with indignation.

"Fellow had Blue Nile," Walter explained. The sun beat against his face like a hortator pounding a drum on a Roman galley. "It was an act of mercy. Hey, Abe, the Fourth of July was yesterday. Why the getup?"

"Yesterday is never too late," said the stranger cryptically, pulling a yellowed sheaf from his vest. "Never too late," he repeated as, swathed in the hot, buttery light, he neatly ripped the document in half.

For Walter Sherman, pummeled by the heat, grieving for his lost slave, wearied by the imperatives of mercy, the world now became a swamp, an all-enveloping mire blurring the stranger's methodical progress toward McDonald's. An odd evening was coming, Walter sensed, with odder days to follow, days in which all the earth's stable things would be wrenched from their moorings and unbolted from their bases. Here and now, standing on the crisp border between the fairway and the putting green, Walter apprehended this discomforting future.

He felt it more emphatically as, eyes swirling, heart shiver-

220 ✦ James Morrow

ing, brain drifting in a sea of insane light, he staggered toward the roses.

And he knew it with a knife-sharp certainty as, searching through the rough, he found not Jimmy's corpse, but only the warm hulk of a humanoid machine, prostrate in the dusk, afloat in the slick, oily fluid leaking from its broken brow.

ON DEATH
AND THE DEUCE

◆　◆　◆

Richard Bowes

Richard Bowes has written a number of stories about Kevin Grier-
son, the protagonist of "On Death and the Deuce." Most of the
stories have appeared in F&SF, *and one appeared in* Tomorrow
Magazine. *They all form the basis for his novel,* Minions of the
Moon. *Terri Windling chose this story to appear in the anthology,*
The Year's Best Fantasy and Horror *(Sixth Edition).*
"On Death and the Deuce" marked Rick's first short fiction
appearance, but not his first appearance in print. He has published
three novels: Warchild, Feral Cell, *and* Goblin Market.

In the last days that the Irish ran Hell's Kitchen, I lived in that
tenement neighborhood between the West Side docks and
Times Square. An old lady of no charm whatsoever named
McCready and called Mother rented furnished studios in an un-
derheated fleabag on Tenth Avenue. Payment was cash only by the
week or month, with anonymity guaranteed whether desired or
not. Looking out the window one February morning, I spotted my
Silent Partner heading south toward Forty-second Street.

He was already past me, so it was the clothes that caught my
attention first. The camel-hair overcoat had been mine. The dark
gray pants were from the last good suit I had owned. That morning
I'd awakened from a drinking dream, and was still savoring the
warm, safe feeling that comes with realizing it was all a nightmare
and that I was sober. The sight of that figure three floors down

filled my mouth with the remembered taste of booze. I tried to spit, but was too dry.

Hustlers called Forty-second the Deuce. My Silent Partner turned at that corner, and I willed him not to notice me. Just before heading east, he looked directly at my window. He wore shades, but his face was the one I feared seeing most. It was mine.

That made me too jumpy to stay in the twelve-by-fifteen-foot room. Reaching behind the bed, I found the place where the wall and floor didn't join. Inside was my worldly fortune: a slim .25 caliber Beretta, and beside it a wad of bills. Extracting six twenties, I put on a thick sweater and leather jacket and went out.

At that hour, nothing much was cooking in Hell's Kitchen. Two junkies went by, bent double by the wind off the Hudson. Up the block a super tossed away the belongings of a drag queen who the week before had gotten cut into bite-size chunks. My Silent Partner was not the kind to go for a casual walk in this weather.

Looking the way he had come, I saw the Club 596 sitting like a bunker at the corner of Forty-third. The iron grating on the front was ajar, but no lights were on inside. As I watched, a guy in a postman's uniform squeezed out the door and hurried away. The Westies, last of the Irish gangs—short, crazed, and violent—sat in the dark dispensing favors, collecting debts. And I knew what my Silent Partner had been up to.

Then I went to breakfast, put the incident to the back of my mind, and prepared for my daily session. The rest of my time was a wasteland, but my late afternoons were taken up with Leo Dunn.

He lived in a big apartment house over in the east sixties. Outside, the building gleamed white. The lobby was polished marble. Upstairs in his apartment, sunlight poured through windows curtained in gold and hit a glass table covered with pieces of silver and crystal. "Kevin, my friend." Mr. Dunn, tall and white-haired, came forward smiling and shook my hand. "How are you? Every time I see you come through this door, it gives me the greatest pleasure."

I sat down on the couch, and he sat across the coffee table from me. The first thing I thought to say was: "I had a drinking dream last night. This crowd watched like it was an Olympic event as I poured myself a shot and drank it. Then I realized what I'd done, and felt like dirt. I woke up, and it was as if a rock had been taken off my head."

Amused, Dunn nodded his understanding. But dreams were of no great interest to him. So, after pausing to be sure I was through, he drew a breath and was off. "Kevin, you have made the greatest commitment of your life. You stood up and said, 'Guilty as charged. I am a drunk.' "

Mr. Dunn's treatment for alcoholics was a talking cure: he talked, and I listened. He didn't just talk—he harangued; he argued like a lawyer; he gave sermons of fire. Gesturing to a closet door, he told me, "That is the record room where we store the evidence of our mistakes. Any boozehound has tales of people he trusted who screwed him over. But has there ever been anyone you knew that used you as badly and that you went back to as often as you have to booze?"

We had been over this material a hundred times in the past couple of weeks. "You're a bright boy, Kevin, and I wouldn't repeat myself if I hadn't learned that it was necessary. We go back to the record room." Again he pointed to the door. "We look for evidence of our stupidity."

For ten years, my habit and I had traveled from booze through the drug spectrum and back to booze. Then one morning on the apex of a bender, that fine moment when mortality is left behind and the shakes haven't started, I found myself standing at a bar reading a *New York Post* article. It was about some guy called Dunn who treated drunks.

The crash that followed was gruesome. Three days later I woke up empty, sweat-soaked, and terrified in a room I didn't remember renting. At first, it seemed that all I owned were the clothes I had been wearing. Gradually, in jacket and jean pockets, stuck in a boot, I discovered a vaguely familiar pistol, a thick roll of bills, and a page torn from the *Post*. The choice that I saw was clear; either to shoot myself or make a call.

My newly sober brain was blank and soft, and Mr. Dunn remolded it relentlessly. On the afternoon I am describing, he saw my attention wander, clicked a couple of ashtrays together on the table, picked up the gold lighter, and ignited a cigarette with a flourish. "How are you doing, Kevin?"

"O.K.," I told him. "Before I forget," I said, and placed five of the twenties from my stash on the table.

He put them in his pocket without counting and said, "Thank

you, Kevin." But when he looked up at me, an old man with pale skin and very blue eyes, he wasn't smiling. "Any news on a job?" He had never questioned me closely, but I knew that my money bothered Mr. Dunn.

Behind him the light faded over Madison Avenue. "Not yet," I said. "The thing is, I don't need much to get by. Where I'm living is real cheap." At a hundred a week, Leo Dunn was my main expense. He was also what kept me alive. I recognized him as a real lucky kind of habit.

He went back to a familiar theme. "Kevin," he said, looking at the smoke from his cigarette. "For years, your addiction was your Silent Partner. When you decided to stop drinking, that was very bad news for him. Your Silent Partner wants to live as much as you do." At the mention of that name, I remembered what I had seen that morning.

Dunn said, "Your partner had the best racket in the world, skimming off an ever-increasing share of your life, your happiness. He is not just going to give up and go away. He will try treachery, intimidation, flattery, to get you back in harness."

He paused for a moment, and I said, "I saw him today, across the street. He saw me, too. He was wearing clothes that used to belong to me."

"What did he look like, Kevin?" I guess nothing a drunk could say would ever surprise Mr. Dunn.

"Just like me. But at the end of a three-week bender."

"What was he doing when you saw him?" This was asked very softly.

"Coming from a mob bar up the street, the 596 Club. He was trying to borrow money from guys who will whack you just because that's how they feel at the moment."

"Kevin," said Mr. Dunn. "Booze is a vicious, mind-altering substance. It gets us at its mercy by poisoning our minds, making us unable to distinguish between what is real and what isn't. Are you saying that you had to borrow money?" I shook my head. Very carefully, he asked, "Do you mean you remembered some aspect of your drinking self?"

"Something like that," I said. But what I felt was a double loss. Not only had my Silent Partner discovered where I lived, but Dunn didn't believe me. The partner had broken the perfect rapport between us.

At that point the lobby called to announce the next client. As Leo Dunn showed me to the door, his eyes searched mine. He wasn't smiling. "Kevin, you've done more than I would have thought possible when you first walked in here. But there's what they call a dry drunk, someone who's managed to stop drinking, but has not reached the state beyond that. I don't detect involvement in life from you, or real elation. I respect you too much to want to see you as just a dry drunk."

The next client was dressed like a stockbroker. He avoided looking at me in my street clothes. "Leo," he said, a little too loudly and too sincerely, "I'm glad to see you." And Dunn, having just directed a two-hour lecture at me, smiled and was ready to go again.

Outside, it was already dark. On my way across town, I went through Times Square down to the Deuce. It was rush hour. Spanish hustlers in maroon pants, hands jammed in jacket pockets, black hookers in leather miniskirts, stood on corners, all too stoned to know they were freezing to death. Around them, commuters poured down subway stairs and fled for Queens.

Passing the Victoria Hotel, I glanced in at the desk clerk sitting behind bulletproof glass. I had lived at the Victoria before my final bender. It was where those clothes the Silent Parner wore had been abandoned. Without remembering all the details, I sensed that it wasn't wise to go inside and inquire about my property.

Back on my block, I looked up at my bleak little window, dark and unwelcoming. Mother's was no place to spend an evening. Turning away, I started walking again; probably I ate dinner somewhere, maybe saw a movie. Without booze, I couldn't connect with anyone. Mostly I walked, watched crowds stream out of the theaters. *A Little Night Music* was playing, and *A Moon for the Misbegotten*. Then those rich tourists and nice couples from Westchester hurried into cabs and restaurants and left the streets quite empty.

In Arcade Parade on Broadway, goggle-eyed suit-and-tie johns watched the asses on kids bent over the pinball machines. Down the way a marquee advertised the double bill of *College Bound Babes* and *Bound to Please Girls*. Around a corner a tall guy with a smile like a knife slash chanted, "Got what you need," like a litany.

Glancing up, I realized we were in front of Sanctuary. Built to be a Methodist church, it had gotten famous in the late sixties as a disco. In those days a huge Day-Glo Satan loomed above the former altar; limos idled in front; a team of gorillas worked the door.

Now it was dim and dying, a trap for a particular kind of tourist. Inside, Satan flaked off the wall; figures stood in the shadows, willing to sell what you asked. I could remember in a hazy way spending my last money there to buy the Beretta. My trajectory on that final drunk—the arc that connected the pistol, the money, the absence of my Silent Partner—wasn't buried all that deeply inside me. I just didn't want to look.

At some point that night, the rhythm of the street, the cold logic of the Manhattan grid, took me way west, past the live sex shows and into the heart of the Kitchen. On long, dirty blocks of tenements, I went past small Mick bars with tiny front windows where lines of drinkers sat like marines, and guys in the back booths gossiped idly about last week's whack.

I walked until my hands and feet were numb, and I found myself over on Death Avenue. That's what the Irish of the Kitchen once called Eleventh because of the train tracks that ran there and killed so many of them. Now the trains were gone, the ships whose freight they hauled were gone, and those Irish themselves were fast disappearing. Though not born in the Kitchen, I identified with them a lot.

On Death, in a block of darkened warehouses, sat the Emerald Green Tavern. It was on a Saturday morning at the Emerald Green that I had found myself in a moment of utter clarity with a pistol and a pocketful of money, reading in a newspaper about Leo Dunn. I stood for a while remembering that. Then maybe the cold got to me, and I went home. My memory there is vague.

What I will never forget is the sight of a ship outlined in green and red lights. I was staring at it, and I was intensely cold. Gradually, I realized I was huddled against a pillar of the raised highway near the Hudson piers. One of the last of the cruise ships was docked there, and I thought how good it would be to have the money to sail down to the warm weather.

In fact, it would be so good to have any money at all. My worldly wealth was on me: suede boots and no socks, an overcoat and suit and no underwear. In one pocket were a penny, a dime, and a quarter—my wealth. In another were a set of standard keys and the gravity knife I'd had since college.

Then I knew why I had stolen the keys and where I was going to get money. And I recognized the state I was in: the brief, brilliant period of clarity at the end of a bender. My past was a wreck; my future held a terrifying crash. With nothing behind me and nothing to live for, I knew no fear and was a god.

With all mortal uncertainty and weakness gone, I was pure spirit as I headed down familiar streets. A block east of Death and north of the Deuce, I looked up at a lighted window on the third floor. I crossed the street, my overcoat open, oblivious to the cold.

Security at Mother's was based on there being nothing in the building worth taking. Drawing out the keys, I turned the street-door lock on my third try and went up the stairs, silently, swiftly. Ancient smells of boiled cabbages and fish, of damp carpet and cigarette smoke and piss, a hundred years of poverty, wafted around me. This was the kind of place a loser lived, a fool came to rest. Contempt filled me.

Light shone under his door. Finding a key the right shape, I transferred it to my left hand, drew out the knife with my right. The key went in without a sound. I held my breath and turned it. The lock clicked; the door swung into the miserable room with a bed, a TV on without the sound, a two-burner stove, a table. An all-too-familiar figure dozed in the only chair, shoes off, pants unbuttoned. Sobriety had made him stupid. Not even the opening of the door roused him. The click of the knife in my hand did that.

The eyes focused, then widened as the dumb face I had seen in ten thousand morning mirrors registered shock. "I got a little debt I want to collect," I said, and moved for him. Rage swept me, a feeling that I'd been robbed of everything: my body, my life. "You took the goddamn money. It's mine. My plan. My guts. You couldn't have pulled that scam in a thousand years."

For an instant the miserable straight head in front of me froze in horror. Then shoulder muscles tensed; stocking feet shot out as he tried to roll to the side and go for the .25. But he was too slow. My knife slashed, and the fool put out his hands. Oh, the terror in those eyes when he saw the blood on his palms and wrists. He fell back, tipping over the chair. The blade went for the stomach, cut through cloth and into flesh.

Eyes wide, his head hit the wall. The knife in my hand slashed his throat. The light in the eyes went out. The last thing I saw in them was a reflection of his humiliation at dying like that, pants fallen down, jockey shorts filling with dark red blood. His breath suddenly choked, became a drowning sound. An outstretched hand pointed to the loose board and the money.

"I was just cut down," I told Dunn the next morning. "It wasn't even a fight. I left that knife behind when I had to move, and the fucking Silent Partner had it and just cut me down." It was hard to get my throat to work.

"It was a dream, Kevin, a drinking dream like the one you told me yesterday. It has no power over your conscious mind. You came home and fell asleep sitting up. Then you had a nightmare. You say you fell off your chair and woke up on the floor. It was just a dream."

My eyes burned. "The expression my Silent Partner had on his face is the one I used to see sometimes in the mirror. Those moments when I was so far gone I could do anything."

"Nothing else has reached you like this, Kevin."

"Sorry. I couldn't sleep."

"Don't be sorry. This is part of the process. I don't know why, but this has to happen for the treatment to work. I've had detective sergeants bawl like babies, marines laugh until they cried. Until this, you haven't let anything faze you. Our stupid drinker's pride can take many forms."

"I won't be able to sleep as long as he's out there."

"Understand, Kevin, that I'm not a psychiatrist. I was educated by the Jesuits a long time ago. Dreams or how you feel about your mother don't mean much to me. But I hear myself say that, and spot my own stupid pride at work. If dreams are what you bring me, I'll use them." He paused, and I blew my nose. "What does your Silent Partner want, Kevin? You saw through his eyes in your dream."

"He wants to disembowel me!"

"The knife was the means, Kevin. Not the motive. What was he looking for?"

"My money. He knew where I had it."

"You keep money in your room? You don't have a job. But you

pay me regularly in fairly crisp twenties and hundreds. It's stolen money, isn't it, Kevin?"

"I guess so. I don't remember."

"Earlier you mentioned that in the dream, you went for a gun. Is there blood on the money, Kevin? Did you hurt anyone? Do you know?"

"The gun hasn't been fired."

"I assume it's not registered, probably stolen. Get rid of it. Can you return the money?"

"I don't even know who it belonged to."

"You told me that he was in a calm eye when he came after you. That was his opportunity. You had that same kind of clarity when you found the article about me. You had the money with you then?"

"The gun, too."

"Kevin, let's say that some people's Silent Partners are more real than others. Then let's say that in a moment of clarity, you managed to give yours the slip and walked off with the money the two of you had stolen. Without him holding you back, you succeeded in reaching out for help. The money is the link. It's what still connects you to your drinking past. I don't want any of that money, and neither do you. Get rid of it."

"You mean throw it away?"

"The other day, you said your Silent Partner was borrowing from the West Side mob. If he's real enough to need money that badly, let him have it. No one, myself above all, ever loses his Silent Partner entirely. But this should give you both some peace."

"What'll I do for money? I won't be able to pay you."

"Do you think after all this time, I don't know which ones aren't going to pay me?" I watched his hands rearrange the crystal ashtrays, the gold lighter, as he said, "Let's look in the record room, where we will find that booze is a vicious, mind-altering substance, and that we have to be aware at every moment of its schemes." I raised my eyes. Framed in the light from the windows, Dunn smiled at me and said, "Keep just enough to live on for a couple of weeks until you find work. Which you will."

Afterward in my room, I took out the pistol and the money, put two hundred back in the wall, and placed the rest in a jacket pocket.

The Beretta I carefully stuck under my belt at the small of my back. Then I went out.

At first, I walked aimlessly around the Kitchen. My Silent Partner had threatened me. It seemed my choices were to give up the money or to keep the money and give up Leo Dunn. The first I thought of as surrender; the second meant I'd be back on the booze. Then a third choice took shape. Payback. I would do to him just what he had tried to do to me.

Searching for him, I followed what I remembered of our route on the last night of our partnership. It had begun at Sanctuary. Passing by, I saw that the disco was no longer dying. It was dead. The doors were padlocked. On the former church steps, a black guy slept with his head on his knees. No sign of my Silent Partner.

But I finally recalled what had happened there. Sanctuary was a hunting ground. Tourists were the game. That last night I had run into four fraternity assholes in town with seven grand for a midwinter drug buy. Almost dead broke, I talked big about my connections. Before we left together, I bought the Beretta.

Following the trail, I walked by the Victoria. That's where I had taken them first. "Five guys showing up will not be cool," I said, and persuaded two of them to wait in my dismal room. "As collateral, you hold everything I own." That amounted to little more than some clothes and a few keepsakes like the knife. With the other two, I left the hotel that last time knowing I wouldn't be back. I recognized my Silent Partner's touch. He had been with me at that point.

Turning into an icy wind off the river, I took the same route that the frat boys and I had taken a few weeks before. At a doorway on a deserted side street near Ninth Avenue, we halted. I remembered telling them that this was the place. In the tenement hall, I put the pistol at the base of one kid's head and made him beg the other one to give me the money.

Standing in the doorway again, I recalled how the nervous sweat on my hand had made it hard to hold on to the .25. When those terrified kids had handed over the money, I discouraged pursuit by making them throw their shoes into the dark and lie face down with their hands behind their heads. The one I'd put the pistol on had pissed his pants. He wept and begged me not to shoot. Remembering that made my stomach turn. Right then my partner had still been calling the shots.

The rest of that night was gone beyond recovery. But what had happened in those blank black hours wasn't important. I knew where the search for my partner was going to end. Death Avenue north of the Deuce had always been a favorite spot for both of us. The deserted warehouses, the empty railroad yards, made it feel like the end of the world.

Approaching the Emerald Green Tavern, I spotted a lone figure leaning on a lamppost, watching trailer trucks roll south. Only a lack of funds would have kept a man out on the street on a night like that. Touching the pistol for luck, stepping up behind my Silent Partner, I asked, "Whatcha doing?"

Not particularly surprised, not even turning all the way around, he replied, "Oh, living the life." I would never have his nonchalance. His face was hidden by shadows and dark glasses. That was just as well.

The air around him smelled of cheap booze. "We have to talk." I gestured toward the Emerald Green.

As we crossed the street, he told me, "I knew you'd show up. This is where we parted company. When I woke up days later, all I had were these clothes and a couple of keepsakes." I was reminded of the knife. My Silent Partner knew as soon as that crossed my mind. "Don't worry," he said. "I sold it." He went through the door first.

The Emerald Green was a typical Hell's Kitchen joint, with a bar that ran front to back, a few booths, and beer- and cigarette-soaked air unchanged since the Truman administration. The facilities were the one distinguishing feature of the place. The rest rooms lay down a flight of stairs and across a cellar/storage area. You could organize a firing squad down there, and the people above wouldn't know.

Or care. The customers that night were several guys with boozers' noses, an old woman with very red hair who said loudly at regular intervals, "Danny? Screw Danny," and a couple of Spanish guys off some night shift and now immobile at a table. The dead-eyed donkey of a bartender looked right through me and nodded at my Silent Partner. In here, he was the real one. We went to the far end of the bar near the cellar door, where we could talk. I ordered a ginger ale. My companion said, "Double Irish."

As we sat, he gave a dry chuckle. "Double Irish is about right for us." At no time did I turn and stare my Silent Partner in the face. But the filmed mirror behind the bar showed that he wore the rumpled jacket over a dirty T-shirt. The camel-hair coat was deeply stained. When the whiskey came, he put it away with a single gesture from counter to mouth. Up and in. I could taste it going down.

It was like living in a drinking dream. I touched the back of my belt and said, "You found out where I live."

"Yeah, Billy at the 596 told me you were staying at Mother's. Of course, what he said was that he had seen me going in and out. So I knew." Indoors, my partner smelled ripe. The back of his hand was dirty.

"You owe them money?" The last thing I needed was to get shot for debts he had run up.

"Not even five. My credit's no good," he said. "You left me with nothing. They locked me out of the hotel. Ripping off those kids was something you never could have done by yourself. You needed me." He signaled for a refill. The bartender's eyes shifted my way, since I was paying.

I shook my head, not sure I could have him drink again and not do it myself. "I've got the money on me. It's yours. So that we don't attract attention, what I want you to do is get up and go downstairs. After a couple of minutes, I'll join you."

"Pass the money to me under the bar." He didn't trust me.

"There's something else I want you to have." For a long moment he sat absolutely still. The TV was on with the sound off. It seemed to be all beer ads. "When you come back up here," I told him, "you will be able to afford enough doubles to kill yourself." That promise made him rise and push his way through the cellar door.

For a good two minutes, I sipped ginger ale and breathed deeply to calm myself. Then I followed him. Downstairs, there were puddles on the floor. The rest-room doors were open. Both were empty. One of the johns was broken and kept flushing. It sounded like an asthmatic trying to breathe.

The cellar was lighted by an overhead bulb above the stairs and one at the far end of the cellar near the rest rooms. Both lights swayed slightly, making it hard to focus. My Silent Partner had reached up and bumped them for just that reason. It was the kind of thing that I would not have thought of. He stood where the light didn't quite hit him.

When I reached the bottom of the stairs, I reached back and

drew out the .25. He seemed to flicker before me. "Easy does it," he said. "You know how jumpy you are with guns." His tone was taunting, not intimidated.

I realized I could read him as easily as he could me. My Silent Partner wanted me to try to shoot him and find out that I couldn't. Then, after I failed, we could both go upstairs, have some drinks, and resume our partnership. Carefully, I ejected the clip and stuck it in my pocket. His eyes followed me as I put the empty pistol on the stairs. "You bought this; you get rid of it," I said. "My guess is, it's got a bad history."

"You'll never have another friend like me." His voice, my voice, had a whine to it, and I knew this was getting to him. I reached into my pocket and took out the money and a piece of torn newspaper. "You thought about what it's going to be like to be broke?" he asked. "It's not like you've got any skills."

I had thought of it, and it scared me. I hesitated. Then I noticed that the newspaper was the page with the Dunn article. Taking a deep breath, I riffled the money and told my Silent Partner: "Almost six grand. Just about everything I have." I put the cash on the stairs beside the Beretta and turned to go. "So long. It's been real."

"Oh, I'll keep in touch," he said in a whisper. Looking back, I saw nothing but a blur of light in the shadows.

On the stairs, I felt light-footed, like a burden had been laid down. This was relief, maybe even the happiness Mr. Dunn had mentioned. From his perch near the front, the bartender gave me a slightly wary look, like maybe I had come in at 2:00 A.M., drunk ginger ale, and had a conversation with myself. It occurred to me that if that's what happened, the first one to go take a leak was going to get a very nice surprise.

But as I went out into the cold, the bartender's gaze shifted, his hand reached for the pouring bottle, and I heard the cellar door swing open behind me.

THE HONEYCRAFTERS

◆ ◆ ◆

Carolyn Ives Gilman

Carolyn Ives Gilman has written a number of wonderful short stories for F&SF. Many of them, including "The Honeycrafters," have been cover stories. "The Honeycrafters," which was on the final Nebula ballot in 1993, creates an entire society from something as simple as harvesting honey. Carolyn currently works as the Director of Exhibitions and Design for the Missouri Historical Society in St. Louis, and she is putting the final touches on her first novel, Haven.

T he motherhold of Magwin Ghar had prospered for nine journeys, until the day Renata Oblin came out of the west. The band of beeherders had come to the very brink of Dawn to begin their nectar quest. They were erecting their dome tents on a sparse meadow beside a swift, chalky blue meltwater river. The immobile sun hung low in the east; to the west the sunlight touched the tips of ice peaks under the dark bank of clouds that always hung at the edge of permanent night. Here they were at the beginning of things, where land was born from ice and night. Everything around them was young.

The children were playing with their enormous shadows, when they saw the stranger coming down the pathless slope of scree. They stood still to stare. She was dressed in barbarian leathers, and coming from the west, where only storm and glaciers dwelt. As word spread through the camp, people stepped from their tents to watch her approach. When she drew near, they saw what they had half-feared, half-hoped: a ceramic broodpot in a pouch strapped to her chest.

She raised an arm in greeting and called in a clear, strong voice, "Whose motherhold is this?"

"Magwin Ghar's," someone answered.

She dropped to one knee to touch the ground in thanks. When she rose, her eyes swept them all in. "I am Renata of Oblin Motherhold. Many whiles ago I journeyed into the Dawnlands to seek my future. I have found it. I bring you a new hive mother!"

She touched the broodpot at her breast, then looked around, exhilarated, as if she expected them all to cheer at her hero's deed. But the people's looks were grave and uncertain. Because of her, their lives were all about to change.

Dubich Rhud had always known the day would come. Ever since he and Magwin Ghar had walked the marriage line together, it had been there, somewhere in the future: the day a challenger for the motherhold would come, and Magwin would have to face death. But he had never guessed how full of helpless rage he would feel.

His voice sounded eerily calm as he told her the news. They sat inside her tent with their favorite pillows drawn close together. The beeswax candles cast a soft light on the intricate patterns of the woven wall-rugs and the comfortable layers of carpet on the floor.

"I am not ready to die just yet," Magwin said grimly. She still had the look of the wrestler she once had been—strong neck; solid, muscular torso; stocky legs. But now her close-cropped hair was the color of granite, and her face was leathery from years in the sun.

"There cannot be two leaders in the same motherhold," Dubich said, fingering the long braids of his gray beard. "*Someone* is going to die. Unless you step aside."

"Ha!" was Magwin's response. She raised her arm, clenching her fist and staring at her bunched biceps. The skin was loose, mottled with age spots. But there was nothing old about the flash in her eyes.

"Why not give way, Magwin?" Dubich said quietly. "It is the way of nature. Youth should replace age."

"When age has nothing more to offer," Magwin said. "I built this motherhold. I know how to run it."

It was not what she had said nine journeys ago, when *she* had been the one challenging old Borsun Ghar for control of the motherhold. She had been a whirlwind then: a swift temper, a loud laugh, forthright and bold, with a tender side only Dubich and a few others knew about. Gods, he had been so proud of her.

"So you will fight her?" Dubich said unwillingly.

Magwin reached out for his hand. There was a teasing twinkle in her eye. "Don't worry, old man. I still have some brain cells that are as good as new, you know."

She loved it—the challenge, the conflict. Once, Dubich had enjoyed watching her, advising from the shadows. But lately he'd lost his taste for battles. It had been so quiet, the last journey since their children had left for other motherholds. He had grown used to a maturer marriage and the slower rhythms of age. He did not want to lose it all. The stakes in this battle were just too high.

Someone shook the door rattle, and Magwin shouted, "Enter!" It was two of the master honeycrafters, come to get good seats for the confrontation everyone expected. Magwin welcomed them from her pillow, and Dubich rose to serve some hydromel in carved horn cups. Soon more arrived, and more, till the tent was crowded, and people began to collect outside, where they could hear through the tent sides.

When Renata Oblin entered, Dubich was startled at how young she was—younger than their own daughter. Yet she stood at the entrance with a careless self-confidence. She was tall and agile, with a long braid of brown hair. An archer, Dubich thought, or a climber.

"You are welcome to my tent, wanderer," Magwin said formally.

Dubich held out a cup of hydromel. Renata shook her head and, in a supple movement of tanned limbs, settled down, legs crossed. Now everyone knew how the land lay. Renata would not accept hospitality from someone she intended to kill.

"What is that around your neck?" Magwin asked.

In answer, Renata placed the broodpot on the soft carpet, then opened it.

People leaned forward to see. Slowly, a large insect crawled free of the pot, too young yet to fly. There were several indrawn breaths, for she was a larger mother bee than any in Magwin Ghar's hives; and stranger yet, she was a glossy black all over.

"That is a fine creature," Magwin said. Her voice was bland, but Dubich could hear the envy in it. It had been a long time since their own hives had had an infusion of new bee blood. A motherhold could not last long with puny, inbred bees. "How did you find her?"

"I left Oblin Motherhold a journeypiece ago," Renata said. "I had five companions, young women like me who had all reached the wander-age. They went to find new homes among other motherholds, but I was not content with that. I turned toward the land of Dawn. I set out to find a new hive mother and bring her back.

"The Dawnlands are wide and cold, and constant storms rage along the boundary where night begins. I traveled through unmapped new lands, along the edges of the glaciers. I lived among the rockfalls, eating lichen and beetles; the sun was only an orange ball on the horizon. I always looked for a nest where a mother bee was hatching from her winterlong slumber. Once, I found a nest, but the mother had flown east hours before I got there. I thought I was cursed.

"But I would not give up. At last, as I lay too tired to pull myself upright, the ground began to rock under me. There was a roar fit to bring the sky down, and near me a hillside collapsed into a valley. Afterward I staggered out onto the fresh brown slope and saw there a mother bee climbing from her nest. The avalanche had cleared away a thick layer of gravel the glaciers had left. Without it the mother would have perished, buried; and so would I."

She looked around at her spellbound audience, and her voice became forceful. "I set out to find my own people then, for I knew I was fit to lead a motherhold." Her eyes turned to Magwin Ghar.

"That may be true," Magwin said in a voice of calm and ice; "but you will not lead *my* motherhold."

"Then we will quarrel," Renata said. "Look at my bee. Have you got her equal?"

No one answered. Everyone knew they hadn't.

"I can have your bee," Magwin said.

"Do you challenge me?"

Dubich held his breath, hoping Magwin would not be impetuous. She must not challenge; she needed to choose the weapon.

Magwin said nothing. "I smell old blood here," Renata gave the ritual taunt. "Are you afraid?"

Still no answer.

"Very well, then," Renata said, impatient. "I will challenge you. Prove your fitness to lead this motherhold."

"All these people are witness that you have made the challenge." Magwin smiled, a predator who had trapped her prey. "It is my right to choose the contest."

Renata straightened in surprise at the sudden vigor of her opponent's voice. She looked as if she suspected trickery. "Choose, then," she said.

"The times are gone when a holdmother needs brute force to rule. Leadership skills are what count now. I challenge you to a test of leadership. Each of us will take a swarm and the people to tend it. We will compete for one journey. At the end, whoever produces the best honey wins."

"Who will judge?" Renata asked, narrow-eyed. It was a highly unusual proposal.

"The honey brokers of Erdrum," Magwin said.

"Will you give me the right to pick from your swarm?"

"They are all good bees. You may pick if you please."

"And what of the honeycrafters—the hivekeepers, blenders, and refiners?"

"Persuade as many to follow you as you can."

A smile flashed across Renata's face, as if this challenge were to her liking. "And equipment?"

"We will share fairly."

"This is not a bad proposal, old woman," Renata said. "It is realistic."

"Then you accept, little girl?"

"I do."

The listeners looked troubled, for the decision would be on their shoulders, in a sense. Each one would have to choose whom to support. It would be the strangest journey a motherhold had ever taken.

Renata rose to leave, but before reaching the tent flap, she paused. "What about the loser?" she said.

Magwin Ghar hesitated. There was only one proper answer. "It must be an honorable death."

To die by one's own bees was the only way to be sure of honor. It was a painful death, but natural.

For the first time that night, Renata looked less than sure. With a slightly exaggerated confidence, she said, "Very well."

When all the witnesses were gone, Magwin turned to Dubich. "Ah, she's strong and brave, Dubich. But she can't match me in wits."

Dubich moved slowly around the tent, gathering the horn cups the visitors had left. Her plan gave him a deep foreboding.

Magwin said, "Dubich? Are you criticizing me?"

"I didn't say a word," he said.

"No, you just freeze the air with your silence. What is your problem with my plan?"

"This contest will set the young against the old," he said. "The youth of the motherhold will want to follow her."

"So? I will have wisdom, experience, and skill on my side."

"She will have energy and creativity on hers. And a new mother bee. She has a chance of winning, Magwin."

Magwin grinned. "It would not be a contest if she didn't."

Dubich wanted to smash the cups and roar. He held it back. It was not the right way. He must be clear-minded, clever, and quiet if he was to help her. She must never know. He picked up a cloak.

"Where are you going?" she asked.

"To the extraction tent," he said.

But he lied. He was going to start fighting for her.

On the edge of camp, remote from traveled paths, lay the hive tent. At the start of each journey, the bees were kept there till they acclimated to Dawn, resetting their biological rhythms and starting their life cycles over. It was a dark and buzzing place. The tall ceramic cylinders were stacked in shadowy ranks, so thick they left only a small circle open in the center. There, alone as usual, Hivekeeper Yannas No-Name paced the claustrophobic circle of her skull.

Normally, the quiet music of the bees calmed her, drew her from her thoughts. She pressed her palms, then her cheek, against the side of a hive, to feel the soft vibration of their humming. On good days she could sense their love radiating out, washing her clean of the past. But not today. She mouthed a silent profanity at herself. Her life was a rotten tooth, existing only to cause her pain. The hive circle, her last refuge, her cocoon, had trapped her in an empty round of ritual self-delusions.

She picked up a metal bar and pried loose the lid of the nearest hive. Inside, it was dark, crawling with buzzing shapes, like the memories inside her head. Her skin prickled, overactive nerves fighting for her attention. She reached in, picked a bee at random from the comb, and took it to her table, where a candle burned.

The bee was a healthy worker, sleek and yellow. It was half the size of her thumb, and a vestige of caution made her wonder if it was too large for her purpose. With a shrug of careless self-riddance, she rolled up her sleeve, then placed the bee over the prominent blue vein near the elbow. Her forearm was pocked with old red puncture marks.

She took a sliver of wood from the tangle of gray hair behind her ear and bent forward to tease the bee. At first it was quiet, sluggish with cold. When at last it raised its unsheathed stinger in warning, she aimed a threatening jab at its head. It sank its barb into her arm.

She clenched her teeth, enjoying the pain. Her hand twitched in spasms as the muscles convulsed. Her face grew slick with sweat. The bee was trying to withdraw its stinger, but the barbs prevented it; it thrashed about, its last throes pumping out all that remained in its venom sac. At last the stinger ripped from its body, and it fell twitching to the floor.

The vein stood out, deep blue all up her arm. She panted for breath, her heart racing unevenly. In another person a sting so severe would have caused convulsions. Yannas clenched her teeth to keep from emitting a sound as the poison spread. If there was no seizure, the lancing pain would wear away; and as it did, the gnawing void inside her would fade. She would be able to hear the bees sing to her again.

There was a footstep outside; someone was coming. Yannas quickly rolled down her sleeve and flicked the dead bee into the shadows. She turned away from the entry to seem busy and hide the trembling of her hands.

Dubich Rhud stood for a moment holding up the tent flap to let the sunrise light in. He watched Yannas's tall, lean form moving restlessly among the shadows. "Have you heard?" he asked.

Yannas turned. Her face was flushed; angular brows, nose, and cheekbones jutted out from the gaunt, obscure landscape of her face. "Heard what?" she said too alertly.

Dubich frowned suspiciously and crossed the tent. He seized the hivekeeper's arm and bared it to the candlelight. The stinger was still embedded in the skin. With an exasperated oath, Dubich took a clip from his cloak and used it as a tweezers to pull the barb out, careful not to touch it himself. At last he looked at Yannas's eyes. They were glassy, bright, pain-free. Dubich's pent-in anger erupted, and he slapped Yannas in the mouth.

"Damn you! I don't care what you do to yourself, but it's Magwin's life you're playing with now. She has trusted your loyalty to save her. God, what a delusion! Her secret weapon, her genius—nothing but a wretched addict. If Renata knew, she would laugh her sides out."

The hivekeeper backed away, startled, fingering her face. Her flush was gone; she was clear and cold now. "It's not as if you didn't know."

"You promised to cut down."

"I have," Yannas said; but Dubich could tell it was one of her many lies. He and Magwin had gotten used to them over the years.

It had been seven journeys since they had come across her in the Summerlands, lying in a roadside ditch, a skeleton wrapped in skin. She had been dehydrated, near death, but when she came to consciousness in one of their tents, it was not water she asked for, but sinnom. Then they had known the fault lay with one of the motherholds. For sinnom was a kind of honey—dangerous, addictive, forbidden, and fabulously valuable. Someone, lured by wealth, had perverted their bees into distillers of liquid death.

Magwin had still been new as a holdmother then. Partly from a keen sense of honor, partly from rough kindness, she had adopted Yannas and sworn that she would turn the evil act of some unknown beekeeper into good. No one had ever lived to give up sinnom; but coached by Magwin, Yannas had done it. The bee venom had been the key: it dulled the craving, yet brought no pleasure itself, only pain. Seven journeys had passed, and each one had taken two journeys' worth of life from Yannas, yet the grip of the old addiction failed to fade.

Dubich already regretted having lashed out; it only gave her the excuse to lie. He breathed in and tried to draw on the reserves of patience he had used raising children. Though no child had ever given them the trouble Yannas had.

"You have to give it up, Yannas. If not for yourself, do it for the rest of us. You're the greatest hivekeeper this motherhold has ever had. You may be the greatest one living. And Magwin has made a foolish bargain trusting her life to you."

He told Yannas about Renata then. Yannas watched, immobile, her face complex with shadows as her life was with falsehoods.

"She can't win this contest without your help," Dubich finished.

Yannas was silent a long time. She would not look at Dubich's face. "She was wrong to trust me," she said at last.

"She had reason to. She saved your life. She would never ask for your thanks, but you owe it to her."

"I suppose I do." Yannas's voice was soft, but thick with irony.

Dubich studied her face, searching for a glimmer of love or loyalty. Droning, monotonous music filled the silence—the voice of the fine swarm Yannas had created, first as apprentice, then as assistant, finally as master hivekeeper.

Dubich turned away, defeated. "How is the swarm?" he asked.

"They weathered the last journeypiece well," Yannas said. "One hive is raising a new mother. We will be able to start a new hive soon." Her voice warmed when she spoke of them, as it never did for any mere human. Not even a human who needed her gratitude. If only, Dubich thought desperately, she felt toward us as she feels toward the bees.

"We will have a new mother bee soon, one way or another," he said; the words ached. "You will have to choose sides. I hope you will choose Magwin's."

He waited for an answer, but Yannas said nothing, and he had to leave without knowing her choice.

When Yannas gave out word that the bees were ready to dehive, the whole camp began to stir. Spirits were high; it was the beginning of the human journeycycle as well as the bees'. Soon a procession of wicker litters was winding up the path to the hive tent. A crowd of workers helped shift the heavy hives onto litters, each bound for a preselected site on the plain around them. Yannas stood at the center of the hubbub, passing out directions. For a space around her, everything was quiet, as if her presence stilled the chaos and vitality of the day.

She had marked the hive sites carefully in advance, and each pair of workers set off surely over the uneven ground with a sealed hive slung between them. Soon the hives would be scattered to the alpine meadows nestling in sheltered spots amid the glacial washwater and scree. The nectar from these Dawn flowers was too earthy for human tastes; but the bees needed it to strengthen them for their long pilgrimage east.

The hive tent was only half-empty when Yannas called a halt; the rest of the hives were marked as Renata's. When the crowd had gone, Yannas slung a pack of tools over her shoulder, fastened a pouch of food to her belt, and set off to open the hives. She always did this part alone.

Up out of the river valley, the land was flat as far as the eye could see—a vast, glacier-scoured plain. A cold wind swept down off the ice from the west, unimpeded by anything but a few solitary boulders. It was not the same place they had come to start the last journey. That place had passed on into morning. This was new land, released only recently from the grip of night. Over their lifetimes, the children in camp might see this spot mature, bear fruit, and pass on into searing day; but they would never live to see it reborn. That was left to their descendants.

Yannas strode like a grim specter through the rock-and-water world. Her distended shadow leaped from rock to rock like something younger than she. She wore a one-piece suit, the legs tucked into high boots, and the neck and cuffs cinched tight to prevent stray bees from entering. Her dark bee veil was draped shawllike over her shoulders, but as she neared the first set of hives, she made no attempt to draw it over her face.

The hives lay in a valley, sheltered by a snaking ridge of gravel. Yannas checked to make sure each hive entrance faced the low sun, and that the cylinders were firmly placed on the rocky ground, tilting slightly forward so no rain would run inside. Where the tilt didn't satisfy her, she shimmed up the back with a flat piece of shale. Then she cracked open the tops with her pry bar to check the bees' supply of feed honey, noting down hives that were low. Last, she took the netting from over the broad hive mouth and sat down on a nearby rock to watch the bees emerge.

They were tentative at first, unsure of the new world that lay outside their doorway. At last a few began circling the hives on unpracticed wings. When Yannas saw one fly off toward a nearby clump of blooming everweep, she smiled. It transformed the gloomy landscape of her face like sun on a leaden lake.

She had never believed that any human was responsible for rescuing her from the ruins of her past. It was the bees who had done it. They had taught her to stop seeing herself everywhere, and to look at the world as they did.

Yannas studied the spot beneath her feet, making herself mentally into a bee. The apparent barrenness of the land was an illusion. It was a human mistake to see nothing here, for humans looked on the wrong scale. It was a world for the small and subtle. In every crack and nook, life had taken hold. Lichen first, then mosses with tiny white flowers, then grasses that grew more down than up. In the silence, Yannas could almost hear the burrowbugs sliding through the thin soil, the roots rustling and sipping water, the earth breathing in, released from the weight of winter.

When she set off toward the next hive site, she no longer stared gloomily at the ground ahead, but breathed the fresh air, head back. She went out of her way to visit a spring-fed pool where a few maiden's-tears bloomed. The names of the Dawn flowers were all sad. Yannas had named some herself, following the tradition.

The second cluster of hives had been carelessly placed, probably by youngsters who knew no better. Yannas set about righting the damage. This time she had to light her smoker to calm the bees in one hive where the comb tubes inside had been jostled from their places.

It was not until she reached the third cluster of hives that she realized she was being followed. Looking up from her work, she saw a shadow move against a faraway rock. Its source was invisible; but it was an old mistake in this country, to hide yourself and forget your shadow.

She sat down near the hives to eat her dinner and think about whoever followed her. She was a long way from the camp. If it was one of the roving barbarians, the hives were her best protection, for they knew and feared the bees. But she guessed it had to do with events in Magwin Ghar's motherhold.

There was a patter of falling gravel to her left. She looked up. Standing with one foot on a nearby boulder was Renata Oblin, one elbow on her raised knee, the other hand on her hip. She looked like the dashing heroine of an old story, ready for anything.

"Are you sitting there out of recklessness or bravado?" she asked. She had some pebbles in one hand, and was working them around, scrape, clack.

"No," Yannas said. She turned back to her brown bread and nuts.

"You're three feet from a hive, and not wearing gloves or veil. I watched you. You didn't even put on the veil when you opened the hive."

"The bees know me. And the stings don't bother me as much as most."

"That's lucky. Most people would be long dead before they could get back to the motherhold if they were swarmed out here."

She came forward, but stopped five paces from Yannas. "I am Renata Oblin. Pardon me if I don't shake your hand."

"I am Yannas." She nodded in Renata's direction, barely polite.

"Yannas No-Name," Renata said. "I know. I heard about you even in Oblin Motherhold. Our hivekeepers were in awe of your Sweettooth and Morning Green blends. They used to say you were possessed."

Yannas's jaw muscles clenched as she chewed over the nuances of that statement.

"You should be back taking care of your bees," she said, putting the rest of her dinner back in its pouch. "They'll start to pine if you leave them sitting in the hive tent. They want to be free."

A smile crossed Renata's handsome face. "Offering advice to the enemy? What would Magwin Ghar say?"

"I am saying it for your bees' sake, not yours. Not that you'll listen." Yannas sounded sour and elderly even in her own ears.

"Oh, I will listen," Renata said seriously. "I will listen carefully to whatever you say."

Yannas turned a sharp, skeptical gaze on her. "What do you want?"

"I should think that was obvious. I want you on my side."

There was a long silence. The drone of bees and the distant, ever-present trickle of water were the only sounds in the chill, birdless air.

Renata spoke first. "In the camp, they told me not to try. They said you owed too much to Magwin Ghar. But it seemed to me you had another loyalty as well: to your craft. And I can make it possible for you to do things Magwin Ghar would never dream of."

She threw down her handful of pebbles and walked restlessly around, too full of energy to keep still. "This motherhold is lax; the standards are low. They don't produce nearly as much honey as they could, nor as high quality. It's not a lack of talent; it's a lack of leadership, of drive. I want to organize things more efficiently. I'll give you helpers for the drudgery, so you can concentrate on the creative part. I will improve the processing and distilling so it's equal to your hive culture."

She turned to face Yannas intently. "I want to give you a chance to achieve the recognition you deserve. We can set standards here. You're a brilliant artist working with poor tools. I can give you better ones."

It was as though someone had snipped time with a scissors and overlapped the edges, so that Yannas was faced with an earlier version of herself. She could remember how magical those words had been: ambition, achievement, success. She, too, had set out to be the best once, but not at hivekeeping. The bees were a refuge— an end, not a beginning.

"You've misjudged me," she said. "There is nothing I want to accomplish. I learned long ago that the world never thanks you for doing well. If you raise your head up above the rest, you're only more likely to get kicked in the face."

"That's not true!" Renata said positively. "You've got to have goals. You have to fix your eyes on something, then put every ounce of skill and strength into achieving it. Your success is in your own hands."

"Is it?" Yannas said. "How do you know?"

"If I didn't believe that, life would be like this land here—"

"Yes," Yannas said, looking out over the scoured plain where life was taking hold against all odds. "Life would be like this."

"—a barren, desolate plain. No peaks, no valleys, nothing noble or useful in it. Well, *my* life isn't going to be like that."

Yannas could remember when she had yearned for crags and gorges, for dangerous rapids and rainbows. Those had been years of glorious, self-destructive gestures. Now the bees had taught her to see fine textures, to praise little things.

"I had goals once," she said. "As lofty and compelling as yours."

"What happened?"

"The world paid not the slightest attention."

"Don't blame it on the world. It was you who gave up."

Gave up. The words chafed a spot still raw after all these years. "Yes, I gave up!" Yannas bit off the words. "Because I couldn't have made myself what I wanted to be."

"I don't believe that."

"Of course you don't. Why should you believe me just because I have lived twice as long and seen twice as much as you?"

She got up, hefted her pack to her shoulder, and started off. She heard a step behind her, Renata following. She wheeled around, angry and bitter.

"Prove, prove, prove!" she said. "You youngsters always want to prove something, as if that's all that can make you solid and real. You all want to set yourselves apart, draw lines around yourselves and say, 'Here, that's where I begin and the rest of the world leaves off. This is *my* achievement. *I* am real.' And it never makes a damn bit of difference."

She turned and stalked off, stones crunching under her boots. I am a bitter, cynical old woman, she thought. I am dry and twisted like a brittle-root. I am a scarecrow on her path, with a sign hung under my neck: "Don't pass this way."

The grasses bent unheeded under her heels, then sprang up again when she had passed.

When the bees were safely out, the master honeycrafters met in Magwin Ghar's tent to plan the journey. For the first time in memory, Magwin posted sentinels to keep their deliberations from reaching the wrong ears.

The six who arrived were each experts, representing the 103 things one could create from bee culture: there was Brahm, the fermenter of wines and liqueurs; Bogdan, the chandler of sweet-scented beeswax; Zabra, the mixer of soaps, lotions, and pomades; and Reema, the creator of medicines and rubs from the potent honey of plants that calmed the heart, thinned the blood, or purged the digestion. Extractor Dubich Rhud was there, who purified, cured, and stored the raw honeys in his vast tent—now almost empty, but soon to become an archive of varietal honeys, each culled from a distinct blend of flowers. Last of all, Yannas came in and sat in the shadows by the tent flap.

As was customary, Magwin Ghar served a rich mead from the last journey. They sat awhile, tasting the sunny meadows in their cups, remembering the peaceful days spent gathering the honey they now drank. It had been a good journey, and they had had huge wagonloads of products to sell as they had retraced their steps west from day to dawn. Now the honey was almost gone, and the wagons were instead rich with grain, cloth, and tools bought from the towns and farms along their route.

"Ah, you should have seen the honeys we gathered in my third journey," old Brahm said, as if to forestall anyone impertinently suggesting that their last journey had been the best. "Why, we must have had fifty wagons, and our vats were twice as tall as I. We lived sweetly then!"

Not to be outdone, Bogdan spoke up with a reminiscence of his favorite journey, a story all of them had heard a hundred times, till they knew even the pauses and where to laugh. And all of them did laugh, except Magwin, who seemed preoccupied, and Yannas, who never laughed at anything.

The tent was filled with memories brighter than the candles, and everyone was expecting Magwin to refill their glasses, when instead she said, "We need to put our minds to strategy, my friends. We need to plan a honey that will humble young Renata Oblin and win us her queen."

"The upstart chit!" Zabra grumbled. "She knows no more about honey than my elbow does."

"Maybe so," said Brahm, "but my best apprentice has gone off to join her."

This led to a long series of complaints and recriminations. Half the young people in the motherhold seemed to have defected; the other half were getting forward about proposing crazy new ideas. Three girls who had reached the wander-age, inspired by Renata, had set off to seek a mother bee despite all their mothers' dissuasion. The young men thought of nothing but jockeying for Renata's attention. At last, Magwin held up her hands impatiently. "There is nothing we can do. We knew it would be like this."

"I never heard of such a duel," Zabra said, half under her breath. "Dragging the whole motherhold in—"

Magwin spoke loudly to drown her out. "I thought of using our Crystal Dew. We've done well with it for three journeys now, and it's a favorite in Erdrum."

"I can't keep our apothecary honeys stocked without going farther south to get some forest-flower honey," Reema said. "It's been
two journeys since we've gotten any bloodbloom or hoar. My stores
are almost gone."

Others spoke up with objections. Journey plannings were always
contentious, and the final route was inevitably a compromise ham-
mered out to balance conflicting needs.

After much wrangling, Magwin squinted into the shadows by
the door. "You've said nothing, Yannas. What do you think?"

Yannas had been thinking how much like mollusks they all were:
all crusted round with shells of experience. Every experiment they
had tried, every idea explored, had formed another layer of crust.
By now, Magwin's honeycrafters were nearly impervious to mistake, but paralyzed by the accretion of things they had tried. Yannas
could feel her own experience dragging like a dead weight on her.
She didn't want to add more.

"I think Crystal Dew is a bad idea," she said at last.

"But it's your own formula!" Magwin protested.

"It's become too familiar. Can we win with an old honey if
Renata creates something novel and new?"

"She hasn't got the experience," Zabra said, as if that settled
everything.

Magwin raised a hand to silence her, eyeing Yannas curiously.
"So you think we should try a new formula?"

"I think we need a honey like none that has ever been tasted. A
honey so bewitching, a single drop captures the senses. It must be
a distillation of rain, time, sun, and the souls of flowers."

Their faces showed that they had all dreamed of such a honey,
once. Perhaps, in their youths, they had even believed it was possible.

"What formula do you have in mind?" Magwin asked softly.

"You will not believe me if I tell you."

"Try us."

So Yannas began to recite the list of flowers whose nectars she
would blend through the alchemy of the bees. The others listened,
concentrating. They had all learned as children to decipher the
formulas, composing little songs to remember the hard ones. Every
child in the motherhold carried in his or her head the formulas for
the staple honeys; but only the honeycrafters knew the hundreds
of specialized formulas passed down through the generations.

When Yannas finished, there was silence; it had been a long time since any of them had had to critique a new formula, other than the brash and clumsy inventions of the apprentices. This one was not clumsy, but there was a recklessness to it.

"You depend heavily on the border flowers, those at the edge of night and day," Magwin said at last.

"Those are the flowers whose tastes are deep," Yannas said; "they are the ones who have suffered."

"Meadowmatch?" Brahm asked. "It's a stimulant nectar, not a culinary one. It stings in the mouth, like nettles."

"It will be very dilute in a comb blend with primweed and shattercup. You will scarcely taste it, but it will leave a tingle in the mouth that will cleanse the palate like springwater."

They raised more objections. At first, Yannas justified her choices; but as the criticism kept coming, she became touchy, then defensive, then finally lapsed into a glowering silence.

When they had demolished virtually the whole formula and suggested a dozen substitutions, Magwin said, "Well, what is your verdict? Dubich?"

"It might work," he said, "but with so much hanging on the outcome, it is terribly risky."

"Brahm?"

"Not without revisions."

"Zabra?"

"It's a reckless experiment. We can't afford it."

"Reema?"

"The route would be too hard."

"Well." Magwin looked around. Yannas's eyes were on the smoke hole, her jaw clenched. "Yannas?" Magwin said softly. "Has Renata approached you?"

They all looked at her. Yannas stared at Magwin, knocked from her self-absorption by the bluntness of the question. At last she said, "Yes."

There was a hiss of indrawn breath from Zabra. "The bitch!"

No one else spoke. The next question was on all their minds: What had Yannas answered?

Magwin did not ask it. Instead, she leaned back against her pillows and said, "I have decided on our journeycourse. We will follow the route of Yannas's formula, without revision. It will be hard on us, and there will be little chance to gather the ingredients for our staple honeys. We will have to cope. It is for a good cause."

Her tone closed off discussion. Zabra rose abruptly, then turned to the tent flap, sparing only a single suspicious look at Yannas. The others followed more slowly. Yannas sat frozen, staring at Magwin Ghar. Last of all, she turned to go.

"Yannas," Magwin said.

Yannas turned. They were alone.

"Did you think you could goad me into giving you an excuse to join Renata?" Magwin said.

It was true, yet not true. Yannas felt a surge of anger that Magwin knew her so well. "Renata?" she said contemptuously. "She's a vain, reckless dreamer. A child. I would no more work for her than . . ."

"Than what?"

Than grasp after lost youth? Yannas was silent.

"Well, I hope you will work for me now," Magwin said seriously. "I have put my life in your hands."

Yannas looked down, scowling. There was so much past between them that their shells were fused. There was no pulling apart.

"Don't worry," Magwin said. "I am content with the risk. Just do your best."

After Yannas had gone, Dubich returned to the tent. He blew out the candles, then sat down and watched Magwin sip a horn of mead. "You're taking a big risk," he said. "Zabra is saying that Yannas is a turncoat and her formula was planned to make us lose. She is saying you took Renata's bait."

"Jealous old whiner. We have to stop her, Dubich. Everyone must have absolute faith in Yannas."

"What about you?" Dubich asked. "Do you have faith in this formula?"

"I was about to ask you."

"I told you already: risky. It might be inspiration or delusion. Now you."

"I don't know, Dubich. But I've learned over the journeys that if you have a genius on your hands, you don't try to steer her. Just leave her alone. That's what I'm going to do."

"I'm glad it's not my life staked on it."

A smile spread across Magwin's face. "I'm glad it's not yours, too. Come here." He took the pillow next to her. She ran a finger down his cheek, then playfully kissed his nose. Not in the mood for joking, he drew her against him, aware how every knot and hollow of their bodies fit together. All the things he had taken for granted—the softness of her skin where the sun had not touched it, the contented little "Hmmm" she gave—all seemed impossibly precious. They rolled back on the pillows together, every touch poignant with the knowledge that there would be no long forever together.

Before long, Renata's group packed up their hives, tents, and equipment, and pulled out of camp, bound for the first stop on whatever journeycourse they had chosen. People gathered to watch them go, expecting to see amateurish disorder—but they didn't. The move was smoothly run, without a single voice raised.

Yannas stood at the entrance of the hive tent, glumly watching a troop of bare-chested young men hoisting the last of the hives onto litters. She had tried to offer them advice to avoid jarring the bees, but they had told her they knew what they were doing. The galling thing was, they did. Yannas knew her own hives would not be moved with such swift efficiency.

"Sure you won't change your mind?"

Yannas turned; it was Renata. She was dressed in leather: tight-fitting boots and elbow-length gloves that glistened as she moved.

"Whose formula are you following?" Yannas asked. She wondered which of this group was capable of more than mimickry.

"Several of us have ideas," Renata said. "I gather Magwin Ghar will follow yours?"

Yannas nodded.

"Then I suppose you are my mortal enemy," Renata said. Her tone was light, but her eyes were serious.

It came to Yannas that if she succeeded, Renata would die. All of that boundless daring, arrogance, hope, silly flamboyant gloves—all would cease to be. Utterly extinguished, never more to tempt or tease her with memories. Dead as surely as that other youth like her, that youth Yannas had once been.

"Go away," Yannas said harshly.

Renata stood watching her, puzzled.

"Go on! Go join your young heroes and athletes. Leave me to my crones and codgers."

A smile flashed across Renata's tanned face. She turned and

trotted down the slope after the litter-bearers, like a frisky young colt. When she came up to the last one, she clapped him on the back with a comradely gusto. Yannas could hear their laughter faint on the air.

They saw no more of Renata's group for a long time. Even at the well-known meadows where they often encountered other motherholds, there was no sign of her. "She must have led them far away," Magwin Ghar said to Dubich. "Too bad. I was counting on some defections."

"Maybe she foresaw that," Dubich said.

Magwin shook her head. "She's clever, damn her."

For Magwin's group the journey started out badly. Lacking many strong young workers, Magwin had to transfer the hard work onto older shoulders. Grandfathers who had happily retired to camp work were again pressed into carrying hive litters and scouting. To free up young mothers with children, Magwin organized a child wagon and persuaded some grandmothers to take on its wailing load.

As the journeypiece passed, the grumbling grew. Everyone was working harder, yet the vats of honey in the mixing tents were not as full as they should have been. Long after the motherhold should have passed east into the gentle plains of Morning, they were still seeking out rare stands of flowers in the rough, unmapped country on the edge of Dawn.

The cold began to get into Dubich's bones. It took them fifteen long whiles trudging through torrents of rain to reach their fourth stop, and at the end, people set up the tents wherever they fell, in a bedraggled line. After supervising the erection of the mixing tent, Dubich came home to find his and Magwin's tent no more than a heap of soggy canvas on the ground. Silently cursing, he wrestled the sopping cloth over the poles, then went inside to start a fire. Another supper of pea soup was ahead, for there were no farms from which to buy better fare in this country.

Magwin arrived soon after. "Damned stubborn *artist*," she said, and Dubich knew she had been speaking to Yannas. "There was an easier route, you know. But she had to have the sweet-memory with the blue veins, even though no one but she can tell it from the regular kind."

"Close that tent flap," Dubich said irritably.

Magwin took off her dripping cloak and hung it up, though everything was equally wet. "The scouts say this river we're camped on leads down to a nice, fertile prairie," she said glumly. "Lots of marsh-crowns and meadowcup there. Birds, game. Sunshine." Dubich said nothing. That was how their quarrels always started, with him silent and icy. It drove her into a rage.

This time she didn't rise to it. "What are people saying, Dubich?" she asked wearily.

"What do you suppose? They're cold and tired and angry, and they're blaming Yannas's formula."

Magwin was silent awhile, then came to a decision. "We're going to leave this country. I have more to consider than just her formula."

Suddenly afraid he had persuaded her, Dubich said, "The formula is your life, Magwin."

"I know. But I'm still holdmother."

The way down the river valley proved to be a steep, rocky trail. The wagons could barely get through. Magwin walked back and forth along the slow-moving line in the driving rain, joking to encourage people. From his seat in the vat wagon, Dubich wondered how she managed to hide how low her own spirits were.

Ahead, the trail plunged into a torn shred of mist. As the hive litters passed a slippery patch, one exhausted litter-bearer stumbled. The heavy ceramic cylinder teetered, hit the ground, then fell. It toppled slowly, end over end down the steep slope.

While Dubich still watched, frozen in horror, a streak of gray rain gear appeared from nowhere, flying down the slope. It was Yannas. Dubich jumped from the wagon and clambered after. When he arrived, a small crowd of people had gathered. He saw with a sickened heart that the hive was cracked open, irreparable. The hivekeeper was kneeling beside it; confused bees circled dizzily. When Yannas looked up at Magwin, her face was streaming wet, and Dubich did not think it was just the rain.

"We will have to sacrifice the mother bee," she said in a tight voice. "We have no spare hives."

Magwin looked grim. Mother bees were scarce enough without losing healthy ones. "Do what you have to," she said.

"Get away, all of you," Yannas said fiercely. "Leave me alone."

Magwin motioned them away. From a distance they watched as

Yannas located the mother of the broken hive. For a moment she bowed her head over the large, helpless insect, then smashed her with a rock.

It took a long while to coax the swarm into another hive. Many of the bees would not leave their old home, where their mother's eggs lay in their broken combs. There was nothing to do but leave them to perish.

It was a silent camp that night. They had lost a hive. Such a thing had not happened in ten journeys. Only a slovenly, ill-kept motherhold could be so careless. Shame slunk from tent to tent, and people began talking of the ill luck that followed them.

As they traveled east, pausing often to let the bees feed, the sun gradually rose higher in the sky, and the broad, level plains spread before them. Morning was a pleasant, settled land where they came across farms, villages, and even slowly moving cities—since, as Ping turned, everything on its face turned with it. Everyone welcomed them—especially the children, who saw only the confectionery wagon—but also the bakers, cooks, and canners, who haggled for the special blends. Everyone needed honey. There were sometimes rumors of plants or trees with sap sweet enough to make sugar; but most people laughed at the thought of anything replacing honey.

But this journey they could not loiter long in Morning. Yannas's formula called for few of its rich, sanguine honeys.

They passed quickly through the time of primweed and aspen groves, then skirted the fertile wineberry bogs. They were making for the Straits of Carriwell, the narrow bridge between the seas that lay across their path to the Summerlands. The motherholds often met there and celebrated the midjourney Festival of Flowers together. Everyone was looking forward to it.

As they neared their final Morning camp, Yannas traveled ahead to locate sites for her hives along the Windroot River. The Dawnlands had left a glacial chill inside her. She had come away to warm her mind—not in the sun, but in the sight of the maturing land. She halted at the edge of a marsh, letting the healing breeze wash over her. Nearby, a pair of whoorowits was courting. The male erupted from the reeds, a flash of iridescent green scales. The female met him in midair, and they pirouetted together, synchronized as jugglers, the biology of youth in rushing flight. Yannas smiled at the sight. Her face felt cracked, like a statue trying to smile.

She waded in knee-deep among a flaming stand of marsh-crowns, pinching off spent blooms to help the new buds grow. They were skinny-stalked flowers, awkward adolescents, brash and still a bit vulnerable, like the rest of this land. As she reached out for another bloom, she stopped—for a bee was already working this stand. There was no way to tell, but somehow she felt it was one of *her* bees—or had been.

When she looked, the hive was there, sheltered under the gentle bluff. It was a Ghar hive; Renata was here. For a moment she hesitated, for it was bad form to inspect another motherhold's hive; but her desire to be sure her bees were not being mistreated overcame her manners.

The bees seemed active, shuttling in and out of the hive entrance with their burdens of pollen and nectar. But as she watched, it occurred to Yannas they were almost *too* active. A pungent smell hung about the hive. Suspicious, she took her stout pry knife and cracked open the hive cover. As she lifted it, the smell enveloped her.

"Get back!" a male voice ordered.

Yannas looked up to see Hudin, Zabra's son, standing bare-chested on the lip of the bluff several yards away. He had a bow and arrow, drawn and pointed at Yannas.

"Put that thing down!" Yannas ordered angrily. "Didn't your mother teach you anything?"

Instead of obeying, he gave a loud whistle. Two figures appeared nearby, then came dashing through the grass toward them.

"Get away from that hive," Hudin ordered, gesturing with his bow. His voice was tough and arrogant. Yannas lowered the hive cover and moved away. He came up and took her stick and knife. As the other two arrived, he said, "I caught a spy."

"Stop this playacting," Yannas said. "You make me laugh."

He gave her a rough shove. "Move."

Guarded by the three young men, Yannas walked north.

They came upon Renata's camp where the river broadened into a placid lake, dammed by its own delta. The camp was compact, laid out with discipline; Yannas could not help but think of the straggling collection Magwin Ghar's camps had become. Hudin left them to run on ahead.

"So Magwin Ghar has finally caught up," Renata said as she strode toward them across the camp circle. Her hair was swept back and her sleeves rolled up. She walked side by side with Hudin, hips almost touching, with a bravura that reminded Yannas of the whoorowits.

"We've been on the lookout for you," Renata said. "You took your time in the Dawnlands. The Festival of Flowers is over; the other motherholds have gone on."

"We were following a plan," Yannas said sourly.

"While you froze your bees, we have been enjoying ourselves," Renata said airily. "We have learned a lot, and tried out many new ideas."

"Like drugging your bees?" Yannas accused.

Renata glanced at Hudin. He said, "We caught her snooping in one of our hives."

There was a pause. "It's a distillation of meadowmatch," Renata said at last. "We put it in a tray at the bottom of the hive, and it stimulates the bees. We get a third more honey in the same time."

"Did no one tell you about the harm to your bees?"

"There was some old wives' tale. But we tried it, and our bees don't seem harmed." She paused. "Will they be?"

She was pumping for information. Yannas felt outrage; they had experimented on their bees without even knowing the risks.

"Old wives' tales are there for a reason. Your bees will be fine this journey, but you will wear them out. You will get nothing from them next journey."

Renata shrugged. "It's *this* journey I'm worried about."

"A good holdmother always worries about next journey."

"Tell me that when I'm holdmother."

Yannas wanted to slap her. Irresponsible, self-confident girl, so full of her sense of control. She did not know how quickly events could take it from her. How could she know? She had never failed.

Hudin was whispering to Renata. He looked restless. Renata nodded. "Far better to hold her. Without her hivekeeper, Magwin Ghar would be doomed."

The words made Yannas's heart hum with anxiety. But she knew Renata, knew her too well. In a proud, slightly contemptuous tone, she said, "It would be a dishonest way to win. Everyone would say you could not win fair."

They were the right words. Renata said, "She is right, Hudin. We don't need to use tricks. I have a better idea." She whispered into the young man's ear. He frowned, but turned and walked off. "Come with me," Renata said. "You will not leave without tasting our hospitality."

Renata's tent was spartan and functional, the tent of a field commander. But the food she served was good and plentiful, better than Yannas had eaten for journeypieces. She tried not to look like she was enjoying it.

As they were finishing the meal, Hudin came in with a honeypot. Renata opened it and spread some pale honey on a rice cracker. She held it out. "We just finished this blend."

Yannas took it, consumed with curiosity. It had a delicate aroma. "Sweet-memory," she said.

"Yes, we've got quite a lot of it."

Yannas let a drop of the sunshine-colored liquid fall onto her tongue, letting the smell drift up her nostrils. Then she bit into it. The honey had been blended with striking originality. It was a simple formula that tasted of dawn and early blooms. It filled Yannas's mouth with a distillation of young things, long-legged flowers and a land that had never known failure. Memories rushed to her head. She could never make a honey like this. Not now.

"You like it?" Renata said.

Yannas looked down to hide her face. For the first time, she realized she might not win this contest. Renata had no expertise, but, with simple green vitality, she might prevail.

"I am no judge," Yannas said. "This is a young honey. Too young for me."

All the way home, as she pushed through the tall grass, the memory of that taste haunted her.

They had come to the sunbaked shortgrass prairie, when the epidemic struck. It started among the children. One moment they were swimming and running half-dressed in the sun, brown as mud; the next they lay shaking with a fever, dry cough, and rash. Reema, the apothecary, brought the diagnosis to Magwin Ghar's tent. The motherhold was camped by a wide, muddy river that meandered through the plains till it disappeared in the blue distance. Dubich had rolled up the sides of their tent to let in the cool eastern breeze, and now sat cross-legged, repairing some leather. The sun hung unblinking in the sky.

"Spotted fever," Reema said. "And I used the last of my hoar-honey today. We took a risk not going south to replenish our curative honeys. Our grandchildren may pay for our mistake."

Magwin Ghar said nothing to the reproach, but Dubich knew how she flinched inside. Everyone had something to blame her with these days.

"It is not too late to go south," she said.

"It is if we want to spend time gathering desert honeys."

"We can do both."

Dubich's bones ached at the thought. He said quietly, "It is a long way to the forests where the hoarflowers grow. We cannot get there and back again in time."

"We will have to," Magwin Ghar said doggedly. "I will not have my grandchildren die."

It was a hellish journeypiece. Half the motherhold was sick, the other half worn out with doctoring, yet Magwin still pushed them to travel fast. By the time they reached the forest, two children had died, and some said it was the journeying that did it.

"But if we hadn't hurried, more might have died," Magwin said desperately to Dubich. "What do they expect from me?"

They stayed to milk the hoarflowers only till the sickness had crested. When they turned wearily toward the desert again, they met the other motherholds heading for the Erdrum market, their wagons heavy with brimming honey vats, ready to trade. A third of Yannas's formula was still ungathered.

Their last camp lay in a dusty canyon under the glaring forenoon sun. The desert flowers had never seemed more scattered or fleeting. Yannas worked like a fiend, scouting out the stands of flowers and checking the hives. She would come in after long, solitary trips, her hair and eyebrows white with desert dust, her face and hands black from the sun. Then she would work feverishly with Dubich in the hot mixing tent, experimenting with new combinations whose ingredients she refused to reveal.

The boys who went out to fetch in the combs told of a pungent odor emanating from the trays Yannas had placed in the hives. Their grandmothers hushed them and said, "Don't you repeat stories like that." When Dubich mentioned the rumor to Magwin Ghar, she simply said, "I don't believe it." But her eyes said that she did, and didn't care.

But there was another secret Yannas kept closer. There was one hive whose location no one but she knew. On the edge of a wind-scoured gully, she had found a stand of spike-leaved plants, spiral cones with a single white flower on top. The first time she came upon them, she stood looking for a long time. Their name was sinnom, and it did not appear on any lawful formula. A few drops of honey from this plant would bring such pleasure and comfort that a lifetime of happiness crowded into a minute could not equal it.

The smell of sinnom honey came back to her as vividly as if it were yesterday. She had kept it in a thin-necked green bottle. At first she had taken it only in leisure, lying entranced in its spell instead of sleeping. Then she had started taking it in waking times, and all the little miseries and defeats of life became lost in its glow. The honey had been her success, her fulfillment. She could see it even now, the color of gold and more precious, the antidote to everything.

She turned away, feeling the aching cavity the sinnom had left. She stumbled blindly down the path toward the nearest hive. When she reached it she seized one of the guard bees from the entrance. Furious, it stung her hand, and she sank to her knees, clutching her wrist, letting the pain burn through her till it had cauterized her nerves. Then she closed up the hive, strapped it to her back, and, cursing herself, moved it to the gully where the sinnom plants stood.

Since then the bees had slowly been filling their hive with the priceless, deadly nectar. Whenever she came to check the hive, Yannas soaked a rag in liquor and tied it over her face to keep herself from smelling its intoxicating perfume. She told herself she needed it only for insurance, only as a last resort. She would never really use it.

The combs filled too slowly, and time passed too fast. At last they had to take what scant honey they could get. The hives were brought in, and the half-filled combs were taken out and marked; then, in the busy extractor tent, workers loaded the cylindrical comb frames one by one into the spinner. Everyone took turns pushing the treadle lever that kept the spinner constantly going through sleep and waking, till all the combs were empty.

They were the last motherhold to arrive in Erdrum. The broad plain south of the city bubbled with white dome tents as if someone had lathered it with soap. All the shady camp spots were taken, so Magwin Ghar's motherhold had to camp on a sunbaked spot far from the well. As they moved slowly to erect their tents, her people looked like leaves blown in off the desert: dry, dusty, cracked-leather-skinned. They were like wizened relics among the crowds of visitors and shoppers.

Their task was far from over. As soon as the mixing tent was erected, a new stage began. The pots of labeled honeys were sorted and strained; then Dubich banished all visitors but Yannas, and set about the task of measuring and mixing. His worktable was a labyrinth of glass vessels, gleaming with bottled sunlight. Each honey had its signature: clear as water, milky as wax, diamond, gold, garnet, and amber. Some were thick as reluctant syrup; others poured like wine. Some were sweet, others spiced or heady. He knew them all.

Every motherhold in the huge camp soon knew of the strange battle brewing. As he toiled side by side with Yannas, scarcely sleeping, Dubich knew the other honeycrafters were probably sitting around their campfires speculating on strategy. Would the combatants gamble on one of the new spiced blends—Amberfoil, perhaps, or Cinnabar? Would they modify their stronger honeys by heating them first, or use them raw? Would they strive for a striking color, or emphasize bouquet and flavor? Through the haze of weariness, Dubich sometimes smiled to think how surprised they would be.

For it was a honey like no other. As he tasted and tested, Dubich alternated between manic confidence and fear. Sometimes he thought it was inspired. At others, insane.

Word came that Renata had visited Magwin's tent to bargain over the time and place of the contest, the identities and number of the judges.

"She was shrewd," Magwin said when he came, exhausted, to her tent to rest. "I wonder what happened to that reckless youngster who came down out of the hills." As he drifted off to sleep, his last sight was of Magwin curled on her cushions like a wily old lizard. Her hair had gone entirely white since the journey started.

Yannas could not sleep. She had been at Dubich's side for many whiles; now she sat alone in the closely guarded mixing tent. Her masterwork was almost done. She dipped a tasting-stick into the glass beaker and let a drop of honey fall onto her tongue. A drama of conflicting flavors unfolded in her mouth. Dark, brooding spices followed by a tingle of shattercup like the near passage of death; then a hint of aftertaste, fleeting as intuition, that might be fresh-born flowers, and might not. It was a masterful honey; but one addition could make it irresistible. Hidden deep in her inside pocket was a small flask of sinnom honey. She had extracted it herself when Dubich was asleep in his tent. One drop mixed into the pot would be impossible to detect. But it would make the judges crave the honey beyond reason, yearn to recapture the taste as if it were youth itself.

The flask felt hard against her ribs. She rose and walked out into the hot sun, her eyes burning from dust and overwork. She wandered aimlessly among the tents, past a boy washing clothes and a noisy marriage party, past a jeweler from the city hawking golden bees.

"Yannas No-Name," a voice said at her side. She turned and saw Bosna, Reema's daughter, who had left a journey ago to become one of Renata's troupe.

"Is your honey ready?" the girl asked. But no, she was no longer a girl. There were frown lines in her forehead, and her mouth had a pinched look.

"Almost," Yannas said, distrusting the woman.

"Renata's is done," Bosna said. She waited as if expecting a question; when Yannas said nothing, she continued, "It is very good."

"I have no doubt," Yannas said.

Bosna glanced around. "Would you like to taste it?" She unbuttoned a pocket and drew a glass flask out. "I managed to get a sample from the mixing tent. I want Magwin Ghar to have the advantage. I never thought she was a good holdmother till I had to put up with Renata. She's an arrogant bitch, that one."

And you are a treacherous viper, Yannas thought. She took the flask, intending to dash it to the ground, but its color caught her eye: a light gold, like a young child's hair. She clutched it, overcome with the desire to taste.

"You won't tell anyone, will you?" Bosna whispered.

"No," Yannas said. She was already an accomplice. She turned and walked away. Oblivious of all around her, she threaded through the busy camp till she found a deserted cul-de-sac and crouched down, gazing at the contraband flask. Slowly, she uncorked it and let the aroma drift up to her nose. It was unspiced. Renata had wagered on simplicity. Yannas tilted the flask and let the honey drop to her tongue.

Its flavor was faint at first and Yannas groped to place it; but it grew more vivid as it warmed and dissolved on the tongue. Yannas took a second taste, then a third. A sharp, nostalgic ache pierced her. She was surrounded by long-gone years of rustling grass, and wind-pleated lakes, and birds playing catch-'em in the sky out of sheer joy in their wings. It was a cordial of youth, of exuberance. It was simple, yes, but astonishingly original. There was even a hint of tree sap in it. Yannas had never thought of feeding her bees on tree sap.

She realized there were tears in her eyes. No honey had ever moved her like this, not since the old days. She wondered if she had been beaten. Beside this, her own honey was like the tears of tortured flowers, a honey of pain and endings. Would it be enough to kill the spell of Renata's youth? Yannas fingered the other flask in her pocket, longing to let it erase the terrible choice before her.

The judgment was held under the walls of Erdrum, in a broad space cleared of tents for the occasion. When Magwin Ghar arrived, surrounded by her master honeycrafters, the crowd was already large; toward the back, people perched on wagons and barrels to see. The three judges were waiting, seated on campstools in a wagon. Magwin Ghar took her place beside Renata. Behind them, their respective hivekeepers waited, each with a buzzing broodpot that carried death.

Renata went first. As her extractor came forward with the flask, she stood watching confidently, arms crossed and head thrown back. The judges passed the flask around to scan its color, and held it up to the sun to test for clarity. Then they uncorked it, and each sampled its aroma. At last they took glass tasting-sticks and dipped them into the flask.

Dubich watched their expressions intently. One was smiling, a faraway look on his face. Another was slowly nodding. The third looked deeply impressed. The honey was clearly not the amateurish, patched-together job Dubich had desperately hoped for. The judges tasted again, then discussed it among themselves. At last they took water to cleanse their mouths for the second honey.

Dubich stepped forward from Magwin's side. He kept the flask veiled till he was before the judges, then swept away the silk cover and revealed its deep garnet color. There was a murmur of admiration from the crowd. The judges took it, smelled, then finally tasted. One frowned in concentration; then, as the aftertaste came, his expression changed to surprise. The judges tasted again, avidly. Their discussion this time was animated. At last one stood. The crowd fell still.

"These are both excellent honeys," he said. "Each has broken new ground that we hope other motherholds will follow. But the choice is clear. For skill, drama, and subtlety, the prize must go to Magwin Ghar."

The crowd hummed like a thousand bees. Giddy with relief, Dubich put his arm around Magwin and gave her a quick squeeze. It had worked. Renata turned with unbroken poise to concede, offering her hand. Magwin took it, then quickly turned away.

Two men stepped to Renata's side. She greeted them without a hint of fear. They led her to a cleared spot, then brought forward the pot of bees that would have been hers. Her face serious, she stripped off her gloves and rolled back her collar and sleeves. A woman came forward to rub her arms and neck with the extract that would simultaneously attract and madden the bees. The crowd melted back, clearing a wide space around her.

Raised voices came from near the judges' wagon. A heated debate was going on amid the honeycrafters who had gathered to taste the contesting honeys. One of the judges called out, "Stop! There has been a serious challenge."

The extractor from the Borg Motherhold emerged from the crowd, holding the wine-red flask. "This honey has sinnom in it!" she announced.

Magwin Ghar wheeled around upon Yannas. The hivekeeper's face was waxy with astonishment. "No!" she said. "It doesn't!"

"Liar!" Magwin growled low. "Damned crazy addict! Did you think you could get away with it? They'll have my life for this."

"There is no sinnom in it!" Yannas strode toward the judges' wagon. People hastily made way for her. She took the flask and faced the judges. "I will prove it. If I had put sinnom in this honey, I would not dare to taste it." She took a long draft.

As the honey took effect, she froze, her face rigid. The flask slipped from her senseless fingers and shattered on the ground. Her eyes glazed in the unmistakable grip of sinnom addiction.

"Damn you, damn you," Magwin whispered, her fists clenched.

"This is shameful!" Holdmother Alphra Borg stepped from the crowd, other holdmothers close behind. "This crime will slur all the motherholds unless we punish it swiftly. We cannot allow sinnom in our tents." Her voice dropped, but kept its metal edge. "I would not have thought it of you, Magwin. You know the penalty. You and your hivekeeper will die together."

Magwin's jaw muscles knotted. Nearby, Yannas stood like a statue. There were tears streaking down her face.

"No!" Dubich stepped foward, and his weary voice made them all fall silent. "Magwin knew nothing about it. It was I who put the sinnom in the honey. I stole it from Yannas; she never knew."

Magwin stared in disbelief. "Dubich! You?"

He turned to her, unable to meet her eyes. His gamble had lost; he had turned her victory into unspeakable dishonor. "I'm sorry, Magwin. I couldn't bear the thought of your losing."

He would not have blamed her for denouncing him. He had betrayed her, dissolved her lifelong reputation in a single drop of sinnom. But she took his hand and gripped it in her strong fist. Quietly, she said, "I pressed you too hard, and you broke. Broke out of love and loyalty. You're too good for me, old man."

"Is this your defense?" Alphra Borg demanded. "That Dubich Rhud is the one to pay?"

Magwin paused. She looked out at the horizon and took a deep breath, as if savoring life and the vitality still in her. Then her eye fell on Renata, standing to one side. Renata, who had accepted the consequences and faced death so coolly a moment ago.

"No," Magwin said. "I am responsible. The whole crazy contest was my idea, my plot to cheat nature just a little longer. But I couldn't win without breaking those who love me, and whom I love." She looked at Dubich, and suddenly her eyes were glassy with tears. But she spoke on, turning once more to Renata, her voice swelling: "I have one consolation. I have created myself a worthy successor."

Alphra Borg said slowly, "Then you and Dubich Rhud will pay the price."

Magwin turned to Dubich, a pang in her look. He said softly, "I am willing."

Tenderly, she reached out and touched his hair. She looked as if she were seeing him for the first time in many months. "It's all white, Dubich. Your hair. You've gotten to be an old man. So old, so tired. And still a romantic fool."

They embraced then, pressed close against each other with the darkness at their backs. Then, holding hands tightly as new lovers, they turned together to where the broodpot stood waiting.

The drug was leaving. Yannas knew it, though the taste still lingered on her tongue, sweet with oblivion. She was falling away, falling back into the world of longing and loss. She struggled not to return to it, but someone was gripping her hand and urging her back. It was Magwin Ghar. So many times over the journeys, she had dragged Yannas back against her will, forcing her to bear the emptiness of the sunlit world.

"Go away," she said.

"No," the voice replied.

It was not Magwin Ghar. Yannas looked down and saw it was not Magwin holding her hand, either. It was Renata. "What are you doing?" she said.

They were sitting on campstools in the open field beneath the walls of Erdrum. There were no crowds any longer; a last few people were filing away or standing about in clumps, talking.

"I am seeing to my hivekeeper," Renata said.

"Your—" Yannas stopped, realizing what must have happened. Grief seized her, sharp as a beesting, numbing her even to the drughunger. She bent over in pain.

"Is she gone?" Yannas asked at last.

"Yes," Renata said. "And Dubich Rhud, too."

A tear dropped on Renata's hand. "I loved her," Yannas said.

"A lot of people loved her," Renata said softly. "I hope someday I can say the same." She tightened her grip. "Yannas, you have to help me now. I have a lot to learn. I need you."

Yannas wanted to howl out, No! I can't! I am too tired. I can't start over again.

"We all need you," Renata said.

There was no strength left in her to push back hunger, and age, and emptiness, and try to go on.

The sunlit field swam before Yannas's eyes. She rose, clenching her jaw. "I have to see to my bees," she said.

MA QUI

◆ ◆ ◆

Alan Brennert

Alan Brennert is a TV writer ("LA Law," "China Beach"), novelist (Time and Chance), *and short story writer (whose story "Her Pilgrim Soul" was adapted as a musical for the off-Broadway stage). He has written several strong stories for F&SF, including this powerful tale—a Nebula Award winner—about some remarkable casualties of the war in Vietnam.*

At night the choppers buzz the bamboo roof of the jungle, dumping from three thousand feet to little more than a hundred, circling, climbing, circling again, no LZ to land in, no casualties to pick up. Above the roar of the rotorwash come the shrieks of the damned: wails, moans, plaintive cries in Vietnamese. It's real William Castle stuff, weird sounds and screaming meemies, but even knowing it's coming from a tape recorder, even hearing the static hiss of the loudspeakers mounted on the Hueys, it still spooks the shit out of the VC. "The Wandering Soul," it's called— the sound of dead Cong, their bodies not given a proper burial, their spirits helplessly wandering the earth. Psychological warfare. Inner Sanctum meets Vietnam. Down in the tunnels Charlie hears it, knows it's a con, tries to sleep but can't, the damned stuff goes on half the night. The wails grow louder the lower the choppers fly, then trail off, to suitably eerie effect, as they climb away. Until the next chopper comes with its cargo of souls in a box.

What horseshit.

It's not like that at all.

I watch the last of the choppers bank and veer south, and for a while, the jungle is quiet again. Around me the ground is a scorched blister, a crater forged by mortar fire, a dusty halo of burnt ground surrounding it, grasses and trees incinerated in the firefight. The crater is my bed, my bunk, my home. I sleep there—if you can call it sleep—and when I've grown tired of wandering the trails, looking for my way back to Da Nang, or Cam Ne, or Than Quit, I always wind up back here. Because this seared piece of earth is the only goddamned thing for miles that isn't Nam. It's not jungle, it's not muddy water, it's not punji sticks smeared with shit. It's ugly, and it's barren, and it looks like the surface of the fucking moon, but it was made by my people, the only signature they can write on this steaming rotten country, and I sleep in it, and I feel at home.

I was killed not far from here, in a clearing on the banks of the Song Cai River. My unit was pinned down, our backup never arrived, we were racing for the LZ where the dust-off choppers were to pick us up. Some of us got careless. Martinez never saw the trip wire in the grass and caught a Bouncing Betty in the groin; he died before we could get him to the LZ Dunbar hit a punji beartrap, the two spiked boards snapping up like the jaws of a wooden crocodile, chewing through his left leg. I thought Prosser and DePaul had pried him loose, but when I looked back I saw their bodies not far from the trap, cut down by sniper fire as they'd tried to rescue him. The bastards had let Dunbar live, and he was still caught in the trap, screaming for help, the blood pouring out between the two punji boards. I started back, firing my M-16 indiscriminately into the tree line, hoping to give the snipers pause enough so that I could free Dunbar—

They took me out a few yards from Dunbar, half a dozen rounds that blew apart most of my chest. I fell, screaming, but I also watched myself fall; I saw the sharp blades of elephant grass slice into my face like razors as I struck the ground; I watched the blood spatter upward on impact, a red cloud that seemed to briefly cloak my body, then dissipate, spattering across the grass, giving the appearance, for a moment, of a false spring—a red dew.

Dunbar died a few minutes later. To the west, the distant thunder of choppers rolled across the treetops. I stood there, staring at the body at my feet, thinking somehow that it must be someone else's body, someone else's blood, and I turned and ran for the choppers, not noticing that my feet weren't quite touching the ground as I ran, not seeing myself pass through the trip wires like a stray wind.

Up ahead, dust-off medics dragged wounded aboard a pair of Hueys. Most of my unit made it. I watched Silverman get yanked aboard; I saw Esteban claw at a medic with a bloody stump he still believed was his hand. I ran to join them, but the big Chinooks started to climb, fast, once everyone was on. "Wait for me!" I yelled, but they couldn't seem to hear me over the whipping of the blades; "Son of a bitch, wait for *me*!"

They didn't slow. They didn't stop. They kept on rising, ignoring me, abandoning me. Goddamn them, what were they *doing*? Motherfucking bastards, come *back*, come—

It wasn't until I saw the thick, moist wind of the rotorwash fanning the grass—saw it bending the trees as the steel dragonflies ascended—that I realized I felt no wind on my face; that I had no trouble standing in the small hurricane at the center of the clearing. I turned around. Past the treeline, in the thick of the jungle, mortars were being lobbed from afar. Some hit their intended targets, in the bush; others strayed, and blasted our own position, unintentionally. I could hear the screams of VC before and after each hit; I saw Cong rushing out of the trees, some aflame, some limbless, only to be knocked off their feet by another incoming round. By now I knew the truth. I wandered, in a daze, back toward the treeline. I walked through sheets of flame without feeling so much as a sunburn. I saw the ground rock below me, but my steps never wavered, like the old joke about the drunken man during an earthquake.

At length the mortars stopped. The clearing was seared, desolate; bodies—Vietnamese, American—lay strewn and charred in all directions. I walked among them, rising smoke passing through me like dust through a cloud . . . and now I saw other wraiths, other figures standing above the remains of their own bodies; they looked thin, gaseous, the winds from the chopper passing overhead threatening their very solidity.

Prosser looked down at his shattered corpse and said, "Shit."

Dunbar agreed. "This sucks."

"Man, I *knew* this was gonna happen," Martinez insisted. "I just got laid in Da Nang. Is this fuckin' karma, or what?"

I made a mental note never to discuss metaphysics with Martinez. Not a useful overview.

"So what happens now?" I asked.

"Heaven, I guess." Dunbar shrugged.

"Or hell." Martinez. Ever the optimist.

"Yeah, but when?"

"Gotta be anytime now," Prosser said, as though waiting for the 11:00 bus. He looked down at our bodies and grimaced. "I mean, we're dead, right?"

I looked at Dunbar's mangled leg. At Martinez's truncated torso. At . . .

"Hey. Collins. Where the hell are *you?*"

I should have been just a few feet away from Dunbar's body, but I wasn't. At first I thought the half a dozen rounds that had dropped me had propelled my body away, but as we fanned out, we saw no trace of it, not anywhere within a dozen yards. And when I came back to where Dunbar's body lay, I recognized the matted elephant grass where I had fallen—recognized too the tears of blood, now dried, coloring the tips of the grass. I squatted down, noticing for the first time that the grass was matted, in a zigzag pattern, for several feet beyond where my body fell.

"Son of a bitch," I said. "They took me."

"What?" said Martinez. "The VC?"

"They dragged me a few feet, then"—I pointed to where the matted grass ended—"two of them must've picked me up, and taken me away."

"I didn't see anyone," Dunbar said.

"Maybe you were preoccupied," I suggested.

Prosser scanned the area, his brow furrowing. "DePaul's gone, too. He went down right next to me—we were near the river, I remember hearing the sound of the water—but he's gone."

"Maybe he was just wounded," I said. At least I hoped so. DePaul had pulled me back, months before, from stepping on what had seemed like a plot of dry grass on a trail, but what revealed itself—once we'd tossed a large boulder on top of it—as a swinging man trap: kind of a see-saw with teeth. If not for DePaul, I would've been the one swinging from it, impaled on a dozen or more rusty spikes studding its surface. DePaul had bought me a few extra months of life; maybe, when I'd run forward, firing into the tree line, I'd done the same for him, distracting the snipers long enough for him to get away.

"Hey, listen," said Dunbar. "Choppers."

The mop-up crew swooped in, quick and dirty, to recover what bodies it could. The area was secured, at least for the moment, and two grunts pried loose Dunbar's mangled leg from the punji beartrap and hefted him into a bodybag. The zipper caught on his lip, and the grunt had to unsnare it. Dunbar was furious.

"Watch what you're doing, assholes!" he roared at them. He turned to me. "Do you believe these guys?"

Two other grunts gingerly disconnected an unexploded cartridge trap not far from Martinez's body, then scooped up what remained of the poor bastard—torso in one bodybag, legs in another—and zipped the bags shut. Martinez watched as they loaded them onto the chopper, then turned to me.

"Collins. You think I should—"

I turned, but by the time I was facing him he was no longer there.

"Martinez?"

Dunbar's body was hefted onto the Huey, it hit the floor like a sack of dry cement, and I could almost feel the air rushing in to fill the sudden vacuum beside me.

I whirled around. Dunbar, too, was gone.

"Dunbar!"

The Huey lifted off, the branches of surrounding trees shuddering around it, like angry lovers waving away a violent suitor, and I was alone.

Believe it or not, I enlisted. It seemed like a good idea at the time: lower-middle-class families from Detroit could barely afford to send one kid to college, let alone two, and with my older sister at Ann Arbor I figured a student deferment wasn't coming my way anytime soon. So I let myself swallow the line they feed you at the recruiter's office, about how our *real* job over here was building bridges and thatching huts and helping the Vietnamese people; they made it sound kind of like the Peace Corps, only more humid.

My dad was a construction foreman; I'd been around buildings going up all my life—liked the sound of it, the feel of it, the smell of lumber and fresh cement and the way the frame looked before you laid on the plasterboard. . . . I'd stand there staring at the girders and crossbeams, the wood-and-steel armatures that looked to my eight-year-old mind like dinosaur skeletons, and I thought: The people who'll live here will never see, never know what their house *really* looks like, underneath; but *I* know.

So the idea of building houses for homeless people and bridges for oxen to cross sounded okay. Except after eight months in Nam, most of the bridges I'd seen had been blown away by American air strikes, and the closest I'd come to thatching huts was helping repair the roof of a bar in Da Nang I happened to be trapped in during a monsoon.

All things considered, enlisting did not seem like the kind of blue-chip investment in the future it once had, just now.

For the first few days I stuck close to the crater, wandering only as far as I could travel and return in a day, searching for a way back—but the way back, I knew, was farther than could ever be measured in miles, and the road was far from clearly marked. I tried not to dwell on that. If I had, I would have never mustered the nerve to move from my little corner of hell. I wasn't sure where the nearest U.S. base was in relation to here, but I remembered a small village we'd passed the previous day, and I seemed to recall a Red Cross jeep parked near a hut, a French doctor from Catholic Relief Services administering to the villagers. Maybe he would show up again, and I could hitch a ride back to—the question kept presenting itself—*where?* What the hell did I do, ask directions to the Hereafter? With my luck, the Army was probably running *it*, too.

(Now that was a frightening thought; frighteningly plausible. This whole thing was just fucked up enough to be an Army operation. Had I forgotten to fill out a form somewhere down the line?)

I headed back down the trail we'd followed to our deaths, but this time, along with the usual sounds of the jungle—the rustling in the bush that you hoped was *only* a bamboo viper, or a tiger— I heard the jungle's other voice. I heard the sounds the choppers, with their souls-in-a-box, only played at.

I heard weeping.

Not moaning; not wailing; none of that Roger Corman, Vincent Price shit. Just the sound of grown men weeping, uncontrollably and unconsolably—coming, it seemed, from everywhere at once. And slowly, I began to see them: VC, blood spattered over their black silk pajamas, crouched in the bush in that funny way the VN sit—squatting, not sitting, on the ground—and crying. I stopped, dumbfounded. I'd never seen a VN cry before. I'd seen them scared, hell, I'd seen them fucking terrified, but I never saw them cry. All that crap you heard about how the VN are different from us, how they don't *feel* the way we do, I knew that was bullshit. They felt; they just didn't show it the way we did. But goddamned if these guys weren't giving our guys a run for their money. Maybe, if you're a VC and you're dead, it's okay to cry. Maybe it's expected. I moved on.

And somewhere along the trail, as I followed the Song Cai in its winding path south, I began to consider that I might not, in fact, be among the dead; that I might just be alive, after all.

Maybe, I thought, the rounds that had dropped me had just wounded me; maybe the VC took my body so they could get information out of me, later. The more I thought about it, the more reasonable it sounded. They take me, nurse me back to health, so they can torture me later. (That sounded as logical as anything else in this screwy country.) And somewhere along the way, I split off from my body. Got left behind, like a shadow shaken loose from its owner. I listened to the weeping all around me—Christ, I almost wished they *were* wailing and moaning; I could've borne that a lot easier—and I decided that I wasn't, couldn't be dead.

Up ahead, the trail widened briefly into a clearing, in the middle of which stood what looked like a giant birdhouse: a bamboo hut, little more than a box really, perched on the stump of a large tree trunk. There were spirit houses like this scattered all over Nam, small homes erected for the happiness of departed relatives, or for embittered spirits who might otherwise prey on hapless villages. The Army briefed us on the local customs and superstitions before we even arrived over here—things like, you never pat a VN on the head 'cause the head, to the Vietnamese, is the seat of the soul; and *whatever* you do, don't sit with your legs crossed so that your foot is pointing toward the other person's head, because that's the grossest kind of insult. Shit like that. Some dinks would even name their male babies after women's sexual organs to try and fool evil spirits into thinking the kid was a girl, because boys were more valuable and needed to be protected. Jesus.

So I knew about spirit houses, and when we passed this one the other day I remember thinking, hey, that's kind of neat, even better than the treehouse I built in my grandparents' yard when I was twelve, and went on walking.

Today I stopped. Stared at it.

Today there were people inside the birdhouse.

One was an elderly papa-san, the other a young woman, maybe twenty-eight, twenty-nine. They were burning Joss sticks, the sweet fragrance carried back on the thick wind, and around them I saw candles, tiny hand-made furniture, and a few books. I started walking again, more slowly now, and as I got within a couple yards of the birdhouse, the papa-san looked up at me, blinked once in mild surprise, then smiled and held his hand over his chest in a *gassho*— a traditional form of greeting and respect. His other arm, I now noticed, was askew beneath its silk sleeve, as though it had been broken, or worse.

"Welcome, traveler," he said. He was speaking in Vietnamese, but I understood, somehow, despite it.

"Uh . . . hello," I said, not sure if this worked both ways, but apparently it did; he smiled again, gesturing to his woman companion.

"I am Phan Van Duc. My daughter, Chau."

The woman turned and glared at me. She was pretty, in the abstract, but it was hard to get past the sneer on her face. So fixed, so unwavering, it looked like it'd been tattooed on. And since I wasn't sure if her anger was directed at me or not, I decided to ignore it, turned to the old man.

"My name is William Anthony Collins," I said. I wasn't sure if having three names was requisite over here, but I figured it couldn't hurt.

"May we offer you shelter?" Phan asked cordially. His daughter glowered.

There was barely enough room in the birdhouse for two, and I had no desire to be at close quarters with Chau. I declined, but thanked him for the offer.

"Have you been dead long?" the papa-san asked suddenly. I flinched.

"I'm not dead," I said stubbornly.

The old man looked at me as though I were crazy. His daughter laughed a brassy, mocking laugh.

I explained what had happened to me, what I *thought* had happened to me, and how I was heading for the village downriver to see if the Vietcong had taken my body there. Phan looked at me with sad, wise eyes as I spoke, then, when I'd finished, nodded once—more out of politeness, I suspected, than out of any credence he put in my theory.

"What you say may be true," he mused, "though I have never heard of such a thing. I would imagine, however, that rather than take a prisoner to a village, where he might easily be discovered, they would take him to one of their tunnel bases."

The VC had hundreds of tunnels running beneath most of I-Corps: a spiderweb of barracks and underground command posts and subterranean hospitals so vast, so labyrinthine, that we were only just beginning to understand the full scope of them. If I had been taken prisoner in one of them, the odds of finding myself were about equal to winning bets on the Triple Crown, the World Series, and the Super Bowl, all in one year.

"In that case," I said, not really wanting to think about it, "I'll just wait for my—body—to die, and when it does, I'm gone."

Papa-san looked at me with a half-pitying, half-perplexed look, as though I had just told him the sky was green and the moon was made of rice. Hell, come to think of it, maybe the dinks *did* think the moon was made of rice.

"What about you?" I said, anxious to shift the topic. "Why are you—here?"

Phan showed no trace of pain, or grief, as he replied.

"I was mauled by a tiger and left to bleed to death," he said simply, as though that should explain everything. Then, at my blank look, he explained patiently, "Having died a violent death, I was denied entry to the next world."

I blinked. I didn't see the connection.

"Getting mauled by a tiger, that's not your fault," I said, baffled.

He looked as baffled by my words as I was by his. "What difference does fault make? What is, is." He shrugged.

I opted not to pursue the subject. Phan and Martinez would've gotten along just fine. "And your daughter?"

He looked askance at her, she threw me a nasty look, then she scrambled forward into the birdhouse, hands gripping the lip of the floor, spitting the words at me: the hard edges of the Vietnamese consonants as sharp as the bitterness in her words.

"I died childless," she snapped at me. "Is that what you wanted to hear? Are you happy? I died childless, worthless, and I am condemned because of it."

278 ◆ Alan Brennert

"That's crazy," I said, despite myself.

She laughed a brittle laugh. "You are the crazy one," she said, "a *ma qui*, thinking he is alive. I pity you."

"No," the papa-san said gently, "you pity no one but yourself."

She glared at him, her nostrils flaring, then laughed again, shortly. "You are right," she said. "I pity no one. I don't know why I let you keep me here. I can do anything I want. I can bring disease back to the village, kill the children of my former friends. Yes. I think I would like that." She grinned maliciously, as though taking relish in the wickedness of her thought.

"You will not," Phan warned. "I am your father, and I forbid it."

She muttered a curse under her breath and retreated to the rear of the birdhouse. The papa-san turned and looked at me sadly.

"Do not judge my daughter by what she is now," he said softly. "Death makes of us what it wishes."

Jesus Christ; these people actually believed that. And so, I guess, that's just what they got. Well, not me. No fucking way, man. Not me.

I backed away. "I have to go."

"Wait," Phan said. I halted, I'm not sure why; he leaned forward, as though to share something important with me. "If you go into the village . . . you must be careful. Do not walk in the front door of a house, because the living keep mirrors by the doorway, to reflect the image of those who enter. If a spirit sees himself in the mirror, he will be frightened off. Also, if red paper lines the entrance, stay away, for you will anger the God of the Doorway. Do you understand?"

I nodded, numbly, thanked him for his advice, and got the hell out of there, fast.

I hurried down the trail, past the weeping guerrillas in black silk, feeling a sudden, black longing for something as violent and mundane as a mortar strike; yearning for the sound of gunships, the bright spark of tracer fire, the crackling of small-arms fire, or the din of big Chinook choppers circling in for the kill. God *damn*. This was the dinks' Hell, not mine; I wasn't going to be a part of it, I would *not* buy into their stupid, superstitious horseshit. The weeping around me grew louder. I started running now, phantom limbs passing harmlessly through trip wires and across punji traps, even the elephant grass not so much as tickling my calves as I ran along banks of the Song Cai—

The weeping changed. Became different: deeper. I knew instantly that it was not the cries of a Vietnamese; knew, suddenly and sickeningly, that it was an American's cries I was hearing.

I stopped; looked around. I saw no one lying wounded in the bush, but heard, now, too, a voice:

"—Jesus, Mary, and Joseph, *help me*—"

Oh, Christ, I thought.

DePaul.

I looked up. He was floating about five feet above the muddy water of the river, like a tethered balloon, his big, six-foot frame looking almost gaseous, his black skin seeming somehow pale. His hands covered his face as he wept, prayed, swore, and wept again. At first I thought he was moving upstream, but I soon realized that it was the water flowing under him that gave the illusion of movement; he swayed back and forth slightly, but was utterly motionless, completely stationary.

It took me a moment to recover my wits. I shouted his name over the roar of the rapids.

He looked up, startled.

When he saw me—saw me looking at *him*—his face lit up with a kind of absolution. "Oh, Jesus," he said, so softly I almost couldn't hear it. "*Collins?* Are you real?"

"I sure as shit hope so."

"Are you alive?"

I dodged the question. "What the hell happened to you, man? Prosser said you went down right next to him, but your body—"

"Charlie hit me in the back." I could see the hole torn in his skin at the nape of his neck, and the matching one in front, just below his collarbone, where the bullet had exited. "I couldn't breathe. Couldn't think. Got up, somehow, ran—but in the wrong direction. Dumped into the river. Christ, Bill, it was awful. I was choking *and* drowning, and the next thing I knew—" His hand had gone, reflexively, to his throat, covering the ragged hole there "—my body had floated downriver, then got snagged on some rock. Over there."

I followed his gaze. His body was pinned between two rocks, the waters flowing around it, flanking it in white foam. I turned back to Depaul, floating in place above the river, and I took a step forward.

"Christ, De," I said softly. "How—I mean, what—"

"I *can't get down*, man," he said, and for the first time I heard the pain in his voice; "I been here two, three days, and it *hurts*. Oh Christ, it hurts! It's not like floating, Jesus, it's like treading water, every muscle in my body aches—I'm so *tired*, man, I'm so—" He broke off in sobs; something I'd never seen him do. He looked away, let the tears come, then looked back at me, his eyes wide. "Help me, Collins," he said softly. "*Help me.*"

"Just tell me how," I said, feeling helpless, horrified. "Why— why are you *like* this, man? You have any idea?"

"Yeah. Yeah, I know," he said, taking a ragged gulp of air. "It's—it's 'cause I died in water, see? You die in water, your spirit's tied to the water till you can find another one to—"

"*What?* Jesus Christ, De, where'd you *get* that shit from?"

"Another spook. VC, half his head blown away, wanderin' up and down the river. He told me."

"You bought *into* this crap?" I yelled at him. "These dinks believe this shit, man, *you* don't have to—you're an *American*, for Chrissake!"

"Collins—"

"You believe it, it happens. You stop believing, it stops happening. Just—"

His eyes were sunken, desperate. "Please, man. Help me?"

No matter what I thought of this shit, there was only one thing that mattered: he'd saved my life once; and even if there was no more life in him to save, I could, at least, try to ease his pain I *had* to try.

"All right," I said. "What can I do?"

He hesitated.

"Bring me a kid," he said quietly.

"Why?"

He hesitated again; then, working up his nerve, he said, "To release me. A life for a life."

My eyes went wide. "*What?*"

"It's the only way," he said quickly. "You die in water, the only way to be set free is to—drown—a kid, as an offering." His eyes clouded over, his gaze became hooded and ashamed even as he said

it. For a long minute the only sound was the rushing of water past
the dam of DePaul's corpse, and the distant sounds of weeping
carried on the wind.

Finally I said, "I can't do that, man."

"Bill—"

"Even if I believed it'd work—*especially* if I believed it'd work—
I couldn't—"

"Not a healthy kid," DePaul interrupted, desperation and pleading creeping into his tone, "a sick one. One that's gonna die anyway. Shit, half the gook kids over here die before they're—"

"Are you crazy, man?" I snapped. "Gook or not, I can't—"

I stopped. Listened to what I was saying.

DePaul's face was ashen; in torment. "Collins . . . please. I hurt
so bad—"

I was buying into this crap. Just like him. Someone'd filled his
head with dink superstition, and now he was living—or dying—
by it. That was it, wasn't it? You die, you get pretty much what
you expect: Catholics, heaven or hell; atheist, maybe nothing, non-
existence, loss of consciousness; dinks—this. And we'd been over
here so long, wading knee deep in their fucking country, that we
were starting to believe what they believed.

But the DePaul I knew would never kill a kid. Not even to save
himself. Maybe the only way to shake him loose from this bullshit
was to show him that.

I waited a long minute, thinking, devising a plan, and then, finally
I spoke up.

"A sick kid?" I asked, carefully, as though I actually believed all
this.

He looked up, hopefully. "One that's gonna die anyway. You've
seen 'em, you know what they look like, you can see it in their
eyes—"

"I won't bring one that's gonna live."

"No no, man, you don't have to. A sick kid. A real sick kid."
God, he sounded pathetic.

I told him I didn't know how long it would take, but that I would
head into the village we had passed through a few days ago and
I'd see what I could do. I told him I'd be back as soon as I could.

"Hurry, man. Hurry." It was the last thing I heard before I
headed back into the bush once again. He'd bought the line. Now

all I had to do was show him he'd bought another—and, more important, that he could buy out of it.

The village was about two hours up the road. There was no Red Cross jeep in sight, no Catholic Relief doctor handing out aspirin and antibiotics; just the squalid little huts, the half-naked kids running through muddy puddles probably rife with typhoid, tired-looking women doing laundry in a small stream tributary to the Song Cai. There was a huge crater at the edge of town—the mortar strike that was too late to save me and Dunbar and DePaul. Nearby roofs were scorched, at least two huts had been burned to the ground. Friendly fire. Any more friendly, and half the village would be greeting me personally. I walked up the main road, peeking in windows. If I was going to make it look genuine I'd have to bring back a genuinely sickly kid; though exactly how, I still wasn't sure.

Outside one hut I heard the sound of a mother comforting a squalling baby, and decided to go in and take a look. Sure enough, just as the old papa-san had predicted, the doorway was lined with red paper to ward off evil spirits. I stepped across the threshold. Big fucking deal. Up yours, God of the Doorway. I turned—

I screamed.

In the mirror positioned just inside, I saw a man with a foot-wide hole blasted in his chest; the torn edges of the wound charred to a crisp, the cavity within raw and red as steak tartare. A pair of lungs dangled uselessly from the slimmest of folds of flesh, swaying as I jumped back, reflexively; beside them, a heart riddled with half a dozen jagged frag wounds throbbed in a stubborn counterfeit of life.

And behind me in the mirror, a glimpse of something else: a shadow, a *red* shadow, red as the paper above the doorway . . . moving not as I moved but looming up, and quickly, behind me.

I ran.

Out of the house, down the street, away from the huts, finally collapsing on a patch of elephant grass. At first I was afraid to look down at myself, but when I did, I saw nothing—saw exactly what I'd seen up till now, the drab green camouflage fatigues stained with blood. All this time, I realized, I had seen everyone else's wounds but mine. Not till now.

I sat there, gathering my wits and my courage, trying to work up the nerve to enter another hut. I didn't think about the mirror, didn't dwell on what I'd seen. Better just to think of myself this way, the way some part of me *wanted* to see myself. When I finally got up and started round to the huts again, I steered well clear of the doors.

There was the usual assortment of sickly kids—malaria, mostly, but from the look of them, a few typhoid, influenza, and parasitic dysentery cases as well. I felt gruesome as hell, trying to choose which one to take, even knowing this was only a ruse, something to shock DePaul back to normalcy. *Just get it over with.* I looked in one window and saw what appeared to be a two-year-old girl— in a dress made of old parachute nylon, an earring dangling too large from one tiny lobe—being washed by her mother. It was only when the mother turned the child over and I saw the small brown penis, that I remembered: the mother was trying to deceive the evil spirits into thinking their sickly boy-child was really a girl, and thus not worth the taking.

Jesus, I thought. Said a lot about the place of women over here. But it did mean the kid was probably seriously ill, and after I'd used her—him—to get DePaul back to normal, I could take the poor kid to the nearest Evac . . . leave it on the doorstep of the civilian ward with a note telling the name of his village.

Assuming I could *write* a note.

Assuming I could even *take* the kid in the first place.

I took a deep breath and, once the mother had left the room, walked through the wall of the hut. I didn't feel the bamboo any more than I'd felt the trip wires I'd run through. I stood over the infant, now worried that my hands would pass through him, too . . . then slowly reached down to try and pick him up.

I touched him. I didn't know how, or why, but I could touch him.

I scooped the boy up in my arms and held him to my chest. He looked up at me with old, sad eyes. All the kids here had the same kind of eyes: tired, cheerless, and somehow knowing. As though all the misery around them, all the civil wars and foreign invaders— from the French to the Japanese to the Americans—as though all that were known to them, before they'd even been born. Rocked in a cradle of war, they woke, with no surprise, to a lullaby of thunder.

I walked through the wall of the hut, the child held aloft and carried him through the window. When we were clear of the building, I hefted the boy up, held him in my arms, and headed into the bush before anyone could see.

I wanted to stay off the main road, for fear that someone might see me: not me, I guess, since I *couldn't* be seen, but the kid, the boy. (What, I wondered, would someone see, if they did see? A child carried aloft on the wind? Or an infant wrapped in the arms of a shadow, a smudge on the air? I didn't know. I didn't want to find out.) Every once in a while, I'd see a dead VC look up from where he was squatting, on the banks of the river or in the shade of a rubber tree, and look at me, sometimes with curiosity, sometimes resentment, sometimes fear. They never said anything. Just stared, and at length went back to their mourning, their weeping. I hurried past.

About half a mile from DePaul I caught a glimpse of a squad of still-living VC about a dozen yards into the jungle, carrying what looked like an unconscious American GI, probably an LRRP. I immediately squatted down in the bush, hiding the kid from view as best I could, dropping a fold of blanket over his face to protect him from the prickly blades of grass. I watched as one of the VC bent down, reaching for what looked like a patch of dry dirt, his fingers finding a catch, a handle of some sort, and then the earth lifted and I saw it was actually a trapdoor in the ground itself—a piece of wood covered with a thin, but deceptive, layer of dirt. One by one the VC crawled headfirst into the tunnel, until only two were left—the two carrying the unconscious GI. I debated what to do—was there anything I *could* do?—but before I could make a decision, I saw the GI's head tilt at an unnatural angle as he was lowered into the ground . . . and I knew, then, that I'd been mistaken. He wasn't unconscious; he was dead. And, very quickly, lost from sight.

Psychological warfare. Drove Americans crazy when we couldn't recover our dead, and Charlie knew it. Just like we played on their fears with the Wandering Soul, they played on ours, in their own way. I got up and moved on.

Less than half an hour later I was back at the river. DePaul still floated helpless above the rapids. He looked up at my approach,

the torment in his face quickly replaced by astonishment and—
fear?

I brought the kid to the edge of the river, looked up at DePaul,
made my voice hard, resolute—all that Sergeant York shit.

"He's got malaria," I said, tonelessly. "You can tell when you
pull down his lower eyelid, it's all pink; he's anemic, can't weigh
more than twenty pounds. They could save him, at the 510 Evac.
Or you can take him, to save yourself." I stared him straight in the
eye. "Which is it, DePaul?"

I'd known DePaul since boot camp. Faced with the reality of it,
I knew what he'd answer.

And as I waited, smugly, for him to say it, his gaseous, wraithlike
form spun round in midair, rocketed downward like a guided missile, and slammed into me with vicious velocity, sending me sprawl-
ing, knocking the kid out of my arms.

Stunned, I screamed at him, but by the time I'd scrambled to my
feet he had the kid in a vise grip and was holding the poor sonofa-
bitch under the water. I ran, slammed into De with all my strength,
but he shrugged me off with an elbow in my face. I toppled backward.

"I'm sorry, man," he kept saying, over and over; "I'm sorry. . ."

I lunged at him again, this time knocking him off-balance; he
lost his grip on the kid, and I dove into the water after the boy. It
felt weird; the water passed *through* me, I didn't feel wet, or cold,
nothing at all; and the waters were so muddy I could barely see a
foot in front of me. Finally, after what seemed like forever, I saw
a small object in front of me and instinctively I reached out and
grabbed. My fingers closed around the infant's arms. I made for
the surface, the kid in my arms; I staggered out of the water, up
the embankment—

I put the boy down on the ground. His face was blue, his body
very still. I tried to administer mouth-to-mouth, but nothing happened; and then I laughed suddenly, a manic, rueful laugh, at the
thought of me, of all people, trying to give the breath of life.

I looked up, thinking to see DePaul towering above me . . . but
he was nowhere to be seen. And when I looked up at the spot above
the river where he had been tethered, helplessly, for so long—

I saw the spirit-form of the little boy, floating, hovering, crying
out in pain and confusion.

I screamed. I screamed for a long time.

And knew, now, why I'd been able to touch the child, when I hadn't been able to touch anything else: I was the *ma qui*, I was the evil spirit come to bear the sickly child away, and I had done my job, followed my role, without even realizing I'd been doing it. I thought of Phan, of his daughter Chau, of DePaul and of myself. *Death makes of us what it wishes.*

I wept, then, for the first time, as freely and as helplessly as the VC I'd seen and heard; wept like the Wandering Soul I knew, at last, I had to be.

I must've stayed there, on the banks of the river, for at least a day, trying to find some way to atone, some way to save the soul of the child I'd led to perdition. But I couldn't. I would've traded places with him willingly, but didn't know how. And when I went back to the spirit house where Phan and his daughter dwelled, when I told him of what I'd done, he showed no horror, expressed no rage; just puzzlement that it had taken me so long to realize my place in the world.

His daughter, on the other hand, gleefully congratulated me on my deed. *"Ma qui,"* she said, and this time, hearing the word, I understood it not just as ghost, but as devil, for it meant both. "Did it not feel good?"

A terrible gladness burst open someplace inside me—a black, cold poison that felt at once horrifying and invigorating. It was relief, expiation of guilt by embracing, not renouncing, the evil I'd done.

Chau, as though sensing this, laughed throatily. She leaned forward, her spiteful smile now seductive as well. *"Yêu dâu,"* she said, *"yêu quái."*

Beloved demon.

"Together we could do many things," she said, twisting a lock of long black hair in her fingers. Her eyes glittered malevolently. "Many things." She laughed again. Cruel eyes, a cold-blooded smile. I felt betrayed by my own erection. I wanted her, I didn't want her. I loathed her, and in my loathing wanted her all the more, because perverse desire was, at least, desire; I wanted my cock, dead limb that it was, inside her, to make me feel alive.

When I realized how badly I wanted it, I ran.

She only laughed all the louder.

"Beloved demon!" she called after me. "You shall be back!"

But I haven't been back. Not yet. Nor back to the crater, the place of my death, not for many months. I still search for my body, but I know that the odds of finding it, in the hundreds of miles of tunnels that honeycomb this land, are virtually nil. I search during the days, and at night I come back to my new home to sleep.

I have a birdhouse of my own, you see, just outside the village; a treehouse perched on a bamboo stump, filled with joss sticks and candles and little toy furniture. I come back here, and I fight to remind myself who I am, what I am; I struggle against becoming the *yêu quái*, the demon Chau wishes me to be. Except, that is, when the bloodsong sings to me in my voice, and I know that I already *am* the demon—and that the only thing that stops me from acting like one is my will, my conscience, the last vestiges of the living man I once was. I don't know how long I can keep the demon at bay. I don't know how long I want to. But all I can do is keep trying, and not think of Chau, or of how wonderfully bitter her lips must taste, bitter as salt, bitter as blood.

Damn it.

Above me, the Wandering Soul cries out from its box, wailing and moaning in a ridiculous burlesque of damnation, and I think about all the things we were told about this place, and the things we weren't. Back in Da Nang, when anyone would talk about the Army's "pacification" program—about winning the "hearts and minds" of the Vietnamese—the joke used to be: Grab 'em by the balls, and their hearts and minds will follow. Except, no one told us that while we were working on their hearts and minds, they were winning over our souls. The Army trained us in jungle warfare, drilled us in the local customs, told us we'd have to fight Charlie on his own terms—but never let on that we'd have to die on his terms, too. Because for all the technology, all the ordnance, all the planning that went into this war, they forgot the most important thing.

They never told us the rules of engagement.

NEXT

✦   ✦   ✦

Terry Bisson

Terry Bisson has won the Hugo, Nebula, and Theodore Sturgeon Awards for his short fiction. He has written four novels, including the offbeat, winsome Talking Man *(which was a finalist for the World Fantasy Award).*

"Next" is part of a group of all-dialogue stories, some of which appear in his excellent collection, Bears Discover Fire. *In a few short pages, "Next" manages to be a cautionary tale, as well as a treatise on human nature.*

N ext!"
        "We want to get a marriage license, please."
"Name."
"Johnson, Akisha."
"Age?"
"Eighteen."
"Groom's name?"
"Jones, Yusef."
"Yusef? You with *him*? Honey, you kids are in the *wrong* line."
"We are?"
"Try that line over there, on the other side of the Pepsi machine. And good luck. You're gonna need it, child. Next!"

"Next!"
        "We want to apply for a marriage license."
"For who, might I ask?"
"For us. For me and him."

"I beg your pardon?"

"She told us to get in this line. I guess because . . ."

"I can't give you a marriage license. He's black."

"I know, but I heard that if we get a special permit or something . . ."

"What you're talking about is a same-race certificate. But I can't give you one, and I wouldn't if I could. The very idea of blacks marrying *each other*, when . . ."

"So why'd she tell us to get in this line?"

"This line is for same-race certificate *applications*."

"So what do we have to do to get one of those?"

"Under the law, just ask for it. Even though there's something disgusting about . . ."

"So look, lady, I'm asking."

"Here. Fill this out and return it to window A21."

"Does that mean we have to start in line all over again?"

"What do you think? Next!"

"Next!"

"Hello, I'm not even sure we're in the right line. We want to get one of those special certificates. To get married."

"A same-race certificate. You're in the right line. But under the Equal Access Provisions of the Melanin Conservation Act, we can't just hand those out. You have to have an Ozone Waiver to even apply for one."

"I already have the application filled out. See? That white girl over there told me about it."

"She told you wrong. What you filled out is the application for the *waiver*. But you can't get the waiver without 12.5 minutes of counseling."

"Can't you just stamp it or whatever? We've already been standing in three lines for hours, and my feet are . . ."

"Excuse me? Maybe you know more about my job than I do?"

"No."

"Good. Then listen up. I'm trying to be helpful. What I'm going to give you is an appointment slip to see the marriage counselor. Take it to Building B and give it to the clerk at the first desk."

"We have to go outside?"

"There's a covered walkway. But stay to the left, several panels are missing. Next!"

"Next!"

"We have an appointment slip."

"For what?"

"Counseling. To get a waiver, so we can apply for a certificate, or something. So we can get married."

"Sit down over there. The Sergeant Major will call you when he's ready."

"The Sergeant Major? We were supposed to see a marriage counselor."

"The Sergeant Major is the Marriage Counselor. Has been ever since the Declaration of Marital Law, under the Ozone Emergency Act. Where have you been?"

"We don't get married every day."

"Are you getting smart with me?"

"I guess not."

"I hope not. Take a seat, in those hard chairs, until I call you. Next!"

"Next! At ease. State your business."

"We need to get the counseling for . . ."

"I wasn't talking to you. I was talking to him."

"Me?"

"You're the man aren't you?"

"Uh, yes, sir! We, uh, want to get married, sir!"

"Speak up. And don't call me sir. I'm not an officer. Call me Sergeant Major."

"Yes, sir; I mean, Sergeant."

"Sergeant Major."

"Sergeant Major!"

"Now tell me again what it is you want."

"This is ridiculous. Yusef already told you . . ."

"Did I ask you to speak, young lady? Maybe you think because I'm black I'll tolerate your insolence?"

"No. Sergeant. Major."

"Then shut up. Carry on, young man."

"We want to get married. Sergeant Major!"

"That's what I thought I heard you say. And I guess you want my approval as your marriage counselor? My blessing, so to speak?"

"Well, yes."

"Well, you can forget it! For Christ's sake, boy, show a little backbone. A little social responsibility. You kids are the kind who are giving our kind a bad name. You don't see white folks lining up trying to evade the law, do you?"

"They don't need to line up."

"Watch your mouth, young lady. And nobody told you to sit down. This is a military office."

"She's been standing for hours, Sarge. Major. My fiancée is, uh . . ."

"I'm pregnant."

"Will you quit butting in, young lady! Now, let me get this straight. Is she pregnant?"

"She is."

"Why didn't you say so in the first place?"

"That's why we want to get married. Sergeant Major."

"You're in the wrong office. I'll need to see a Melanin Heritage Impact Statement and a release from the Tactical Maternity Officer before I can even begin to counsel you. Take this slip to Office 23 in Building C."

"Outside again?"

"Only for a few yards."

"But the sunscorch factor is eight point four."

"Quit whining. Show a little pride. Imagine what it's like for white people. Next!"

"Next!"

"We were told to come here and see you because I'm . . ."

"I'm a woman too, I can tell. At ease. Sit down, you both look tired. Want a cigarette?"

"Isn't smoking bad for the baby?"

"Suit yourself. Now, how can I help you? Captain Kinder, here; Tactical Maternity."

"All we want is a certificate so we can get married."

"Negative, honey. No way. If you were both sterile, or over-age, *maybe*. But nobody's going to give you kids a same-race if you are already PG. Not with active replicator AAs in such short supply. Who are all us white folks going to marry?"

"Each other?"

"Very funny. And watch our kids fry. But seriously, you don't have to get married to have a child. You can have all the AAs you want OW. What's the problem?"

"We want to keep it."

"Keep it? Negative. You know that under the Melanin Heritage Conservation Act, Out-of-Wedlock African American children must be raised in Protective Custody."

"You mean prison."

"Haven't you heard that old saying, 'stone walls do not a prison make'? And this is not like the bad old days; since the Ozone Emergency, AA children are a precious resource. You should be glad to see them in such good homes."

"But they *are* prisons. I've seen them."

"So what? Does an NB, that's newborn, know the diff? And it's for the child's own good as well as the good of the society. Do you realize the culture shock for African American youth when they find themselves in prison at age sixteen or so? If they are raised in prison from infancy, the TA or Transitional Adaption goes much more smoothly. Besides, they get out as soon as they marry, anyway."

"What if we don't want our kid to go to prison at all?"

"Whoa, Akisha! Do you mind if I call you Akisha? Are we back in the Dark Ages here, where the parents decide the child's future even before it is born? This is a free country and kids as well as parents have rights. Sure you don't want a cigarette?"

"I'm sure."

"Suit yourself. Let's cut the BS. You're nice kids, but under the Melanin Distribution Provisions of the Ozone Emergency Act, the law is clear. If you want to raise your own children, you'll have to marry legally."

"Which means marry a white person."

"As a white person myself, I'll overlook your racist tone of voice, which I'm sure you didn't mean. Is there something so terrible about marrying a white person?"

"No. I don't guess so."

"Okay. Now why don't you get with the program. Don't you know some nice white boy to marry?"

"Then I can keep my baby?"

"Not this one, but the next one. This one's double M and belongs to Uncle Sam, or at least to the Natural Resources Administration of HEW and M."

"But what if I don't want to marry some damn white boy!"

"Jones, I was hoping we could handle this without emotional

outbursts of naked bigotry. I see I was wrong. You are in danger of making me feel like an inadequate counselor with this racist attack on my professional self-image. Is it because I'm white?"

"It's because I want to marry Yusef."

"Who just *happens* to be black? Let's get real, girl. There's nothing subtle about you same-race couples. The way you strut around, as if daring the world to rain on your disgusting little intraracial parade."

"But—"

"Whoa! Before you go blaming all white people because of your personal problems, let me warn you that you are already in violation of several applicable federal Civil Rights statutes. I'm afraid you've taken this matter out of my hands. I have no choice but to send you up to see the Colonel."

"The Colonel?"

"The Civil Rights Prosecutor. In the big office on the top floor of the main building."

"What about me?"

"You can go with her if you want, Yusef. But if I were you—"

"You're not."

"—I'd find a nice white girl and get married. Fast. Before you both get in more trouble than you can handle. Dismissed. Next!"

"Next!"

"We're here to see the Colonel."

"I am the Colonel. I'm here to help you if I can. And let me begin by warning you that anything you say will be used against you."

"Will be?"

"Can be, will be, whatever. Young lady, are you splitting hairs with me?"

"No."

"Good. Now, I see you are under indictment for Discrimination and Conspiracy."

"Conspiracy? All we wanted to do was get married."

"Which is against the law. Surely you knew that or you wouldn't have gone to the Marital Law Administration in the first place."

"We were trying to get a special license."

"Precisely. And what is that if not trying to evade the Melanin Redistribution Act which prohibits black intramarriage? The mere presence of you two in line A21 is in itself evidence of a conspiracy to circumvent the provisions of the Melanin Hoarding Ban."

"But we were trying to *obey* the law!"

"That makes it even worse. The law is a just master, but it can be harsh with those who try to sabotage its spirit by hypocritically observing its letter. However, I'm going to delay sentencing on Conspiracy and Hoarding because we have an even more serious charge to deal with here."

"Sentencing? We haven't been convicted yet."

"Young lady are you splitting hairs with me?"

"No."

"Good. Now let's move on to the Discrimination charge. Deep issues are involved here. You two aren't old enough to remember the Jim Crow Days in the South, when blacks weren't permitted to swim in the public pools. But I remember. Do you know what Discrimination is?"

"I read about it in school."

"Well, then you know that it is wrong. And blacks who don't marry whites are denying them the right to swim in their gene pool. Discriminating against them."

"Nobody's denying anybody the right to do anything! I just want to marry Yusef."

"That's a conveniently simplistic way of looking at things, isn't it? But it won't wash in a court of law. You can't marry Yusef without refusing to marry Tom, Dick or Harry. It's the same difference. If you marry a black person, you are denying a white person the *right* to marry you; and that's a violation of his rights under the Fourteenth Amendment. Do you recognize those two pictures on the wall?"

"Sure. Martin Luther King and John Kennedy."

"John *F.* Kennedy. Somehow your generation has lost sight of the ideals they died for. Let me pose a purely hypothetical question—would it be fair to have a society in which one racial grouping, such as yours, had special rights and privileges denied to the rest of us?"

"It never bothered anybody before."

"Are you getting smart?"

"No. But what about the Fourteenth Amendment. Doesn't it apply to me?"

"Certainly it does. To you as an individual, and to your young man as well. But as African Americans you are more than just individuals; you are also a precious natural treasure."

"Huh?"

"Under the Melanin Heritage Act, your genetic material is a national resource, which America is now claiming for all its people, not just for a privileged few. It is the same genetic material that was brought across the ocean (bought and paid for, I might add) in the 18th and 19th centuries."

"But the slaves were freed."

"And their descendants as well. But genetic material, being immortal, can be neither slave nor free. It is an irreplaceable natural resource, like the forests or the air we breathe. And whether you kids like it or not, the old days when our resources were squandered and hoarded by special interests are over. Your genetic heritage is a part of the priceless national endowment of every man, woman and child in America, not just your private property to dispose of as you please. Am I making myself clear?"

"I guess."

"You guess! Would it be fair to have an African American child born double M, while a white child, denied his or her Melanin Birthright, was doomed to twice the chance of skin cancer and god-knows-what-else?"

"Nobody ever worried about white kids being born with twice everything before."

"Enough, young lady. I am sentencing you to nine months at Catskill Tolerance Development Camp, or until our baby is born, followed by nine years at Point Pleasant Repeat Pregnancy Farm. I sincerely hope you will use your time at Point Pleasant to think about how racist attitudes such as yours threaten the rainbow fabric of our multi-ethnic democracy."

"What about me?"

"I'm putting you on probation, Yusef, and taking you home for dinner as soon as court is over. I want you to meet my daughter. Marshall, put the cuffs on this one and take her away. Pay no heed to her crocodile tears: they are masters of deceit.

"Next!"

THE FRIENDSHIP LIGHT

◆ ◆ ◆

Gene Wolfe

Gene Wolfe is probably the most critically acclaimed SF writer of this decade, for such award-winning work as The Book of the New Sun *series. His most recent novel is* Lake of the Long Sun. *Mr. Wolfe's short fiction is of equally high quality, and here is a spooky and compelling tale of friendship and retribution.*

For my own part I have my journal; for my late brother-in-law's, his tape. I will refer to myself as "Ty" and to him as "Jack." That, I think, with careful concealment of our location, should prove sufficient. Ours is a mountainous—or at least, a hilly—area, more rural than Jack can have liked. My sister's house (I insist upon calling it that, as does the law) is set back two hundred yards from the county road. My own is yet more obscure, being precisely three miles down the gravel road that leaves the county road to the north, three-quarters of a mile west of poor Tessie's drive. I hope that these distances will be of help to you.

It began three months ago, and it was over—properly over, that is to say—in less than a week.

Though I have a telephone, I seldom answer it. Jack knew this; thus I received a note from him in the mail asking me to come to him on the very day on which his note was delivered. Typically, he failed to so much as mention the matter he wished to discuss with me, but wrote that he would be gone for several days. He was to leave that night.

He was a heavy-limbed blond man, large and strong. Tessie says he played football in college, which I can well believe. I know he

297

played baseball professionally for several seasons after graduation, because he never tired of talking about it. For me to specify his team would be counterproductive.

I found him at the end of the drive, eyeing the hole that the men from the gas company had dug; he smiled when he saw me. "I was afraid you weren't coming," he said.

I told him I had received his note only that day.

"I have to go away," he said. "The judge wants to see me." He named the city.

I offered to accompany him.

"No, no. I need you here. To look after the place, and— You see this hole?"

I was very tempted to leave him then and there. To spit, perhaps, and stroll back to my car. Even though he was so much stronger, he would have done nothing. I contented myself with pointing out that it was nearly a yard across, and that we were standing before it. As I ought to have anticipated, it had no effect upon him.

"It's for a friendship light. One of those gas things, you kow? Tess ordered it last fall. . . ."

"Before you had her committed," I added helpfully.

"Before she got so sick. Only they wouldn't put it in then because they were busy tuning up furnaces." He paused to wipe the sweat from his forehead with his index finger, flinging the moisture into the hole. I could see he did not like talking to me, and I resolved to stay for as long as I could tolerate him.

"And they don't like doing it in the winter because of the ground's being frozen and hard to dig. Then in the spring it's all mushy."

I said, "But here we are at last. I suppose it will be made to look like a carriage lamp? With a little arm for your name? They're so nice."

He would not look at me. "I would have cancelled the order if I'd remembered it, but some damned woman phoned me about it a couple of days ago, and I don't know— Because Tess ordered it— See that trench there?"

Again, I could hardly have failed to notice it.

"It's for the pipe that'll tap into the gas line. They'll be back tomorrow to run the pipe and put up the lamp and so on. Somebody's got to be here to sign for it. And somebody ought to see to

Tess's cats and everything. I've still got them. You're the only one I could think of."

I said that I was flattered that he had so much confidence in me.

"Besides, I want to visit her while I'm away. It's been a couple of months. I'll let her know that you're looking after things. Maybe that will make her happy."

How little he knew of her!

"And I've got some business of my own to take care of."

It would have given me enormous pleasure to have refused, making some excuse. But to see my old home again—the room in which Tessie and I slept as children—I would have done a great deal more. "I'll need a key," I told him. "Do you know when the workmen will come?"

"About nine-thirty or ten, they said." Jack hesitated. "The cats are outside. I don't let them in the house anymore."

"I am certainly not going to take any responsibility for a property I am not allowed to enter," I told him. "What if there was some emergency? I would have to drive back to my own house to use the telephone. Do you keep your cat food outside, too? What about the can-opener? The milk?"

"All right—all right." Reluctantly, he fished his keys from his pocket. I smiled when I saw that there was a rabbit's foot on the ring. I had nearly forgotten how superstitious he was.

I arrived at the house that for so many years had been my home before nine. Tessie's cats seemed as happy to see me as I was to see them—Marmaduke and Millicent "talked" and rubbed my legs, and Princess actually sprang into my arms. Jack had had them neutered, I believe. It struck me that it would be fairly easy to take one of the females—Princess, let us say—home with me, substituting an unaltered female of similar appearance who would doubtless soon present Jack with an unexpected litter of alley kittens. One seal-point Siamese, I reflected, looks very like another; and most of the kittens—possibly all of them—would be black, blacks being exceedingly common when Siamese are outcrossed.

I would have had to pay for the new female, however—fifty dollars at least. I dropped the idea as a practical possibility as I opened the can of cat food and extended it with one of tuna. But it had set my mental wheels in motion, so to speak.

It was after eleven when the men from the gas company came,

and after two before their supervisor rang the bell. He asked if I was Jack, and to save trouble I told him I was and prepared to sign whatever paper he might thrust under my nose.

"Come out here for a minute, will you?" he said. "I want to show you how it works."

Docilely, I followed him down the long drive.

"This is the control valve." He tapped it with his pencil. "You turn this knob to raise and lower the flame."

I nodded to show I understood.

"Now when you light it, you've got to hold this button in until it gets hot—otherwise, it'll go out, see? That's so if it goes out somehow, it'll turn off."

He applied his cigarette lighter, and the flame came on with a *whoosh*.

"Don't try to turn it off in the daytime. You'll ruin the mantle if you light it a lot. Just let it burn, and it'll last you maybe ten years. Should be hot enough now."

He removed his hand. The blue and yellow flame seemed to die, blazed up, then appeared almost to die once more.

"Flickering a little."

He paused and glanced at his watch. I could see that he did not want to take the time to change the valve. Thinking of Jack's irritation, I said, "It will probably be all right when it gets a bit hotter." It flared again as I spoke.

"Yeah. I better turn it down a little. I got it set kind of high." The sullen flickering persisted, though in somewhat muted fashion.

The supervisor pointed. "Right over here's your cut-off. You see how long that valve-stem is? When the boys get through filling in the trench, it'll be just about level with the ground so you don't hit it with the mower. But if you've got to put in a new light—like, if somebody wracks up this one with his car—that's where you can turn off the gas."

I lingered in the house. If you knew how spartanly I live, in a house that my grandfather had thought scarcely fit for his tenant farmers, you would understand why. Jack had liquor, and plenty of good food. (Trust him for that.) My sister's books still lined her shelves, and there was an excellent stereo. It was with something of a shock that I glanced up from *A Rebours* and realized that night had fallen. Far away, at the very end of the long, winding driveway, the new friendship light glared fitfully. It was then that I conceived my little plan.

In the morning I found the handle of the cut-off valve that the supervisor had shown me and took it off, employing one of Jack's screwdrivers. Though I am not really mechanically inclined, I had observed that the screws holding the plate over the control valve had shallow heads and poorly formed slots; they had given the supervisor some difficulty when he replaced them. I told a clerk at our hardware store in the village that I frequently had to retighten a screw in my stove which (although there was never any need to take it out) repeatedly worked loose. The product he recommended is called an anaerobic adhesive, I believe. It was available in four grades: Wicking, Medium (General Purposes), High Strength, and Permanent Installation. I selected the last, though the clerk warned me that I would have to heat the screw thoroughly with a propane torch if I ever wished to remove it.

Back at my sister's, I turned the flame higher, treated the screws with adhesive, and tightened them as much as I could. At that time, I did not know that Jack kept a journal of his own on cassette tapes. He had locked them away from my prying ears before he left, you may be sure; but I found the current number when the end-of-tape alarm sounded following his demise, and it may be time now to give old Jack the floor—time for a bit of fun.

"Well, here we are. Nicolette's in the bedroom switching into something a lot more comfortable as they always say, so I'm going to take a minute to wrap things up.

"The judge said okay to selling the beach property, but all the money's got to go into the fund. I'll knock down the price a little and take a finder's fee. Nicolette and I had a couple of good days, and I thought—"

"Jack! Jack!"

"Okay, here's what happened. Nicolette says she was trying out some of Tess's lipsticks, and looking in the mirror when she saw somebody down at the end of the driveway watching her. I told her she ought to have shut the drapes, but she said she thought way out in the country like this she wouldn't have to. Anyway, she saw this guy, standing there and not moving. Then the gas died down, and when it came back up he was still there, only a little nearer the house. Then it died down again, and when it came back up he was gone. She was looking out of the window by that time, she says in her slip. I went down to the end of the drive with a flashlight and looked around, but there's so many footprints from the guys that put up the friendship light you can't tell anything. If you ask me it was Ty. He stopped to look when he saw lights in the windows. It would be just like that sneaky son of a bitch not to come by or say anything, but I've got to admit I'm glad he didn't.

"Well, when I got back to the house, Nicolette told me she heard the back door open and close again while I was gone. I went back there, and it was shut and locked. I remembered how it was while Tess was here, and I thought, that bastard has let those cats in, so I went, 'Kitty-kitty-kitty,' and sure as hell the big tom came out of the pantry to see if there was anything to eat. I got him by the neck and chucked him out."

"Got some good pix of Nicolette and me by using the bulb with the motor drive. What I did was put the bulb under the mattress. Every once in a while it would get shoved down hard enough to trip the shutter, then the motor would advance the film. Shot up a whole roll of twenty-four that way last night. She laughed and said, 'Put in a big roll tomorrow,' but I don't think so. I'm going to try to get her to go back Thursday—got to think about that. Can't take *this* roll to Berry's in town, that's for sure. I'll wait till I go sign the transfer of title, then turn it in to one of the big camera stores. Maybe they'll mail the prints to me, too.

"She wanted me to call Ty and ask if anything funny went on while we were away. I said okay, thinking he wouldn't answer, but he did. He said there was nothing funny while I was gone, but last night he was driving past, and he saw what looked like lightning at an upstairs window. I said I'd been fooling around with my camera equipment and set off the flash a couple of times to test it out. I said I was calling to thank him and see when I could drop by and get my key back. He said he'd already put it in the mail.

"If you ask me he knows Nicolette's here. That was him out there last night as sure as hell. He's been watching the house, and a few minutes ago on the phone he was playing a little game. Okay by me. I've loaded the Savage and stuck it under the bed. Next time he comes snooping around, he's going to have bullets buzzing around his ears. If he gets hit— Hell, no jury around here's going to blame a man for shooting at trespassers on his property at night.

"Either there's more cats now, or the coons are eating the cat food again."

"Nicolette got real scared tonight as soon as it got dark. I kept saying what's the matter? And she kept saying she didn't know, but there was something out there, moving around. I got the Savage, thinking it would make her feel better. Every so often the phone would ring and keep on ringing, but there'd be nobody on the line when I picked it up. I mixed us a couple of stiff drinks, but it was like she'd never touched hers—when she finished, she was just as scared as ever.

"Finally I got smart and told her, 'Listen, honey, if this old place bothers you so much, why don't I just drive you to the airport tonight and put you on a plane home?' She jumped on it. 'Would you? Oh, Lord, Jack, I love you! just a minute and I'll run up and get packed.'

"Until then there hadn't really been anything to be scared of that I could see, but then something really spooky happened. The phone rang again. I picked it up out of habit, and instead of nobody being there like before, I heard a car start up—over the goddamned phone! I was mad as hell and banged it down, and right then Nicolette screamed.

"I grabbed the rifle and ran upstairs, only she was crying too much to say what it was. The damn drapes were still open, and I figured she'd seen Ty out by the friendship light again, so I closed them. Later she said it wasn't the guy she'd seen before, but something big with wings. It could have been a big owl, or maybe just her imagination and too much liquor. Anyway we wasted a lot of time before she got straightened out enough to pack.

"Then I heard something moving around downstairs. While I was going down the stairs, I heard it run—I guess to hide, and the sack of garbage falling over. After I saw the mess in the kitchen, I thought sure it was one of those damned cats, and I still do, but it seemed like it made too much noise running to be a cat—more like a dog, maybe.

"Nicolette didn't want to go out to the garage with me, so I said

I'd bring the car around and pick her up out front. The car and jeep looked okay when I raised the door and switched on the light, but as soon as I opened the car door I knew something was wrong, because the dome light didn't come on. I tossed the rifle in back, meaning to take a look under the hood, and there was the god-damnedest noise you ever heard in your life. It's a hell of a good thing I wasn't still holding the gun.

"It was a cat, and not one of ours. I guess he was asleep on the back seat and I hit him with the Savage when I tossed it inside.

"He came out of there like a buzz saw and it feels like he peeled off half my face. I yelled—that scared the shit out of Nicolette in the house—and grabbed the hammer off my bench. I was going to kill that son of a bitch if I could find him. The moon was up, and I saw him scooting past the pond. I chucked the hammer at him but missed him a mile. He'd been yowling like crazy, but all of a sudden he shut up, and I went back into the house to get a bandage for my face.

"I was a mess, too. That bastard took a lot of skin off my cheek, and a lot of blood had run onto my shirt and jacket.

"Nicolette was helping me when we heard something fall on the roof. She yelled, 'Where's your gun?' and I told her it was still out in the goddamned car, which it was. She wanted me to go out and get it, and I wanted to find out what had hit on the roof, but I went out first and got the Savage. Everything was O.K., too—the garage light was still on, and the gun was lying on the seat of the car. But when I tried to start the car, it wouldn't turn over. Finally I checked the headlights, and sure enough the switch was pulled out. I must have left the lights on last night. The battery's as dead as a doornail.

"I was pulling out the folding steps to the attic when the phone rang. Nicolette got it, and she said all she could hear was a car starting up, the same as I'd heard.

"I went up into the attic with a flashlight, and opened the window and went out onto the roof. It took a lot of looking to find what had hit. I should have just chucked it out into the yard, but like a jerk I picked it up by the ear and carried it downstairs and scared Nicolette half to death. It's the head of a big tomcat, if you ask me, or maybe a wildcat. Not one of ours, a black one.

"O.K., when I was outside and that cat got quiet all of a sudden, I felt a breeze—only cold like somebody had opened the door of a big freezer. There wasn't a noise, but then owls can fly without making a sound. So it's pretty clear what happened.

"We've got a big owl around here. That was probably what Nicolette saw out the window, and it was sure as hell what got the cat. The cat must have come around to eat our cat food, and got into the garage sometime when I opened the door. None of this has got anything to do with the phone. That's just kids.

"Nicolette wanted me to take her to the airport in the jeep right away, but after all that had happened I didn't feel like doing it, so I told her it would be too late to catch a flight and the jeep wasn't running anyhow. I told her tomorrow we'll call the garage and get somebody to come out and give us a jump.

"We yelled about that for a while until I gave her some of Tess's sleeping pills. She took two or three. Now she's out like a light. I've pulled the jack on every goddamned phone in the house. I took a couple of aspirins, but my cheek still hurt so bad I couldn't sleep, so I got up and fixed a drink and tried to talk all this out. Now I'm going back to bed.

This is bad—I've called the sheriff, and the ambulance is supposed to come out. It will be all over the damned paper, and the judge will see it as sure as hell, but what else could I do? Just now I mopped up the blood with a couple of dirty shirts. I threw them out back, and as soon as I shut the door I could hear them out there. I should've opened the door and shot. I don't know why I didn't, except Nicolette was making that noise that drives me crazy. I damn near hit her with the rifle. I've done everything I can. She needs an ambulance—a hospital.

"Now, honey, I want you to say—right into here—that it wasn't me, understand?
    "Water. . . ."
    "I'll get you plenty of water. You say it, and I'll get it right away. Tell them what happened."

"The tape ran out. Had to turn it over.
    "O.K., then I'll say it. It wasn't me—wasn't Jack. Maybe I ought to start right at the beginning.
    "Nicolette shot at a coon. I was sound asleep, but I must have

jumped damned near through the ceiling. I came up yelling and fighting, and it was dark as hell. I hit the light switch, but the lights wouldn't come on. The only light in the whole place was the little crack between the drapes. I pulled them open. It was just the damned friendship light way down at the end of the drive, but that was better than nothing.

"I saw she had the gun, so I grabbed it. She'd been trying to work it, but she hadn't pulled the lever down far enough to chamber a fresh round. If she had, she'd probably have killed us both.

"I said. 'Listen, the power's just gone off—that happens a lot out here.' She said she got up to go to the bathroom and she saw eyes, green eyes shining. She turned on the hall light, but it was gone. She tried to wake me up but I just grabbed her, so she got the gun. Pretty soon all the lights went out. She thought she heard it coming and fired.

"I got my flashlight and looked around. The bullet went right through the wall of Tess's room and hit the bed—I think it stopped in the mattress somewhere.

"Nicolette kept saying, 'Give me the keys—I'll go to the airport by myself.' I smacked her good and hard a few times to make her shut up, once with the flashlight.

"Then I saw the green eyes, too, but as soon as I got the light on it, I knew what it was—just a coon, not even a real big one.

"I didn't want to shoot again, because even if I'd hit it would have made a hell of a mess, so I told Nicolette to open the door. She did, and that's when I saw them, two or three of them, flying around down by the friendship light. Jesus!"

"They're outside now. I know they are. I took a shot at one through the big window, but I don't think I hit it.

"Where the hell's the sheriff's guy? He should've been here an hour ago—the ambulance, too. It's starting to get light outside."

"The coon got in through the goddamned cat door. I ought to have guessed. When Ty was here he had the cats in the house with him, so he unbolted it—that was how Marmaduke got in last night.

"I tried to switch this thing off, but I'm shaking too bad. I damn near dropped it. I might as well get on with it anyway. This isn't getting us anywhere. I gave her the keys and I told her, 'O.K., you want to go to the goddamn airport so bad, here. Leave the keys and the ticket in the dash compartment and I'll go out and pick it up when I can.'

"I didn't think she'd do it, but she took the keys and ran outside. I went to the window. I heard the jeep start up, and it sounded like she was tearing out the whole damn transmission. Pretty soon she came roaring down the driveway. I guess she had it in second and the pedal all the way to the floor. I didn't think any were close to her, and all of a sudden there was one right above her, dropping down. The wings made it look like the jeep was blinking on and off, too.

"The jeep went across the road and into the ditch. I never thought I'd see her again, but it dropped her on the front lawn. I shouldn't have gone out to get her. I could've been killed.

"It was looking for something in her, that's what I think. I didn't know there was so much blood when you cut a person open like that. What the hell do the doctors do?

"I think she's dead now."

"The sheriff's men just left. They say the power's off all over. It looks like a plane hit the wires, they said, without crashing. Jesus.

"Here's what I told them. Nicolette and I had a fight. I keep the gun loaded in case of prowlers, and she took a couple of shots at me. They said, 'How do we know you didn't shoot at her?' I said, 'You think I'd miss a woman twice, with my deer rifle, inside the house?' I could see they bought it.

"I said I gave her the keys to the jeep and said to leave it at the airport—the truth in other words. They said, 'Didn't you give her any money?' I told them, 'Not then, but I'd given her some before, back when we were still in the hotel.' I told them she floorboarded it down the drive and couldn't make the turn. I saw her hit and went out and got her, and brought her back into the house.

"They said, 'You ripped her up the belly with a knife.' I said, 'No way. Sure, I slapped her a couple times for shooting at me, but I never knifed her.' I showed them my hunting knife, and they checked out all the kitchen knives. They said, 'How'd she get ripped up the middle like that?' and I said, 'How the hell should I know? She got thrown out of the jeep.'

"I'm not supposed to leave the country, not supposed to stay anyplace but here. They took the Savage, but I've still got my shotgun and the twenty-two."

"Power's back on. The tow truck came out for the jeep and gave me a jump for the Cadillac.

"The way I see it, they've never even tried to get into the house, so if I stay in here I ought to be all right. I'm going to wait until after dark, then see if I can get Ty to come over. If he gets in okay, fine—I'll string him along for a while. If he doesn't, I'll leave tomorrow and the sheriff can go to hell. I'll let his office know where I am, and tell them I'll come in for questioning any time they want to see me."

"I just phoned Ty. I said I'd like to give him something for looking after the place while I was gone. And that I was going away again, this time for quite a while, and I wanted him to take care of things like he did before. I told him I've been using the spare key, but the one he mailed was probably in the box, down by the friendship light, because I haven't picked up my mail yet. I said for him to check the box before he came to the house. He said O.K., he'd be right over. It seems to be taking him. . . ."

Ty again. At this point in the tape, my knock can be heard quite distinctly, followed by Jack's footfalls as he went to the door; it would seem that he was too rattled to turn off his tape recorder. (Liquor, as I have observed several times, does not in fact prevent nervousness, merely allowing it to accumulate.) I would be very happy to transcribe his scream here, if only I knew how to express it by means of the twenty-six letters of the Roman alphabet.

You took him, as you promised, whole and entire. I have no grounds for complaint upon that score, or indeed upon any. And I feel certain he met his well-deserved death firmly convinced that he was in the grip of demons, or some such thing, which I find enormously satisfying.

Why, then, do I write? Permit me to be frank now: I am in need of your assistance. I will not pretend that I deserve it (you would quite correctly care nothing for that), or that it is owed me; I carried out my part of the agreement we made at the friendship light, and you carried out yours. But I find myself in difficulties.

Poor Tessie will probably never be discharged. Even the most progressive of our hospitals are now loath to grant release in cases of her type—there were so many unfortunate incidents earlier, and although society really has very little invested in children aged two to four, it overvalues them absurdly.

As her husband, Jack was charged with administration of the estate in which (though it was by right mine) I shared only to a minuscule degree through the perversity of my mother. Were Jack legally dead, I, as Tessie's brother, would almost certainly be appointed administrator—so my attorney assures me. But as long as Jack is considered by law a fugitive, a suspect in the suspicious death of Nicolette Corso, the entire matter is in abeyance.

True, I have access to the house; but I have been unable to persuade the conservator that I am the obvious person to look after the property. Nor can I vote the stock, complete the sale of the beach acreage, or do any other of many such useful and possibly remunerative things.

Thus I appeal to you. (And to any privileged human being who may read this. Please forward my message to the appropriate recipients.) I urgently require proof of Jack's demise. The nature of that proof I shall leave entirely at your discretion. I venture to point out, however, that identifications based on dental records are in most cases accepted by our courts without question. If Jack's skull, for example, were discovered some fifty or more miles from here, there should be little difficulty.

In return, I stand ready to do whatever may be of value to you. Let us discuss this matter, openly and in good faith. I will arrange for this account to be reproduced in a variety of media.

It was I, of course, as even old Jack surmised, whom Jack's whore saw the first time near the friendship light. To a human being its morose dance appeared quite threatening, a point I had grasped from the beginning.

It was I also who pulled out Jack's headlight switch and put the black tom—I obtained it from the Humane Society—in his car. And it was I who telephoned; at first I did it merely to annoy him—a symbolic revenge on all those (himself included) who have employed that means to render my existence miserable. Later I permitted him to hear my vehicle start, knowing as I did that his would not. Childish, all of them, to be sure; and yet I dare hope they were of some service to you.

Before I replaced the handle of the valve and extinguished Tessie's friendship light, I contrived that my Coleman lantern should be made to flicker at the signal frequency. Each evening I hoist it high into the branches of the large maple tree in front of my home. Consider it, please, a beacon of welcome. I am most anxious to speak with you again.

SUSAN

◆　◆　◆

Harlan Ellison

For years, Harlan Ellison has served as F&SF's film columnist and all-around gadfly. He wrote the introduction to our 40th Anniversary Best from Fantasy & Science Fiction *collection, and he has given excellent advice—and criticism—to the F&SF staff.*

"Susan" comes from a challenge Harlan set himself after seeing the work of Jacek Yerka, the Polish artist. Harlan wrote thirty-three new stories around thirty-four of Yerka's paintings between February and November of 1993. The Yerka painting that inspired this story appears on our December 1993 cover. The primary inspiration, though, comes from Harlan's lovely wife . . . Susan.

A s she had done every night since they had met, she went in bare feet and a cantaloupe-meat-colored nightshift to the shore of the sea of mist, the verge of the ocean of smothering vapor, the edge of the bewildering haze he called the Brim of Obscurity.

Though they spent all of their daytime together, at night he chose to sleep alone in a lumpy, Volkswagen-shaped bed at the southernmost boundary of the absolutely lovely forest in which their home had been constructed. There at the border between the verdant woods and the Brim of Obscurity that stretched on forever, a sea of fog that roiled and swirled itself into small, murmuring vortexes from which depths one could occasionally hear something like a human voice pleading for absolution (or at least a back-scratcher to relieve this awful itch!), he had made his bed and there, with the night-light from his old nursery, and his old vacuum-tube radio that played nothing but big band dance music from the 1920s, and a few favorite books, and a little fresh fruit he had picked on his way from the house to his resting-place, he slept peacefully every night. Except for the nightmares, of course.

And as she had done every night for the eight years since they had met, she went barefooted and charmed, down to the edge of the sea of fog to kiss him goodnight. That was their rite.

Before he had even proposed marriage, he explained to her the nature of the problem. Well, the curse, really. Not so much a *problem*; because a problem was easy to reconcile; just trim a little nub off here; just smooth that plane over there; just let this bit dangle here and it will all meet in the center; no, it wasn't barely remotely something that could be called a "problem." It was a curse, and he was open about it from the first.

"My nightmares come to life," he had said.

Which remark thereupon initiated quite a long and detailed conversation between them. It went through all the usual stages of good-natured chiding, disbelief, ridicule, short-lived anger at the possibility he was making fun of her, toying with her, on into another kind of disbelief, argument with recourse to logic and Occam's Razor, grudging acceptance, a brief lapse into incredulity, a return to the barest belief, and finally, with trust, utter acceptance that he was telling her nothing less than the truth. Remarkably (to say the least) his nightmares assumed corporeal shape and stalked the night as he slept, dreaming them up. It wouldn't have been so bad except:

"My nightmares killed and ate my first four wives," he had said. He'd saved that part for the last.

But she married him, nonetheless. And they were extremely happy. It was a terrific liaison for both of them. But just to be on the safe side, because he loved her very much, he took to sleeping in the lumpy Volkswagen bed at the edge of the forest.

And every morning—because he was compelled to rise when the sunlight struck his face, out there in the open—he would trek back to their fine home in the middle of the forest, and he would make her morning tea, and heat and butter a muffin, or possibly pour her a bowl of banana nut crunch cereal (or sometimes a nice bowl of oatmeal with cinnamon or brown sugar sprinkled across the surface), and carry it in to her as she sat up in bed reading or watching the Home Shopping Channel. And for eight years she had been absolutely safe from the nightmares that ripped and rent and savaged everything in sight.

He slept at the Brim of Obscurity, and he was a danger to no one but himself. And whatever means he used to protect *himself* from those darktime sojourners, well, it was an armory kept most secret.

That was how they lived, for eight years. And every night she would go barefoot, in her shift, and she would follow the twenty-seven plugged-together extension cords—each one thirty feet long—that led from the house to his night-light; and she would come to him and kiss him goodnight. And they would tell each other how happy they were together, how much every moment together meant to them, and they would kiss goodnight once more, and she would go back to the house. He would lie reading for a time, then go to sleep. And in the night, there at the shore of fog, at the edge of the awful sea of mist, the nightmares would come and scream and tear at themselves. But they never got anywhere near Susan, who was safely in her home.

So as she had done every night since they had met, she followed the extension cords down through the sweet-smelling, wind-cooled hedges and among the whispering, mighty trees to his bed. The light was on; an apple ready to be nibbled sat atop a stack of books awaiting his attention; the intaglio of a tesseract (or possibly a dove on the wing) lay in the center of a perfectly circular depression in his pillow where he had rested his head. But the bed was empty.

She went looking for him, and after a time she found him sitting on the shore of fog, looking out over the Brim of Obscurity. But she heard him crying long before she saw him. The sound of his deep, heartfelt sobbing led her to him.

And she knelt beside him, and he put his arms around her, and she said, "I see now that I've made you unhappy. I don't know how, but I can see that I've come into your life and made it unpleasant. I'm sorry, I'm truly sorry."

But he shook his head, and continued to shake it, to say no . . . no, that isn't it . . . you don't understand.

"I'm so sorry . . ." she kept saying, because she didn't understand what it meant, his shaking his head like that.

Until, finally, he was able to stop crying long enough to say, "No, that isn't it. You don't understand."

"Then what *are* you crying about?"

He wasn't able to tell her for a while, because just trying to get the words out started him up all over again. But after a while, still holding her, there at the Brim of Obscurity (which, in an earlier time, had been known as the Rim of Oblivion), he said softly, "I'm crying for the loss of all the years I spent without you, the years before I met you, all the lost years of my life; and I'm crying that there are less years in front of me than all those lost years behind me."

And out in the roiling ocean of misty darkness, they could both hear the sound of roving, demented nightmares whose voices were now, they understood, less filled with rage than with despair.

GUIDE DOG

✦   ✦   ✦

Mike Conner

*Mike Conner wrote a handful of distinctive stories for F&SF and three novels (*The Houdini Directive, Groupmind, *and* Eye of the Sun*) in the mid-eighties, then sort of retired for a time until he returned in 1991 with "Guide Dog," a very different and moving tale about a young human who is trained into a kind of benign servitude on a strange world. The story won a Nebula Award and became the basis for several sequels.*

When I was fourteen years old, my parents sold me. I don't blame them for it. They got a lot of money for me. Mom and Dad ran an import company, and they were at a disadvantage because, while they were never big enough to compete, they always did just well enough to keep from going under. And they had another son to worry about that they could not sell yet. So the contract was a good thing for the family.

The night I left, Dad cried and said that when I turned twenty-five and had worked off the term, I could come home, and he would pay me back every cent. I told him he didn't have to do that. I was at the age where you don't care much about leaving home, anyway. So, one morning in December, Dad drove me over to the compound in the old vegetable truck. His eyes were still red, but he wasn't crying anymore. He told me to be careful in town, pay attention to my teachers, and wash all the fruits and vegetables I ate. I thought he ought to know about that because he imported food, so I thanked him and said I would see him in about ten years. He gave me a tiny blue pocketknife then that had a fingernail file in it and a pair of scissors. I still had that knife until last night. It was so small they never believed I could actually use it as a weapon. It was the last thing Dad ever gave me, and I stood turning it over with one hand and waving good-bye with the other.

At first I missed the folks. Anybody with half a heart misses their family no matter how awful they are. But the Academy had developed plenty of ways to make you forget about them. They got you busy with the academic stuff, and they put you in the social program, too. They arranged your rooms and your classes to put you with people they calculated you would get along with. They wanted you to fall in love as soon as possible. It didn't matter with whom. Here you were, lonely as hell, and they gave you a roommate, also lonely, and they look the other way and hand you every opportunity, so how could you resist? Then, when you thought you were set all right, they fix it so one of you moves up a class or transfers out to another dorm. So you moan and groan and then look around and find somebody new. Somehow it ate up whole years.

Eventually, though, you passed your exams and got a chance to see what you were there for. Like everything else, it was pretty much sink or swim (though after three years they were pretty certain about who would sink and who could do the swimming). What they did was take you out early in the morning into the Tree. They landed you on top and said all you had to do was make it back to the gate of the Academy. No time limit. No life or death. If you freaked, you could call in on a beeper, and they'd pick you up, and you were free to try again as many times as you wanted. But everyone knew getting to that gate meant getting out of school. And after three years of being jacked around, manipulated, and otherwise educated, there wasn't anybody who wasn't ready for that.

I know I was. I'd spent hours studying the tapes and maps. I'd put on phones and gotten used to the noise they made. I knew all the best routes to take on foot, and how to ask for directions and read the answers from the little dances they did. I had a pack of food and a list of districts in the Tree where our people were allowed to work or live. So when they came for me, I thought it would not be a problem. They flew me in and let me out directly at the top of the Tree.

Oh my! The perches at the top are narrow and wind-worn slick, rounded like branches; and even cleated, gum-soled slippers and practice on the balance beams couldn't prepare you for the sheer power of thousands of them swarming by, wings buzzing—to say nothing of the way they turned their heads and panned their eyes when they looked at you, and how you thought they wanted you to fall, and then, and even worse, realized that they *didn't care* whether you fell or not, that you were nothing to them, while they were everything to each other. It was the emotion that was hard to take and still carry on the task of moving down. In spite of the perches and platforms, there were millions of places you could crash and fall through, bouncing down like a ball in a pachinko machine all the way to the ground.

My first five minutes up there, I slipped and hung, legs swinging onto a slippery perch, fighting a total despair that sapped the strength in my arms and made me want to let go. Then I told myself no, this is what you're up here for, to survive this, and it's the only way you'll ever see the end of that contract. *This is what you've been going to school for!* And so I swung my legs up and stood and spread my arms to keep the ones flying by off of me, and sure enough, they commenced to veer because their radar told them I had position. And I started picking and hopping my way down until I reached a fountain I remembered from the tapes, got myself oriented, and eventually made it back to the gates of the school. It took six and one-half hours. Later they said it was some kind of record. I don't know. It seemed to have lasted forever.

The next day they called me in and gave me an assignment in a nest.

A guide dog lives in a nest for two years. You continue your studies, but the idea is to learn all you can about how they live. At the end of the two years, you are supposed to be used to their ways. My nest lay about twenty miles outside the Tree, near a river. It was nice, lush country, with lots of flowers and paths that you could walk along and almost fool yourself into believing you were home—until a couple of them flew over.

The nest family is where you wear a harness for the first time. The harness is the mark of a guide dog. It is the means of communi-cating with your client. The word *client* is a hard one to get around.

You want to learn to forget what you think you mean by the word, and try to really understand the concept of service. As a guide, your purpose is to help the client to live as normally as possible. In the nest, you learn not to feel ashamed of that, and to take pride in what you are and enjoy it. That way you can understand the kind of appreciation they give you in return. I admit this appreciation can be difficult to handle. However, you cannot live as a guide dog without it. It is as if you were a plant and had to learn to *appreciate* the light before you could grow and thrive.

I had a good nest. They had worked with the Academy for many years and had boarded many student guides, and they knew how to train us. They were an older nest, and lots of the kids were almost grown. With a nest, it is the kids who really do most of the teaching. They laugh at you when you first feel the thousands of tiny needles in the top of your back from the harness translator that turns their buzzing into shapes that you interpret as words. They demonstrate the body language. You make your first moves in a harness with the kids, too. They hold the grab bar and press their knees into the cups on either side of your hips. If they are old enough and strong enough, they fly with you, too, or try to. Sometimes you make it across the room. Sometimes you crash and lie there in a heap, pushing and trying to untangle yourself just like you would with any other kid.

The biggest thing they teach you, though, is about the emotion. I'm talking about what you feel and what you have to go through if they accept you even a little. In school they say it is possibly the result of a chemical reaction. They would. Anyone who's ever felt it knows that there is nothing chemical about it. It is a spiritual rush of love and gratitude that hits you so hard your toes curl. You think that you understand everything. You know it is all worth it, no matter what it is.

I remember when I felt it the first time. I was with one of the young ones, and we were playing a kind of catch game with a long scoop and a sticky ball. I made a move and caught one behind my back and flipped it right back at him, and he just stood there looking at me, his flat eyes shining like china. And it hit me so hard then I thought I would just burst with it.

Of course, once you feel it like that, you want to feel it again. That's why the Academy teaches you to channel your feelings. That feeling of belonging is what holds everything together for them. It pulls them in and keeps them healthy. *You*, however, are meant to have only a taste of it. That's how they put it at school. *Tasting.* When you feel it coming on, you're supposed to sidestep and take a taste. You must not let it get to you. That first time in the garden with the kid, I got in all the way, and I paid. Inside-out of that burning glow of belonging is black, empty desolation that hits even harder. It just about knocked me out for good. I was so down with it, I spent three days trying to figure out how I could kill myself with the little pocketknife Dad gave me. In the end, though, I came back, and from then on I was really careful. I made sure to take only a taste.

You get to know how much you can have, and I pushed that to the limit, but stayed safe. There were some who wanted more, though. They took all they could get, and built up a tolerance. They didn't care about the consequences. They were renegades. Eventually I would run into them.

By my second year with the family, I was doing pretty well. I got so I didn't feel the harness anymore, and the pictures pressed against my back turned easily into words and pictures in my head. I was fond of my nest. The father would take me out flying in the harness, and we got to be pretty good together. Of course, he could see, and his radar was sharp, so it was not like guiding him. But he helped me to figure out the traffic system and how they worked the right-of-way. The father told me I was the best dog that had ever come into his nest. *Dog.* That's how the harness translated their sound for what we were. He got emotional about it, too. I could feel it coming on, and got all cold inside and had just the smallest taste. I knew it was hard for him getting attached to a guide and then having to let go. It was hard for me, too. But that was the way it was.

A couple of days after the father paid me that compliment, the Director asked me to come around to his office. When I came in, he was sitting behind his desk wearing a pair of big glasses. Which was a good thing, because small eyes were starting to look strange to me.

"You've been an outstanding, outstanding student," the Director began.

"Thank you, sir."

"You could not ask anyone to do any more than you've done here." He was speaking emotionally. It always surprises me how we demonstrate emotion so visibly—eyes misting, voice trembling—with so little of the feeling coming through.

The Director began to clean his glasses. "We have been approached by the representative of a very, very special client. A very, very important personality in this world. We have never had an opportunity to serve someone of this stature until now. Fortunately, I believe we are ready to meet the challenge. I believe you are ready to guide. I believe you are the one person here who can guide this client." He put both his hands on my shoulders and looked deep into my eyes. "What do you say?"

"I'll give it a shot," I said.

I called him Henry. Henry was an artist. By artist, I mean painter and sculptor. He was the most famous artist who had ever lived on their world. Part of the reason was that he was so old. He had lasted longer than all of his immediate relatives, and now he lived alone. That was the second reason for his fame. It was absolutely astonishing and incomprehensible to them that someone would *choose* to live alone. They were always asking him about it, and he always said that he did not live alone, but with anybody who had ever seen his work. But he did actually live alone, and that was a marvel to them.

The third reason Henry was so famous was that he was damned good. Maybe he flew around and spoke by buzzing and making little dances, and lived by chewing on the edges of big leaves—but Henry could flat out paint. His canvases were a kind of silky cloth stretched over various geometric frames, including rectangular ones. For as long as anyone could remember, he had covered them with beautiful pictures.

Henry was a great master, and would have been on *any* world. Unfortunately, old age had got him. He had gone blind. The big eyes were milky saucers now, and Henry could make out only rough shapes and distinguish light from dark. His sight had been failing a long time, but he had continued to paint. Then his radar went out on him, too. The feathery shoots above his head withered and curled, and Henry was in darkness and, for the first time, truly alone. But he was still strong. Henry had no intention of biding time in an old-age nest waiting to die. He had things to do! And so he had contacted the Academy, and the Academy had sent me to him.

I called his house the Atelier, because that's what it was. It sat on a high bluff and had a magnificent view of the Tree, with its branches sparkling like the facets of a snow crystal. Inside, the rooms had enormously high ceilings and huge windows. There were four or five rooms for living and three for working. And in every corner were the paintings and sculptures.

Henry estimated he had done a quarter of a million pictures, not counting sketches, studies, painted-over first tries—to say nothing of the statues, prints, plaster casts, and the pen-and-ink drawings that were piled up everywhere. Henry was not very organized. Again, that was unusual for them because generally they are neat as pins. Not Henry. His carapace was covered with paint, some of it very old paint, layers like you get on the stair post of an old hotel. He never bothered cleaning it off. It was his trademark. He told me, though, that when he was young and just leaving the nest, his sloppiness had caused him a lot of hardship. He had trouble finding a job, or holding one when he did find it. It was the old story. The ones that don't fit in are the ones who try the hardest to make sense of everything. That is why you have pictures and books and plays and songs and everything else that isn't business or food. If you can't fit into the world, then you try and make it into a place that fits you.

When they brought me to the Atelier, the Director was there, cleaning his glasses and blowing his nose because of his allergies. They had a Minister of Education around. (And yes, they had all of it— government offices, places of business, places of worship, universities, just like we did. It was all organized differently, and not necessarily inside monumental buildings, but they had them, all right, as I was to discover.) There were reporters from their media, and some from ours. Our people took pictures and asked me how it felt to have such a heavy assignment, and the Director blew his nose and made eye contact with me, and I remembered to be polite and humble, though inside I was getting impatient with all the fuss. Finally they brought me inside, and there he was, standing in the middle of the first big room of the Atelier with his long hands in front of him, cocking his head a little because he didn't quite know what was going on. One of them went over to him—I found out later he was Henry's Business Manager—and buzzed something at him. Henry nodded and came forward and stood over me.

"What's up?" he said in English.

He must have been practicing a long time. It is very hard for them to make the sounds we use when we speak, but Henry just loved that expression. He told me once he thought it summed up his philosophy of life better than anything he could say in his own language. You see, "up" was just like right or left to them. But Henry figured out it had a greater meaning for us, in terms of escape and climbing and falling and trying and failing. Plus, he liked being able to make the sound. Anyway, that was when I felt the first wave coming from him. From that moment I loved Henry and everything about him.

I couldn't wait to get started. Finally, a couple of hours later, when they had taken their pictures and gathered in the scene at the Atelier for their media, and all the necessary documents had been executed by the Director and Business Manager, they left us alone. I helped Henry touch the grab bar.

"That's it," I said. The harness translated for me. He could still hear all right. "How are you?"

"Good," he replied. I could feel the needles tingling against my back.

"You understand me?"

"I believe I do."

"O.K.," I said. "Let's get to work."

They had given Henry a lot of training, too, I discovered. He had studied "Physiology of Dog" and "Psychology of Dog" and "History of Dog." He had tons of scrolls around on how to care for me, and Business Manager had hired a contractor to make me a perfect room. It was a pretty good try. But the result was a little like what happened when the committee of blind men described what an elephant looked like. Right in the middle of the room, for instance, they installed a commode that was big enough to swim in. And the bed was in the wall. I slept in the room only a couple of nights. Then I moved my bed into a shop that Henry had used for wood carving. He had not done much carving lately, but the shop still smelled like pine shavings. It was small, and I liked the smell and how the chips and sawdust felt under my feet.

Henry never asked why I had moved. He had a supreme ability to mind his own business. Again, that was so unusual for them, close-knit as they were, and completely lacking in anything that would correspond to our concept of tact or politeness. When I was with the nest, the kids all had to know everything I did and why and what for. Finally you got tired of the questions and told them to shut up. Even then they would ask you why, but not Henry. You had the feeling he knew you would tell him what he wanted to know without his ever having to ask.

Henry had been blind for around ten of our years. At first he accepted his condition with good humor and contented himself sculpting in clay and plastic. I have seen some of his pieces from this period, and they are graceful, rounded forms. He was good as ever, but he wanted more. He wanted his freedom back, and for that, he had to be able to fly. You must understand: flying is the one thing they do alone. And yet, by flying around, they become part of the Tree and of their world. In that respect, Henry was no different than the rest of them. Without flying, he was lonely.

Right away Henry and I began practicing in the big room of the Atelier. This room was the treasure-house of Henry's art. There were canvases of all sizes and shapes from his Blue and Orange Periods. He told me these "periods" were not solid blocks of time. When a "blue" mood came on, he would paint in those tones and in that style, and the historians and critics would assign the piece to the "Blue Period."

We spent hours in that room, and I went there when Henry was resting or out somewhere with Business Manager, just to look at all the stuff. There were hundreds of pieces, some of his most famous works, like "Waterfall at Night" and the "Huskers," that were familiar to anybody who liked art. And this was where we began to work with the harness. It was a little like playing handball in the Médicis room at the Louvre.

There were perches in the room spaced close so that we could handle the jumps without Henry having to fly very far. Henry took the bar, tucked his knees in a little as I looked back at him over my shoulder.

"Where to?" I said.

"You choose."

"You sure? I don't want you to fall."

"Who does?" Henry replied with vast amusement.

I made the first jump. They are very agile, and so strong and quick that he had no trouble reading the direction or the distance from the way my body shifted under his light pressure in the knee cups. He wasn't afraid. He trusted right away that my moves would be good. And sometimes we did fall, but Henry somehow always got his wings out in time. Right away I could tell we were a good team. And it wasn't long before we were using his wings for more than braking a fall. Henry flew, riding the harness like a saddle, and I moved my body this way or that, and he would know when he had to turn, and how much or that he must slow and pull up and land. We flew to the top perches in the Atelier. It was a fatal fall to the floor from up there, but with Henry, I felt safe. We landed, and I stood there looking out at the Tree in the early evening, listening to the click of Henry's breastplates as they rose and fell. He was still a little out of shape for flying, and was breathing hard. But he was happy.

Then one day we went out. It was early morning, the sun up just long enough to burn off some of the mist, and there was plenty of traffic. The Tree looked like a bubble of boiling water, all misty at the edges with so many of them flying in and out. Henry let me collect myself for a long time. He must have been nervous, too. Finally I heard him come up behind me, and felt him take the grab bar.

"What's up?" he said.

I looked back at him. His head was cocked a little, and the clouded-over disks of his eyes looked like pearl buttons. I wondered what *was* up. I wasn't sure if I would have trusted someone to lead me around the room if I had been blind, much less fly.

"I'm ready," I said.

Henry tucked his knees in against me. I heard the dry scrape of his back plates as he unsheathed his wings. And then he sprang out easily, and we were off. He rolled, spiraling toward the Tree, and he was laughing, tumbling both of us through the air like a kid in a nest.

At first I didn't have much to do. Then we got closer to the Tree, and the traffic really got thick. They all had their radar going, and there was a tingling in the air from it that made the hair stand up on the back of your neck. But you had to forget about that and work with your eyes and your ears and your anticipation. It was like riding into a beehive, except the bees all weighed three hundred pounds. I ducked and turned and twisted the way I had been taught and in ways I had never dreamed of, and all the time Henry drove on, plunging straight through the avenues and dropping right into the core at the busiest time of the day. Nobody flew like we were flying now. We had fifty near misses and caused a dozen near accidents, and I was waiting for their cops to come after us. After a while I noticed they started to give way and pull up and watch when we went by. At first I thought it was just a lull in the traffic, but then I realized: *Word had gone around!* They knew that Henry was back. He had come back from the worst thing that could happen to one of them, and they wanted to see how he had done it.

All morning we flew. Then Henry asked me where we were in relation to certain landmarks of the Tree and began to guide *me*. We left the Tree and followed a deep canyon above a river for a while. The walls were slate and spalled off, and in the crevasses, twisted trees grew thickly wherever they could take root. The canyon grew deeper, and narrower, and a canopy of green covered the top, so that the light turned a dusky gray-green. By now you could hear the sound of a waterfall. Suddenly Henry pulled back on the harness, and we flew straight up, blasting through the foliage up to a wide ledge that was shaded by another layer of spreading branches and walled in by the canyon. I heard a buzz of activity. We landed on the ledge, and Henry caught a breath.

"What is this place?" I said.

"Well, I suppose you would call it a café," he said through the harness. "*Kaaff,*" he repeated in his own voice.

I hesitated. It was one of their private places. They had clubs and the like, but we were never allowed near them.

"Do you think it's a good idea for me to go in? I mean, I can wait out here for you." Like a good dog, I thought.

"Don't be silly. I'm one of the owners. Maybe the only owner. The others may all be dead now."

He gave a little push on the harness, and I led him in. There were tables with long stone benches that were crowded with them. When they saw me, they all stopped talking. *They don't like us*, I thought. *We're nothing to them.* And then the place exploded because they realized it was Henry. They were all over him. He let them touch him, preen him, look at his eyes and withered stalks on his head. And then, holding the harness so I could understand, he told them all that he had flown here with my help. I felt the rush then, but I did not back too far away. After all, we were in a café.

They sat us down and brought Henry and me each a platter piled high with leaves and bowls of yellow mead fermented from flower nectar. Henry tore right into his, then he noticed that I wasn't eating. He got up, and I made out through the harness that he wanted some food for his friend. Someone went out and brought back a bowl of fruit and berries, so that I could eat with the rest. I was starving after all the flying, and I ate not caring if it was any good for me or not. I figured that if Henry could trust me to guide him while he flew, I could trust him not to poison me. As it happened, the fruit did contain some alkaloid dust in low concentration, so that soon I was singing along with them, and dancing on the tabletops, and Henry flew me around and let some of his friends have a turn with the harness, too. Henry taught them all how to say "dog," and they made up a song about it. Then Henry showed me some of his stuff that was hanging on the walls. Most of it was real old, done on boards with cheap paint that was already cracking. Henry described each one. They hadn't touched a thing since the last time he had been there.

The paintings were mainly landscapes or still lifes with a nature theme. One really got to me, though. It was of two of them, an adult and a child. The adult stood behind the child and looked down at him with his head bent. The child tilted his head and raised his eyes. There was just something about the way they looked at each other that reminded me of my own dad, and I started to cry. This caused a sensation. It had never occurred to me that they would be sensitive to *my* emotions. In a moment they were all around me, stroking me and trying to get a little sample of my tears. I would have had to cry a river to supply them all. There was so much coming back from them that for a second I felt myself slipping away. That was when Henry stepped in. Firmly, he ordered everyone to get away from me. He made them be quiet and let me get myself together.

"What's up?" he said after I came around.

"It's the painting. Something about it makes me feel awfully sad—and happy, too, at the same time."

"Is that so?"

"Yes. It's an awfully good picture."

"Would you like it?"

"Oh, I couldn't. It belongs here."

"We'll give them another one. Would you like it? It would give me pleasure to give it to you."

"O.K.," I said.

He had them take it off the wall, and we took it with us when we left.

I put the painting up above my bed in the carving room. I liked the feeling it gave me when I looked at it. It was good to have a picture in the room where you could see it accidentally when coming in or getting out of bed in the morning. That was the way to see a painting. In museums, when you made a point of visiting them and stood around respectfully with a lot of other people, it was like gawking at animals in a zoo. It gave you an uneasy feeling because ordinarily you would never see animals that way. Paintings were made for money or to please the artist, not to be exhibited with a lot of other paintings. That's what I thought, anyway. I told it all to Henry one night, too.

"Is that your theory about art?" he asked.

I said it wasn't exactly a theory. It was more like an opinion. He cocked his head then because there was no exact translation for "opinion" in his language. After a while he sat back a little.

"You mean it is your idea," he said.

"That's about the size of it."

"The guide dog and I think alike," he said. "I wonder if we *see* alike."

I always liked to remind him how smart I was, and so I began explaining that my eyes had only one lens, while his had 256. But he stopped me.

"*See*," he said, tapping the plate on top of his head. "Inside. You look out through the door into the big room. Tell me what you see."

"The edge of that bench."

"Why?"

328 ◆ Mike Conner

"I don't know. Maybe it's because the wood's split. I always wonder what made it split like that."

"Color?"

"Well, that changes, Henry. I can see it from my bed, you know. Sometimes—early in the morning if it's been raining, say—the wood looks gray and brown together with a little blue. *Vast*, I'd call it."

"Vast?"

"What the light looks like inside a big church when the sun isn't shining through the windows. That's what I mean."

"Vast," Henry repeated.

He didn't say any more, but went out and left me alone. I read a book for a while, and then wrote a letter to my folks. I told them not to feel too proud about my assignment. I suppose they had a right to feel proud, but I didn't want them bragging about me. I wrote that I was lucky to get in with Henry, but that when you got right down to it, I was working off my contract just like anybody else. I tried not to be too blunt. But it is not a bad thing every once in a while to remind someone gently of the things they have done to you. There are plenty of ways to say such things without using the actual words. After dozens of letters to my family, I was still finding new ones all the time.

I finished the letter and sent it off into the link, and then I wandered around the Atelier looking for Henry. I found him out on the back terrace. He was sitting in his net chair, working his jaws on the end of a stick. He had a tray of sticks in front of him, and I realized he was chewing out brushes. Henry had a species of shrub growing around the house that sent out straight green stalks packed full of silky fibers that made nice bristles if you broke them down a little. Depending on what size shoot you picked, you could chew out any brush you wanted, from hairline to one you could use to paint a house. Henry had made up about a dozen, brand-new.

"Good," Henry said, touching the harness. "I was just about to call you." He pressed the new brush against the back of his hand, chewed it a few more times, and then put it into the tray with the others.

"Take this, please?"

I took up the tray, and he grabbed the bar and steered me into the big room. There he had set up his stool and another chair and a flat canvas on an easel in the middle of the room.

"Put the tray down and sit," he said.

I sat. My heart was starting to beat faster. Henry sat to my left and a little behind me. He took up a palette and squeezed out colors from tubes. They were like the paint tubes we used. Henry knew which colors he wanted. He had learned, when he was going blind, to put everything he needed in the same order every time.

"Clouds today?" he asked.

"Yes."

"Today we paint the bench," he said. "How far away?"

I told him.

"Where?"

I wasn't sure what he meant.

"If you square your shoulders to the canvas, where?"

"A little off-center to the right."

He took a pencil then and reached past me and made a sketch. It took him about a minute to block out the shape of the bench. The perspective, the angle, even the shadow lines, were perfect. It was amazing.

"How can you do that?"

"Inside. Old as I am, long as I've lived here, I'd better remember. But anything new"—he shook his head—"I need my guide dog."

"You're going to try to paint?"

"No. I *am* going to paint. With you."

"But I can't paint. I can't even draw a straight line!"

"Yes. And you cannot fly, either," he said.

I had to smile as I thought about it. In a way, it was a bigger responsibility than flying him around. Henry was one of the most famous artists ever to live. Anywhere.

"It would make me very happy," he said, and I felt a flood of emotion from him that almost knocked me off the stool.

"All right," I said. "I'll try."

"Good," Henry said.

"But how do we do it?"

"We learn. Like flying. The first lesson is color. Take this brush. I want you to mix a color for me on the palette."

"Which color?"

"Look at the bench. Give me the darkness with the light inside of it. Mix me the color you called *vast*."

We did that first painting in a couple of hours. Henry wasn't one of those artists who worry a piece to death. He liked to work quickly, and, in fact, I had to get him to calm down on that first one because we hadn't worked out a system yet. Henry listened to me. He stopped fussing and began to ask what things in the painting looked like, and showed me where the colors ought to go, and how I should mix them differently for different times of the day. I never thought you could actually teach a thing like painting, but Henry had a way of making you understand one thing by talking about something else. And sometimes he let my hand go free, and said I should do whatever I wanted. I said no, but Henry said the paintings couldn't be considered only his, and if I was really going to help him, I had to be in there, too. So I did the best I could. As we worked, I had to tell him everything: how big the shapes were and where they were on the canvas. Eventually we worked out a way of plotting out a grid in proportion to the dimensions of a canvas. That way, Henry could reckon the composition and know where he was, and tell me where to go. We made a scale of colors, too, with the primaries and shades mixed like notes on a piano. Voicing the colors, Henry called it.

It was all about communication and breaking everything down so that you could tell a lot with a minimum of description. It took awhile, but we got to be good at it, as good as we were at flying. I was his guide. Henry said that he felt such pleasure coming from me when we were working together that he didn't care if he saw the pictures or not. He could *feel* what they looked like, and set them up in his mind.

We brought the first painting of the bench back to Henry's club in exchange for the one we had taken away. Everyone there was thrilled about it, and said it was as good a piece of work as any he had done. Henry gave me full credit. This was the first painting of his *vast* period. From now on, we were going to be painting vast works using vast colors. Eventually we did do a whole series of pictures in that same green-sand color. I got to be almost as paint-spattered as Henry was. And I was beginning to understand why he never wanted to wash it off.

* * *

So far this has been mostly about Henry. That's natural. When I first came to the Atelier, all I thought about was Henry. But don't think that I ever for a minute forgot who or where I came from, or the number of days that were left on my contract. Henry knew how I felt. He waited until word about the paintings had got out. Then he arranged for us to visit the Academy.

It was pleasant to go back. I was the big success of the school. They had photos up of me and Henry together, and old pictures, too, of a skinny, long-haired me wearing a training harness. They held a big assembly, and Henry gave a speech, which I translated, and then I followed up with a speech of my own. I told them how we were all the same underneath, and how anyone who had seen with another person's eyes would know that. I added that when you had to look out for someone else all the time, you automatically took care of yourself. I was real inspirational. They got a good dose of Henry, too. Up in the top row, I saw Mom and Dad hugging each other until they were both red in the face.

Afterward there was a reception in the library, where I stood around and tried to be polite and answer questions. I said that guide dogs were going to be a big thing, and that it might help the colony pay its way more. Since we were all the same under the skin, there was no reason to think we couldn't be guides for other races, too. Maybe we had a talent for it, although it didn't take much talent when the clients were as nice as Henry. I got even more maudlin than that, even, until Henry drew me aside a little.

"Tired?"

"I'm all right."

"That last answer was a little much."

"You heard me?"

"I could feel you getting emotional," he said.

"Well," I said, "you might as well share the warmth."

"Why don't you go off and see your friends?"

"But you need me here."

"Oh, they're not going to let me go anywhere. And I have Business Manager to translate for me. You go on awhile." And he shushed me out with those big hands of his.

My friends and I went off to a coffeehouse on the edge of campus. You could see the Tree glowing off in the distance. We all sat around, and it was a little awkward at first. A lot of them were training to be guides, too. I still had my harness on, and I could tell it bothered some of them to see me wearing it, but by and by we had our coffee and started laughing, and it was like I had never left. One of the girls I had known pretty well before wanted me to sit close to her. Every now and then, she tried to kiss me. I didn't mind. Being with a girl was one of the things you missed plenty, if you started to think about it.

Everyone asked me questions. They were pretty much the same ones I had answered before, until this boy named Scott asked me what Henry was really like.

"What do you mean?"

Scott was someone I had never cared for much. He was the kind that could twist anything around to get a look at its bad side. He had been a class behind me, and thought he had to compete. I never thought that, which drove him crazy, I suppose.

Scott said, "I mean, when he lets loose. How is he?"

"He doesn't 'let loose,' " I said, feeling myself tightening up.

"Right. He's only the most famous thing they've ever had. All of them buzz about him. Don't they start buzzing when you fly by?"

"I guess they do."

"You *guess* they do! You must get a good dose every time you go out—not to mention what you've had today."

Scott said this with a sneer, and it was interesting: I got mad. He was talking about emotion, and here was one I hadn't felt for a long time.

"Just what are you getting at?"

"I'm talking about you living for the taste. Why, you're no better than a renegade down inside the Tree!"

I should have just ignored him, but I couldn't. The one thing I hadn't done was taste any more emotion than was good for me. In fact, I gave myself tons of credit for tasting a lot less. So I got up and grabbed his collar and lifted him up into the air, practically.

"It *is* strong," I said. "It's plenty strong, and you've got to have it when you're living out there by yourself. But I don't, because if ever I did, I *would* be a junkie. I'd be living down inside the Tree. I wouldn't be able to help Henry, and I wouldn't be able to help myself, either."

"You're so high and mighty," Scott sputtered. "But you don't fool me. Maybe you won't admit it—"

I pushed him back down in his chair. His arm hit the table, some of the coffee spilled, and they all jumped up. The whole place got quiet. I said that I'd better go.

"*Junkie*," Scott yelled after me.

Scott was a fool, but what a fool says can eat at you, too, and anyway, there was some truth in it. To be a guide dog, you did have to forget about yourself. When you were flying, sometimes it seemed as though it took every cell in your brain to keep going and avoid a crash. It taxed you to the limit, and even then, you felt a disaster was coming any second—that there was all this responsibility, and you never quite measured up. That's why sometimes you would see guide dogs flying with faces clouded over, looking to the side and avoiding your eyes. That's why every so often a guide could lose his grip. You thought you really deserved to have all that love after what you went through.

I was thinking things when we left the school that night. I guess Henry could tell something was up. We were riding in a car with Business Manager. Henry respected my feelings and didn't say anything until Business Manager dropped us off at the Atelier.

"Another reception," Henry said. "Just like all the rest."

"Been to a lot of them, have you?" I said sharply.

He had got some leaves from the cooler and was working his jaws on them, and now he stopped and turned his head in my direction.

"We have receptions. Just like yours. For exactly the same reasons."

"Good for you," I said.

"What's up?" Henry said. I swear he had even learned to make that hiss of his sound sympathetic. But at the moment I hated him for trying.

"Nothing."

"Did something happen while you were off with your friends?"

"They aren't my friends. I don't have any friends."

He chuckled softly. "Oh, I don't think that's true."

"Don't start, Henry. I'm not your friend. I'm your *dog*. Do you know what a *dog* is, Henry? We can't have them here because we can't afford to keep them, but do you know what they are? They're *pets*. We love 'em because they're smart enough to remember us and dumb enough to love us no matter what we do. So we love them back. But we don't respect them, Henry. Because we think we're better than they are. The dumbest, most low-down one of us is still better than the best dog, Henry. And that's what you call me. *Dog*."

He let me go on awhile. He had never seen me angry before, and I think he wanted to watch. At last he said, "*Dog* is just a word. We don't have *dogs*. *Dogs* is your word. It's what is in your head when you hear us speak of you. I would never call you a *dog*, the way you mean."

"What would you call me?"

"Eyes," he said. "Hands. *Friend*."

He was right. I was all those things to him. I felt ashamed for lighting into him, and said I was sorry, and I vowed privately never to let my feelings get the better of me again. I told myself they had got built up out of a lot of other unhappy things. Now that I had got them off my chest, everything would be all right again. And for a while it was. We did a few more still lifes of flowers and trees on the grounds of the Atelier. Sometimes Henry would feel around to "see" their texture and general positions, but now he more often let me block the pictures out alone, and put in only a brush stroke or two. I didn't care if he did. After that reception, I had begun to take a kind of permanent, different view of everything.

After a few days of this, Henry declared we were getting stale, and said we should go out. And so we flew around. It was getting to be winter, and it rained or sometimes it was cold and blew pretty good. Henry didn't care. We just bundled up, and out we went.

By this time I had got used to the flying and began to take more notice of where we were going and who and what was around us. I was proud of myself for being able to do it; I thought that I had grown and detached myself from the job of being a guide dog. What I had really detached myself from, of course, was Henry. He knew it, too. But he never complained. He just let me have my own way, and waited to see how things would go.

One day we flew deep into the Tree. It was dark and raining, with flashes of lightning that seemed to come from all directions at once, green and cold and throwing long, slow-fading shadows. We were headed for a shop that wanted Henry to sign some art books. It was one of our shops, and I think Henry agreed to do it to make me feel a little better.

We didn't say much on the way in. I pretended to concentrate because there really was a lot of traffic. I still felt bad about Henry. I thought the way I was feeling about him was serious and forever. It was just one of the cycles a friendship goes through. You have the euphoria and enthusiasm piled up in the beginning, and then the reaction sets in. You feel horrified by the feelings, and you try to deny them and deny the other person. It goes away, though, if you let it. It would have with Henry if I had just given it a chance.

Down inside the Tree, it was really dark. We were in the oldest part of the city, and where the flyways became bores worn smooth by the centuries of brushing wingtips. They had a few lights, which were like sparklers, set up at the head of the runs, and they had little buzz boxes, also at the head of the runs, that bounced noise off the surfaces and helped the radar along. We bounced around for a while, and then came to an intersection. There was an avenue that led to the open part of the Tree, and three bores, all pitch-black, headed straight down. I described where we were to Henry, and he said we should take the middle bore, which dumped into the quarter where the bookshop was.

"Oh Henry, I don't know," I said.

"Why? What's up? It's fine. You're doing fine."

It was fine for *him*. Henry was enjoying himself. Why shouldn't he? This was like a trip down memory lane for him. His ancestors had spent a couple of aeons chewing out the insides of logs.

"It's too dark. I don't have a lamp. You should have told me about this."

"We'll go slow. I know these streets like home."

He sounded a little impatient, and I felt it, and felt myself wanting to please him. Right then and there, I hated him. Most of all I hated myself. I *was* an addict. I might as well admit it. No matter how little I took, I still lived for his approval.

"All right, Henry. You're the boss. Let's do it." He took up the grab bar and pressed his knees in and lifted his wings, and we were off.

Down and down we dropped. I couldn't see anything. I heard

Henry grunt in surprise a time or two when we bumped the wall, and I was glad about it. I made myself into a load for him, the way a bad rider is a load on the back of a horse. It seemed to take forever to get to the end of the run, but finally we dumped into a big square—or what would be a square in one of our towns. It was a public place where people without jobs could sit while everybody else went to work. In this case the people sitting there were renegades. About six of them, with their backs to the wall, bored and dead-looking until we lighted on the square. Then it was like someone had thrown the switch. Up they popped, grinning and elbowing each other, ready for no good. I swore under my breath. I had never seen so many lousy-looking guys in one place before.

"What's up?" Henry said.

"Renegades," I said. "Earth dogs."

"Really!" he said. "What do they look like?"

"They look like scum, Henry, all right?" They were coming over now. "I think it would be a great idea if we just went back the way we came."

"Don't believe I can do it just now, unfortunately. Need some rest."

"Could you handle a straight run?"

"I believe so."

"There's a hole straight across the square. Let's go for it."

He lifted his wings, and we buzzed off—but we were slow, and I was dragging. Still, we might have gone through them, because they had been sitting a long time, and Henry with his wings out was no small thing. But one of them caught my eye.

"That's it," he called after me. "Good doggy!"

And I lowered my legs and stopped us.

"What did you say?"

"I said *doggy*, which is what you are. In fact, you're worse than a dog. A dog doesn't know any better."

I should have ignored him. Who was he to tell me anything? He was a low-down junkie who had probably been a guide dog once himself. But the way he looked at me and the way he said it and the way I was feeling meant I couldn't let it pass.

"Let go of the harness, Henry," I said.

"I think not."

"If you don't let go, then it's true and I am your dog," I said. "Let go!"

I yanked away. I never thought that he might have been afraid. He was the old one. He was the one standing there blind and alone. All I cared about was how I felt. I waded into that crowd of louts, and went up to the one who had called me out, and I swung at him. They were on me in a second. They were weak and slow, and I was fast and strong—but there were too many of them, and I didn't stay up long. Henry figured out what was happening to me before I did. They have a way of sounding an alarm with their wings, and they can tell who is in trouble by the sound—and they all knew it was Henry, and hundreds of them came, more than could fit in the bores feeding into the square. It was a swarm of them. It was just what the junkies wanted. They left off before they had kicked me to death, and lay back with their arms spread and their eyes shut, soaking all that emotion in with the biggest and most beatific smiles upon their faces.

The next morning I was called in to see the Director at the school. I was sore. My ribs were cracked, and one of my eyes was swollen shut. The Director paid no attention. He wanted to take the opportunity to let me know exactly how I had let everyone down. I didn't say much at first. I thought I would let him get it off his chest. If I had known what he had in mind, though, I might have tried to say something in my own defense.

"A guide does nothing that would endanger the safety of a client!" the Director began. "That's what we taught you. That is the essence of everything we do here! And you, you especially! Didn't we impress upon you day after day the enormous responsibility you took on? He is the most important personality of this world! And our reputation stood to rise or fall depending on how you succeeded with that trust!"

I had to say something then.

"Maybe that's the problem," I said. "Why do we advertise ourselves as servants? They'll never respect us that way."

"Because that is what we are. We have to succeed as what we are. Then we can advance."

"You mean they'll give us a *promotion*?" I laughed right in his face. "Like, if we get good grades, we get to move up a class?"

He was getting red now. He had thought it all out.

"They'll never promote us," I went on. "Why should they? I'm as close to one of them, this 'leading personality,' as you say, as

338 ◆ *Mike Conner*

any of us here have ever got, and what good has it done? Henry hasn't said, 'Don't be my guide.' He's never said I was his equal. He knows what he is. He doesn't have any idea what we are. That's because *we* don't have any idea! So how could he? All this talk about responsibility. Well, who's responsible for the fact that all we thought about was getting here? We had no idea what to do after that. Absolutely none at all! So now we live as outsiders and cook up schemes to make ourselves useful. Great. And you sit there and hope we'll be promoted to *necessary!*"

"I was hoping for some sign of contrition on your part," the Director said. "But I can see that's too much to expect from you."

"You got that right. Can I go?"

He had a file open in front of him.

"Go? Where do you think you're going?"

"Home," I said. "Henry needs me."

The Director smiled a little. He had been saving this.

"Whatever gave you the idea you would be going back there?"

I sat up. "What do you mean?"

"You left a client alone while you engaged in a fight. And caused a riot," he said. "The whole basis of the relationship between a client and his guide is trust. And you have shattered that trust. Your relationship with this client is therefore over."

"I'm fired?"

"Oh, you are still under contract. And you have shown that you can be an excellent guide under certain circumstances. Therefore, we are giving you a second chance. We have a new assignment with another handicapped person, a regular citizen this time. One whose life is not subject to the same level of scrutiny—"

"They are *all* under scrutiny!"

"Nevertheless—"

"Have you asked Henry? Is this what he wants?"

"A new guide has already been assigned to 'Henry,' as you call him."

"Who?"

"That information is confidential."

"Who!" I jumped up, and he jumped back, pale and sweating. It is easy to decide things alone in an office. I swept up the file and had a look.

"Scott? You're sending *Scott*?"

"He is the most qualified—"

"He's a dick. He'll never work out. Henry won't want him around."

"I can call Security," the Director said. "I can void your contract, and your family will be in a work farm by tomorrow afternoon. Is that the way you want it?"

I stood there with the file in my hand. My temper had been getting a big workout lately. Maybe that had taken some of the edge off. I stood there a moment, and then I closed the file and handed it back to him.

"You're making a big mistake," I said.

"I think not."

"Henry and I understand each other. We're a team. I'm helping him paint again. It would break his heart—"

"The client understands the situation," the Director said.

"You mean he *knows*?"

"I met with him myself," the Director said smugly.

That finished it for me. If Henry didn't care, why should I? I felt the rest of the fight draining out of me. But I did have one faint hope left.

"I'll have to get my things."

"We've already had them delivered back here," the Director said.

They gave me a room at the school, and I lived there with my stuff in boxes in the corner. I didn't go to class, and nobody checked up on me. I blamed myself and said that I would take it all back if I could. That had the effect on reality it always does. At the end of the week, they moved me into an apartment in a suburb of the Tree with my new client. I called this one Lester.

Lester was a chemist who had been blinded in an accident at work. He had just come out of rehab training, and his insurance had provided him with the cost of a guide. Unfortunately, Lester was not interested in having a guide. He was in a postinjury phase of great depression, and insisted on living away from his nest. All he wanted to do was stay in all day and be blind. As I was feeling more or less the same way, we made a great pair. But Lester needed somebody to make him get off his abdomen. In the mood I was in, I was not up to being a cheerleader. So, with Lester not wanting any help, and me not interested in giving him any, you could see where things were headed.

Which is not to say I never tried to get him out. We actually did some harness work, and one day even went around the neighborhood. In the end, though, it only seemed to make him sadder. And that meant I was going to have plenty of time on my hands.

Lester's place was small, and it was depressing, too. No air, no windows. I couldn't sit alone inside, and as he didn't care what I did, I started to go out alone into the Tree. I wasn't being a renegade. I wore my harness and carried my ID, and if any one of them or any human stopped me, I explained I was out on an errand. I went all over just looking around. Up at the top, you had to do a lot of climbing because of the distance between perches, and I started to get into pretty good shape. And I got my harness light hooked up, too, and went into the bores as deep as I could go. I was really hoping to run into the louts who had ruined me with Henry. I went back to the square a couple of times, and once I even stayed all day, hanging back in the shadows and waiting. But they never were there. Maybe that was just as well. I have to admit that I didn't have a real good idea of what I would do if I did catch them.

Then one day I saw Henry. There was no mistaking that big head and those cloudy, milk-white eyes. I was up in the crown of the Tree, watching the clouds pile up like they did every afternoon that time of year. And he came along with his wings out, turning his head slowly from side to side as if his radar were still working. But he didn't have any radar, of course. What he had was his new guide dog in a harness. I leaned forward, and sure enough, it was Scott, flailing around and looking like he was going to crash them any second. The buzzing got louder. They always started in when Henry passed by. He was like a seltzer tablet dropped into the water wherever he went. And then, finally, they came close enough to where I could see the bastard's face.

Henry was guiding *him*. He could sense what was giving Scott problems, and sort of point him in the direction that made him the least nervous, and that is where they went. They flew in big spirals, practicing together, so I got to watch them for a while. It was almost worth what had happened to watch Scott sweat like that. But in the end my satisfaction was bitter. I felt lonely and cheated, and for the first time wished for what I had lost. I watched them until they flew out of sight. Then I made up my mind that I would go and see Henry that night.

The tricky part wasn't getting away from Lester. I just told him that I wanted to go out. He didn't care. I'm not sure he even heard me. Even if he *had* heard me and he did care, I knew he wouldn't bother reporting me. He was glad I was gone.

So I went off. There were routes out of the Tree where transports flew, and I waited above one that pointed in the Atelier's direction. Finally came a lorry with a soft-topped trailer that I took a leap for and made. I banged my arm pretty good hitting a rib under the tarp when I landed, and almost bounced off. But I was strong and determined. The thought that I might kill myself somehow did not occur to me at all.

That was good, because the transport really took off once it was out of the city, and I had to hang on tight to keep from being blown off. Then, just as I started to worry about how I would get off, the transport got caught in a snarl of traffic. So I was all right. I just slid down and started walking. I could see the Atelier perched on the cliff up ahead of me, glowing in the twilight.

It was a nice, fresh evening with the damp cool you get after the rains have come. There were peepers in the bushes on the sides of the path, and the sound of the traffic moving slowly above my head. The ground was all mine. I was glad for the weeks of training I had put in when it came to climbing up to Henry's. Several times I got stuck under overhangs that I didn't have the knack of getting around, and had to backtrack and try again. Finally, though, I reached the terrace wall and looked into the big room.

Everything was as it had been. I felt touched, but then I laughed at myself. Who was going to rearrange the furniture? I decided to wait. What I wanted to do was alert Henry, but leave Scott out of it. I waited and watched, and after a while I saw that nobody was home. So I went in and headed for the kitchen to see what supplies they had for a guide dog. I did find some orange sherbert sitting in a pan of dry ice. That made me madder than anything, because of Henry being so nice and Scott such a woos. I had paid for that ice cream by trying to eat what Henry ate.

Since I was getting worked up about Scott anyway, I decided to poke around my old room. Scott had cleaned it out. All the wood was stacked up according to size on the shelf underneath the bench, and the tools were hanging in the rack. The place had been swept, and it looked as though he had even washed down the walls. It was disgusting. People have no business being that neat. If they do, it is only because they want to show up the rest of us.

Scott had set up a desk, too. It was all polished on the top, with a short row of reference books squeezed between a pair of lead slabs that were spray-painted gold. The desk drawers were locked. It was such an insult to Henry. As if he cared about what Scott had in his desk! I cared, though. I found a long, straight chisel on the tool rack, and when I popped out the drawer in the middle, the rest of them came free, too. The inside of the drawers were just as neat as the rest of the room. I found a steel box with money inside, files of school records, a receipt book, a ledger, a journal, a calendar and a log, plus pens and paper and supplies. There was also a chewed-up baseball that looked about a thousand years old. Well. Everybody always keeps at least one thing that isn't like the rest of him.

I laid it all out and looked everything over and decided the journal would probably be most interesting to start with. I sat down on the bed and began to read. It was slow going though. Scott wrote down what he ate every day and how much money he spent, and how hard he studied what, and how many hours he slept and what the dreams were. There was no reason to hide that journal, because it would put you right to sleep. I started skimming and got all the way to the end, and then I found something that made me yell out loud. "He and H. are going to bookstore tomorrow," I read. "I have arranged a surprise on the way. We'll see how he does when he meets the boys."

The entries were all dated, and on a hunch I opened up the account ledgers and had a look. And sure enough, there were six payments of one hundred gold dollars, with receipts clipped to the page, for "personal services." And the signatures on all of them looked pretty rocky. Just what you would expect from renegades.

Well, that was it for me. They say that if you find out something by snooping around, you have no business getting mad at the person you are snooping on, but this was my business. Scott had hidred those thugs to wait for Henry and me! He knew what would rile me most, and he had done it, and it had worked, and now he had got what he wanted. Oh, I wanted to kill him!

But he wasn't around, and I paced for a while and gradually grew cooler and began to consider what I ought to do. It was better to be cool about such things. I left the desk ransacked and threw some of his books around and pulled down the tool rack. That last was for spite. Then I went out and found a good perch under a thicket on a ledge up above the Atelier, and I settled down and waited.

It was dark by the time they came back in Business Manager's car. Scott got out first. His hair was messed, and his harness was twisted around on his back. He went right inside and up to his room while Business Manager led Henry in. Then the lights came on, and I got to see him stare at the desk and whirl around and tear down to get Business Manager. Business Manager did not appear impressed by the damage. To him, it probably looked the same as when I had lived there. But Scott made him bring Henry, and then they were all three looking around, Scott putting Henry in touch with the harness and jabbering away at him. Henry felt around a little, and I could see him speak to Business Manager. Scott meanwhile was cleaning up. He just could never stand to have anything out of place at all.

After a while they left him alone, and Scott went to bed. Henry and Business Manager were in the big room having some mead. Then Business Manager stretched out his wings and said good night. Henry didn't sleep much, but the rest of them usually had to have around eight hours just like we do. Business Manager drove off, and I waited some more. It was deep-dark now, with the stars spread across the black sky like blistered paint. I waited some more. Then I went inside and found Henry working on a canvas.

It almost broke your heart to see him do it. He was feeling with his left and putting it on with his right, and then getting the shape from where the wet paint was; but he was missing, and the colors were all wrong because he had no one to help him lay out his palette. He must have known; he was drooping a little, but he kept on. I think he did because he liked the feel of the brush dragging across the canvas with the load of paint on it. I watched him for a long time before I saw what he was getting at, and realized it was a portrait. It was a face. My face.

I came up behind him and touched his shoulder. He gave a start. Then I made him take up the grab bar, and said, "What's up, Henry?"

Oh, I got it then. I had never felt it so strong or so pure. It was just like hot liquid gold poured right in through the top of my head. My heart was hammering, and my knees felt like water. Fortunately, Henry knew what was happening to me, and backed off. When I came to, he was stroking my head and saying my name over and over, not through the harness, but in his hissing English.

"Ohhh. You got to watch that, Henry." I knew I would probably be worthless for a week after a dose like that. He helped me up. I was just glad to see him. I didn't care anymore about the rest of it.

"What are you doing here?"

"I had to make sure you were getting along all right."

There was a moment of silence. Then I said, "So how's the new dog working out?"

"He's not you."

"Well. Not many people are."

That made him laugh.

"I saw you trying to paint," I said. "Just now, I mean. I've been waiting here for you for a while."

He cocked his head. "Don't you have a new client?"

"He doesn't like to go out. Truth is, I don't think he's so happy to have me around."

"So you ran away."

"No. I asked if I could go."

"You didn't tell him you were coming here, though."

"He wouldn't care."

I felt him looking at me.

"No, I didn't."

"You'll be in more trouble," Henry said. He sounded tired and worried. Worse than that: he sounded old. I knew it was my fault. I knew he missed me, and I knew I had let him down. If I had followed my training, I would still be with him, and Scott would be with Lester or somebody else.

"You were in Scott's room, weren't you?" Henry said severely.

"Yes. I was mad. I wanted to get even."

" 'Get even' for what? He had nothing to do with what happened."

I bit my tongue. I wanted to tell him what Scott had done, but I couldn't. I had to accept responsibility for what *I* had done. I had played into Scott's hands. His plan would have come to nothing if only I had kept my temper. If I told Henry what I knew, I would only disappoint him more.

"Scott was very upset."

"I know."

"You should make it right," Henry said. "You should go up and offer to clean up the room."

The truth I was holding in was practically making my head pop, but I couldn't say a thing. Because everything *he* was telling me was the more important truth.

"O.K. But he's sleeping, Henry, and—"

"Yes?"

"Henry, I'd just like to fly with you one more time. Would that be all right?"

He chuckled a little. They had a way of doing that that sounded just like your mother.

"Please, Henry! We never had a chance to end it ourselves. They just came in and took me away. Did they even ask how you felt or what you thought they ought to do? I know there's nothing we can do about that, but at least we could fly one last time. Maybe it would be easier for you then. Maybe it would be easier for me to accept things. Then I wouldn't always be thinking about what happened. Please, Henry."

"All right," he said. "One more time, for you and for me."

I took him out to the terrace. There were so many stars you could have read a book. Henry hooked up with the grab bar and tucked in his knees and lifted his wings, and we took off. I had never felt him so strong before. The sound of his wing beats was a pitch higher, and he made his turns with authority and climbed with such ease that I thought we would fly up until we ran out of air. We climbed and climbed, up above the Tree, until the city was nothing but a fuzzy ball of light. Henry didn't say much. He just kept climbing, and then all of a sudden pointed us down in a steep dive. I leaned into it with him, not thinking about the danger in it. We flew straight down together right through the outskirts of the Tree, right through the traffic and into the core. I shifted on pure instinct and guesswork, and I was right every time. We plunged deeper and deeper into the bored-out avenues and out again, spiraling down around the shaft, until at last he pulled up and used all the energy we had gathered in our long plunge to swoop upward again in a curving, effortless arc out toward the Atelier. It was thrilling. It was as if he had summed up all of his life into that one flight. He sent out about it, too. In the cool evening, gliding almost without a sound with the Atelier in view, you could hear them buzz. All of them knew what Henry was doing. Maybe they knew what he would do. I didn't know anything. I was just grateful for the chance to fly again.

We came closer, and I turned the harness light on, and there on the terrace, I saw Scott and Business Manager. Scott was pointing at us, and I thought, He's probably called the Director, and that broke the feeling I had and made me forget all my good intentions. I was going for him as soon as we hit ground, and to hell with anything else. So as we came in, Henry spreading out his wings to pull us up, I got my legs ready, and then Henry twisted a little, suddenly enough to snap the safety release on the harness, and dropped me. I landed on the terrace as he rose off, climbing away, flying blind.

It is funny about momentum. Henry's carried him up and away. Mine sent me right into Scott, and we sprawled together past Business Manager. I popped to my feet, and I had enough left to pull him up, too, all ready to yank his head off. Then I realized that Henry was free of the harness. I looked up. You could see him spiraling up and out against the stars that sparkled like diamond sand on a black marble floor. He made a wide right turn, and you could see him beating his wings to pick up speed. Then it was like the mountain just got up and put itself in front of him. Henry flew right into it.

A couple of rocks and small stones rattled down the steep slope and came to rest. After that came the silence.

They had a system of laws and justice, and a forum like a court, and they put me on trial. I was the first human being to come under their jurisdiction. Ordinarily, we were not worth the trouble, but because Henry was so important, they declared me a citizen and brought me up on charges.

I went in thinking that I would defend myself. But after a couple of days, I saw that they were interested only in reconstructing the circumstances of the crime. You couldn't blame them, I guess. Since it is impossible for them to lie to each other, proving guilt was ame up with. Nobody questioned it. The laws weren't even written down. They were bred into you.

According to custom, the accused could select the venue, and so I picked the auditorium at school. I had a lawyer, and they had a prosecutor, and the witnesses came in and gave statements and answered questions. They called the Director, who said that I had been relieved because I had abandoned my post to fight with bums, and so had endangered my master's life. He actually said *master*. My lawyer tried to turn that around by saying I was only attempting to save Henry from renegades, but they brought the scuzzballs in, and they all swore they weren't interested in Henry at all, but had merely made a joke at my expense. I waited for my lawyer to do something with that; he didn't, though, and so I jumped in.

"Say, weren't you guys tipped off that we were going to that bookstore?"

"Who woulda done that?"

"Him," I said, pointing dramatically at Scott, who had come to the trial every day.

"What about him?"

"Didn't he pay you to jump us?"

"Naw," the lout said. "Why would he do that?"

"Because you're scum," I said. "And scum are always available for the right price."

He smiled at me. "Maybe so," he said. "How much they pay you to wear that collar?"

I guess I didn't help myself then when I went after him. It took a couple of them to hold me while I shouted it was all a lie: that I had found out about the payoffs from a ledger in Scott's room, and that they should call him and ask about it; that Henry and I had loved each other, and that I had tried to get him out of the square, and that he had *dropped* me on purpose in the end because he wanted to fly alone; and nobody lived forever, not even Henry, and that if they really wanted to honor him, they should not insult his memory by making out that he would ever have let anyone get away with killing him. I was eloquent, all right, in between the biting and kicking. Finally they got me tied down to a chair and took a few more witnesses. Lester came in and said I had run away. Scott stepped up—eyeing the ropes on the chair all the time to make sure I couldn't get loose—and testified I had ransacked his room and had even destroyed a painting that he and Henry had done together. He just went up there and lied. I suppose it didn't matter. They knew we could lie. And because we had the talent for it and they did not, they assumed that all of us *were* liars.

After a couple of days, they closed out the testimony and put it to the vote. Everyone who had followed the trial or read the transcript could get in on the decision. They put their heads together, millions of them, and came up with a unanimous verdict. I was guilty of murder through negligence. My sentence was to be put out on the Rock and to remain there until I expired.

They gave me one evening at the school before the sentence would be carried out. I stayed in my old room with a guard posted outside and entertained a few visitors. Nobody really had much to say. I ended up patting backs and doing most of the talking. I didn't mind making them feel better. Somebody had to do it.

But it was hard when Dad finally showed up late in the evening. Mom couldn't take seeing me in person, I guess; Dad took a snapshot to bring back to her. We chatted a little about the new house they were building and how well my brother was doing in the merchant marine. Then there was that awkward waiting you get when one person wants something and the other one knows it but doesn't know what. What I wanted was for him to thank me at least for being a good son and trying to work my contract off. He didn't say any of that, though. What he finally came up with was that I should not be afraid when the end came.

"You mean when I die?"

"When you realize it's all over."

"That ought to be right about when I die," I said.

"Don't think about it now. Just remember to be brave. When the time comes."

How brave is he gonna be? I thought.

"Son," he said.

"Yeah, Dad."

"Remember the day I brought you here? I gave you something. A little knife. Do you remember?"

"Yeah, Dad, I remember."

"Do you still have it?"

I looked at him.

"They want me to get it from you."

"Christ, Dad!"

"Even if they didn't, I'd still like to have it. It would mean a lot to me."

"Would it, Dad?"

"Yes."

So I gave it to him. Weak as he was, I could never really get angry at him.

They gave me a nice dinner. Stuff from home like lobster and a bowl of radishes. I ate as much as I could. I wanted to last a long time out there on the Rock. They probably had a record for how long somebody had made it out there. Whatever it was, I wanted to try and break it. There was beer, too, and some brandy with the dessert, and I felt pretty sleepy by the time I finished. I lay on the bed with my arm over my eyes. After a while I heard the door open. I looked up. It was one of them, looking too big against the frame of the door. I sat up and saw that someone had cleared the dinner plates away.

"Oh, get out of here, will you?" I said. Then I saw that it was Business Manager. He was holding my harness. He didn't move. He just looked at me, trying to see how I was. When I reached for the harness, he handed it to me, and I put it on. It felt a little stiff, but warmed right up when I powered it on, the needles pressing lightly against the top of my back.

"How are you?" he said.

"Oh, I'm just great. Never better."

I guess he knew about sarcasm, because he didn't say anything. Finally I asked him what he was doing here.

"I came to bring you the harness. You should wear it tomorrow."

"Now, why should I do that?"

"You are a guide," he said. He was looking at me, and suddenly I felt bad. He was someone who had always tried to help Henry, and I knew Henry was fond of him.

"I'm sorry about what happened, you know," I said.

"You have nothing to be sorry about."

"You're the only one who feels that way."

"Not the only one," Business Manager said.

"Nobody spoke up."

"That is not our way."

"No. I guess it isn't."

He turned, ready to go. "Wait a minute. Can I ask you something?"

He looked back. His eyes were shiny, like black glass.

"What do you think happens? After you die?"

"Why ask me that? What do you think happens?"

"I don't know. You change. But I think you're still around somewhere in a different form."

"Do you think it would be any different for us?"

"No. I guess it wouldn't."

"We believe that you can remain. And see and act through another. If you want to and if you are strong enough."

"Henry was strong, wasn't he?"

"Wear the harness tomorrow," he said.

What they did was put me on the Rock. It is a smooth basalt dome that is in the middle of a large caldera. It is very high and steep and polished like marble by the wind. There are no handholds. They valley floor is littered with the shells of the ones who have come before me. If you're one of them, they clip your wings and leave you here, shunned by the rest. Then the loneliness and the humiliation get to you. Eventually you give up, and the wind pushes you off. The floor of the caldera is littered with the bodies of dead criminals.

I sit on the Rock and think about jumping.

The sky is that brown-green color Henry called vast. Off toward the Tree, I see something tiny flash against the clouds. It gets bigger. It is one of them, flying toward me. I wish it were Henry, come to take me home to the Atelier, but of course it is not.

It is Business Manager. And I am wearing my harness.